INTO THE ABYSS

HELL ON EARTH, BOOK 2

BRENDA K DAVIES

Copyright © 2018 Brenda K. Davies

ALSO FROM THE AUTHOR

Books written under the pen name
Brenda K. Davies

The Vampire Awakenings Series

Awakened (Book 1)

Destined (Book 2)

Untamed (Book 3)

Enraptured (Book 4)

Undone (Book 5)

Fractured (Book 6)

Ravaged (Book 7)

Consumed (Book 8)

Unforeseen (Book 9)

Forsaken (Book 10)

Coming 2019/2020

The Alliance Series

Eternally Bound (Book 1)

Bound by Vengeance (Book 2)

Bound by Darkness (Book 3)

Bound by Passion (Book 4)

Bound by Torment (Book 5)

Coming 2020

Redemption (Book 5)

Broken (The Captive Series Prequel)

Vengeance (Book 6)

Unbound (Book 7)

The Kindred Series

Kindred (Book 1)

Ashes (Book 2)

Kindled (Book 3)

Inferno (Book 4)

Phoenix Rising (Book 5)

The Fire & Ice Series

Frost Burn (Book 1)

Arctic Fire (Book 2)

Scorched Ice (Book 3)

The Ravening Series

The Ravening (Book 1)

Taken Over (Book 2)

Reclamation (Book 3)

The Survivor Chronicles

The Upheaval (Book 1)

The Divide (Book 2)

The Forsaken (Book 3)

The Risen (Book 4)

This book is dedicated to all the butterfly chasers in the world.

GLOSSARY OF TERMS

- **Adhene demon** <Ad-heen> - Mischievous elf-like demon. Corson and Wren are the last adhenes.
- **Absenthees** – Center of the Abyss and its main focus of power.
- **The Abyss** – The Abyss is another plane. The jinn can open a doorway into the Abyss and enter it. Absenthees is at the center of the Abyss and main focus of power in the Abyss.
- **Akalia Vine** <Ah-kal-ya> - Purple black flowers, orange berries. Draws in victims & drains their blood slowly. Red leaves. Sharp, needle-like suckers under leaves. Behind the 6th seal.
- **Barta demons** <Bartə> - They were locked behind the 55th seal. Animal of Hell. Now part of Lucifer's guard.
- **Calamut Trees** <Cal-ah-mut> - Live in the Forest of Prurience.
- **Canagh demon** <Kan-agh> - Male Incubus, Female

Succubus. Power thrives on sex but feed on souls on a less regular basis than the other demons. Their kiss enslaves another.

- **Ciguapa** (see-GWAH-pah) – Female demon with backward feet.
- **Craetons** <Cray-tons> - Lucifer's followers.
- **Crantick demon** – Crazy. Often run head first into walls and throw themselves off ledges for fun. Howl in a pack. Like to fight but mostly innocuous.
- **Drakón** <Drak-un> – 101st seal. Skeletal, fire breathing dragons. They now protect the varcolac's Chosen.
- **Erinyes** (furies) <Ih-rin-ee-eez> - demons of vengeance and justice. 78th Seal.
- **Faerie/Fae** – Empath demons who were slight in build, fast, and kinder than the other demons. The fae bloodline still exists in mixed demons but the purebred fae died out thousands of years ago.
- **Fires of Creation** - Where the varcolac is born.
- **Forest of Prurience** <Proo r-ee-uh nce> - Where the tree nymphs reside. Was also the original home of the canaghs and wood nymphs.
- **The Gates** - Varcolac demon has always been the ruler of the guardians of the gates that were used to travel to earth before Lucifer entered Hell.
- **Ghosts** - Souls can balk against entering Heaven, they have no choice when it comes to Hell.
- **Gobalinus** (goblins) <Gab-ah-leen-us> - Lower level demons, feed on flesh as well as souls. 79th seal.
- **Hellhounds** - The first pair of Hellhounds also born of the Fires of Creation, with the first varcolac who

rose. They share a kindred spirit and are controlled by the varcolac.

- **Jinn (Singular form is jinni)** – 90th seal. Beautiful creatures. They'll grant a wish, make it more of a nightmare, and tear out their victim's heart as payment. Feed on the life force of others as well as on wraiths.
- **Lanavour demon** <Lan-oh-vor> - The 3rd seal. Can speak telepathically and know people's inner most secrets and fears.
- **Leporcháin** <Lepor-cane> - Leprechaun looking creatures. Half on Kobal's side, the other half are on Lucifer's. Only ten in existence.
- **Macharah** – 103rd seal. Creature with 30 plus tentacles at the bottom.
- **Manticore** – 46th seal. Body of a red lion, human/demon head.
- **The Oracle** – The oracle is a lake of fire, deep in the bowels of Hell, where earth could be looked on. Few made the journey as the lake was also the central focus of all the heat in Hell.
- **Ouroboros** - 82nd seal. Massive, green serpent.
- **Palitons** <Pal-ah-tons> - Kobal's followers.
- **Púca** <Poo-ka> - 80th seal. Shape changers which can take on animal or human form. Could also be the source of vampires as they drain their victim's blood.
- **Skelleins** <Skel-eens> - Guardians of the Gates.
- **Spiny Clackos** – demon who is known to have spikes in every part of their anatomy.
- **Tree Nymphs** – Live in the Forest of Prurience. Men and women. Striking and very free sexually. Smaller than wood nymphs and live in the trees.

- **The Wall** - Blocks off all of Washington, Oregon, California, Arizona, New Mexico, Texas, Louisiana, Mississippi, Alabama, Georgia, Florida, South Carolina, North Carolina, Virginia, Maryland, Delaware, New Jersey, Connecticut, Rhode Island, Massachusetts, Vermont, New Hampshire, and Maine. Blocks parts of Nevada, New York, Pennsylvania, and Arkansas. Similar wall blocks off parts of Europe.
- **Wraith -** A twisted and malevolent spirit that the demons feed from. On earth they only come out at night.
- **Varcolac demon** <Var-ko-lack>- Born from the fires of Hell. Only one can exist at a time. When that one dies another rises from the Fires of Creation. Fastest and most brutal of all the demons. They are the only kind that can create and open natural gateways within Hell as well as close them. They control the hellhounds.

Demon Words:

- **Mah lahala** 'Mɑ: <la-hall-a> - My Love.
- **Mohara** <Mo-har-ah> – Mother
- **Paupi** <Pow-pea> - Father.
- **Unshi** <Un-she> – Uncle

PROLOGUE

"Sometimes...."

"Sometimes?" the woman prompted when the man's voice trailed off.

The paliton camp was only half a mile away, but they were alone out here in the woods, which was just the way she liked it. The woods were a place of peace, and she didn't want anyone to interrupt them.

The rays of the sun filtering through the trees danced across the ground around them. When the barren branches swayed and clacked together overhead, they made a sound like dancing skelleins. Not that she'd ever seen the skeletal demons dance, but she'd heard them charge into battle, and their teeth clacked when they got excited, and their bony feet clicked on hard surfaces.

The man's fingers dug into the rotting log they sat on as he stared at the forest. When bits of wood broke away beneath his hands, the scent of rotting wood, moss, and earth rose around them. He seemed not to notice any of it though.

She batted her lashes at him in the hopes he would look at her, but it seemed as if he were caught in another world when all she wanted was to catch him up in *her*.

"Sometimes?" she prompted again.

He shook his head as if he were clearing it. "Sometimes I wonder if things could have been different in this world."

"Oh, me too," she replied with a sigh. "Every day I daydream about how this world should have been, how it once *was*. It's all so... so terrible now."

"Yes," he agreed.

A bird fluttered between some of the branches above them. It chirruped before taking flight. Beneath her ass, the damp log leeched the heat from her, but she didn't move. "What would you change?" she inquired.

"What wouldn't I change?"

She chuckled. "True."

"What would *you* change?"

"All of it."

"Hmm," he murmured, and his pinky finger brushed her hand.

She glanced down as he continued to rub the outer edge of her hand. He may have been lost in his thoughts earlier, but she had him now. She gave him a sultry smile from under her half-lowered eyelashes.

"I think," he said. "I would change it so demons never came to Earth."

"Oh, what a difference that would have made." She leaned closer until she smelled the mint on his breath. "I think about it often."

"Think about what often?" he asked.

They were so close now she could feel his breath on her lips. His hand stilled against hers.

"What it would have been like if the demons never came to Earth," she said.

"I often wish...."

"For?" Her tongue flicked out to wet her lips, and his gaze fell to her mouth as she'd hoped it would. Sliding her tongue over her mouth again, she teasingly licked the edge of her full bottom lip to entice him further.

"I don't know. There are so many things I'd change that I don't know where I'd start or what I'd wish for."

Disappointment filled her when he leaned back a little and bowed his head. *So close!* She'd been *so close!*

Then he leaned closer again, his hand sliding over hers once more. *Gotcha.* Excitement hummed through her when his fingers dipped between hers.

"I know what I'd wish for," she said.

"And what is that?" he asked as his lips brushed her forehead before moving lower to her temple and down her cheek.

"Every day, I daydream about what it would have been like if the gateway never opened and we were *all* anywhere but here. Every day, I wish we could all experience the lives we want most, the lives we were supposed to lead before Hell came to Earth."

"Who is all?" he inquired.

"All the people in the camp and the demons too, I suppose. I bet some of them would like their old lives back too."

"Oh, how *perfect.*" Placing his finger under her chin, he lifted her head until she gazed into his striking, electric blue eyes.

"And you? What would you wish for?" she asked.

"I know better than to make wishes, but *your* wish is my command."

She giggled, but when she leaned closer, he abruptly rose and wiped the bits of bark from his mouthwatering ass. Confusion swirled through her as she watched him step over the log and stroll further away from her. She'd been so certain she was about to get laid by this delicious man.

They'd just met, but she'd had sex with plenty of men she barely knew or hadn't known at all since that demon murdered her

Ricky. No man would ever matter after Ricky; they were merely a way to forget, if only for a few minutes.

"Where are you going?" she asked.

"I have what I came for," he replied with a backward wave of his hand.

She tried to rise, but a wave of darkness slid over her, and she collapsed onto the ground.

"YOUR WISH IS MY COMMAND, isn't that a little cliché?" Eron asked.

Olgon smiled as he clapped his younger brother on the shoulder. "It is, but as we've learned during our time on Earth, it is what these ridiculous humans expect from the jinn, and who am I to disappoint?"

"At least it finally got us the wish we required."

"It did. Come now, we have a wish to fulfill for so many others."

They grinned at each other before separating to sow their misery.

CHAPTER ONE

Magnus

"What happened? What the *fuck* happened?" Corson hissed.

The woman's dead weight on my shoulder shifted when I grabbed Corson's arm to hold him back before he could plunge heedlessly into the clearing. I dodged the talons he swung at me when he lashed out. I didn't blame him for trying to attack me; we'd left his Chosen, Wren, at the camp when we went out to hunt for the day.

We'd found plenty of game, and stashed it in a cave nearby, but it seemed as if everyone who stayed behind at the camp was....

Well, I wasn't sure what they were, but they definitely weren't with *us* right now.

"Easy," I cautioned, my hand constricting on Corson's arm as I gazed at the bodies sprawled around the small clearing. Judging by the number of bodies, not everyone in the camp was here, but I suspected we'd find them somewhere nearby and just as unmoving as those here. "Losing it isn't going to save anyone or help anything."

Whatever happened to those at the camp while we were gone occurred quickly as none of the affected tried to break their fall before hitting the ground. There were no outspread hands, no one was braced against anything, and just as many lay on their backs as on their faces.

Most of their chests still rose and fell with their breaths, but one man didn't move at all and his head lulled at an unnatural angle. When he fell, he'd slammed his head on a rock and broken his neck before collapsing across the boulder that killed him.

Usually, there was chatter in the camp, the clink of plates being washed after a meal, or the shuffle of cards as the players looked to kill some time. Silence hung like a thick fog over everything now, not even the song of a bird pierced the air as they seemed to have taken flight or hidden somewhere.

Typically, there would have been guards to greet us or lookouts spread through the woods. We'd encountered one of the lookouts on our way into camp after storing the game we'd hunted. Sitting in a tree, she was slumped over its branch. I'd removed her from the tree and, uncertain about what happened to her, carried her back to the camp. She remained draped over my shoulder.

What happened here?

My mind spun at the possibilities. Demons and humans alike had fallen where they stood or sat. I didn't think this phenomenon was spread throughout the Wilds. Otherwise me, Corson, Caim, and Raphael would be napping too.

So it's something that only took out our camp.

A sinking sensation filled my gut when I realized this was a personalized attack against the palitons who followed and were closest to my king, Kobal. However, if the craetons who followed the fallen angel Astaroth did this, then why was anyone here still alive?

What better time to slaughter them all than when they were so defenseless?

That question brought me back to what happened here and *why*?

Carefully examining those who slumbered to see if anyone else was dead, my gaze fell on Bale. Her red hair was splayed around her as she lay on her side. To say we grated on each other's nerves was an understatement, but as much as the two of us would gladly chop off each other's body parts, seeing her vulnerable like this made my blood boil.

I didn't know who'd done this, but I'd make them pay for attacking us in such a cowardly way.

Corson jerked his arm away from me, and stalking forward, he made his way through the group of Wilders and demons. I didn't try to draw him back. He had to know what happened to Wren, and trying to keep him restrained would only result in an unnecessary fight between us.

Bending, I lowered the woman's body carefully to the ground. I lightly slapped her pale cheeks and shook her, all things I'd already tried, but they had the same effect as before, nothing. If it weren't for the rise and fall of her chest, I'd believe her dead. I checked her pulse and found her heartbeat slow but steady.

What kind of demon or fallen angel power was this? How long had they been like this? And would the length of time they were unconscious matter on how easy it would be to wake them again?

I didn't know the answers to any of those questions, but whatever this was, it was unlike anything I'd ever seen before.

I inspected the woman more closely for any sign of an answer, but it was impossible to tell if she'd been unconscious for hours or minutes. This could have occurred shortly after we left camp at daybreak, or it could have happened minutes before our return when the sun started sinking toward the horizon. I saw no marks on the woman, but I didn't remove her clothes.

I turned the woman onto her side and then carefully onto her front before rolling her over again. She never so much as twitched while I examined her. I was born in Hell, fought beside Kobal and against Lucifer, but her utter stillness was one of the creepiest things I'd ever encountered.

What the fuck is going on here? And what if it's impossible to wake them again?

Nothing scared me, but the idea of losing most of our camp in this one, strange, fell swoop made my skin crawl. Not only would we lose them, but also Corson as he'd never survive the loss of Wren if she were involved in this too.

A rustle of wings alerted me to Raphael's descent before the angel landed noiselessly beside me. His white wings rippled outward, and he shook the golden angel dust from them. The movement revealed the sun symbol pattern of gold feathers on his inner right wing.

Curiosity once compelled me to ask him about those feathers and if they were on all the angels. He'd simply replied, "I am unique among my kind," in his flat, emotionless tone before walking away.

His response only piqued my curiosity and annoyance, but I hadn't bothered to ask him again. I didn't want to end up fighting with a celestial being who could draw on life and fire it into my ass. My ass was far too nice to be blown off.

Raphael's violet eyes surveyed the bodies with an air of detachment. When he rested his hand on the handle of the broadsword at his side, he covered the blue jewel set into it. His white-blond hair hung to the shoulders of the brown shirt he'd modified to fit his wings. Over top of the shirt, he wore a silver plate of chest armor.

"Did you see anything nearby?" I asked him.

"There are more bodies in the woods."

"Bodies like these?"

"Yes. They are all sleeping, and they are all our followers."

They're all Kobal's *followers*, but I decided now was not the time to argue semantics with him. We had far more important things to handle.

"Did you see anyone or anything else nearby?" I asked.

"If I had, I would have stopped them or brought them back," he replied.

"Can you heal those who are affected?" I inquired.

"I shouldn't."

My temper started fraying, but fighting with this golden prick would only waste valuable time. That didn't mean I didn't want to choke him like a goddamn chicken.

"I understand that." I smiled at him, refusing to let him know he'd annoyed me. "But is it even possible for you to heal them?"

If it were, one way or another, I'd *make* him work his ability to heal them.

"I do not know," he replied.

I'd assumed I would have to prod him further, but Raphael crossed over to kneel at Bale's side. He brushed aside the fire red hair covering her face before placing his hand on her forehead and closing his eyes. Bale's chest continued to rise and fall, but she showed no other signs of life.

After a minute, Raphael released her and turned to the human closest to him. He touched the man's forehead and closed his eyes again. He stayed beside the human for a few minutes before removing his hand and rising.

"I cannot," he answered. "Whatever happened to them is beyond my abilities. This isn't physical; it's something else entirely."

But what?

Striding forward, I knelt at Shax's side, and resting my hand on his shoulder, I turned him over to see his face. Dirt caked his golden blond hair, crusted blood had dried under his nose and upper lip, but the injuries that caused the bleeding were already healed. Shax was a fast healer, but I suspected at least an hour had passed since they were all struck down.

I squeezed Shax's shoulder before rising to walk over and kneel at Hawk's side. The former human turned canagh demon had fallen on his back. He had one arm draped across his chest, and oddly enough, a smile tugged at the corners of his mouth. That smile was almost as confusing as the numerous sleeping beauties.

"What the...?"

My voice trailed off as I lifted my head to gaze at the rest of the bodies. We were missing something here, but what?

"Where's Caim?" I asked Raphael as I rose from Hawk's side.

He waved at one of the trees and the massive three-foot-tall, one-hundred-pound raven perched on a branch there. The raven's claws almost encircled the entire limb as it twisted its head to survey the scene below. Rainbow colors danced across the raven's black feathers, and the same colors danced within its onyx eyes.

"Wren!" Corson shouted.

My attention returned to Corson as he leapt over the fallen bodies and ran fifteen feet into the woods. Wren's pale blonde hair shone in the sun when Corson rolled her over. My throat went dry as his hands skimmed her face to brush away the debris clinging to her.

"He's going to lose his mind," I muttered.

"He must maintain control now more than ever," Raphael stated. "So far, we are the only four unaffected."

"Aren't you observant?" I drawled.

Raphael frowned at me before nodding. "I am."

Apparently, sarcasm was lost on angels. Unwilling to hear anything more from Raphael, I made my way across the clearing toward Corson. Placing my feet carefully between the bodies, I managed to avoid stepping on any of them. I was fifteen feet away from Corson when he lifted his head and his blazing orange eyes locked on mine.

He would murder everything he got his hands on if we didn't figure out what was going on and fix it soon... if it could be fixed.

"*What did this?*" Corson snarled.

When I looked at the bodies again, I realized some more of them were smiling while others grimaced. In Corson's arms, Wren's mouth pursed and her brow furrowed. Whatever held her within its grasp troubled her.

"I don't know," I admitted.

"What could have the power, the strength, the *need* to do this?" Corson demanded.

Before I could reply, Caim launched himself out of the tree and, with a loud caw, dove into the woods. Branches snapped as he plummeted with the speed of a meteor toward the ground and out of view.

A startled, female cry followed his disappearance.

CHAPTER TWO

Magnus

I ONLY BEAT Corson to where Caim vanished because he paused to lift Wren into his arms and carry her through the woods. Raphael soared overhead before arcing toward the ground.

When I saw Caim again, he wasn't in raven shape but had resumed the form of a man. He darted back and forth in front of a woman as he used his open wings to block her from running past him.

The silver spikes protruding from the upper and bottom tips of his wings flashed as he moved. Like in his raven form, his ebony hair and coal black eyes shimmered with hints of rainbow color. Unlike the other fallen angels, who regrew more bat-like, veined wings after shearing them off when they first fell to Earth, Caim's wings had regrown feathers, but those feathers grew back black instead of white like the non-fallen angels.

The woman ducked to the side before spinning and dashing past the edge of one of Caim's wings. She plummeted into the woods with her hands out to stop any branches from slapping her face. I didn't think she had any idea where she was going or what lay ahead of her as she charged forward with the recklessness of an immortal.

Speeding after the woman, I kept my gaze locked on her so I wouldn't lose her in the forest. As she ran, her ginger hair trailed like a banner behind her and revealed its numerous colors. It appeared redder one moment, blonder the next, and the color of a pumpkin in the following instant. I realized her hair was like the sky at sunset, ever-changing and multi-hued. The sides of it were pulled back into two braids that became one as they ran down the center of the thick mass.

I couldn't see her face, but if it was anything like her hair, then this woman was magnificent.

I wasn't overly thrilled with having to run, it wasn't an exercise I partook in often, but I *had* to catch her because I had to *see* her. I poured on the speed as curiosity about this creature propelled me onward.

Slender, the woman moved with the grace of a demon, but I didn't know which kind. The bottom of her short-sleeved, yellow dress beat against her ankles when she leapt over a fallen log and around the body of a woman. The past week had been unseasonably warm for February, and her clothes, as well as my own short-sleeved shirt, reflected this.

"Corson, I'll get her. Check the woman!" I shouted over my shoulder.

The shadow of an angel swept over us again. I didn't know it belonged to Raphael until he plummeted out of the trees. A cloud of dirt and leaves billowed up around his feet when he landed before the fleeing woman. She made such an abrupt right that I nearly collided with Raphael when she changed course.

If the woman wasn't at least five-foot-five-inches tall, I would have assumed she was a tree nymph, given the grace and speed with which she moved. However, I'd never seen a tree nymph who stood over five feet.

Watching her, I had the sinking suspicion I knew what she was and what happened to the others at the camp. This woman might be the only chance we had to save some of the others, and she could not be allowed to escape.

Tired of running, I planted my feet and bowed my head. In my mind's eye, I conjured the image of a wall before the woman. Lifting my head, I watched as the mirage formed ten feet in front of her, but it developed too late, and she ran straight through it.

"Shit," I snarled before sprinting after her again.

In raven shape, Caim dove at her and cut off her forward path. Staggering back, she spun away, but he turned to the side. One of his wings skimmed the ground, clearing the forest floor of debris as he flew around her in a circle.

She was turning to head back toward the camp when I dove at her. Wrapping my arms around her waist, I tackled her. Without thinking, I turned to shelter her and took most of the impact with the ground as we bounced across the dirt.

When we finally came to a stop, I wanted to lay for a minute, catch my breath, and try to get this situation under control. The squirming Hell monster in my arms had other plans as she kicked my shins, clawed at my hands, and fought like a cornered hell-hound to get away from me.

Rolling, I pinned her stomach to the ground. Her fingers tore chunks of soil away as she tried to pull herself free of me. Her tiny feet continued to batter my shins as she wiggled beneath me.

"Enough!" I yelled at her.

Caim landed beside us and transformed into a man. "Fiery little thing," Caim murmured with his head canted admiringly to the side.

"Hmm." I grunted when she almost succeeded in driving my

nuts into my body with her heel. "I could use some help!" I snapped at Caim.

"She's a tiny thing; you can handle this," Caim replied with a smirk.

If I'd been able to wield fire, I would have torched the fallen angel's ass all the way back to the pits of Hell. I could only settle for a brief scowl at him before the witch almost launched me off her back with a vicious buck of her hips.

Finally succeeding in pinning her down, I sat on her back as she squirmed like a worm beneath me. I caught my breath while I kept her hands clasped against the small of her back. After a few minutes, her struggles ceased, and she lay panting beneath me.

A twinge of regret filled me as her forehead lowered to the ground and her glorious hair fell forward to shield her features. Seized by the urge to know what she looked like, I carefully adjusted my hold on her, rose slightly, and rolled her over.

My breath caught when I found myself staring into almond-shaped eyes the same color as her hair. I'd never seen eyes like hers before, but then I'd never seen anyone like *her* before. From her slender, pert nose to her rose-red lips and round cheeks, she was exquisite. Yet the dusting of freckles across her nose and cheeks gave her an innocent air that contradicted her inherent nature, as the jinn were anything but innocent.

And I did not doubt that for the first time in my life, I found myself face-to-face with a jinni, a member of the jinn race. The involvement of the jinn in whatever happened to the others was the only thing that made some sense.

None of us knew much about the jinn. Their powers were mysterious and frightening, which was part of the reason one of Kobal's ancestors locked them behind the ninetieth seal in Hell. The jinn were set free when all the seals collapsed.

The woman stared at me with a mixture of annoyance and fear, but if she could do something to me like what she'd done to those at the camp, I'd already be sleeping somewhere.

How does the jinn power work?

I didn't think we'd get any answers from her, but I didn't plan to release her anytime soon. All jinn would happily torment and kill any who fell under their spell, but something about this small, deadly woman intrigued me.

"Well, hello," I greeted; her glower deepened. "And where were you running off to?"

When Corson skidded to a halt beside me, the bird earring dangling from the tip of his pointed ear swayed back and forth. Corson's foot-long talons protruded from the backs of his hands as he leveled the jinni with a stare promising death.

Cradled against his chest, Wren's pale hair fell over his arm. Her matching earring to Corson's twirled around before coming to a halt. The anguished look on Corson's face was one I'd never seen before. As an adhene demon, Corson lived for laughs and to fight, but once he claimed Wren as his Chosen, he also started living for her. Her death, if it happened, would devastate him.

I would *not* allow that to happen. Love wasn't something I ever planned to experience in my life, but I wouldn't lose one of the few friends I had, or his Chosen.

"What did you do to those in our camp?" Corson demanded.

Beneath me, the woman sagged, and most of the fight went out of her as she gazed from Corson to Wren and back again. Sadness crept over her features, but I knew better than to think a jinni would ever regret their actions. I may not have dealt with them before, but their ruthlessness and trickery were legendary.

"I didn't do anything to them," the woman murmured.

"Liar!" Corson accused. "Whatever you did, *fix it!*"

The woman glanced at me and nervously licked her lips. My gaze fastened on the glistening wetness she left on her full bottom lip. Despite this horrible situation, I found myself growing aroused as I inhaled her scent. She held the fiery aroma of Hell, but also something else...

Then, it hit me. She smelled of the promise of spring, a warm, cloudless day on Earth, and better things to come, and I wanted *more* of her.

CHAPTER THREE

Amalia

I REFUSED to let them see my apprehension as I glanced from the striking demon perched on my chest to the grief-stricken one holding the woman in his arms. Though the woman looked entirely human, I sensed something more powerful beneath her surface.

I was tempted to fight against the demon on my chest again but exhausting myself further wasn't going to help me in this situation. If the fallen angel hadn't gotten in the way, I could have outrun him, but now that he had me, there would be no escape. He was stronger than I was.

Besides, I wasn't much of a fighter. It went against who I was, but if I got the chance, I would fight for my life.

To get out of this, I had to keep my wits about me, and I didn't think they'd let me go anytime soon, not while their brethren remained trapped in the Abyss.

I'd finally experienced freedom from the seal, and already it was being yanked away from me. I should never have gone near the encampment, but though they didn't tell me what they planned, I'd known the jinn were up to something there today. I had to see what they'd done, even if I hated their actions.

And seen I had, but then I'd also *been* seen. I hadn't expected to discover anyone here free of the Abyss, but I still would have gone to see what the jinn had done; I just would have been more careful about my approach.

Grinding my teeth, I steadied myself as, behind the man sitting on me, one of the angels moved. He was as golden as the sun, and the one who landed beside him was as black as the raven he assumed the form of when he attacked me. I'd heard stories of the golden angel, Raphael, who descended from Heaven recently. Raphael left Heaven, but he wasn't considered one of the fallen angels, unlike his brother, Caim, who'd been evicted from Heaven six thousand years ago with the rest of the fallen.

I'd believed the stories of the angels to be nothing more than rumors. How could a fallen angel and a golden one work together without trying to kill each other? And how could they be working with the palitons?

A golden angel and a fallen one following the king of Hell sounded ludicrous, but there they stood as opposite as they could get from each other, but both magnificent, powerful, and terrifying in their own way.

Until the seal fell, I'd never dealt with any demons outside of the jinn, and I most certainly hadn't encountered any humans, horsemen, or angels. Since being freed, I still hadn't met any of the fallen angels or horsemen. I'd met only a few humans, and the demons I encountered, I got away from as quickly as I could.

But at least those I'd met wouldn't consider me their enemy; I couldn't say the same about those gathered around me. I'd fallen into the hands of the palitons, and I didn't see it going well for me.

The jinn were locked behind the seal years before the fallen angels entered Hell and the newest varcolac demon, Kobal, rose from the Hellfires to become the king of Hell. Before we were freed, we knew nothing of who ruled Hell, the angels, or what was happening within Hell. What the jinn learned of Kobal and his followers came from other craetons on Earth.

Once freed from the seal, we'd learned fast that things had changed a *lot* over the years. And now, the varcolac who'd sealed the jinn away was dead. Hell was in ruins, and the fallen angel Astaroth, some demons, seal creatures, and the horsemen had aligned to become a threat to the newest varcolac's rule. My parents and most of the jinn had chosen to align with those craetons, leaving me... lost.

I didn't want to be a craeton, but I didn't want to leave my family either, especially while I was still mortal and therefore susceptible to death more than most demons. Once I stopped aging, became immortal, and my empath ability strengthened further, I might have no choice but to leave them as I feared their penchant for cruelty might ultimately destroy me.

Behind the seals, there wasn't anyone for the jinn to persecute; on Earth, there were so many they could destroy, and I couldn't stand by and watch it happen.

But that was a problem for another day; I had a far larger one looming over me. What had I gotten myself mixed up in here with these palitons? Most of their allies were trapped in the Abyss, but these were still some of the most powerful creatures on the planet, and they had *me*. I cursed my curiosity and empathy as I tried and failed to plot an escape.

Why wasn't I faster? But I knew the answer. Jinn were extremely fast, but I wasn't immortal yet, and I hadn't fully come into my abilities.

Cursing my inability to outrun them, I glared at the demon restraining me. His smile didn't falter. I'd never seen a demon quite like him before. Even the jinn, who were some of the best-looking demons, couldn't boast one as sculpted as this man.

His ice blond hair and dark blond eyebrows emphasized the

chiseled planes of his face and silver eyes. His hair mostly covered the black horns curving back against the sides of his head, but the polished, sharp tips poked out, and I guessed them to be about six inches in length.

I bit my lip as I wondered what it would be like to run my fingers over those horns. I'd love to discover if they were as smooth as they appeared. Lithe in build, I couldn't stop my eyes from raking over his broad shoulders and tapered waist as desire spread through me. I'd experienced desire before, of course, but not toward a man who would probably prefer to kill me just because of my jinni status.

Get it together, Amalia, or you'll die today.

Lifting my chin, I pushed aside my lust and stared defiantly back at the demon as an arrogant smirk curved his full lips. I could pretend he didn't intrigue me, but he *knew* he did. Well, of course he did, I wore my emotions on my face and in my eyes. If I spent enough time with my captors, it wouldn't take them long to figure that out.

The fact I wore my emotions openly for everyone to see hadn't been an issue in Hell, but now it was a curse.

The demon with the black hair holding the woman stepped closer to us, drawing my attention to them. I didn't need my empath ability to know he loved the woman; I recognized love when I saw it. Even if I hadn't been an empath, the jinn were adept at reading emotions.

Then, I saw the marks on his neck and hers and caught their mingled scents.

Chosen! No wonder he was so desolate; he probably felt like a big part of him was dying.

My heart twisted as his sorrow beat against me, and yet again I cursed my empath ability. Some might see my ability to feel another's emotions as a weapon; I saw it as a burden but one I couldn't rid myself of as I'd been born with the Fault that ran through the jinn lines.

Behind the seal, being one of the Faulted didn't matter as jinn had empathy toward each other, but most of them felt nothing for anyone outside our breed of demon. Outside the seal, with so many more emotions and other creatures to deal with, my empath ability made me feel weaker than most of the other jinn as I didn't possess their ruthlessness.

There were other Faulted jinn who were also empaths, but they'd branched off and gone their own way a few months after being freed from Hell. I'd yearned to go with them, as I fit in more with the Faulted than the jinn I remained with, but I wasn't ready to leave my parents.

And now I was in this mess because of my empath ability—which was stronger than the rest of the Faulted despite my young age—and what my family did to the palitons today. I had no idea how to get out of it either.

Even if I could get out of it, I couldn't leave this demon in such misery. I couldn't stand the idea of a Chosen losing their mate. My parents were Chosen. I'd grown up surrounded by their love, and if something happened to one of them, the other would die.

I may not completely fit in with my parents, and they may not understand me, but we deeply loved each other.

"Who are you?" I asked the man on my chest.

His smile somehow managed to be arrogant and seductive all at once. This guy knew exactly how gorgeous he was, which only made me want to kick him more.

"I think the better question is, *who* are *you*?" he asked.

"I am Amalia, and you?"

"Pretty name," he murmured.

The liquid silver of his eyes deepened to a nearly black hue when they latched onto my mouth. My breath caught as my body reacted to the desire he emanated. I contemplated trying to wiggle

INTO THE ABYSS 23

out from under him again, but I wouldn't succeed, and I might only arouse him further.

"Stop flirting with her, Magnimus!" the demon holding the woman barked.

"Magnimus," I muttered.

Magnimus sat further back as he tilted his head to survey me. "I prefer to be called Magnus," he said.

"Magnus," I repeated the familiar name. He was a close friend of the king, but that was all I knew about him.

My eyes flickered to the demon with the lethal talons who looked about to gut Magnus and me.

"That is Corson," Magnus said.

Corson was one of the king's second-in-command, I knew.

"Fix this!" Corson snarled at me.

"I can't," I whispered.

"Yes, you can! Undo whatever you sick fucks did and bring her back to *me!*" Corson commanded.

Taking a deep breath, I focused on Magnus. He was far more rational than Corson, and I suspected he would be easier to deal with. "Please, let me up."

Magnus snorted with laughter. "I don't think so."

I gritted my teeth against my frustration. "I'm not going to run. You'll only catch me again."

"Maybe you won't run, and we *would* catch you, but we also can't have you casting any spells or whatever it is you jinn do."

I rolled my eyes. "We don't cast spells; we seep into minds."

Though his expression remained arrogant, I felt a tendril of unease waft from him. "You *seep* into minds?"

"Yes, kind of. Let me up and I'll explain."

He studied me before releasing my hands and rising to his feet in one fluid movement. Sitting up, I rubbed my wrists together while I surveyed those gathered around me.

"Do you know nothing of the jinn?" I asked.

"No one does; it's one of the reasons you were locked away," Magnus replied.

"Because you feared what we could do?"

"Because our ancestors did. Until recently, we've had zero interaction with your kind."

"And what are the other reasons we were locked away?"

"Because you're sadistic, manipulative liars who take joy in tormenting others," Magnus stated.

I forced myself not to wince at his harsh assessment of the jinn. "Aren't all demons like that?"

"Many demons don't turn on each other the way the jinn and other craetons do; we focus our need to wreak havoc on warping souls into wraiths. The jinn, and everything else once locked behind the seals, would have destroyed Hell and all the demons in it if they weren't caged."

Not all jinn are like that.

"None of this matters," Corson interjected.

"But it does," I said. "I can't fix this. It's not a spell woven over them, but something deeper. Only the affected can break themselves free of the Abyss. If they're strong enough to escape the Abyss, then they'll survive; if not, they'll die."

CHAPTER FOUR

Magnus

"No!" I shouted and leapt in front of Corson when he charged toward Amalia.

The sound he emitted would have made a barta demon cower, but I remained in front of him, blocking his path to her. Even with Wren cradled against his chest, I had no doubt he could slice Amalia's head from her shoulders without getting a speck of blood on his Chosen.

"Killing her isn't going to solve anything," I told him. "And we may be able to get her to help us."

Corson's talons extended and retracted as he gazed at Amalia with a look of pure hatred.

A rustle caused me to glance back as Amalia rose. Caim and Raphael moved to flank her, but she didn't try to run again. Instead, she held Corson's gaze while she smoothed the front of her dress.

I kept one eye on Corson and one on her. I didn't trust either of them not to do something reckless. "What is the Abyss?" I asked her.

Her fine-boned hands stilled on her dress. "It's our world, kind of."

"What does that mean?" Corson demanded.

"It's another plane; one only the jinn can open a doorway into and where they trap their victims."

Victims? What an odd choice of word for her to use. I would have thought the jinn saw those they snared more as prey or play-things, but *never* victims.

Is she putting on a show for us? But I didn't think so as she seemed unaware she'd used the word.

Lifting her hand, she held it sideways in front of her face. Then, she weaved her fingers in a slow wavy line from her forehead to her chin. As she did so, a ripple stirred the air before she wiped it away with her hand. She lowered her hand and folded it into the skirt of her dress.

"And in the Abyss, the jinn hold those they trap," she said.

But they're all still here. Amalia followed my gaze when I looked at where Wren lay nestled in Corson's arms.

"Not physically hold them; they mentally trap them in the Abyss," she said as she seemed to guess at my thoughts. "The jinn possess a form of mind control, but it only works on those who allow them in with a wish."

"I've seen humans screw themselves to death while the jinn watched. They were moving freely and not trapped in any Abyss. Why is Wren there?" Corson demanded.

Amalia sighed. "The bodies of those humans may have still moved, but their minds were in the Abyss."

"So, jinn are somehow capable of separating the mind from the body?" Raphael asked.

"Or conscious awareness at least," Amalia said. "Depending on what someone wishes, the jinn are capable of doing many things. If someone wishes to be good at sex, then the jinn may make it so they practice it over and over again, until they die.

The wisher might not even be aware of their body's deterioration."

"Those humans were miserable and aware of what was going on," Corson spat.

"The jinn are also capable of allowing that to happen," Amalia whispered. "They can keep the mind in the body but give the mind no power over the body. Some jinn take great pleasure in pain."

"And what about you?" I demanded.

"What about me?" she retorted.

"Do you take great pleasure in pain?"

"I'm not like most of my kind."

Corson stepped toward Amalia. "Oh, I'm sure you're different."

An almost pleading look came into her eyes when she looked at me. "I *am* different."

I wanted to believe her, but one thing we all knew about the jinn was they were manipulative creatures capable of almost anything.

"Fine, don't believe me," she muttered when none of us responded to her.

"How can we get them out of the Abyss?" I asked.

She refused to meet my eyes as she spoke. "I told you, only the affected can free themselves, and when they do, their mind will return to their bodies."

"There has to be something we can do to *help* them get free."

Her fair eyebrows drew together over the bridge of her slender, freckled nose. "I'm not sure if I would be able to do anything, but I *can* enter the Abyss and at least see what they're going through or maybe try to do... something."

"And to do that, you would separate your consciousness from your body?" Caim asked.

"No, I can physically enter the Abyss."

"You expect us to let you out of our sight for one second?" Corson demanded.

I shot him a warning look over my shoulder, provoking her wouldn't do us any good, but the panicked gleam in his eyes silenced my censuring words. Not only did Wren's life hang in the balance, but so did his.

When I turned back to Amalia, her attention was focused on Wren, and if I hadn't known any better, I would believe the sad look in her eyes, which had become a more ochre hue, was real.

"No," she murmured. "I don't. But it might be the only hope you have."

"Can you take someone into the Abyss with you?" I inquired.

She held her palms out before her. "I don't know. I've never entered the Abyss before."

"Liar," Corson accused.

Her eyes deepened to a reddish hue. "I understand your Chosen is in danger and you're terrified, but you don't know me, so *back* off! I don't have to offer to help at all, and if you keep talking to me like that, I won't!"

I planted my palm firmly in Corson's chest when he stepped toward her again. "Enough," I growled at him and worried he'd slice my hand off at the wrist. The appendage would grow back, but I'd prefer not having to deal with a missing hand for the next few days. "We'll see if I can go into this Abyss with her."

"I'll go with her," Corson said.

"No. You will stay with Wren and keep her protected."

"But if Wren's in there, I might be able to pull her back through our bond."

"I'm not taking you with me," Amalia stated before I could reply.

Fury darkened Corson's features as he scowled at her.

"I don't trust you not to hurt me should you fail in freeing her," Amalia continued.

"You don't have a choice," Corson hissed.

"She does," I said. "And it will be *me* who goes. The angels are needed here to keep watch from the sky and get word back to Kobal should it become necessary. You *have* to stay with Wren." I turned away from Corson before he could protest my decision. "Will you take me?" I asked Amalia.

She bit her bottom lip and studied me intently before replying, "Yes."

"And how do you plan to get back?" Corson asked me.

"I'll bring him back," Amalia said, as if the answer was completely obvious.

It was not so obvious to me or the others. She could easily take me into her Abyss and leave me there to rot.

There wasn't anything Corson wouldn't do to get Wren back, but I saw the doubt and hesitation in his eyes when they met mine. He'd do anything for Wren, but he didn't want someone sacrificed in his place if that was Amalia's plan for me.

"Magnus, once you're in there, she can take you anywhere," he said. "For all we know, she can open another portal somewhere else in the world and leave you there. Or it could be nothing but a trap that will spring and destroy you the second you enter."

"You don't know what you're talking about," Amalia said. "The jinn can only open a portal in and out of the Abyss to where they were on Hell, Earth, or the Abyss. If we leave this spot, we will return to *this* spot. If we return here and then go back to the Abyss, we will emerge in the last place we left."

"And what if you open the portal into some trap for him?" Caim inquired.

Amalia's agitation grew as she fiddled with her dress. "There is no trap."

"And we're just supposed to believe you?" Raphael inquired.

"No matter what I say, you won't believe me, so make up your own minds about that," she retorted.

"If you've never been to the Abyss, then where will the portal open?" I asked.

She looked helplessly at me. "I have no idea where or what we'll be stepping into. That is a risk we both have to take."

CHAPTER FIVE

Magnus

"I DOUBT this Abyss of yours was designed to harm the jinn in any way," Corson said. "So I doubt it's much of a risk to you."

Amalia's jaw locked, and her eyes deepened to a more reddish hue as she focused on the woods.

The idea of stepping into a plane I'd never heard of and knew nothing about was less enticing to me than having sex with a spiny clackos demon—and the clackos were known to have spikes on *every* part of their anatomy. But there was one simple fact in this: "We don't have a choice," I reminded him.

"*I* will go," Corson said again.

"What if she does to you what was done to the others?" Raphael asked me.

"I *will* bring him back the way he is! And I didn't do this to the others! I had no hand in this!" Amalia stared at all of us, but when no one responded to her words, she continued, "I also can't do to him what was done to the others because he didn't call me to him."

"What does call you to me mean?" I asked.

"If someone is desperate enough for something, the jinn are attracted to them. They can often manipulate those who call them into wishing for something. Once that wish is made, the victim is susceptible to the jinn's power and pulled into the Abyss."

There's that victim word again.

"I have no sway over you and can't ensnare you," she said to me.

"And how do we know you're telling the truth?" I asked.

"I *am* different from most of the jinn, but I can't make you believe me. So, we'll all stay here and get to know each other better while we wait to see if any of those in the Abyss are strong enough to come back to us."

Corson didn't look at all happy with that idea.

"Has anyone escaped the Abyss before?" Raphael inquired.

"Some did before the jinn were sealed away. I'm not sure if anyone has broken out of the Abyss since the jinn were freed. I stay out of this aspect of the jinn's lives."

She held my gaze while I stared skeptically at her, Corson snorted derisively, Caim smiled in amusement, and Raphael remained straight-faced. Something about her made me want to trust her, but only a fool believed a jinni, and I was no fool.

"What do the jinn do with those they have in the Abyss?" I asked.

"Like you feed on the wraiths, and so do I, the jinn also feed on the life force of those they trap," she said, "but I suspect you already knew the answer to that."

I had known the answer, but I was curious to see if she would admit it to me. "Will there be other jinn in the Abyss?"

"Most likely."

"And they'll most likely be feeding on our friends."

She bowed her head, and though it hadn't been a question, she replied, "Yes."

Corson held Wren closer as I rubbed my forehead. I could well be walking into my death, but Corson wasn't stable enough to go, and Raphael and Caim were needed here. Plus, I wasn't sure Raphael would intervene to help someone in the Abyss if he felt he might be interfering with their fate, and I didn't know if Caim could be completely trusted.

I was the only option.

"After Amalia and I go, you'll have to gather everyone and move them somewhere they'll all be together and easier to protect. You know the place," I said to Corson.

"I do," Corson replied.

I refused to say the location or that it was a cave out loud as I wouldn't give this jinni any clue about where the bodies would be hidden. And I couldn't stay to help them get everyone to safety without giving away the location to her. They would have to handle this on their own.

"It's not only the jinn we have to worry about; they're all vulnerable to *any* enemy now," I said.

Corson's jaw clenched, but he didn't protest my words.

"We will keep them safe," Raphael vowed.

Caim inspected his nails, but when he felt the weight of all our stares, he lifted his head. "What?" he asked.

"Did you hear what I said?" I demanded of him.

"Oh, yes, we will keep the others safe," he said distractedly. Then, he tilted his head to study Amalia. "There's something about you...."

When Amalia stared back at him, her eyes lost their reddish hue to become the color of a sunrise. With a start, I realized her eyes appeared to shift with her emotions, and I found myself questioning what each color revealed about her.

Who cares? She's a jinni and someone to stay far away from. That's the only thing that matters about her. Sometimes, I couldn't deny I was as intelligent as I was good looking.

"What do you mean; what is there about her?" I asked Caim.

Caim seemed to rouse himself from somewhere else as he

blinked and unfurled his wings. "I should keep watch," he said before taking to the sky.

"Is he losing his mind?" I asked Raphael as Caim circled overhead in ever-widening arcs. He vanished over the trees before reemerging in raven form.

Raphael shrugged and rested his hand on the hilt of his sword. "Caim is as he is, and as he will be."

"Angel riddles, delightful," I muttered before turning to Amalia. "Let's get on with this. What do we have to do?"

~

Amalia

I didn't tell Magnus I wasn't sure I could do any of what was necessary to enter the Abyss. Corson was staring at me like he intended to gut me, and unlike the other jinn, I wouldn't recover if those talons eviscerated me.

I hadn't been lying; I'd never entered the Abyss before. Within the seal, our ability to enter the Abyss was shut down, and since being freed, I'd never had a reason to enter the plane. Out of curiosity, I once opened a doorway into the Abyss, but I never went through the portal, and I'd never considered taking a non-jinni with me. I'd heard it was possible, but I wasn't fully matured, so who knew what I could or couldn't do.

But I had to do something before they decided I was useless and killed me. I'd just gotten my freedom, and I wouldn't lose it now.

The only thing I could do was open the Abyss, and if Magnus couldn't enter with me, at least I might have a chance of fleeing into it to get away from them. If I failed, they'd probably kill me, but if I succeeded in escaping, maybe I could do something to help them.

They hate you simply because of what you are; why would you bother to help them?

It was true, but as Corson's anguish beat against me, I knew I would help them because, whether they believed me or not, I was different from most of the jinn and I couldn't stand the suffering of another.

Then, a possible way to help those affected by what the jinn did today occurred to me. However, none of those around me would go for it, so I decided to keep it to myself. If they didn't kill me, maybe I'd get the chance to put my idea into action later. And if they did kill me, then screw them for not giving me the opportunity to help because they despised my kind.

I'd prefer not to die for the sins of my brethren though.

Taking a deep breath, I threw back my shoulders and lifted my hand before my face. I closed my eyes as I drew on the well of power flowing through the veins of all the jinn. While I concentrated, the creaking branches, bird song, and whisper of the wind faded until there was only the Abyss and me.

Even though I'd never entered the Abyss and only opened a portal into it once before, I *knew* the jinn were the Abyss, and the Abyss was us. Even locked behind the seal, I'd felt it in my being.

The power of my connection to the Abyss spread warmth through my arms, down my thighs, and into my fingers and toes. Turning my hand sideways in front of my face, I made a weaving motion with it as I ran it down to the center of my chest.

The fabric of the air pulled silently back when I opened a doorway between this world and the next.

Opening my eyes, I stared into the portal before me. Roughly the size of a doorway, it was a gray canvas blocking out the scenery beyond it and revealing nothing of what lay within the Abyss. No breeze flowed in or out of the portal; no noise sounded in my ears in this world or the next, but the Abyss beckoned me to enter it.

When I opened the doorway before, the unknowing of what lay

beyond was too frightening for me. I'd quickly closed it before something could escape or something that didn't belong inside it could enter. The unknowing still unnerved me, but I no longer had a choice; I had to step into the Abyss.

Tearing my eyes away from the portal, I turned back to find Magnus's gaze riveted on it. "Can you see it?" My voice rang louder than normal in my ears.

Magnus strode forward to stand beside me. "Yes."

"We all can," Raphael said.

Easily eight inches taller than me, I had to tip my head back to meet Magnus's eyes as I spoke to him. "I'm not sure if it's necessary or not, but I think I should hold onto you while we enter."

Uncertain of how he would react, I hesitated before slipping my hand into his. I started when a small current of something ran through me, but instead of disrupting the flow of my power, it swelled my ability within me.

I couldn't stop my fingers from stroking his hand. His skin warmed mine, and for a second, I almost stepped closer to him as a frisson of need rocked me. Magnus's emotions caressed my skin as his surprise faded to curiosity then desire. When he met my gaze again, his thumb stroked the back of my hand.

"Are you ready, Amalia?" he inquired.

The way he said my name sent a shiver down my spine, but was I ready? Throughout all of this, I hadn't stopped to think about the consequences of my actions. I was bringing an outsider into the Abyss, and not just any outsider, but a paliton close to the king. The jinn would be *furious* with me, but they would forgive me. Would they forgive me if something went horrifically wrong though?

"I won't tolerate the jinn being hurt," I said to him. "We are going to find your friends, not to fight the jinn. I'll bring you back immediately if you try to hurt them, and know that I *am* your only way back here. None of the other jinn would allow you to go free, but I will."

Magnus's silver eyes narrowed at me. "I won't purposely hurt anyone, but I will defend my life and the lives of my friends if it becomes necessary."

I absorbed the emotions coming from him. He was uncertain about this, but his words were true, and that was the best I could hope for.

"Okay, let's go."

Keeping his hand in mine, together, we stepped into the Abyss.

CHAPTER SIX

Amalia

I DIDN'T KNOW what I'd expected to discover in the Abyss: nothing, fog, chaos, floating brains, or conscious thought streaming through until one mind couldn't be separated from another, but none of that unfolded before me.

Instead, I found myself standing beside Magnus in a meadow with waves of waist-high, violet grass flowing around us. No breeze caressed my cheeks, but the grass bowed and swayed as if currents of air stirred it. Before us, the grass covered a steep hill rising into the air until it seemed to touch the red sky.

When I glanced back through the portal, I spotted Corson and Raphael leaning close together with their eyes narrowed as they watched us. Then, the edges of the portal started closing in on each other until the door-sized hole became nothing but a pinprick before fading completely.

Beyond where the doorway was located lay a large body of reddish water. I couldn't tell if that was the natural color of the water or if it was reflecting the sky. Pink sand surrounded the shore of the lake stretching as far as the eye could see in that direction. Beyond the twenty feet of shoreline, the meadow started, but unlike the grass, the water was as still as glass.

The second the portal closed, noise returned. I still didn't feel a breeze, but the sighing sounds of the feathery grass ends filled my ears as they danced. Something about the music they created sounded melancholy, and a twinge of sadness tugged at my heart as I released Magnus's hand to caress a fluffy tip.

When it slid across my palm, the seed head was as soft as a butterfly's wings. On Earth, those colorful insects had fascinated me, as almost everything on Earth did, but something about butterflies intrigued me more than anything else.

One day, when they were especially active, I'd lain by a pond watching the creatures flutter and dance around me in the sunlight. The longer I lay there, the more some started settling on me until I was shocked to discover myself covered in them. Their supple wings stroked my skin, and their multi-colored hues captivated me. It had been one of the best days of my life topped only by the day I was set free of the seal.

When I released the grass, it bowed its head as if it were mourning something, but grass couldn't grieve. That was impossible. But no matter how impossible it was, my empath ability insisted this field was mourning something.

But what?

Unfortunately, the grass couldn't answer that question, and I had no idea how to figure it out.

"The grass sounds like the ocean," Magnus murmured as he studied the field.

"The what?" I inquired.

"The ocean. It's numerous bodies of salty water on Earth located near the shores of the land. Where we are on Earth is pretty far from the closest sea."

"I've never seen it. Does the ocean sound sad too?"

"I suppose it could sound sad to some. You think the grass sounds sad?"

"Yes. Don't you?"

He listened for a minute before shrugging. "Maybe it does. You don't know much about the human world, do you?"

"I know what I've had the opportunity to learn since being freed, but I haven't really traveled, and I didn't have the chance to see much while locked behind a seal," I retorted.

"No, you didn't," he said.

Before I knew what he intended, he lifted his hand to run his fingers over my cheek. I tried to recoil from him but found myself unable to move as his touch sent a thrill through me.

"The ocean is sort of like the River Asharún," he said. "Except the ocean is bigger and blue instead of red."

"I don't know what the River Asharún is either."

His hand stilled on my face. "You never saw or heard about the Asharún?"

"I was *born* behind a *seal*," I reminded him impatiently.

When he lowered his hand, I almost snatched it back to place it against my face again. For some reason, the loss of contact inexplicably saddened me, but I restrained myself from reaching out to him again. Getting closer to this demon was an even worse idea than bringing him here in the first place.

"And none of the jinn told you about it?" he asked.

"Why would they? I never expected to see it, and why would they torment me with things I could never experience? The jinn told me about the Abyss because I could feel it inside me." I placed a hand on my chest. "And I had to know what it was I felt, so they explained it to me. Once we were free of the seal, the jinn told me what I needed to know about other demons, the varcolac, craetons, and palitons, but there was no point in learning about Hell when we wouldn't be returning to it."

"I'm surprised they didn't tell you about what you were missing behind the seal for the fun of it; I thought jinn feasted on cruelty."

"You know nothing about my kind. Some of them can be cruel to those outside our species, but we *don't* inflict hurt on each other."

"Some of them *can* be cruel to those outside the jinn? Are you saying there are jinn who don't enjoy torturing others?"

"I already told you there are some who don't," I retorted, growing annoyed with the stubborn demon. "But I know you won't believe me, so what does it matter?"

His eyes ran over me in a leisurely perusal that escalated my pulse and made my breasts feel heavier all while I resisted kicking him for his constant skepticism.

"I suppose it doesn't," he finally said.

"Then you'd suppose right." I couldn't stop the twinge of disappointment I felt over his continued inability to look past *what* I was to *who* I was, but then, I knew how manipulative many jinn could be, so I couldn't blame him for being a stubborn asshole.

"Where are we?" he asked and turned his attention to the meadow.

"The Abyss."

"But *where* in it?"

"I... ah... I'm not sure. I didn't expect to find anything like this here, but then I'm not sure what I expected to discover here."

"You've really never been here before?"

"Do you have difficulty hearing, or are you purposely being obtuse?" I demanded. "I already told you I haven't been here. And now you're going to accuse me of lying, so let's bypass the bullshit and start walking. If we climb to the top of the hill, we should be able to see more."

I didn't look back at him as I started through the soughing grass. The ends tickled my arms, and when I ran my fingers over the tips, some of the seeds spilled free. I caught them and lifted them to examine the tiny, deep purple seeds. When I poked at them, I discovered they were hard to the touch.

The unfelt breeze moving the grass stirred the seeds in my palm but didn't take them. Stopping, I lifted the seeds close to my lips and blew on them. They danced before me, swirling higher while the currents of air spun them.

When I turned to watch them floating away, I came face-to-face with Magnus. He glowered at me as he folded his arms across his chest. He looked formidable in a way he hadn't before.

For the first time, a trickle of apprehension ran through me. I was in an unfamiliar place with a demon who was stronger than me. This was my world, but I knew how to use it to my advantage as well as I knew this man.

He didn't trust me, he feared my kind, and though he'd acted easier going than the other palitons, and I perceived no murderous intentions from him, anyone could change in an instant.

I almost stepped away before rethinking the action. I refused to be intimidated by him.

"Are you creating this?" he asked.

I blinked at him in surprise. "Creating this? How could I possibly do that?"

"Perhaps a jinni's ability works in much the same way as mine."

"And how does yours work?" Leaning forward, I inspected his horns a little more closely. They were so shiny, but there were plenty of demons with horns and none of them had captivated me this much. "What type of demon are you, or what *types* of demon? I know many demons are mixed now."

Hence, my Fault.

"I'm not a mix," he said.

Oddly entranced by them, and determined to know what they felt like, I stretched my fingers toward his horns before coming to my senses and snatching them back. I despised the heat creeping into my cheeks when I glanced away from him.

"Then what are you?" I asked.

"I'm a demon."

He's not going to tell me.

Not that I blamed him, I wouldn't trust me either, but it only reinforced the truth I'd learned since arriving on Earth; I didn't fit in with most of the jinn, I didn't fit in with other demons, and I didn't fit in with humans.

At least behind the seal, my differences hadn't separated me so much from my family, and I'd had no contact with other demons. But my small seal had been blown apart, and now I knew nothing of the world or those in it.

Feeling a lot sadder than when we first entered, I turned away from him and trudged up the hill through the grass.

Magnus

I COULDN'T SHAKE the twinge to my conscience Amalia's defeated air created. Happiness had exuded from her while she watched the seeds floating in the air; now, she looked dejected.

Is this really her first time here?

She'd insisted it was, but I found it impossible to believe her. If this was where the jinn came to inflict their torment, they would spend as much time here as they spent hunting for their victims on Earth. The jinn would never wait until they fed on and tortured their victims to death in here before returning to Earth to find new prey. No, a hunger like what the jinn possessed would propel them to hunt for more and more targets.

But Amalia had looked so enchanted with the grass that I almost found myself believing she'd never been here and she *wasn't* the same as the rest of her ravenous kind.

Maybe there really were jinn who were different. So very little was known about the creatures, it could be possible they weren't *all* destructive and malicious.

But then, she was jinn, and one thing I knew about the jinn was they were manipulative. This may all be an excellent act on her part.

Maybe it made me a fool, but I wanted to believe it wasn't.

My gaze dropped to the curve of her round ass, emphasized by the flow of her dress. I didn't think she realized it as she hadn't tried to use her looks to her advantage against me, but she was the most enticing woman I'd ever met.

Watching her, I couldn't help but visualize my hands cupping her ass as I rubbed my horns over her silken flesh. I'd never considered doing such a thing with my sensitive horns before, but I wanted to stroke every inch of her with them until she begged for more.

I'd gotten a hint of what her arousal would smell like before we stepped into this place and the fiery aroma was seared into my nostrils. If I dipped my head between her thighs to feast on her, she'd grip my horns, and her scent would increase until it engulfed me. I *craved* that with this woman.

When my growing erection started making walking difficult, I was torn from my fantasies of Amalia.

Idiot! For all I knew, Amalia was somehow feeding such fantasies into my mind, though I doubted it. I was well aware of what was going on around me, and her effect on me, whereas it seemed those in the camp were not. However, this was the world of the jinn, and if I wasn't careful, I wouldn't make it out of here alive.

I didn't look at her again but kept my gaze focused on where the land met the sky as we climbed.

When Amalia reached the top of the hill, she lifted her head, released a small cry, and stumbled back. The revulsion on her face told me I wasn't going to like what I saw before I reached the apex, but I could never have prepared myself for what lay beyond.

CHAPTER SEVEN

Magnus

"This is why others fear us," Amalia whispered.

If others saw this, they would do far more than fear the jinn; they would make it their mission to eradicate them. When Kobal learned of this, he may decide to eliminate the jinn completely, and I would help him.

Then, my gaze fell on Amalia's trembling lower lip, and the tears sliding down her cheeks. Her eyes were the color of ochre; it was a color that suggested heartache. I almost rested my hand on her shoulder to offer her comfort, but I couldn't fall into her trap if she were playing games with me.

Bowing her head, she turned from the scene below us and wiped away her tears. She threw back her shoulders and lifted her chin before meeting my gaze.

"I think your friends will be below," she said.

"I think you're right."

The only problem was I'd prefer not to enter what lay before us, and from the look on her face, so would Amalia, but I had no choice. I couldn't return to Earth without at least attempting to rescue as many of my friends as possible.

If I didn't do something to try to save them, so many could be lost, and I didn't have many friends. Corson would also join the status of lost or dead if I failed to save Wren. Shax was my friend for centuries before I retreated from the war we'd engaged in with Lucifer to work on honing my ability to create illusions.

I knew Lix before I retreated, but I wouldn't have called him a friend; I would now. Erin, Vargas, and Hawk had become my friends in the time since I first met them. Bale was not my favorite demon, and though I wouldn't call us friends, I'd never leave her to the fate of what lay below us, and she wouldn't leave me to it either.

Born and raised in Hell, I'd witnessed and created some pretty horrific things over the centuries. I'd seen the collapse of the seals and the slaughter Lucifer unleashed when he reached Earth, but none of it could have prepared me for the jinn's Abyss.

This place was a nightmare come to life.

The pathway unfurling before us meandered like a serpent through the rock walls lining it. From our position, I could see at least ten more pathways cutting across the barren valley in a sidewinding pattern that caused many of the paths to vanish in and out of view. I suspected it was all the same path stretching throughout, but it was impossible to tell.

On top of the jagged rocks the paths cut through stood thousands of scraggly trees over what must be miles of Abyss. Once we entered the pathway, the height of the walls would block most of the trees from us. The trees were bent over as if the air itself pushed down on their blackened branches, and irregular formations stuck up between their wilting trunks. Something about those formations tugged at my mind as I tried to place them.

They're rib bones. And that is a skull, but I don't think I've ever seen a creature shaped like that before.

"They're bones." Amalia placed her hand over her mouth as she came to the same conclusion I had.

"Are there any unusual beasts in this land?"

"Not that I know of. I was only ever told it was a land for the jinn."

So the jinn probably brought creatures into hunt and slaughter. *Is that why she brought me here? Am I their next hunt?*

That could be an excellent possibility, but dwelling on it would only make me paranoid, and I had far more significant problems to contend with. Besides, none of the skeletons looked demon or human, and most of them were small.

I turned my attention away from the trees and skeletons and back to where all the paths converged in the center of the Abyss. There, rising from a large crater was a multi-sided, metallic black, monolith.

The monolith rose at least a thousand feet into the air before ending in a pointed top. From here, I could see faint lines on it that I assumed were etchings marking the surface of it, but I was too far away to know for sure. Hovering in the air beside the primary structure, three more elongated, diamond-shaped monoliths orbited the massive one in the center like they were its moons.

All the same color as the main one, each of them was sharp enough to split a demon or Hell creature in two. As I watched, a fourth one rotated into view, and one of the others disappeared behind the central monolith.

Though I saw no sun, the Abyss was a scorched, barren wasteland. However, it wasn't shrouded in darkness. I didn't cast a shadow, but enough light emitted from somewhere that we could navigate the pathways.

When I glanced behind me, the purple grass continued to sway and dip. The red sky over the field and lake mirrored the one over the pathways and monolith, but the sky over the grass seemed less foreboding. Over the monolith, the sky had the appearance of a festering sore and looked prepared to strike down any who ventured into the inhospitable environment.

For a second, I pondered if the Abyss was real or if all this was something created to fuck with my mind. *Am I just like everyone else in the camp and playing out my role in the jinn's game?*

The possibility caused my mind to spin. Then, I recalled the way Amalia opened the portal and felt the grass brushing against my fingers and waist. No, the Abyss was real, and it was another plane, just as Earth, Hell, and Heaven were different planes residing alongside each other until the humans opened the gateway. Except, unlike those planes, the Abyss could be manipulated, and the jinn were adept at doing that. I had a feeling the Abyss evolved with the jinn or the jinn with the Abyss.

A part of me knew the Abyss could still be some elaborate deception, and I could be trapped like the others, but if I stayed focused on it, it would drive me mad. If this were a game, then I would have to play until I could break free, and if it wasn't, then it wasn't; but either way, I had to continue.

"Why the grass and lake and then this shithole? Why are there two such entirely different places in the Abyss?" I asked.

Amalia lowered her hand from her mouth and inhaled a shuddery breath. "I... I don't know."

Is she telling the truth? I didn't think she was capable of being this good of an actress, but trusting a jinni was what landed their victims in this place.

But I couldn't figure the Abyss out. It made no sense the jinn were trying to lure their victims into a false sense of security by bringing them into the field of grass before revealing *this* to them. They already had their victim here, there was no need for that, but perhaps it was their way of playing with them like a cat with a mouse.

Still...

I turned my attention back to the monolith as a bolt of silver lightning ripped from the sky. It pierced straight into the top of the main monolith. From there the lightning sizzled all the way down the structure, before racing back up to the top where it burst out in four different bolts that struck the heads of the orbiting moons.

Those smaller structures froze in place and started glowing before suddenly erupting and sending a flash of light across the land. Illuminated by the wave of light the bolt created, the red sky pinkened before becoming an angry red again. The original bolt sizzled when it hit the structure, but everything following it remained disconcertingly hushed.

Amalia gasped and rubbed at the goose bumps covering her flesh as she huddled into herself. She somehow looked smaller and was more than a little repulsed.

"What was that?" I asked.

"I don't know," Amalia murmured. "But I felt the... power and... the *wrongness* of whatever it was go through me. Didn't you?"

"No. What *do* you know about this place?"

Some of her revulsion vanished as she shot me an irritated look. "I've told you everything I know."

Turning away from the pathways, she continued to rub her arms while she stared across the field of swaying grass. "Maybe the two sides of the Abyss are so different because there are different jinn," she murmured. "This side—" She waved a hand at the grass. "—resonates with something inside *me*. But that side...." Her voice trailed off, and she didn't look back as she waved a hand behind her. "I don't want anything to do with it."

Is she lying to me? I despised this not knowing if I could trust her more than I loathed the barren land before us.

"But, the only choice we have is to go deeper into it," she said and faced the monolith again. "It's only grass and water back there. And here... well, here are pathways leading somewhere. I can't imagine there's anything good down there, which means its where we have to go."

"But what lies between here and where the pathways lead?"

Her troubled eyes met mine before darting away. "I don't know, but if the jinn are in this place, I suspect they're in the pit or close to that thing."

I didn't have to ask what she meant by that thing; I knew it was the monolith.

"Let's go." I didn't look back before starting onto the pathway.

CHAPTER EIGHT

Amalia

Everything about this place made my skin crawl, and I was afraid the lump clogging my throat might become a permanent condition. The jagged red, black, and gray rocks jutting from the walls surrounding us leeched any happiness from me.

I *despised* this place, yet a part of me belonged here as I couldn't deny something about the Abyss called to me. I didn't understand what that meant, or what about this stark place could resonate so deeply inside me when the Abyss represented everything I disliked about being a jinni.

Perhaps I was more like my family than I'd realized, but that answer didn't feel right. There was *something* here. What that something was, I didn't know, but I wouldn't back down from the wrongness of the Abyss, and I would *not* leave anyone trapped here if I could help them.

After seeing this place, I no longer cared what the consequences of getting involved in this might be for me with the other jinn. No one deserved to endure anything that happened here.

As we wound our way deeper into this place of despair, it became increasingly clear that though I loved my parents, I didn't fit in with them. When this was over, I would go to the Faulted and live with them.

Lifting my head, I was met with only more rock walls and the dead branches of the trees overhanging the pathway in some areas. In a few places, we had to step over the broken and nearly pulverized remains of small skeletal creatures. I kept my gaze diverted from those bones, but I couldn't forget the skeletons I'd seen scattered between the trees.

"Where are they?" I didn't realize I'd spoken the question out loud until Magnus replied.

"Are you hoping to find the jinn?"

"No!" I blurted. "I meant where are those who are trapped here? They have to be here somewhere, don't they?"

His eyes were questioning when they met mine, and then his gaze slid over me. I sensed he had no idea what to make of me, but in the end, his distrust would never allow him to see me as anything other than a jinni.

"I would think so," he replied before focusing on the path again. "I hope so anyway, as it means we're heading toward nothing otherwise. Can you open a portal out of here from this spot?"

"On the other side, we can open a doorway from anywhere, so I assume it's the same here." I stopped and lifted my hand before my face, but he grasped it before I could attempt an opening.

"Do the jinn know when someone opens a portal in and out of this place?"

"No."

His silver eyes were remorseless on mine as he tried to ascertain if I was telling the truth or not. While he silently debated this, his thumb slid over the back of my hand. It was a gesture I didn't think he was aware of, but my pulse picked up.

A prickle of awareness came to life in my breasts, and when my nipples poked against my dress, they drew Magnus's gaze to them. There was nothing I could do to hide them as, unlike humans, I didn't wear anything under my dress.

In Hell, we never wore clothing, but once on Earth, the jinn adapted to it. Most humans didn't trust anyone wandering around nude, and jinn needed to earn their trust to get their wish. I didn't have to do that, but I'd taken to wearing clothes because I liked the different colored dresses and the way they felt against my skin. Even the thin, pink slippers I wore were comfortable and fun, but I found the human's undergarments restrictive.

Besides, I didn't care if I was exposed more than a human would think acceptable. It was impossible to be shy when locked behind a seal with forty-six other jinn. My parents were Chosen and only with each other, but none of the other jinn were. They'd happily bounced from jinni to jinni, sometimes having orgies for endless periods of time.

As I grew older, I'd watch the things they did to each other and absorbed the enjoyment they took in it. I'd yearned to come of age and join them for something to break the monotony of my existence, but also because their sensual cries stimulated me in much the same way Magnus's gaze did.

If I'd never been caged behind the seal, I would have been free to experiment with demons closer to my age, but behind the seal, *all* the jinn were thousands of years older than me. While I was still aging, they'd seen me as too young to join them, but it was clear Magnus didn't see me as too young and would teach me things I'd only witnessed before.

The image of gripping Magnus's horns while pulling his mouth between my legs burst through my mind. I'd watched men and women enjoy the act with each other behind the seal and was impatient to experience it. But I didn't desire it with them, not anymore. I wanted it with *this* man.

It stunned me to realize that no matter how curious I'd been about having the jinn do to me what they did to each other, I'd never craved any of them as badly as I did Magnus.

Lust emanated from Magnus as his eyes slid from my breasts to my stomach before settling on the juncture between my thighs. He may not trust me, but he desired me. If we weren't in this awful place, I had no doubt I'd lift my dress and let him have me.

As it was, it took all I had not to lean against the rocks and beckon him closer, but I didn't think a quick taking by this man would be enough to satisfy me. And once it was done between us, I'd want to do it all over again.

What an odd thought to have.

I'd seen enough of demons to know they freely rotated through partners, it's what *I'd* planned to do once I got the chance, but I didn't think I'd easily move on from Magnus. Confusion rolled through me as I tried to process the odd thought while fighting my hunger for this man.

Then I realized I probably only thought it because Magnus was the first demon I'd encountered, outside the jinn, who didn't scare me.

Since being free of the seals, I had little contact with other demons. Those I did encounter were all craetons, and the maliciousness I'd sensed in them frightened me. They were also nowhere near as attractive as the man standing before me. A man who refused to see past what I was to *who* I was.

I should have gone with the Faulted; I thought, not for the first time since entering this place.

At least amongst them I was accepted, and they would shelter me from those who would have my empath ability going haywire. And once I stopped aging, they would stop treating me like a child and start treating me like a woman.

And they wouldn't desire me while completely distrusting me

as Magnus did. That reminder strengthened my resolve against him.

"We should go," I said and strode away from him.

Magnus

When Amalia found a side tunnel etched into the rocks surrounding us, I followed her into it.

"I need a break," she murmured.

Her shoulders were hunched up, and whereas the dress flowed about her before, it now hung limply against her slender frame as she walked. She couldn't fake this dejected air, could she?

"I hate this place."

I didn't think she'd meant for me to hear those words, but I did. Or maybe she *had* meant for me to hear them and they were part of the game she played. This wanting to trust her but unable to aspect of Amalia frustrated me.

"How do you know you can take a break here?" I asked.

"I don't. But I think it will be safer to relax off the main path than on it, don't you?"

When she glanced at me over her shoulder, her eyes were that sad, ochre color. Her colorful hair was a beacon of warmth in the gloom of this place that my fingers itched to run through.

"I don't know," I said.

"Well, I think it—"

Her voice broke off, and she halted abruptly as, before her, the path opened to reveal a lake of water the same bleak color as the rocks surrounding it. Then, she was moving forward with a nimble grace not entirely unlike the jinn, but that somehow struck me as different. When she fell beside the lake, it must have been painful for her knees to hit the rocks, but she didn't acknowledge it.

Leaning over, she gazed at her reflection before stretching her fingers toward the water. She snatched her hand back before she touched the lake and lifted her head to stare at me.

"What is it?" I asked her.

"I'm not sure, but there's power here."

Leaning back, she rested her hands on her knees and looked at the monolith in the distance. From here, only the top quarter of the structure was visible above the walls. When a new bolt crashed into the top of it before splintering off, Amalia hunched in on herself as she had before.

My head snapped around when voices pierced the quiet following the bolt. *Are the jinn coming? Did she set me up?*

Grinding my teeth together, I stalked to Amalia's side, grabbed her arm, and helped her rise. The movement caused strands of her hair to billow out and tickle my cheek. The scent and silken feel of it shoved my apprehension aside as I found myself momentarily enthralled by her.

Then the approaching voices and loud laughter pulled my attention away from her. *Get it together, you moron. She's no different than any of the numerous women you've seen and bedded over the years.*

But she wasn't like any other. There was something more to this woman, and that something more might get me killed if I didn't watch out. I was above lusting after a woman like this, and I was certainly above falling for one.

Falling for one? I didn't have time to ponder where that thought had come from.

Amalia looked frantically around before pointing toward a rocky outcropping. "There."

For all I knew, it could be where she planned to spring her trap on me, but I had no other choice. We were out in the open here. If she tried to take me down, she'd be in for a surprise as I had more than a few tricks up my sleeve when it came to my illusions.

I led her around the lake and toward the rocks. Slipping around the corner of one, I drew her into the alcove. I tugged her down beside me when I knelt and kept her against my side so I could see everything she did.

CHAPTER NINE

Amalia

THE WALL of the alcove pressed against my side as I craned my head to look out for the approaching voices. My heart hammered while I waited to see who was coming, and I bit my lip while I resisted tapping my foot.

I had no idea what I would do if we were discovered. I'd have to get Magnus out of here as fast as possible, but if the jinn learned I'd brought him here, what would they do?

Bringing someone into the Abyss wasn't forbidden, or at least I didn't think it was, but what did I know? I'd been told what this place was, but not much more about it, and everything with the jinn was so different since we fled Hell.

The warmth of Magnus's body against mine pulled my attention away from whoever was approaching as I focused on the feel of him against me. Closing my eyes, I inhaled the fiery scent of Hell on his flesh. Beneath the fire, I detected the more pleasing, earthy aromas of pine and leaves.

I'd only been on Earth for a short time, but it was already more of a home to me than Hell ever was, and I liked the fact Magnus's scent had mingled with the humans' woods. No, I more than liked it, I realized as I inhaled deeply.

During my time on Earth, I'd grown fascinated by the colorful, vibrant plane and tried to learn as much about the human world as I could. It was a difficult undertaking as I'd avoided humans once the jinn realized they could manipulate them into the Abyss like they did demons. So I absorbed as much knowledge as I could on my own and peppered the jinn who moved more freely amid humans and demons with endless questions.

When Magnus's scent lulled me closer, I lifted my hands and rested them on his arm without pausing to consider the action.

What is wrong with me?

I didn't know if my strong attraction to him was from my pending immortality, and therefore increasing libido, or if it was the man himself, but I couldn't get enough of him. Leaning closer to him, one of my breasts brushed his arm. I didn't realize I'd turned my mouth into his neck until his head turned toward me and his lips caressed my temple.

Startled by the contact, my mind yelled at me to move away, but my body stubbornly remained where it was. Demons didn't deny themselves the pleasures they sought, but this was not the time or place for such things.

Still, I found myself unable to pull away from him. And then, my tongue flicked out, and I tasted his flesh. The saltiness of his skin on my tongue caused my eyes to roll back.

When his hands fell on my waist, I thought he was going to push me away, but he drew me closer until I was flush against the lean length of him. Out of control, I licked him again before nipping his flesh. The swelling evidence of his arousal against my belly caused my heart to beat faster.

Shifting, I partially rose, and my dress fell back when I slipped my legs around his waist while he remained crouched on the ground. The new position caused his cock to nestle in the junction between my thighs.

Demons took what they wanted, when they wanted it, and I wanted *him*.

My body thrummed with excitement as I ground against the rigid length of his erection. His fingers gripped my waist, and a shudder went through him when I rotated my hips and thrust against him.

Tugging at his shirt, I pulled buttons free until I exposed enough of his skin to rest my hands against his chest. The heat of his flesh seared into my fingertips and branded the feel of him onto me until I became more out of control than I'd ever been in my life.

I would have him. Pulling slightly back, my hands fell to his brown pants, and I was starting to undo them when girlish laughter sounded from only a few feet away from us.

Capturing my hands, Magnus halted my tugging on his button. My breath came in rapid pants against his neck as I resisted licking him again.

What was I thinking?

I'd completely forgotten the approaching voices and the danger we were in with my eagerness to have this demon inside me.

I didn't have to feel Magnus's self-recrimination; I could see it in his eyes. And then, anger wafted off him. I held his gaze, refusing to be embarrassed or apologetic about what happened. It was the completely wrong time and place, but we'd both wanted it. He probably believed I'd done it to try to trap him or kill him or something, yet he was still alive.

For now. I had no idea what was on the other side of those rocks.

Untangling myself from him, I kept my chin raised as I straightened my dress before crouching beside him once more. For the first time, I became aware of an unfamiliar tingling sensation in my gums. When I prodded at my teeth, the tingling stopped, but I had no idea what caused it.

While struggling to catch my breath, I leaned away from Magnus and turned to look as a man and woman ran around the water. The woman's laughter trailed behind her as the man chased her.

I'd never seen either of them before, but they were human. The woman squealed when the man caught her and swept her into his arms.

"I know her," Magnus murmured.

"I don't," I said.

He glanced at me before moving closer to the end of the crevice. "She's one of the humans from camp, but I don't know the man."

The man lowered the woman, and they kissed each other with an obvious love that made my heart ache. I couldn't imagine what it would be like to have someone love me like that. My parents loved me; even if we were completely different, they still loved me. And I loved them though I *loathed* their cruel streak and that they'd aligned themselves with the craetons.

However, I doubted I'd ever have someone *be* in love with me as this couple so obviously was with each other. The sexual parties of the jinn fascinated me behind the seals, but it was my parents' love for each other, and the times when they sat in a corner speaking with their heads bent close together, that I truly longed for one day.

Even trapped within the seal, my parents were happy in a way none of the others were because they had each other. And though I'd seen all the other jinn rut more times than I could count, I'd never seen my parents. I was sure there were times they were together, I wouldn't be here otherwise, but they somehow did it without me knowing, and I suspected the other jinn were shut out from it too.

Their time together was private and unique, and they didn't share it with anyone else.

The woman laughed again as the man lifted her and spun her around. While they twirled, the world around them started to shift. At first, it was so subtle I didn't notice it, but slowly I noted the green grass sprouting forth to replace the gray, rocky ground. The woman, probably in her early to mid-thirties, started to age backward as if the hands of a clock were rewinding her through the years.

Her brown hair lengthened until it cascaded to her ass. Her hollow cheeks plumped out and took on a rosy hue while a sparkle lit her brown eyes. The man, perhaps in his early twenties, remained the same while the woman looked eighteen again.

Then the man was taking her down into the grass next to a lake that was now a deep blue. They tugged at their clothes until they were both naked from the waist up.

"What is going on here?" Magnus asked; his gaze was distrustful when it came back to me.

"I don't know, but this is something private. We should leave them be."

We'd have to step out into the open to leave here, but the couple was too far gone in each other to notice us. Magnus seized my hand when I stepped forward. He drew me back as a hideous, lower-level demon appeared near a rocky outcropping on the other side of the lake.

My breath sucked in; I was about to shout a warning to the couple when Magnus clamped his hand over my mouth. I struggled against his hold, unwilling to not at least try to help them, but his grip was as solid as the walls of the seal.

Had I really desired this asshole? I'd castrate him for this!

"The demon materialized from out of nowhere," he hissed in my ear. "Something's not right here. Let it play out."

My resistance weakened against him until I slouched in his

arms. He didn't remove his hand from my mouth as the demon closed in on the couple. He was right about that, but still, I couldn't stop myself from crying out. Muffled by his hand, the sound didn't reach beyond us.

The man was tugging the woman's pants down her thighs when the demon rushed forward, cinched his arm around the man's throat, and lifted him off the woman. Screaming, the woman used her elbows and feet to propel herself back across the ground as the man released a choked cry.

Turning over, the woman leapt to her feet, but her movements were awkward due to the jeans hugging her lower thighs. She nearly went down before catching herself and tugging her jeans up. The demon broke the man's neck and let his body fall limply to the ground.

When the demon turned toward the woman, its snout pulled back in a leering grin as its foot-long penis rose to jut out from its yellow-tinted body. Screaming, the woman pulled a gun from her back pocket and opened fire on the demon. She shot off its manhood before turning her attention to its eyes.

The demon roared and charged at her, but three of her shots hit it dead center in the right eye, and the fourth hit it in the forehead. The final bullet, in its left eye, knocked it off its feet. It landed on its back, and its feet kicked limply against the ground. Yanking a knife from the holster at her side, the woman rushed forward and fell beside the demon. She didn't hesitate before sawing its head off.

Tossing the knife away, she raced to the man's side. Tears spilled down her face as choked sobs shook her slender frame. Drawing his head into her lap, she cradled it there. The low wail issuing from her tore at my heart and wrenched tears from me. She leaned over the man and rocked him as she begged him to come back to her.

Releasing me, Magnus rose and stepped away from the crevice. I pressed my fist against my mouth to keep my sobs muffled while I crept out behind him. As I walked, I became aware of the grass fading away and everything returning to what it was before the couple arrived.

"Mara," Magnus said as he stopped beside the woman who was gradually aging again. "Mara."

When he rested his hand on her shoulder, she lifted her tear-streaked face to meet his gaze. "Bring him back," she implored and held the dead man toward Magnus.

"I can't," Magnus said.

"Why?" the woman choked out as snot streaked from her nose. "My life... it's all... it's been *nothing* since I lost Ricky!"

"Mara, listen to me, whatever is going on here, it's not real. Let him go and step away from him."

"He's real!" she wailed and held the man closer. "He's real!"

I could barely breathe as the woman's suffering battered me until I felt it as acutely as if it were my own. Weaving its way into me, her sorrow rattled my bones and caused my legs to wobble.

Then, the man's body faded to reveal the rocks beneath him before he disappeared.

"NO! *RICKY!*" Mara screamed so loud her voice echoed off the rocks around us. "NO!"

Kneeling beside her, Magnus tried to draw her to him. She smacked his hands away as she kicked her feet.

Magnus sat back on his heels and held up his hands in a conciliatory gesture. "Easy, Mara, I won't hurt you."

"Bring him back!" she screeched.

She tore at her hair until handfuls of it spilled from her fisted hands. Unable to handle anymore, I backed away as blood trickled from her scalp.

Then, Mara vanished too.

CHAPTER TEN

Magnus

I GAWKED in disbelief at where Mara had been in my hands before turning toward Amalia. I opened my mouth to demand answers from her, but my words froze when I saw her face. Huddled in on herself, tears streaked her cheeks as she sobbed soundlessly.

I didn't think anyone could fake the melancholy radiating from her. Her eyes, which turned a vermillion color when she was impassioned earlier, weren't just the color of ochre but they also held a gray hue I'd never seen in them before. It was as if the gray existed when she was so sad the ochre hue alone wasn't enough to convey this.

She was a jinni, they were as trustworthy as the horsemen, but I found myself rising and going to her. Enveloping her in my arms, I held her while her tears wet my shirt. When my hand slid up to grip the back of her head, the silken strands of her hair slipped through my fingers. She clutched my back, drawing me closer until her tears subsided.

Jinn were the most manipulative creatures ever to exist, but this was no act.

She is different from the others. But how is that possible? Why is she different?

My mind spun as I tried to figure it out, but the one thing I did know was that I wouldn't allow this place, or her kind, to destroy her.

"I'm okay," Amalia said after a couple of minutes, but she didn't release me, and though her tremors eased, her tears still fell.

"Can you handle this place?"

Silence met my question, and then she inhaled a jerky breath. "Yes. I wasn't expecting that. If something like it happens again, I'll be better prepared."

"I think it's going to happen often in here," I warned her.

"Yes. Yes." She pulled out of my arms and wiped the tears from her eyes. "You're probably right, but I'm fine."

She was trying to convince herself more than me. She could say she'd handle this, she could dry her tears and lift her chin, but the melancholy color of her eyes belied her words.

A memory niggled at the recesses of my mind as her amazing eyes gradually shifted toward a more ochre color. There was something about those eyes and their shifting colors that I'd seen... or heard... or maybe read before?

Read, I read it somewhere!

When the war with Lucifer was still waging in Hell, I'd retreated from Kobal's forces to work on strengthening my ability to conjure illusions. Over time, I became so adept at creating illusions that I built them into realities. During that period, I'd also spent a lot of time poring over the scrolls documenting the history of demons and fallen angel children who roamed the Earth.

Something about those demon scrolls beckoned me to remember it as I gazed into her eyes, but I couldn't quite put my finger on what it was. There was something there about changing eyes, something....

Laughter floated to me again; I turned as it drew closer. "Mara," I whispered as a couple appeared and grass sprouted beneath my feet once more.

The couple ran around the lake, laughing as they toppled to the ground. From the shadows, the lower-level demon emerged. Releasing Amalia, I stepped forward to intercept the demon before it could attack the couple. Like a ghost gliding through walls, it went straight through me and lifted Ricky.

Unable to stop it, I watched as the demon killed Ricky again and Mara wailed once more.

This time, Amalia knelt at her side and rested her hand on Mara's shoulder. "It's not real," Amalia murmured. "This isn't real. You can pull free of this if you try."

Before Mara could reply, she vanished. Amalia remained kneeling on the ground, her hands on the rocks as she bowed her head. She didn't cry, but I could feel her sorrow across the distance separating us.

"It's running on a loop," I stated.

Taking a deep breath, Amalia lifted her head and met my gaze. "Yes."

"Was this her wish?"

"I doubt it," Amalia replied. "She might have wished for Ricky back, or for things to be different, or any one of a hundred things. I suspect these were her last moments with him and she's trying to change it, but since you can't change the past, she's only reliving the extreme high of their love and the abysmal low of her heartbreak."

"There has to be some way we can stop this. Something we can do to intervene or get through to her."

Amalia gazed helplessly around as the laughter started again. This time, when the couple emerged, I intercepted them and pulled them apart. Like the demon, my hands went straight through Ricky. Gripping Mara's shoulders, I pulled her away from Ricky. Kicking and slapping at me, she fought against my restraining hold.

When the demon materialized, Amalia leapt in front of it and threw out her hands. Like me, the demon ran through her and caught Ricky again. Mara was still in my arms when the demon slaughtered her lover. She turned on me with her fingers hooked into claws. Unprepared for her attack, I couldn't stop her before she tore a chunk of flesh from my cheek.

Then she was gone, and I was left holding nothing. Warm blood streaked my cheek and dripped off my chin. Amalia came to me and, lifting the hem of her skirt, she went to dab the blood from my face. I claimed her wrist before she could touch me.

"It will ruin your dress," I said.

"That's the least of my concerns right now."

Maybe it was, but I didn't want anything staining her. Using the hem of my shirt, I wiped the blood away from my face. Since my skin was already repairing itself, no fresh blood trickled from the gash.

"It will be fine," I assured her and released her wrist. "How is Mara solid while the other two aren't?"

"Because she's still alive and the other two aren't. She can die in here, they can't," Amalia said as the laughter started again.

"We have to figure out some way to break this cycle. If we can do that, maybe we can save the others."

Amalia nodded, but I saw the doubt in her eyes as the scene started playing through again. This time, after Ricky died, I knelt at Mara's side. "Listen to me, Mara. This isn't real. You have to fight it if you're going to break free of this place. You have to fight to *live*."

Tears swam in her eyes, and she seemed not to hear what I said before she disappeared again.

"Shit!" I smashed my hand on the ground as the grass vanished.

"We'll break through to her," Amalia insisted, but I wasn't so sure as the scene started to replay.

I had no idea how much time we spent trying to break through to Mara and end the loop, but I did everything I could think of to stop it. I tried casting an illusion of demons to interfere with the lower-level demon, but they did nothing to deter the monster, and Mara tried to shoot my creations. Whereas her bullets repeatedly knocked the lower-level demon down, they went uselessly through my illusions.

"How did you do that?" Amalia asked when the scene faded once more and I allowed my illusions to dissolve.

"I have my ways," I told her. Her face fell, and she focused on the wall behind me. It was best I kept my distance from her; maybe she was different from the others of her kind, but she was still a jinni. However, I despised the crestfallen look on her face. "I can create illusions."

A tiny smile curved her lips, and she opened her mouth to reply, but before she could question me further, Mara's nightmare started again.

"What do you think Mara wanted most from this?" Amalia asked as Mara and the man went to the ground again. "To have one last time with Ricky, to kill the demon before it killed Ricky, or something else entirely?"

"Does it matter?"

"Maybe if we can figure *that* out we can break through to her somehow."

I allowed the scene to play through before kneeling at Mara's side again. "What is it you want from this, Mara?" I asked.

Lifting her head, she blinked at me before turning her gaze to the lake. "My life back. I want it all to have *never* been this way. Ricky... Ricky is my heart," she whispered tremulously and rested her hand on her chest. "And when that thing killed him, it tore the heart from my chest."

"No one can undo what has already been done. Somewhere deep inside, you know this is true."

"No," she moaned.

I rested my hand on her shoulder and gave it a tender squeeze. "Mara—"

"It can be different. It can. It *can*! I wished for it to be different. There *must* be a way to change it!"

"Mara—"

My hand fell through thin air when she vanished.

"Son of a bitch!" I snarled. My shoulders heaved as I struggled to retain my temper, but I wanted to burn this entire place to the ground before tearing to shreds every jinni who'd had a hand in creating this endless *fucking* nightmare.

Slowly, reeling in my frustration, my gaze fell on Amalia. She'd done better with this whole thing since it first started, but her shadowed eyes and pale skin revealed the toll it was taking on her.

We couldn't stay here much longer. There were numerous others trapped here who required help, and I didn't know how much more Amalia could take, but I couldn't give up on Mara yet. If I had to give up here, then I might not be able to save anyone trapped in this place, and I refused to acknowledge that possibility.

When Mara reemerged again, Amalia leapt forward and yanked her away from Ricky. When Mara kicked and lashed out at her, her punches caught Amalia in her bicep. I lunged forward with the intent of taking Mara down before she could hurt Amalia anymore, but Amalia dragged her to the ground and pinned her there before I reached them.

"Listen to me!" she yelled at Mara as the lower-level demon emerged. "If you don't break free of this, you *will* die!"

Mara flailed against her restraining hold as the scene with Ricky and the demon played out before the demon disappeared without Mara's bullets striking it.

Then, Mara vanished.

Walking over, I sat on the ground beside Amalia as she drew her knees up to her chest and settled her chin on them. "I don't know what to do," she muttered.

"Neither do I," I admitted. "But we're not getting through to her, and there are many others trapped here. Even if we can't help Mara, we might be able to help one of them."

Amalia looked as doubtful as I felt about that, but we were wasting time here, and if there was a possibility we might be able to help one of the others, we couldn't stay.

"You want to leave her to this?" Amalia asked as the scene started again.

"Can you think of anything else to do?"

"No."

The scene faded away, and Mara started weeping. Rising, I extended my hand to Amalia and grasped hers within mine. Mara leapt to her feet and released a shriek that caused Amalia to wince. Before I could say or do anything, Mara bent her head and ran headfirst at the jagged rocks.

"No!" Amalia cried as Mara rammed her head into the wall.

Blood burst from the top of Mara's skull, and she staggered back a few steps. Shaking her head, Mara regained enough control to wipe away the blood streaking her cheeks before bowing her head and rushing forward again. The crack of her neck followed the echo of her skull battering the rocks. Mara fell limply to the ground with her hands and legs splayed haphazardly out at her sides.

This time when Mara's body faded away, I knew she wouldn't be coming back.

In the distance, another bolt slammed into the massive monolith before spiraling out to the other four.

"Oh," Amalia breathed, and I turned to find her paler than I'd ever seen her before. "It's... oh."

"It's what?" I demanded.

"Her life," Amalia murmured. "The lightning is her life force. It went through me along with a rush of power that just feels so *wrong*. That's what I felt when the lightning struck before too. The lightning is the life force of those who perish in the Abyss."

"The jinn are interwoven with the Abyss," I stated.

"And feeding on it." She shuddered in revulsion.

"Is the reason you're different from the other jinn because you've never been here before and therefore never fed on the life force of others?"

Because if that was the case, I had to get her out of here. I wouldn't let Amalia's goodness be eaten away by the malevolent nature of the Abyss and her fellow jinn.

"No," she said. "I'm different because I'm Faulted."

"What do you mean you're *Faulted*?"

"While jinn always empathize and care for each other, most don't care about anything outside of the jinn race, but some jinn are born with the Fault of empathy for those outside the jinn and are also empaths. Before the jinn were locked behind the seal and they still numbered over a hundred, there were fifteen Faulted. Only forty-six jinn survived the battle waged to seal the jinn away, and six of them are Faulted. Neither of my parents is Faulted, but I was born with the curse some of the jinn bear."

I absorbed her words as I studied her. "You're an empath." Her reaction to Mara and her need to help us made more sense now. She couldn't tolerate another in pain because she felt that pain as if it were hers.

"Yes."

"Do you really believe it's a curse?"

"Maybe, if things were different, I wouldn't believe so, but I do now."

"Different how?"

"Adapting to Earth and all the changes has been tougher for the Faulted. The jinn all care for each other, and they've been together for over eighteen thousand years. I came along much later, but behind the seals, we were all equal, and the non-Faulted jinn were unable to unleash their cruelty as they do now. Though we all love each other, the Faulted have trouble standing by and watching what the other jinn do. Three months after we were freed, the Faulted broke off to live on their own. I remained with my parents, but...."

Her voice trailed off, and her eyes took on that ochre color again while she gazed forlornly at the spot where Mara's body had lain. Without thinking, I closed the distance between us and drew her into my arms again. I still didn't entirely trust her, I wasn't an idiot, but I couldn't stay away from her either.

"But staying with them has been challenging for you," I said.

"Yes. And the things they do... this is *awful.*" Her voice broke.

Many demons weren't as callous and ruthless as the jinn, but Amalia acted more caring than the tree nymphs, which many considered the most compassionate of demons.

"If the lightning signals a death, then three have died since we entered the Abyss," she said. "We have to go."

"Yes," I agreed, and reluctantly releasing her, I led her back to the central pathway.

CHAPTER ELEVEN

Corson

RAPHAEL'S WINGS extended as he rested a hand on Mara's forehead. A few minutes ago, she'd started convulsing. When her feet kicked against the ground, Raphael knelt at her side and tried to soothe her.

Then Mara stopped convulsing, she collapsed onto the ground and blood trickled from her mouth. My gaze bored into her chest as I waited to see if she would take another breath; she did, but two other humans had already died. One of them simply stopped breathing, and the other screamed like the hellhounds were on her ass before silencing abruptly.

Raphael hadn't approached either of them, but he'd gone to Mara.

"Can you heal her?" I demanded.

If sudden death could happen to the humans, then it could happen to Wren. Panic constricted my chest; my talons extended and retracted before doing it again. I was unraveling, but there was nothing I could do to stop it. Wren's life was on the line, and I was helpless to save her.

"I am not the Being. It is not my place to alter the course of someone's fate," Raphael replied.

There were times when I'd like to kill both the angels, and this was one of them. "I understand, but this is *not* the natural course of Mara's fate."

"Who am I to judge that?"

I stepped toward Raphael.

"Easy," Caim said.

When he rested his hand on my arm, I yanked it away from him.

"I think, what our demon friend means, Raphael, is if you *wanted* to heal her, would it be possible?" Caim inquired.

Caim gave me a conspiring grin that set my teeth on edge. I'd become more accustomed to working with these angels since the gateway closed, but I didn't overly like either of them.

"No," Raphael said and rose. "I couldn't. Just like I cannot rouse them from whatever state they're in, I cannot fix the damage done to their bodies while they're trapped in the Abyss."

My gaze fell to where I'd left Wren bundled in blankets against the wall of the cave. We'd moved into the area over a week ago and discovered the cave shortly afterward. We'd been using it as a place to store the game we killed, and some slept in it.

It had taken some time, but we'd finally located everyone and carried them deep underground to hide them. Some people and demons were a mile or more from camp when the jinn struck. How the insidious demons managed to trap them all, I didn't know, but we were the only four who escaped them.

We'd encountered no enemies and saw no signs of them as we worked, but I didn't doubt the jinn had some way of watching over their victims. They wouldn't want to miss out on the fun.

Wren's vulnerability almost knocked me to my knees as I

watched her chest rise and fall. I couldn't fight this enemy as I had countless others. I couldn't charge in to save her; I could only stand here as she fought a battle I couldn't see.

The smoke from the fire we'd lit deep within these rocky recesses, drifted down one of the side tunnels on currents of air. Mara inhaled a shuddery breath, then a thin trail of blood trickled from her lips and she went still.

"See if you can heal her now," I commanded Raphael.

He gazed from me to her and back again before kneeling to rest his hand on her forehead. I sensed his power swelling until it beat against the walls with a dull whomping sound. Though no breeze stirred the air, the dancing fire leapt into the air and cast sparks throughout the cave.

Raphael's wings rose as the beat of his power increased until the large cave quaked with it. Pebbles and dirt skittered down the walls and broke free of the ceiling, but I didn't feel them when they pelted my skin and coated my hair.

Then, Raphael's wings lowered. "There is nothing I can do."

"Fuck!" I spat, and before I could restrain myself, I drove my talons into the wall until I was wrist deep in the rocks.

I yanked my hand free and stormed over to kneel at Wren's side. Brushing her pale hair away from her face, I rested my fingers against her cheek.

"You have to come back to me," I whispered to her, but she gave no sign she heard me. Resting my hand over her heart, I took comfort in its reassuring beat.

"Magnus might be able to do something from inside the Abyss," Caim said.

"If the jinni doesn't turn on him and kill him while he's in there," I grated from between my clenched teeth.

"She is different than the others," Caim stated.

"Caim—"

"I will remove Mara's body and place it with the others," Caim said before I could question him about his statement.

He hefted Mara's body over his shoulder and carried it deeper into the cave, which wound miles beneath the earth. When this was over, and we could come and go from this cave without worrying someone might see us, we'd better dispose of the bodies; but for now, we could only hide them.

Gazing at all the bodies gathered in the cave and wrapped up in blankets to ward off the damp chill of this below ground dwelling, I realized the humans couldn't withstand the jinn's effects as well as the demons did. The jinn slaughtered demons too, but demons were stronger and would hold out against them for longer.

As I thought it, Erin's fingers started twitching on the ground, much like Mara's had about an hour before she died.

~

Magnus

"What created the Fault in some jinn?" I asked as we traversed the Abyss.

"Thousands of years ago, a jinni found their Chosen outside of our line. Not only did that bond change some of the jinn, but it also infused our line with something other than jinn blood."

"And what blood was that?" I asked.

From fifty feet ahead of me, Erin careened around a corner of rock and raced down the path toward me. Unprepared for her sudden appearance, my foot froze in midair before falling to the ground. Amalia staggered a few steps back, and her hand flew to her mouth when Erin skidded to a halt in front of me.

Erin's almond-shaped, dark blue eyes widened on me. Her normally sleek, short black hair was a disheveled mess around her beautiful face.

"Where am I?" Erin demanded in a tone more strident than I'd ever heard from her before. "I'm not supposed to be here. *Where am I?*"

"You know you're not supposed to be here?" I asked, unable to keep the surprise from my voice.

"Does this look like a place I should be in?" she demanded and gestured at the rocks surrounding us.

"No, it doesn't." But after Mara, I hadn't expected anyone to see through this place.

"What am I doing here?" she demanded.

"Erin—"

"How do you know my name?"

Words failed me when I realized that though she knew she didn't belong here, she hadn't completely broken free of the control the jinn held over her mind.

"Who are you?" she demanded of me.

"My name is Magnus, and I'm a friend of yours."

"A friend? I have no friends. Not since the war. All I have is my family."

Her voice trailed off as she frowned at the rock walls. "Am I at *the* wall?" she asked.

After the gateway opened, humans and demons built a wall dividing the central areas of the country devastated by the opening of the gateway from the outer regions of the country that weren't as severely affected. Erin volunteered to work the wall when she was sixteen and had stood guard there. Months ago, she left the wall behind to join us in eradicating what remained of our enemies in the Wilds.

"No. This is not the wall," I said.

When Amalia moved closer, she drew Erin's attention to her.

"We can help you," Amalia whispered.

"How? I'm not... something is *wrong*." Erin dropped her head into her hands and slapped at the sides of it as if she were trying to batter the answer into it.

"Don't." Grasping her hands, I stepped closer and held her palms against her temples as her shoulders heaved with her breaths.

Erin was strong, capable, loyal, and one of the most intelligent humans I'd ever come across, but her brain wasn't processing any of this right. Unlike Mara, who was convinced it would get better or she could change something, Erin knew none of this was right, but she couldn't figure out what was wrong, and it was screwing with her mind.

"I can only live where there is light, but I die if the light shines on me. What am I?" Erin murmured.

"What does that mean?" Amalia asked.

"It's a riddle," I explained. "The skelleins are always trying to stump her with them, but they haven't succeeded yet."

Erin's head lifted, and her eyes bored into mine. "*What am I?*"

"I don't know the answer," I admitted.

"A shadow. I'm a shadow of who I was. A shadow in this place that is nothing but shadows, but there are no shadows here," Erin babbled. "It's not real. It's *all* real. But it's not right. Something is wrong here. Not right. No shadows. No shadows in this land."

I could feel her mind unraveling further as she struggled to grasp what was real and align it with what the jinn had done to her.

"We hurt without moving," Erin whispered. "We poison without touching. We bear the truth and the lies. We are not to be judged by our size. What are we?"

"I don't know the answer, but I am your *friend,*" I said.

"This place is lies and shadows."

Erin jerked on her hands as she tried to free them to batter herself again, but I wouldn't let her go. When she lifted her head, her eyes were more dazed than when she first ran into us. I felt her grip on reality loosening as the Abyss worked its way deeper into her mind.

"*What are we?*" she shouted in my face.

"We are *here!*" I yelled back at her, uncertain of what else to do. "*You* are here with us. Listen to me, Erin. Hear what I'm saying to you."

"Erin," she murmured and licked her lips as clarity slipped back into her eyes. "I am Erin, and you are...?"

"Magnus. You know me."

"I know you. I know we are trees."

"Trees?" Her mind was jumping too fast for me to keep up with her.

"Yes, trees, that is what we are."

It took me a minute to comprehend trees was the answer to her last riddle. "Yes, trees."

"Unless it's a calamut tree, and then they *can* move." Her forehead furrowed, and she bowed her head. "Calamut trees, I remember them now."

"Those trees came from Hell," I said.

"Yes. They did. You came from Hell too. Death also came to Earth from Hell."

"Death has always been on Earth."

"Not on horseback," she murmured. "Now, Death rides."

I realized she was talking about Death the horseman and not actually dying.

"Erin?" Lifting her head, she blinked at me.

Recognition lit her eyes. "Magnus."

I grinned at her. "Yes."

She smiled back at me before vanishing.

"What? No!" I grasped at the empty air in a failed attempt to grab for her. Rage vibrated my body when I whirled on Amalia. "*What happened?*"

Amalia gawked at me before looking at the space where Erin had stood. Her gaze traveled over the rock walls before returning to me. "She's not here."

"No shit." I regretted the hostile words as soon as they left my mouth. This was not her doing.

Amalia recoiled before her eyes narrowed and deepened to a livid, red hue. "I mean she's *not* in the Abyss."

"Not in the Abyss?"

"Yes. Is that too difficult for you to comprehend?"

I glared at her, and she glared back.

"Are you saying she's free of this place?" I inquired.

"Well aren't you the cleverest of demons!" she retorted and crossed her arms over her chest.

The motion pulled the material taut over her breasts. Some of my annoyance ebbed when my gaze fastened hungrily on them. Despite my frustration with this place and her kind, the sight stirred me. We were supposed to be doing something, but all I could think about was drawing her nipple into my mouth and feasting on it.

If I stepped into her now, pressed her against the wall, and lifted her skirt, would she let me take her? When I recalled her actions when we were crouched behind the rocks earlier, I thought she might. She was irritated with me, but she wanted me too. However, such an action might get us both killed in this place. Although, we hadn't encountered anything deadly to *us* yet.

A quick rutting would get her out of my head, and I'd be able to concentrate on what was going on around here more when I found my release. But I couldn't do quick with her. No, I wanted to savor every inch of her supple body.

What color will her eyes be when I'm inside her?

Never had I craved a woman so much I ignored any form of danger, but for a brief second, I forgot we were in this place as my mind became consumed with wicked fantasies about the things I longed to do to her. Amalia was a temptation that might lead to my ultimate downfall, but what a downfall it would be.

What is it about her?

I was determined to find out the answer, but first I had to learn what became of Erin.

"Erin is free of the Abyss?" My voice was more guttural than normal, but then my growing erection was pushing uncomfortably against my pants.

Amalia lowered her arms and glanced around her. "Yes, I think so. I believe her moment of realization might have been enough to free herself from this place. Unlike Mara, she wasn't trying to fix something; she was trying to understand and break free. I think she's back with your friends."

"We need to return and make sure she's there. Can you take us back?"

"Yes."

CHAPTER TWELVE

Amalia

MAGNUS STEPPED through the portal before me, and I followed. We reemerged into the clearing we'd left behind. Night had descended while we were gone, no bodies remained, and no one was here.

"Do you know where they went?" I asked.

"Yes, this way."

A small jolt of happiness went through me when I realized he trusted me enough to reveal to me where the others hid. No one who wasn't a jinni trusted the jinn, but he'd just shown more faith in me than I'd ever expected from him. It was such a stupid thing to be so pleased about, yet I found myself smiling as I followed him through the woods.

Magnus continuously surveyed the area for any hint of a threat as we wound our way through the trees in a course I suspected was meant to draw forth or lose any enemies who might be lying in wait. After at least a mile, we arrived at the entrance of a cave.

Standing four feet tall and only three feet wide, I would have missed the entrance set into the gray rocks surrounding it if he hadn't pointed it out. The vines hanging over the rocks were brown and barren now, but they would completely cover the entrance when they were in bloom.

Taking my arm, Magnus led me into the cave. Because it was too narrow, I had to walk slightly behind him, but he kept hold of me. His finger caressed my flesh, and I got the sense he couldn't get enough of touching me as we walked. With every step he took, the bunch and flex of his muscles kept my eyes riveted on him. I didn't know what it was about this demon, but he captivated me even during those times when as I was contemplating punching him in the face.

A hundred feet in, Magnus ducked to avoid banging his head on a low-hanging rock, but he rose to his full height on the other side of it. Afterward, the cave started to widen out until we could walk next to each other.

I stayed close by his side as we wound deeper beneath the earth. The further we went, the more the damp air caused a chill to creep over my flesh and the less light penetrated until we were in complete darkness. Unable to see anymore, I relied on my other senses, and Magnus, to keep me from walking into a wall.

We were at least half a mile into the cave when the scent of smoke wafted to me along with the murmur of voices. Flickering light lit the dark recesses when we rounded a corner of the cave. From around a bend in the stone walls, Raphael stepped into view. His hand rested on the hilt of his sword, and his shoulders hunched as if he were preparing to charge into a fight. Then, he relaxed and his hand fell away from the weapon.

"Magnus," he greeted.

"Raphael," Magnus replied.

Corson arrived at Raphael's side. "What happened?" he demanded.

"Is Erin here?" Magnus inquired, and then Erin emerged from the shadows behind Corson.

Erin grinned as she waved at us. "I had no idea what happened to you."

Magnus released me to embrace the small, slender girl. "I can say the same to you," he said.

A bolt of jealousy tore through me when they hugged, and I looked away before the emotion overwhelmed me. Staring at the cave walls, I concentrated on the differences between the stones of Earth and those of the Abyss. Within the Abyss, the rocks were *wrong* somehow; here, they were a foundation of the planet itself.

"How did you get free?" Magnus asked Erin.

Erin stepped from his embrace and glanced at me. I suspected the others had already informed her what I was and where she'd been.

"I'm not sure. It was all so confusing in there," Erin said. "One minute, I was eating dinner with my family, laughing and joking as we always did, and the next I was at Volunteer Day, waiting to step forward to go to the wall."

Her hands tightened on Magnus's forearms. "My parents were so proud of me that day, and I loved it. I volunteered to make sure they would have enough food for them and my siblings, but I was scared, and I didn't want to leave. Standing there, it was all so familiar, and I could feel my parents' love, yet it all seemed sort of... off. You know?" Erin asked.

"I don't," Magnus admitted.

"I don't either." Erin released him and stepped back. "I just *knew* I shouldn't be there."

"There have always been those with a strong enough mind to escape the Abyss," I said. "Is there anything you desperately long for or would wish was different?" I asked Erin.

They all gave me wary glances, but I didn't need to see their distrust of me, I could feel it.

"Don't make a wish," Corson said and rested his hand on Erin's shoulder.

My fingers dug into my palms as I glowered at him. I almost screamed at him that I wasn't like the jinn who did this, I was trying to *help*, but I bit back the words; he believed he already had me figured out.

"She's not like most of the jinn," Magnus said.

My eyes flew to him, and a wave of relief washed over me. *He believes me!*

What does it matter if he believes me? I knew who I was, no one could take that from me, and that was what counted.

But then I realized it mattered because I desired this demon more than anyone I'd ever encountered, and I didn't want him to see me as a monster.

Crap.

I wanted him, but this could all end horribly with the jinn and everyone else involved.

"She has you believing that?" Corson inquired as he cast me a doubtful glance.

"It's true," Magnus said. "Somewhere along the way, a jinni found their Chosen outside of the jinn population. Because of that, they have what they call..."

"Faulted," I supplied when his voice trailed off, and he glanced questioningly at me. "I'm a Faulted jinni. There are seven of us in total."

"And this Fault makes you different than the rest?" Corson asked.

I chose to ignore the sarcasm in his voice when I replied, "Yes."

"And we're supposed to believe you?"

"You can believe whatever you want, but it's the truth. Behind the seals, my Fault didn't matter. Now, most of the Faulted live on their own, but I decided to stay with the other jinn because of my parents. I'm not sure how long that will last."

"Why, because it hurts you to hurt others?" Corson oozed venom as he asked this.

"Enough!" Magnus snarled in a tone I'd never heard from him before. "I believe her."

My eyebrows rose as Corson's gaze slid from me to Magnus.

"You believe her?" Corson asked incredulously. "The jinn are nothing but manipulative monsters."

"We are *not* monsters!" I snapped. "Maybe the jinn don't have to feed on others the way they do to survive, but in some of them, it is their nature to do so. And that nature is as interwoven into them as your bond to your Chosen is interwoven into you.

"Besides, I don't care if you like what the jinn do or not. Maybe people and demons shouldn't yearn for things they can't have, and then they'd never have to deal with the jinn. Maybe they should realize that nothing worth having comes by simply wishing for it. And if I were you, I'd watch what you're feeling about bringing your Chosen back, because the jinn might be drawn to *you* too!"

Folding my arms over my chest, I scowled at Corson as I tried to control the tumult of emotions rattling me. Not only were my feelings out of control, but so were those of everyone around me.

"I believe her," Magnus said after a protracted silence followed my outburst. "Because I know what caused the Fault in the jinn line."

I shot him a disgruntled look. "Do you now?"

"You're part fae," he stated.

CHAPTER THIRTEEN

Amalia

His words deflated some of my exasperation as I gazed at him. So, he'd paid enough attention to me to figure it out.

"The fae line has been dead for thousands of years," Corson said. He still regarded me like I was a manticore looking to strike, but most of the antagonism had melted from his voice.

"Over five thousand years to be exact," Magnus replied. "That's why I didn't recognize it at first; I should have known what she was just from her eyes, but none of us have seen a fae before."

"How do you know that's what she is?" Caim inquired.

"I've read a lot of the scrolls the demons kept about our history. The demons who wrote those scrolls didn't mention the fae often, as the fae weren't fighters. Their empath ability and pacifistic nature made them easy targets for other demons, but they adapted enough to survive amongst demonkind. After a while, most demons let the fae be; what fun is it to attack someone who won't fight back?

"The fallen angels didn't feel the same way and were the ultimate end of the fae. The angels didn't care if the fae were fun to fight or not. They saw them as inferior because they were demons, so they slaughtered them."

My fingers dug into the skin of my forearms as my heart ached for those distant ancestors who never quite fit in to the environment they were born into. I knew well how difficult that must have been for them. But despite their differences from other demons, the fae learned to survive in Hell until a group of vicious intruders eradicated them.

I couldn't stop myself from glaring at Caim who had his head tilted to the side as he studied me.

"I think I dimly recall these fae beings," Caim murmured. His eyes slid up to meet mine. "With their colorful eyes. They didn't put up much of a fight against us."

"I'm glad you remember slaughtering my ancestors," I muttered.

Caim shrugged. "Only the strongest survived Lucifer. I take no satisfaction from killing; I never have. I simply did what was necessary to survive back then."

"And killing a species who didn't like to fight was necessary?" I demanded.

"Not at all," Caim said. "Surviving Lucifer's wrath was though. He wanted them dead, and nobody said no to him. Your fae or my life, the choice was not a difficult one to make."

"So when you turned on Lucifer, you did it to save yourself?" I inquired.

Caim's eyes and his sculpted face became a wall of ice. "No. I did that to save *all* of us. Turning against my brother was not an easy decision to make." A muscle twitched in his cheek when he glanced at Raphael. Hostility shimmered in the air between them, but when he looked at me again, he smiled. "Your eyes betray your emotions."

My eyes were as much of a curse as my ability to feel the

emotions of others as if they were mine. The rest of the Faulted hadn't inherited the shifting eye colors of the fae—colors that revealed my every emotion to anyone who knew what each of the shifting hues meant.

"I'm sure their eyes were another thing that helped aid in the demise of the fae," I murmured. "I guess it's tough to fight someone when they can figure out your every emotion by looking at your eyes."

"Yes, it would be," Corson murmured. "And you trust her because she is part fae?" he asked Magnus.

"No," Magnus said. "I trust her because she didn't turn on me in the Abyss, and she brought me back here when I asked her to. If she intended to kill me or set me up, she's had plenty of opportunities to do so. I also trust her because I saw what the Abyss does to her."

I couldn't stop myself from grinning at him. I felt like a childish idiot for soaking up his words in this way, but no one, outside the jinn, had ever shown any faith in me, and most of the jinn saw me as nothing more than a child. Magnus saw me as more, and he wanted the others to see it too.

"Then we shall see what happens," Raphael murmured.

"Yes, we will. According to the scrolls, the fae did breed with some other demons, mostly the tree nymphs, before they were eradicated," Magnus said. "Hence, the tree nymphs' powerful call toward nature and their more kindhearted temperament, but I've never seen a nymph with your eyes. That's what threw me off so much in the beginning. I recalled reading about a demon with shifting eyes before, but I couldn't remember where or what they were, and I would *never* have guessed the jinn and fae line crossed at one time."

"That's like mating a lamb with a lion," Corson said.

I released my arms to spread my hands before me. "You can't

pick your Chosen, and the line continues, so the pairing was a strong one."

"Yes," Magnus agreed. "Do all the Faulted have the fae eyes like you?"

"No. Few of the Faulted have had the fae eyes over the thousands upon thousands of years since the fae and jinn bred. I'm the only Faulted with them now."

"And you are an empath like the fae were."

I couldn't tell if this was a statement from Caim or a question, but when he stared at me and the silence stretched on, I answered him. "Ah, yes, I am."

And from what the other Faulted told me, my empath ability would amp up once I came into my immortality. I was looking forward to finally being immortal, but I dreaded the increase of my empath ability. My ability was already stronger than what the other Faulted possessed. The idea of it becoming worse frightened me, but I would cope with it; I had no other choice.

"Are all the Faulted empaths?" Magnus asked.

I contemplated how to answer this. I had to protect my kind and keep them safe, but I could feel their growing trust in me and their lessening hostility. "To some degree," I said. "Do you plan to harm the jinn?"

"I plan to do whatever is necessary to save my friends," Magnus replied honestly. "I will destroy anyone who stands in the way of that."

My parents were involved in this, and so was my uncle, but I'd dug myself into this mess when I took Magnus into the Abyss; I couldn't distance myself from it now. If I did, then a lot of those here could die, along with many other future innocents.

Looking around the cave, I gazed at the numerous faces trapped in the Abyss. There had to be something I could do to help them while making sure none of the jinn were hurt. We couldn't save Mara, but there might be others we *could* rescue, and I refused to walk away from that.

Plus, if I remained involved in this, maybe there was a chance I could talk the jinn into freeing their captives. At the very least, I should be able to ease some of the hostility between the two sides. The jinn were devious, but we were loyal to each other, and though they still saw me as the baby, they might listen to me.

"The jinn have also chosen to side with and follow the horsemen and Astaroth. The craetons can't be allowed to win this," Corson said. "We'll all be dead then."

"We have leaders amongst us, but the jinn don't do well with following others or orders from anyone outside of the jinn. They may have aligned with the craetons, but they aren't following them," I replied. "If it suits the jinn, they will break the alliance."

"And do you think you can get them to break it?" Magnus asked.

"No," I answered honestly. "They see me as the baby and as someone who doesn't understand the way things work with them, but I might be able to get them to listen to me about who they have trapped in there now. No matter what happens in the Abyss though, you must remember the Faulted only seek to live in peace."

"And they will be allowed to continue doing so while they remain peaceful," Corson said, and I believed him.

Besides, the Faulted were extremely well protected where they resided. Anyone who tried to attack them would regret it.

"The scrolls detailed demon history for over fifty thousand years, I didn't get the chance to read them all, but I never saw any mention of a fae and jinn who were Chosen," Magnus said.

"Some say the pairing happened a hundred thousand years ago; others say it was a couple hundred thousand years ago," I said. "But no matter how long ago it was, it did occur, and the jinn line has had Faulted in it ever since. Some of the jinn call us the Fae-aulted."

"Fae-aulted," Erin murmured as her gaze ran inquisitively over me. "Amazing."

"The Faulted often remained in the shadows of the jinn; far preferring to allow their brethren to do what they must rather than get involved. Since being freed, and I'm sure before they were locked away, most of the jinn see the Faulted as weaker and needing protection. But the Faulted don't want to be protected, and we're *not* weaker. However, the jinn aren't complete monsters, we are all very close. The jinn are not the horsemen or the fallen—"

"Careful, you're about to make the mistake of lumping all fallen angels together," Caim said and grinned at me as he ruffled his wings. "Some of us are different."

"*You* are different," Raphael said. "The others are too far gone in their madness to see beyond their mission to destroy us all and enslave the human race."

Caim lifted his hand to admire his nails. "Perhaps, one day, some of our siblings will come around."

"They are not our siblings, not anymore, and I would not hold out hope for that."

Caim blew on his nails and buffed them on his shirt. "I think there is much hope to be found in this world."

Raphael frowned at him while confusion and disbelief drifted from the others. I was struck with the impulse to hug the fallen angel. I didn't get a sense of much emotion from Caim, but something about his words rang true.

"Okay, so the jinn can ensnare people," Erin said. "Some jinn are Faulted and empaths, and you can fly—"

"I can't fly," I interrupted, "and neither can my fellow jinn."

"But I was there. I *saw* you all float out of the gateway," she said.

"We can levitate." Placing my hands at my sides, I held my palms over the floor and pictured my feet rising off the stone. A small wave of power issued from my palms and my feet lifted a few inches off the ground. "I can do this, and continue to go upward, but I'm not like an angel, I can't soar over treetops or navigate. I can float over short distances, but most of the time, because of my fae blood, it's faster for me to run. To escape Hell, it was fastest for us to float out as it was the most direct route, and we avoided much of the chaos raining down."

Erin's eyes were huge as she watched me settle back on the cave floor. "But seeing you do that makes me understand where humans got the idea of a jinni being able to fly," Erin murmured. "What about the magic lamp?"

"What magic lamp?" I asked.

"In some legends of the jinn, they're stuck in magic lamps, and when someone rubs the lamp, a jinni emerges. The jinni then has to grant whoever set them free three wishes," Erin said.

"Well, that's just... ridiculous," I replied. "And untrue. Why would someone make that up?"

Erin laughed as she ran a hand through her hair. "For fun, I guess."

"It must have been someone with a big imagination," Magnus said. "It's time for us to get back to the Abyss."

I focused on Corson again. "We'll try to find Wren."

"I'll come with you," Corson said. "If seeing Magnus helped to jar Erin out of the Abyss, then seeing me will help Wren."

CHAPTER FOURTEEN

Magnus

"No. You have to stay and continue to make sure everyone is guarded," I said. "I'll weave an illusion over the entrance of the cave to make it appear as if it's solid rock, but everyone here is too vulnerable to take away any of their protection. When we find Wren, if it's necessary, we *will* come back for you."

I didn't dare risk taking Corson into the Abyss; he was too unstable. He'd take off in search of Wren, and though it was important we find her, there were others in there who also needed help. We couldn't risk losing Corson in there because of his focus on Wren.

Corson opened his mouth to protest when a human lying against the back wall sat up like a ventriloquist dummy whose strings had been pulled. Caim squawked and danced away from the man so fast black feathers broke free from his wings and floated lazily in the air.

When the man's head turned stiffly toward us, I recognized him as Chet, before he rose in a fluid motion that should have been impossible for a human. He walked woodenly across the cave and toward the entrance.

"What is going on?" Corson murmured. He took a step after Chet before edging back toward Wren. His talons slid free.

"I'll be back," I said and raced after Chet when he walked toward the front of the cave. Everything about him, from his unbending legs to his unblinking gaze, reminded me of a puppet. *But who is pulling his strings?*

Amalia's soft step alerted me that she was following us as we approached the entrance. Caim strolled behind her with his hands clasped behind his back, and Raphael remained stone-faced while he walked behind him.

When Chet went to step outside the cave, I slipped past to block him. I was curious to see where he intended to go, but we couldn't risk something seeing him leaving here. Chet continued his wooden walking, but it got him nowhere as he continuously bumped into me.

"What is he doing?" Amalia murmured, her voice laced with horror.

I clasped Chet's shoulder and held him a little to the side of me to avoid his ceaseless legs. A Wilder, Chet was one of Wren's followers and often dispersed the meals to the humans. He'd always been friendly enough, and we'd spoken a few times, but there was no spark of recognition in his glazed-over eyes.

"Chet," I said.

He didn't blink, but his legs continued to rise and fall. When I eased my grip on his shoulder, he started walking in a circle beneath my hand. In the cramped space, his movements were awkward, and his feet continuously connected with the rock walls, but he didn't stop.

When he was done turning, he started toward the front of the cave again, but I blocked him once more. Placing myself firmly in front of him, I gripped his shoulders.

"Chet!" I gave him a rough shake that did nothing to make him respond. *Blink!* "Chet!"

Nothing.

Chet's head swiveled toward me; his gaze remained deadened and his eyes unblinking while his legs continued to rise and fall.

It repulsed me to continue holding him, but I couldn't let him leave here.

"Do you think you could wake him?" I asked Raphael.

"No."

"Maybe if we let him go, he'll wake up," Amalia suggested.

"And if there's something out there hunting for us?" I asked.

"There was nothing out there when we came in."

"I'll go make sure it's clear." Caim shifted into raven form and took flight from the cave.

"Let's hope no one saw him," I muttered.

A few minutes later, in which Chet continued his awkward stepping, Caim returned to the entrance of the cave and shifted out of his raven form. "It's all clear for at least a mile radius around here; if Chet goes any further, I will search again."

Amalia's appalled gaze met mine when I released Chet and he goose-stepped out of the cave. Taking her elbow, I kept her against my side as we traversed through the trees while staying parallel with Chet. Amalia's scent tickled my nose as her supple flesh warmed my palm. I'd destroy anything that came near her.

I searched for a threat moving into our area, but all I detected were the birds watching us from their perches. The subtle trickle of water flowing over rocks penetrated the air as we approached a stream in the trees. Sparkling blue water came into view, and then Chet stopped at the edge of the stream.

Amalia's hair tickled my arm when she leaned forward to study him. I searched the other side of the stream but saw only the shifting shadows of the swaying trees as they danced across the leaf-strewn ground.

Raphael and Caim spread out to stand on either side of us as Chet remained unmoving. His gaze was fixed across the stream, but he didn't seem to see anything over there. The birds stopped singing as even they appeared to wait to see what he would do now.

"Stay here," I whispered to Amalia.

Releasing her arm, I pushed aside the branches of a tree and walked toward him. I was almost to his side when his head tipped back and a gurgling sound issued from his throat.

"What the fuck?" I murmured as he started swaying back and forth while making that awful sound.

Then, his body jerked as if a hundred rounds of gunfire were hitting it. Lunging forward, I grabbed his shoulders before he could hurt himself, but the spasms jolted his slender body beneath my grasp. His eyes rolled back, and when blood sprayed from his mouth, I realized that's what was clogging his throat.

I shook him roughly, but it was already too late to wake him as his eyes rolled back in his head and his body became a dead weight in my grasp. When I released him, he hit the ground.

I stood and gazed down at him as the blood oozing from his mouth seeped into the water, turning it pink before being washed away. Then, the birds started singing again.

Bending, I scooped up some water and used it to wash Chet's blood from my face and hair before rising.

"Why?" Amalia moaned.

She clasped her head with her hands as anguish shook her slender frame. Consumed by the urge to protect her, I strode over and swept her into my arms. She didn't fight me as she curled up against my chest and buried her face in my neck.

I ignored the allure of her breasts pressing against my chest as I turned to the angels. Raphael's face remained impassive, but sadness shone in his violet eyes. Caim's attention was riveted on Chet's body; his face mirrored the confusion in his eyes.

"What do they do to them in the Abyss?" Caim murmured.

"Nothing good," I said. "Gather his body. We can't leave him here."

Caim didn't tear his gaze away from Chet's body as he spoke. "Why did he walk around before dying while the others die in their sleep, or whatever state they're in?"

"I think the jinn gave him control of his body," Amalia whispered, "to unnerve you and keep you on your toes."

"They're playing with us," Raphael stated.

Amalia bowed her head. I didn't wait to hear any more before I turned and started back to the cave with Amalia nestled safely in my arms.

Magnus

When we returned to the cave, I stood at the front of it while I weaved the illusion of a wall over the entrance. No one passing by here would ever know the entry existed.

When the last rock settled into place, I turned to find Amalia watching me. Her eyes were such a sad shade of orange I wondered if she could return to the Abyss. Knowing what I did about her, this constant sway of different emotions must be battering her. The empath ability was a powerful tool as well as a highly destructive one to whoever possessed it.

"How did you do that?" she inquired.

"I am the last demon of illusions."

A vibrant smile lit her face, and her eyes became a joyful yellow color I vowed to see as often as I could from here on out.

"You told me," she breathed.

Self-hatred swamped me for the way I treated her in the beginning. She had the tenderest heart I'd ever encountered, and I'd treated her like shit.

"I'm sorry for the way I treated you when we first met," I apologized.

"Thank you, but an apology isn't necessary."

"Yes, it is."

"I understand why others fear and mistrust the jinn, more so now that I've been in the Abyss. And you didn't know about the Faulted."

"No, but I suspect the jinn are responsible for keeping the Faulted line a secret. If they are as protective of each other as you say, they wouldn't want other demons to know some jinn aren't as ruthless. Most demons steer clear of the jinn, but if they saw a chance to exploit some of the jinn, they would take it."

"Or, perhaps the jinn kept the Faulted a secret because they see us as the weak link and were ashamed," she said what I wouldn't say to her.

"If they were, then they were idiots."

She smiled again, but this time her amusement didn't reach her multi-hued eyes. "Come now, Magnus, admit it, you see me as weaker than the non-Faulted jinn."

"No," I said honestly. "It takes more strength to open yourself to others, suffer hurt and degradation, and continue, than it does to hide yourself away or be cruel to others. Once free of the seal, you could have retreated with the Faulted or stayed the course of never going against the jinn, yet here you are."

"I didn't have the strength to leave my parents and go with the other Faulted."

"Yet you have the strength to make a stand against what they do. The other Faulted wouldn't interfere and try to help an innocent."

Her mouth parted and the vermillion hue I recognized as passion crept into her eyes. Seeing that color caused blood to flood into my groin as my body instinctively responded to her. Before I could go to her, a sound drew our attention to Erin as she emerged from the shadows.

"We're all set back there," Erin said.

"Then, it's time for us to return to the Abyss." Walking forward, I claimed Amalia's hand and led her through the shadows toward the others.

CHAPTER FIFTEEN

Amalia

I HATED the Abyss more when the second we returned to it, another bolt of lightning pierced the sky and hit the monstrous monolith. A wave of lost life washed over me, leaving me feeling filthy again.

Unfortunately, it was not the last one either. As we traversed the pathway and discovered more side paths, lightning hit the monolith again and again. Some of the bolts we never saw the people or demons whose deaths they signaled, but a few of them belonged to a couple of humans and one demon we encountered along the way.

We'd tried, and failed, to get through to all of them before their deaths were distributed throughout the Abyss. And the closer we got to the monolith, the stronger the force of the lost lives washing through me became.

One thing was certain; I would not return to live with my parents when this was done. I didn't know what I would do, but it wouldn't involve standing complacently by while they and the other jinn destroyed lives.

Trudging beside Magnus, I kept my head bowed as I dreaded and hoped to come across someone soon, but someone we could help, like Erin.

"Why don't we take a break?" Magnus suggested after what felt like hours of roaming the pathway.

He led me into another side path that dead-ended in a rock wall. Settling on the ground, I drew my legs against my chest and dropped my chin on top of them while Magnus leaned against the wall beside me. I didn't require as much sleep as a human, but as a demon who wasn't fully matured yet, I needed more than other demons, and sleep tugged at my eyelids.

"What's this?"

My eyes opened at Magnus's words and alarm shot through me. Then I realized there was no enemy as he was kneeling at my side. My skin came alive when his fingers encircled my arm, and he turned it to the side.

"What's what?" I asked.

"This."

My attention was drawn to the bruise on my arm, and I recalled Mara punching me near the lake. My sleeve mostly hid the bruise, but the deep purple edges of it poked out.

"It's a bruise," I murmured and stifled a yawn. "Do you not know what a bruise is?"

He lifted his head and frowned at me. "I do, but when did you get it, Freckles?"

"Freckles? What does that mean?" I demanded. *Did he just insult me?*

He smiled as he brushed his fingers over my nose and cheeks. "These small marks are freckles."

I tried to understand what he was talking about, and then it dawned on me. "You mean the dots on my face!"

He chuckled. "Humans call them freckles."

"Oh. I never had them until I came to Earth. At first, I thought something was wrong with me, but then two of the other Faulted developed them too."

"The fae were described as very fair," he said. "I'm not sure if they had freckles or not in Hell, but the sun causes some people to develop them."

I almost searched for the big, beautiful orb in the sky before recalling we were in a place more like Hell than Earth. "I didn't know that."

"Now you do, and I like your dots."

I couldn't stop a blush from creeping into my cheeks. I didn't think I'd *ever* blushed before, but his words caught me off guard.

"For not knowing much about humans and Earth, you speak English extremely well. The language wasn't around before the jinn were sealed away," he remarked.

"When we came to Earth, we knew we had to adapt or be destroyed," I explained. "The jinn are highly intelligent and learn fast. However, there are some words we still don't know, like freckles."

"Hmm," he murmured and leaned forward to kiss the tip of my nose before doing the same to each of my cheeks.

My breath caught at the tender gesture as need coiled within my belly. I craved curling into his arms and shutting out everything else. Instinctively, I knew he could make me forget this place and all the horror that came with it. I shouldn't want to forget, I should get up and return to searching, but my legs wouldn't move.

"Magnus," I whispered as his lips brushed across mine.

Demons didn't kiss. My parents did, but I never saw the jinn kissing each other while having sex, and I hadn't seen it from any other demons since coming to Earth. This was different, not wrong, but there was something more here, something I couldn't quite put my finger on....

It felt like fifty jolts of life from the monolith went through me when he took full possession of my mouth. His lips branded mine as liquid heat spread from my belly to between my thighs. When his tongue traced my lips, I opened my mouth to his invasion.

His tongue ran across mine in a slow, torturous dance that had me craving more. I melted against him while our tongues entwined, our breaths mingled, and the kiss hardened. I couldn't get enough of his fiery taste, and when our teeth clicked together, I didn't care. I had to feel this harsh wildness from him.

I needed to know he was as out of control for me as I was for him. And if the sounds he made and the increasing demand of his kiss was any indication, he was as eager to be inside me as I was to feel him between my thighs.

Lowering my legs, I lifted my hands and slid my fingers over the buttons of his shirt. I undid them and pushed them aside so I could touch his smooth flesh.

Oh yes!

I almost screamed the words aloud as I desperately shoved his shirt to get it free. I *had* to feel more of his bare flesh and finally know what it was like to scream in ecstasy while riding someone until we were both too tired to move.

Demons saw sex as a simple scratching of an itch between each other, unless it was with their Chosen. Once demons scratched this itch, they moved on from each other. And I had a *big* itch that I'd been ready to scratch since I was old enough to understand what the jinn were doing while they writhed over each other.

There were plenty of jinn I would have had no problem having sex with before going to the next one. I'd picked out who my first would be. I'd informed him he would be my first, and he agreed to it, but I'd also picked out my second and third. I'd watched them all enough to know which ones I wanted to start with, though I'd planned to use them all.

But would I be able to move on from Magnus, or would he haunt me in ways that no other demon would?

The more I touched him, the less I cared about the answer as I found myself fascinated by his lean body and the way it moved against mine. His desire for me inflamed mine for him until my mind swam with the hunger radiating between us.

I shoved his shirt back from his shoulders and squirmed closer when my hands were finally able to trace the dips and hollows of his etched abs. Lithe in build, every inch of him was rock solid beneath my hands. The power racing through his whipcord frame vibrated against me.

My fingers fell to the button of his pants, and I undid it as he pulled the front of my dress down until my breasts spilled free. Magnus broke our kiss as I slid down the zipper on his pants. His shaft brushed over my hand when it sprang free. Leaning back, his eyes were nearly black when they latched onto my puckered nipples.

"Delicious," he murmured.

His breath sucked in when I wrapped my hand around his shaft. I'd seen many naked men while behind the seal. I'd admired their different shapes and sizes, but I hadn't anticipated how hot and throbbing their cock would be against my palm. Hadn't expected the silken feel of the skin stretched taut over it or how rigid it would be in my hand. I hadn't anticipated feeling each pulse of his heartbeat searing into me while I ran my hand over it.

Leisurely, I explored him and learned what made his breath quicken and his body lean toward me. Most times, I would prefer not to have my empath ability, but this was not one of those times as it helped me to discover how to please him better.

I thrived on holding him in the palm of my hand.

Then, one of his hands cupped my breast, and the balance of power shifted as I lost myself to him once more. Crying out, my back arched into his touch when his thumb traced my aching nipple before he bent his head to run his tongue over it. The torturous tease of it had my hips thrusting toward him.

"Magnus," I murmured as I squirmed against him. I couldn't take this anymore.

Releasing his shaft, I placed my hands against his chest and guided him back against the wall. I hiked my skirt up and straddled his lap as lightning split the sky. Someone's life force rushed through me.

I froze against Magnus, my lips curled back, as my skin crawled with the need to be scrubbed clean. We sat and stared at each other while his dick pulsed against my core. I could so easily ignore what was going on here and take him into me, but more would die while I was doing that. And I would never forgive myself.

When I met his eyes, I knew I didn't have to explain. Reluctantly, I untangled myself from him and rose. I didn't look at him as I adjusted my dress to cover my breasts. If I met his stare, I might stop caring about anything else, curl up in his arms again, and shut out all this atrocity with him.

"Amalia."

Lifting my head, I met his nearly black eyes. He'd also risen and fixed his clothing. "Yes?" I inquired.

"Sometime soon, I will have you."

My breath trapped in my lungs. It burst free when I finally found the words to reply, "That's a very bold statement."

The grin he gave me almost had me saying screw it and jumping him.

"I'm a very arrogant demon."

Why did that make me want him more when I'd always found the most arrogant demons annoying? Before I could respond, his eyes returned to my arm.

"Why isn't that bruise healing?" he asked.

I struggled to ignore the unfulfilled lust coursing through me as

I recalled the bruise in question. "Probably because I haven't stopped aging yet."

His head shot up, and his nostrils flared. "You're not immortal?"

"Not yet."

His eyes shot over the rock surrounding us before he clasped my arm and drew me closer to him. "You can't be here anymore."

"You're at far more risk in the Abyss than I am."

"But this place—"

"Is the place of the jinn. As much as I hate it, and as much as every flash of lightning makes me feel like scrubbing the skin from my body, a part of me does feel as if I belong here. This place will not hurt me. The jinn will be mad if they find me here with you, but they won't harm me."

His body vibrated with tension, and though I was correct in my assessment of our different danger levels here, he didn't release me.

"You should have told me you weren't immortal," he stated.

"Why? What difference would it have made? In the beginning, neither you nor Corson would have cared if I died here."

He opened his mouth, I assumed to protest my words, but he closed it again when he probably realized lying to an empath was pointless.

"Besides, it changes nothing," I continued. "You still need to attempt rescuing your friends, and I'm still the only way you can get in and out of here."

"We can figure something else out so you don't have to be here."

I couldn't deny his protectiveness gave me a small thrill of pleasure, but this argument was pointless and wasting time.

"I'm close to my immortality. It's right *there*." Like a shadow, I could sense it there before me, but I couldn't grasp it yet; I would soon. "And I'm safer here than I am in the human world. I don't know if you've noticed this or not, but the jinn aren't exactly welcomed with open arms. Many would kill me before they ever got the chance to learn anything about me."

A muscle in his eye twitched as frustration rolled off him. "I knew you were young, but I didn't know you were *this* young."

"I'm twenty-three. I may not be some ancient demon or anywhere near as old as the other jinn, but I'm not a child. How old are you?"

"I celebrated my nine hundredth birthday this year."

"You're a babe compared to the rest of the jinn."

A small smile curved his lips, and his eyes turned silver again. "I suppose I am."

"You're still old," I teased, and he released me. I missed the feel of his flesh against mine the second it was gone.

"Not too old to please you though," he replied with a wink.

"Maybe, one day, I'll be the judge of that."

His smile slid away, and he leaned closer to rest his lips against my ear. A shiver ran through me, and any progress I'd made toward getting my body under control vanished as he spoke. "Oh, you will be, and I guarantee you'll judge me very favorably while screaming my name."

"Arrogant demon," I huffed, but I couldn't stop my toes from curling. "We should go."

"Yes," he agreed, but his lips lingered against me for a little longer before he moved away.

CHAPTER SIXTEEN

Magnus

"WHAT WAS HELL LIKE?" Amalia asked as we traversed what was becoming an increasingly twisted pathway through the Abyss.

From this angle, and with the walls closing in on us, I couldn't see the monolith. Being unable to see anything beyond ten feet of our surrounding area had me contemplating climbing the rocks to take a look from above. I could cloak myself while I was up there, but I doubted the view would reveal much more than what I saw from the top of the hill when we first entered the Abyss.

"Magnus," she prodded.

"It was Hell," I said when I recalled her question.

When her delectable mouth pursed, and her eyes slid sideways to meet mine, an increasingly familiar tightening started in my groin. Had there ever been a woman I desired as much as her? I tried to think of the answer, but I couldn't recall anyone before she walked into my life.

I could only remember what it felt like to have her lips against mine and her flesh beneath my hands. And out of all the women I'd been with, she was the first demon I kissed. Some of the humans insisted on kissing during sex, and I obliged when I had to, but I'd never felt the compulsion to taste a woman as I did with her.

And I would taste her again as soon as I got her out of this place, alive.

She's still mortal.

The reminder caused my teeth to clench. She was right, she was safer here than I was, but I hated this vulnerability in her that I hadn't known she possessed until recently. No matter what happened, I would make sure she attained her immortality. My protective feelings toward her had me questioning just what she was to me.

Is she my Chosen?

The more I pondered that, the more it made some sense. I experienced a draw toward her from the beginning. I wanted her, badly; I felt more protective of her than any other, but I'd never wanted a Chosen and wasn't sure how to deal with the possibility of having found mine. I'd seen the loss of a Chosen destroy demons before, and I'd vowed not to be one of them.

I was not a demon to fall in love, but discovering a Chosen didn't guarantee love between them. However, all the mated demons I'd encountered loved each other deeply.

The Chosen bond made demons inherently stronger. It also gave them a weakness they'd never experienced before as they now had someone else walking around whose death would equal theirs.

Lucifer killed my parents, but I'd learned later in life that my father's death propelled my mother into going after Lucifer without any concern for herself. She'd handed me over to Kobal. Then, she went to hunt Lucifer and died. Her love for my father drove her to such reckless behavior, and because of that, I'd always seen love as a weakness.

Amalia could be my Chosen, we could one day complete the bond between us, and I could keep myself from falling in love with her. If she were my Chosen, I would welcome the strength the bond would bring me, but if I kept from loving her, I might also be able to live without her should she perish. The idea of her death caused my teeth to clamp together; it would *not* happen.

"I could see the fires of Hell through the windows of my seal, but what was it really like there?" she asked. "What was Lucifer like? What is *the* king like?"

I stopped walking and turned to face her. "It was a hideous pit of misery. Demons slaughtered demons, angels slaughtered demons, Lucifer was a *prick* who deserved to die, and the day I watched it happen was *the* best day of my life. He slaughtered my parents when I was two."

Her hand flew to her mouth. "I'm sorry."

"Don't be; it was centuries ago."

"Do you remember anything about them?"

"My mother's hair was dark, and my father's was the same color as mine. I recall being hugged between them and sitting on the ground playing with them as they wove illusions around me. They loved me, and I loved them, but that's all I remember." I could still feel the warmth of their love for me, but it wasn't enough to keep my mother alive. "They died before either of them could teach me what I was capable of, and there were no other illusion demons to do that either. I am the last of my kind."

"What happened to you after they died?"

"Kobal, the king, brought me to a Chosen pair of visionary demons who had lost their child ten years before, during a surprise attack from Lucifer and the angels."

"How awful for them," Amalia murmured.

"We should discuss something else," I said when her eyes turned ochre again.

"No. I want to learn more about Hell and you."

Those words pleased me more than I'd expected.

"What happened after that?" she asked and started walking again.

I fell into step beside her. "The visionary demons raised me. They never had another child before they were killed by the craetons twenty-eight years later, a year after I stopped aging."

"That must have been difficult for you."

"It was." I didn't like recalling the sadness their passing caused. "I may not have been theirs, but demon children are rare and precious, and they loved me as if I'd been a product of their love. I started fighting with Kobal once I aged into my immortality, but after their deaths, I plunged into the battle. I wanted Lucifer dead in the worst way, and I was reckless in my youth. When I look back on those days, I know only luck, Kobal, Corson, and even Bale kept me alive throughout those centuries of my life. Then, once my grief, youth, and bloodlust were spent, I started to reevaluate what I was doing."

"And what did you learn?"

"I was doing it all wrong."

Amalia stopped walking, and I faced her. "I don't understand," she said.

"I'm an illusionary demon, and I knew I was capable of conjuring things such as this." Holding out my palm, I brought to life a perfect, red rose in the center of it. She smiled as the rose started spinning in a slow dance over my palm. "Go on, touch it."

She glanced at me before stretching her fingers forward. Her smile faltered when her fingers slid through the rose, but it returned when the flower remained.

"Amazing," she breathed.

"I thought the same, back then, but I knew there was a *lot* more potential in me. Curious about my kind, I decided to read up on what past illusionary demons could do. In the process, I learned I was barely scratching the surface of my abilities. My illusions distracted our enemies for a brief time, but they were parlor tricks at best."

"So what did you do?"

"I knew I wouldn't be able to concentrate on the war with Lucifer and strengthen my abilities at the same time, so I retreated from the war. I hoped our friendship would be enough to keep Kobal from killing me, as I never told him why I abruptly decided to stop fighting."

"Why didn't you tell him?"

"I was afraid if I told him, Lucifer would somehow discover what I was trying to do and come after me. No one wants an enemy who is trying to grow stronger, and back then my illusions weren't a concern to anyone. I also don't think the craetons knew what I was then, or now, as in battle it's almost impossible to tell who is doing what."

"I don't think they know either," she said. "I'd heard of you, but I've never heard anything about what you are capable of doing."

"If Lucifer never learned the truth of what I was doing, he'd remain too busy trying to defeat Kobal than to concern himself with going after the coward many viewed me as. I preferred to let them *all* think I'd tucked tail and run, than to reveal the truth and risk everything."

Amalia seized my other hand and squeezed it. When she went to release it, I held on to hers so I could feel the warmth of her delicate hand within mine. It wasn't a good way to keep my distance from her, but I *had* to touch her.

"I staked out a corner of Hell, claimed it as mine, and started practicing," I said. "I created a demonic carnival meant for Hell alone. I trapped craetons and lower-level demons there, turned them into sideshow freaks, or killed them."

"Kind of like the jinn with the Abyss," she murmured.

"The demons who entered my world weren't tricked into it; they went there to kill me. I may have been flying under Lucifer's radar, but there were still plenty I'd pissed off over the years and others I pissed off after I left the war. Those demons just weren't prepared for what they encountered, but believe me, they all deserved what they got. The jinn are not so discerning."

"No, they're not," she agreed, "but I still don't like it."

"Then it's a good thing I don't need to build any carnivals on Earth, Freckles." As I'd hoped, a small smile tugged at the corners of her mouth.

CHAPTER SEVENTEEN

Magnus

"What is a carnival?"

Reluctantly, I released her hand and knelt. "It's a human thing. A place of games and rides, food, animals, and all kinds of assorted things."

As I mentioned each thing, I weaved a foot-high replica of a carnival over the path. Colorful tents sprang to life, and roller coasters and carousels rose from the ground. The miniature humans strolling the midway pointed to the games and rides. Barkers leaned out to wave at them as they encouraged the humans to spend their money.

When Amalia knelt before me to examine my creation more closely, the colors of the carnival flickered over her face and illuminated her awe-filled, coral eyes. She laughed when the roller-coaster wheels clattered over the wooden tracks and screams echoed from the humans when the cars plummeted down a steep hill.

With two fingers, she tried to touch the top of the carousel as it rotated into life and the proud horses started to rise and fall in rhythm with the music playing. Unlike the malevolent carousal and carnival I'd created in my corner of Hell, this fair held only the delights of the human world. Amalia had witnessed enough ugliness in the Abyss; I would make sure she didn't see any more of it than she had to.

A bell rang as someone slammed a hammer down on the strongman game and a giant teddy bear was handed over to a woman who hugged it. More tents and buildings rose from the ground. Animals stood idly by as people strolled through the barns to admire them.

Amalia clapped her hands when the racetrack materialized and the harness horses and their drivers raced around it. The horse's hooves pounded across the dirt as the crowd cheered them on from the grandstand.

"Amazing," she murmured.

"Humans are creative creatures," I said.

"Yes, they are. How did *you* know these places existed on Earth?"

She never took her eyes off the carnival as I weaved new rides and games into place.

"Once I retreated from the war, I started reading through the scrolls, but they weren't exactly entertaining, so I spent a lot of time watching Earth too."

"How did you do that?"

"I would journey to the oracle." When she gave me a confused look, I realized she didn't know what that was either. "The oracle is a lake of fire in the bowels of Hell, and the focus of all the heat in Hell, but Earth could be looked on from it."

"Oh," she murmured and focused on my illusion again. "And you saw this through there?"

"This and many other things both gruesome and astonishing. Humans are a fascinating, loving, infuriating, self-destructive, angry, and selfish species. Some are as cruel as demons, but as horrendous as some of them can be, far more of them are good and loving. I was fascinated with Earth, humans, and the magnificent things they created before I ever left Hell."

Behind the carnival, I weaved the pyramids, Taj Mahal, Great Wall of China, and Sistine Chapel into creation. "And Earth itself is remarkable." Niagara Falls, the Grand Canyon, and Mount Everest came to life. Above it all, the Northern Lights shimmered over my creations. "Everything about the human world interested me, and I found myself watching it more often with every passing year."

Her striking eyes took on a more ochre hue again when she lifted her head to look at me. "Is it *all* gone?" she whispered. "Did all of it get destroyed when the gateway opened?"

"No." Gradually, the illusions faded away. "Some of it still exists. One thing I've learned about humans over the centuries is they often come back stronger after they face destruction. And much of the natural beauty of this planet remains."

"Since coming to Earth, I've tried to learn as much as I can about it. I find this planet fascinating with all of its creatures, plants, and people, but I haven't met many humans who can answer the questions I have about it."

"I know plenty of humans who will be more than willing to answer your questions."

Hating the sadness in her eyes, I lifted my palm again. Within it, I brought to life a bouquet of lilies that matched her hair and eyes. "I'll answer what questions I can for you and reveal to you anything you ask to see," I vowed.

Offering this wasn't exactly the best way to keep my distance, but if she were my Chosen, I wouldn't be unkind to her; she deserved far better than that, and she would have it.

"Do you miss Hell?" she asked.

"Not at all. Do you?"

"No. I've fallen in love with Earth, especially the butterflies."

Lifting my hand over the flowers, I constructed an orange monarch to perch on top of them. The butterfly's wings flapped, and Amalia laughed.

"It's wonderful, and the flowers are beautiful," she whispered.

"Take them," I encouraged.

She frowned at me before gripping the stems. Her mouth parted as she lifted the bouquet and held it before her. Leaning over the flowers, she inhaled deeply and sighed. Then, she skimmed one finger over the butterfly's wings and gasped.

"It's... it's real!" she cried.

"It's more real than any of the others," I said. "I hated removing myself from the war, despised they considered me a coward, but I became far stronger in the three hundred years I remained in self-imposed exile. I can make illusions a reality now, something *no* other illusionary demon could *ever* do. It takes some time to construct elaborate illusions, but I can weave small ones into existence far faster. Before me, my father was the strongest illusionary demon to exist, but I have grown stronger than he was, in many ways."

"Three hundred years? Why so long?"

"That's how much time it took for me to strengthen. Then, one day, Kobal's queen stumbled into my corner of Hell, and I knew it was time for me to return to the war."

"In what ways aren't you stronger than your father?"

I wiped my palms on my thighs and stood. Extending my hand to her, I waited for her to take it and rise, before speaking. "I'm not very good with cloaking illusions. I can do them, but they're draining for me. My father was a master at them."

She glanced at the flowers in her hand and smiled. "I'd rather have something real than nothing at all."

I couldn't stop myself from bending to brush a kiss against her temple. When the increased beat of her heart thudded in my ears, I remained leaning forward for longer than I'd intended before reluctantly pulling away.

"Can you make a duplicate image of yourself?" she asked.

"I can."

Her eyes widened. "Can you make it as real as these flowers?'

"It would take some work, and the duplicate couldn't talk or reveal emotions, but it would be solid until it was destroyed."

"Amazing," she breathed as she gazed at me from under the lowered fringe of her thick, multi-hued lashes.

"And what of you, Freckles, why do you like the human world so much, aside from the butterflies?"

"It's far better than the four walls of a seal," she said with a laugh as we started walking again. "And what I've seen of it is interesting. The jinn haven't traveled far since being freed, so I haven't seen as much of it as I would like to. For a time, we lived underground, but after some of the jinn met with Astaroth, we moved."

I stiffened at the mention of the fallen angel who had risen to take Lucifer's place. "Why did you move?"

She lowered her bouquet. "I don't know. I'm not exactly kept in the loop. The other Faulted had already split off when the meeting occurred, so I'm not even sure they know about it. I didn't expect the jinn to align with anyone as their loyalty lies with each other, but a lot of them are pissed about being locked away. After eighteen thousand years behind the seal, the jinn were accustomed to their surroundings, they had no other choice, but now that they're free, they want revenge."

"And are you pissed about it?"

"It wasn't the greatest life to have, but it was all I knew. I couldn't be pissed about missing out on something I'd never experienced before like the other jinn were. Sometimes, I'd dream about what it would be like to be free, but I knew it was a waste of time, and that it would destroy me if I did it too often."

Stepping in front of her, I blocked her from continuing and gripped her shoulders. "You shouldn't have endured that."

"You didn't put me there, Magnus, and you didn't keep me there."

"No, but if Kobal had known there were jinn such as you who existed, he wouldn't have kept you there either."

"You're so sure of that?"

"He is tough, but he is not cruel. And he was not the varcolac who sealed the jinn away."

"Wasn't it cruel to lock so many away for so long to begin with? There were two hundred and three seals."

"Perhaps it was cruel, but if the occupants of those seals were all slaughtered outright, you wouldn't be alive."

CHAPTER EIGHTEEN

Amalia

"True," I reluctantly agreed. "It was still a *shitty* thing to do to them though."

"Perhaps, but I don't think the varcolac who created the first seal knew what to do with the demons who stepped out of line. Before the angels, Hell wasn't really a place of slaughter and war. Perhaps that varcolac planned only to keep them imprisoned for a certain amount of time before releasing them, but as the number of seals grew, and new varcolacs rose, the intentions of the first one were lost."

"Maybe," I muttered as I gazed at the bouquet he'd given me. I didn't miss that it matched my hair and eyes, a personal touch of his, I knew.

"Do you hate the king?" he asked, his fingers briefly digging into my skin.

"I can't hate someone I've never met, and willingly or not, his queen did destroy the seals and set us free."

"You've heard the tale then?"

"I think everyone has."

"The act earned River the loyalty of many who were sealed away."

"I have no loyalties in this, Magnus," I said honestly. "I have no grudges, and I'm not much of a fighter. I simply don't want to be judged for what I am, and one day I dream of living in peace. I guess that's the fae in me."

"It's a good dream to have, Amalia."

"But?" I inquired when I sensed more behind his words.

"But sometimes war comes to our door, and we have no choice but to fight it. We can't allow the craetons to win. Not only will they enslave the human race, but the horsemen and fallen will turn on the demons before turning on each other. They will destroy what the palitons have battled to preserve since the gateway opened. They won't care if the fae in you doesn't want to fight; they'll kill you anyway."

"Perhaps, but no matter which side I chose, I will inevitably have to kill, and I don't want to."

Releasing my shoulders, he brushed back the sides of my hair and gripped it against my nape with his hand. His finger traced the curve of my cheekbone before dipping down to run it over my lips.

"You are unlike anyone I've ever met before," he murmured.

"Is that a good thing or a bad thing?"

"Oh, it's a very good thing in most ways."

"And in other ways?"

His eyes met and held mine. "It makes me worry about you."

"I may prefer not to kill, but I *will* defend myself."

"A battered body can heal; a battered spirit might forever be maimed, and if you are forced into something you can't handle, that could happen to you. I'm going to do everything I can to make sure it doesn't."

Before I could respond to his vehement words, he released my hair and turned away. I stood and gawked after his stiff back as he continued down the path. His confusion radiated from him, yet I also sensed he was trying to distance himself from me.

But why?

Amalia

The man sat on a rock, his elbow propped on his knee and his chin on his fist as he watched two children laughing while they played. The children kicked a white ball with black spots back and forth between them. Their mops of shaggy brown hair bounced against their faces as they ran.

"Dana?" Magnus asked, and the man glanced at him before focusing on the children again.

Then, Dana's brown eyes came back to Magnus, and his eyebrows shot into his russet hairline. "Magnus?" he asked incredulously.

"Yes," Magnus said and grinned.

Dana studied him before turning away. "You're not real either," he muttered.

Magnus glanced at me, and I shrugged. He knew as much about what was happening here as I did.

"I'm real," Magnus said.

"Yeah sure, and so are they," Dana waved his hand at the kids. "They're as fake as fake can get. Oh, and yep, here comes the other phony one now."

His words confused me until a pretty woman with her blonde hair pulled into a bun emerged from behind some rocks. She wiped her hands on her checkered apron as she approached the children.

"Dinner's ready, kids!" she called to them before turning to Dana and waving. "Are you hungry, love?"

When Dana lifted his middle finger to her, the woman's smile remained plastered in place. It was a gesture I'd seen before, and I'd figured out what it meant pretty quick.

"We can do the equivalent of that later," the woman said with a laugh, and Dana groaned.

"What is this?" I asked.

Dana glanced at me and turned away before facing me again. "Who are you?" he demanded.

Magnus gave Dana a look that made the man cringe away from him.

"My name is Amalia," I replied.

"She's here to help *you*," Magnus grated, "and you'll talk to her with respect."

I didn't point out that he wasn't exactly respectful in the beginning. There was no reason to bring up the past or argue about it when we might have a chance of helping Dana. The man realized something wasn't right here.

"Yeah, sure she is, and I suppose you're here to help me too," Dana muttered and rolled his eyes.

"I *am* real." Resting his hand on Dana's shoulder, Magnus bared down until the man winced. "Does that woman or those children make you feel pain?"

"*My* wife, *my* children. I've held them, and loved them, and..." Dana's voice trailed off as his attention returned to the laughing family. The woman joined in to kick the ball around with the children. "And I felt their touch on me."

"So why are you sitting here?" I inquired. "If you've felt them, then why do you think they're fake?"

The man's shoulders slumped. "Because I know something's not quite right about them. As much as this family is *mine*, something inside me says they're not. Have you ever seen kids or a woman so perfect before? I mean, kids complain about everything, but not these two. Nope, not my two flawless boys. And my wife is... is... I've known many good women before, but how many of them would smile at you after you flip them off?"

"Not many," Magnus said.

"No, of course not!" Dana cried. "I told her that her cooking sucks—which it doesn't, it's fantastic—but she laughed and told me she'd improve. It's all so perfect and *wrong*. It's like I married a Stepford Wife, and I gotta tell ya, that movie creeped me out as a kid."

I didn't know what a Stepford Wife or movie was, but Magnus sympathetically patted Dana's shoulder.

"What is your wife's name?" I asked.

Dana opened his mouth before a look of consternation crossed his face. "I... I don't know. And there's something really wrong with *that*."

"So this wasn't a family you had before the gateway opened?" Magnus asked Dana.

"The gateway?"

It was then I realized Dana was like Erin. They both knew something wasn't quite right; they just weren't sure what it was, or how to break free of the wrongness.

"The one that allowed demons to roam the Earth," Magnus said.

Dana rubbed his temples. "The gateway," he murmured before his attention returned to the laughing family. "They're exactly the way I pictured my family, from the two boys to the pretty blonde wife. I find that weird too. I mean, no one gets *exactly* what they want in life.

"I used to play soccer; I planned to teach my kids to play it too, but how many kids and wives *all* love soccer and are willing to play it? My father wanted me to play football; I hated it. He wasn't at all impressed with me when I told him I was going to play the European version of the game."

Magnus chuckled, but I gave up trying to figure it all out. I assumed the family kicking the ball around was playing soccer, but the rest of Dana's words went over my head.

"The gateway," Dana said, as if just recalling that part of the conversation.

Another bolt hit the monolith, and I bit back a whimper when more life washed over me. We were losing far more than we were saving in this place.

"Yes, the gateway to Hell," Magnus said. "It opened fourteen years ago. Bombs were dropped—"

"Demons killed my family!" Dana blurted and then shuddered. "That's why I wanted a family like this one. Oh, my mom, my dad, my brothers. They're dead," he moaned and rocked himself forward. "Oh, I remember it all now."

Magnus went to pat him on the shoulder again, but Dana vanished before he touched him. The woman and children disappeared too, but the ball remained rolling across the ground. Then, as if a breeze caught it, it changed direction and came toward us.

I stepped out of the way, but then had to dance back when it zigged and zagged toward my feet. A chill raced up my spine as the sensation of being watched burned into my neck.

CHAPTER NINETEEN

Amalia

THE BALL finally rolled by me, and I braced myself before turning to face the presence I sensed behind me. The ball continued unerringly toward the man standing thirty feet away before it disappeared.

"Amalia," the man greeted in his calm, sultry voice, but his electric blue eyes were crueler than I'd ever seen them before.

This man had tossed me in the air, bounced me on his knee, and patiently let me braid his waist-length, pitch-black hair for hours on end. Many times, I'd experienced his love for me, but now he looked as happy to see me as he would have been to see a hellhound.

"Unshi Olgon," I murmured while trying to control the rapid beat of my heart.

My empath ability wasn't as sharp around the jinn; I still picked up some of their emotions, but far less than I did from other species. However, I didn't require my empath ability to know he was pissed in a way jinn seldom were. Mostly reserved, jinn rarely let their emotions get the best of them, but Olgon couldn't hide the fury radiating from him.

Bending, I carefully placed my bouquet on the ground, and the butterfly took flight. I suspected I would need both hands free for whatever was to come.

"This man is your uncle?" Magnus inquired as he came to stand beside me.

"I am," Olgon purred. "I've watched little Amalia here grow from a babe to a traitor."

"Unshi!" I gasped. "That's not true! I'd never—"

"Silence," he hissed, and my lips clamped together.

Magnus's shoulders went back, and his eyes narrowed as Olgon's gaze pinned me to the spot. At nineteen thousand, Olgon was the oldest jinn alive, a leader, and my family. I wanted to argue further with him and convince him I wasn't a traitor, but no one argued with Olgon.

"You brought a *paliton* into the Abyss." Olgon spat the word paliton at us.

With slow, subtle movements, Magnus positioned himself between Olgon and me. Olgon's eyes slid to Magnus, and his frown pulled his pale skin tighter over the sharp blades of his cheekbones.

"I am nineteen thousand years old, *demon*, you do not want to mess with me," Olgon stated.

"Unless the seal made it so the jinn developed new powers, I don't think there's much you can do to me," Magnus replied.

"We don't need powers to tear you apart. You're in our world now. We've been itching to destroy the bastards who imprisoned us, and you are *far* outnumbered here."

"No!" I grabbed Magnus's arm to halt him when he stepped forward. "Magnus wasn't even alive when you were imprisoned!"

Olgon's lips flattened into a thin line. "That matters not."

"But it does!" I insisted. "You're infuriated at a varcolac and demons who don't exist anymore! You're fighting the same battles that got you placed behind the seal in the first place!"

Closing my eyes, I took a deep breath to steady myself. If I were out of control, I would never get Olgon to listen to me. And if I failed in that, then Magnus could die here.

Magnus

I had to get Amalia away from this man, her unshi. It had been years since I'd heard the demon word for uncle, but then most of the demons I knew didn't have any living family.

"Now, Amalia," Olgon said. "Because of your Fault, we understand why you feel you have to help these creatures, but you must understand you're going against your kind by doing so."

"No, Unshi!" she cried.

When she stepped toward him, I seized her arm. If she got too close to him, he *would* take her from here, and I would be trapped here without her, at the mercy of these creatures. No matter how many illusions I weaved, or how much I fought, they would eventually destroy me if I didn't somehow, miraculously, find a way out.

But even knowing that, I was more worried about Amalia than me.

If she went to him, they would succeed in destroying *her*. I didn't think they would kill her, not outright. I believed her when she said they cared for each other. But being with them and watching them rain down the destruction they so easily unleashed would eventually tear her apart.

I would *not* let that happen. Clasping her elbow, I drew her protectively against my side. I cared for my friends, I would die for my king, but I'd never wanted to shelter someone the way I did Amalia. Nothing would hurt her while I lived, and that included her fucked-up family member.

"Come with me, Amalia," Olgon said, extending his hand toward her.

The power emanating from the ancient creature slid over my skin, but Olgon wasn't stronger than Kobal or Raphael. In a fight, I could take this jinni.

As soon as I thought it, movement caused the shadows to shift, and more jinn emerged from behind Olgon. Most of the taciturn faces were set in nearly identical expressions of disapproval. Many of the jinn were dark-haired, but a few were fair, and one had hair the color of blood. They all wore floor-length black robes.

Locking them behind the seals preserved their numbers I realized. If they'd been allowed to remain free, they would have caused a lot of destruction in Hell, but they also would have been steadily annihilated as so many other types of demons were over the years.

"Amalia," another male jinni said harshly. "Come with us now."

"Paupi." Amalia said the demon word for father in a broken voice.

I stared at the jinni who had spoken, her father. He looked so much like Olgon it was clear they were brothers. The only difference between them was her father's eyes were the sun yellow I'd seen Amalia's become and his black hair, unhindered by a braid, flowed to his waist.

At his side stood a petite woman with orange streaks flowing through her pale blonde hair. Slender and beautiful, her eyes were the pretty coral shade Amalia's could turn. With their similar, delicate features, there was no denying Amalia was her child.

"Amalia." The woman's tone was far kinder, but her eyes were like ice when they met mine. "Come away from him."

Amalia stared at her parents before her ochre eyes met mine. I didn't want her to choose the jinn and have them crush her spirit, but I couldn't keep her from her family.

Reluctantly, I released her arm. This was her choice to make, but I found myself willing her to choose *me*.

"Mohara, please listen to me," she begged her mother.

"Amalia," her mother said more brusquely. "Come to us, *now*."

"Mohara, Paupi, Unshi," she spread her hands before her as she spoke, "the people and demons you have trapped here did *nothing* to us. You know what it is like to be caged. Set them free!" she pleaded. "I only brought Magnus here to try to save his friends."

"Magnus, is it?" her father murmured. "You're one of the king's men. One of those who helped keep us imprisoned."

"He wasn't alive when you were locked away, and neither was the king!" Amalia cried.

"Silence!" Olgon barked, and Amalia's mouth shut.

The low rumble reverberating through my chest caused some of the jinn to exchange glances. Family or not, *no* one would talk to her like that. When I got the chance to go after Olgon without risking Amalia, I'd tear his tongue out and shove it down his throat before unburdening him of his heart.

"Get over here, Amalia, now," Olgon commanded.

"She is *not* yours to order around," I snarled.

"She is my niece, and I am the eldest jinn. She will do as I say, or I'll kill her with you!" Olgon spat.

The jinn gasped, and Amalia's mother paled. "Olgon!" she cried.

"Silence, Vya!" Olgon spat.

Vya didn't speak again, but her Chosen didn't look at all pleased as he shot his brother a fierce look.

"Amalia has put us all in jeopardy by bringing one of the king's men into the Abyss," Olgon said in a calmer tone. "The palitons would like nothing more than to see us all dead or locked away again. That's not going to happen."

"If you don't stand against the king, then no one will bother you," I told him.

"Lies," one of the other jinn hissed.

"Not lies," I retorted. "Things are vastly different now. Kobal's queen is guarded by the drakón who were once locked behind a seal too. If you don't stand against Kobal, he will not come for you."

"And he's going to allow us to roam free, doing what we do best by delivering dreams to the downtrodden in the Abyss?" Olgon murmured, and a handful of jinn chuckled while some of the others stared curiously at us.

"There is no reason for you to continue trapping people and demons here."

"There is the reason that matters most. We *enjoy* it."

"Then yes, Kobal will come for you because your paths will inevitably cross, and he won't tolerate unnecessary cruelty. Neither will I. You have demons and humans here who must be set free."

"Oh, must they?" Olgon inquired.

"Yes."

"We never let those we rightfully claim go," Olgon stated.

"Making an exception now would go a long way with Kobal," I said.

Olgon laughed as he folded his hands inside the sleeves of his black robe. "You think I care what the newest varcolac thinks of us. We were locked behind that seal for eighteen *thousand* years. There is nothing worse than that. We will have our revenge against those who kept us there, whether they were alive when we were sealed away or not. Your king could have set us free; he chose not to. Now, we have chosen to keep those we've caught, and we will align with those who aim to destroy him."

"That poor choice will get you killed."

Olgon's mouth curved into a smile, but behind his eyes, rage slithered like smoke twisting in the wind. Eighteen thousand years had honed this man's thirst for vengeance into a sword that would slice through any who stood in his way, including his niece.

"Amalia, this is your last chance to come away from him, before we kill him," Olgon stated.

"No!" she cried. "Unshi, please! What if we let these palitons go, and then we can find somewhere else to live? What if we leave it all behind? We can forget the king and the angels and find a life somewhere else! Magnus means no harm; he's only trying to free his friends, and there have been enough deaths today!"

Olgon's eyes fell briefly on her before he lifted his chin and stared at the rocks over her head. "Kill him, and if she gets in the way, kill her too."

"No!" Vya cried, and some of the other jinn hesitated at this command.

"Olgon—" her father started.

"I have given my command, Eron."

"She is my *daughter*!" Eron shouted.

"She is a traitor."

"Her Fault—"

"Is no excuse for turning against us!" Olgon bellowed. "*Kill him!*"

While some of the jinn continued to balk at this command, most of them looked more than happy to follow through on it as they came toward us.

"You or them?" I inquired of Amalia.

"What?" she asked as she edged closer to me.

"*You* or *them*, Amalia? Will you stay with them and fight with them, or will you choose yourself and come away with me? You must decide *now*. There is no time to think about it."

Tears filled her eyes as she looked from her parents, to me, to

Olgon. A shiver ran through her slender body when her eyes met Olgon's.

"Me," she whispered.

Turning, I wrapped my arms around her.

CHAPTER TWENTY

Magnus

SLIDING my hand over Amalia's mouth, I covered it as I swiftly weaved a cloaking illusion over us. This illusion may not be my strongest, but I could hold it and keep us hidden from the jinn. The bigger problem was that it drained me far more than any of my other illusions, and I'd be unable to do much else for a little while after this.

The jinn froze when we vanished before them. They glanced questioningly at each other before a few edged away from where we stood and distrustfully surveyed the air.

My hand fell to the knife at my side as I stared at Olgon. He was focused on the area he'd last seen us and where we remained standing though he couldn't see us anymore. The blade was long enough I could decapitate him with it, but I couldn't do it in front of Amalia, and I'd give away our location if I went after him.

The jinn didn't know what I'd done to hide us. For all they knew, I'd somehow transferred us from one place to another, as some *very* rare demons were capable of teleportation. If I killed

Olgon, they'd immediately be on me, and Amalia might turn against me for attacking him that way. Patience had always been my strong suit; there would come a time when I'd have the chance to go for Olgon, but now was not it.

Lifting Amalia, I pinned her against my chest as some braver jinn crept toward us. At first, she was stiff against me, but when her muscles relaxed, I realized she understood what was happening and removed my hand from her mouth.

Her body warmed mine as I edged further away, and I couldn't deny that she felt *right* in my arms. My heart raced with the knowledge she'd chosen herself and *me* over them.

The jinn stopped where we'd stood, and one of them threw out his hands to search for us, but we were a good ten feet away now.

"Where are they?" Olgon demanded.

The one searching for us lowered his hands. "Not here."

"Find them!" Olgon commanded. "And I don't care what it takes, bring that demon to me!"

"What about my daughter?" Vya asked as she stepped toward Olgon. Like a horse running from a wolf, her eyes were wild, and the whites of them showed.

"Unless she gets in the way, she'll be fine," Olgon replied. "If she gets in the way, then she will suffer the consequences."

"She's your *niece!*"

"I am aware of that, Vya, but you must recognize her betrayal cannot go unpunished."

"Punished *how?*"

"We'll decide that when we have them," Olgon replied and turned dismissively away from her.

Eron caught his Chosen by the shoulders when she lunged after Olgon. "Not now," he whispered to her. "We'll discuss this *if* Amalia is caught."

"But they could hurt her!"

"No one is going to hurt her."

"But he said to kill her if she got in the way!"

"Vya." Eron brushed her hair back from her face and clasped her cheeks. "Like it or not, Amalia made this choice and put herself in this position. We'll protect her the best we can."

Vya's head bowed, and tears spilled down her cheeks. Amalia made a move as if to go to her mother before stilling in my arms again.

"We'll make sure she's unharmed, I promise," a female jinni said and rested her hand on Vya's arm. "We all care for Amalia too. Yes, she made a bad decision, but she's young, and we all know she has *too* big a heart. Olgon is mad, but when he calms, he'll see this is because of Amalia's Fault and not because she's seeking to attack us, choosing against us, or trying to see us caged again."

"Yes," a male jinni said as he stepped closer to them. "Amalia is too soft, we all know that. Perhaps, when all is done, she'd be better off living with the other Faulted. We'll all miss her, but our way is not good for her."

I didn't move, not because I was concerned about accidentally drawing the attention of the jinn, but because of a shift in my perception of them. Olgon was the vicious creature I'd expected them all to be, but these were the jinn Amalia had described to me.

They didn't care about anyone beyond the jinn, but they loved each other.

"Come, Vya, Eron, we'll start the search for Amalia. If we find her first, we'll bring her back to Absenthees and keep her safe," another jinni said.

I shifted to flatten my back against the wall as the rest of the jinn departed down a pathway I hadn't seen before, but they must have taken it to get here. I remained where I was, the cloaking spell in place as I tried to understand what I'd witnessed and what it meant for us.

∾

Amalia

Magnus had been unusually subdued since we left the place where we encountered the jinn, but then, I didn't know what to say or do either.

Since we'd seen the jinn, I was certain they would be waiting for us around every turn we made. I loved my family and the jinn, but I couldn't stand by while they killed so many innocents, and I would *not* allow them to attack Magnus.

I was also exhausted and disheartened by the amount of lightning striking the monolith. Were the bolts all lives, or did some of them mean something more?

I felt a blast of energy from each of them, but I held out hope they might mean something more than the death of someone. Maybe I was delusional, but right now, I was okay with delusional.

Trudging behind Magnus, I contemplated what I'd done by choosing *me* and leaving with him. My parents still loved me, I knew the other jinn did too, and they would accept me back again, but I'd taken my first step into severing myself from them and going to live with the Faulted.

And it was a step I had to take. If I stayed with them, they would tear me apart. Not on purpose, they would never do that, but as upsetting as it was, I did belong with the other Faulted more than them.

And I couldn't deny a part of me did it because I wanted to stay with Magnus and make sure he made it out of this place alive.

What did that mean? And why must one more complicated thing be heaped onto this entire mess? Why couldn't it all be simple?

Like it was behind the seal? Because that was about as simple as it got.

I didn't want *seal* simple again, but just yesterday or maybe the day before—I didn't know how much time had passed since we entered the Abyss—my life was straightforward. I woke up, explored Earth, stayed away from anything the jinn might be trying to trap in the Abyss, avoided the craetons, and waited to age into my immortality. Sure, I had some problems, but they weren't *this* big or confusing.

Welcome to life, Amalia, something you wouldn't have had behind the seal, not really.

And that was true. I would have stayed alive and unbothered behind the seal, but I never would have gotten the chance to *live* and experience anything beyond that small world.

"How did they know where we were?" Magnus suddenly inquired.

I frowned at his back as I puzzled his words. He didn't turn to look at me while he strode onward. "Maybe they just lucked on us."

"No. Maybe one or two of them would have lucked on us, but not all of them. They wouldn't *all* leave the monolith at once."

"We're just assuming that's where they all are."

Magnus tilted his head back to gaze at the distant, foreboding structure. "That's where they are."

"Yeah, it is," I agreed, feeling the truth of that in my bones.

"So then how did they know where we were?"

"I don't know." My eyes narrowed on his back. "I didn't somehow tell them, if that's what you're trying to insinuate."

He glanced at me over his shoulder. "It's not, and I didn't say you did, but if they have some way of locating us in this place, we're in danger."

"I think they would have found us sooner if that were the case."

"Maybe they can only find us at certain times, like when one of the wishes is unfolding."

"But we've encountered others going through something like Dana was, and the jinn never found us then."

"I know," Magnus murmured. "That's what makes it more confusing."

I didn't know how to respond, and I had no answers for his question. *How did they find us?*

Turning another corner, I clasped Magnus's hand to draw his attention to me when the distant, familiar scent of water caught my attention. Tingles of awareness raced across my flesh when we connected.

I almost lifted his hand to rub his fingers over my breast when lust like I'd never experienced before rocked me. His gaze fell to my lips before he looked away from me.

Keep it together, Amalia. Remember where you are.

"This way," I forced myself to say.

I made myself release his hand and turn away from him. Hurrying down a side path, I zigged in and out of rocks sharp enough to take out an eye. The scent of water grew stronger until I stepped into a circular clearing.

"Oh," I breathed as I took in the beautiful sight.

A few hundred feet over my head, from the top of one wall, a waterfall crashed and tumbled over the rocks before spilling into a pool. The water in the pool looked dark because of the stones surrounding it, but the spray coming from the waterfall was clear.

A small bubble of hope replaced the heavy weight of despair weighing me down as I realized even in the midst of this stark land-scape, there was still some beauty to be found. Tears pricked my eyes; I ducked my head before Magnus could see them.

"Come," he said and clasped my hand.

"Where are we going?"

If he answered me, I didn't hear it over the thunderous crash of the waterfall as he led me closer to it. Water sprayed my cheeks and dampened my clothes when Magnus pulled me into an alcove behind the waterfall. A good five feet of space separated the wall from the waterfall, but the place had a cozy, safe feeling to it. It was almost as if we'd entered a private world here.

Magnus examined the rock wall before releasing my hand and

pointing up. I followed his gaze to what looked like an opening in the stony face about fifty feet overhead. Before I could say or do anything, he grasped a rock, lifted himself, and scaled the distance in seconds. He disappeared into the opening before coming back and descending to join me again.

Leaning close, he pressed his lips to my ear as he spoke. "There's something you should see."

I frowned at him, but I wasn't willing to try yelling over the waterfall to question him. Nodding, I stepped away from him, and he gestured for me to climb ahead of him.

When I shook my head, he returned his lips to my ear again. "In case you fall, I will be behind you to stop you from hitting the ground."

I couldn't argue with that as breaking bones in here could prove disastrous for continuing. Turning, I gripped a pointed stone and pulled myself off the ground. I could levitate up, but I'd never climbed before and wanted to try it. My hands found grips to lift me higher, and my feet settled on the stones beneath me. When I glanced down, my head spun a little, but the height and the experience thrilled me.

Before I knew it, I was pulling myself up and into the opening. Rising, I ran my hands over the front of my dirt-streaked dress while I lifted my head to take in my surroundings. My hands froze as I understood what it was Magnus wanted me to see.

CHAPTER TWENTY-ONE

Amalia

NOT MUCH LIGHT filtered past the waterfall, but it was enough to reveal the stones lining the walls, ceiling, and floor in here were far different than the ones throughout the rest of the Abyss. I pressed tremulous fingers against a pink stone before resting my other hand over a yellow one.

I rubbed the rocks with my fingers to see if the color would come off or if maybe they were an illusion, but they remained solid and the colors bright. This beauty didn't fit into this world of despair, but somehow, it did. None of it made sense, yet somehow it all made sense.

Confused and feeling a little disoriented, I pulled my hands away and strolled further inside. The rushing water quieted the deeper I traveled until the alcove dead-ended after a hundred feet. Turning, I made my way back toward the front as Magnus's fingers curved over the entrance to the cave, and he hefted himself inside. He glanced behind him before coming to join me in the secluded space.

"We'll rest here for a bit," he said.

"We have to find the others," I protested.

"And we will, but you need a break."

"I'm fine."

"The dark circles under your eyes say otherwise. We have no idea how much time we've spent in the Abyss, and you're exhausted."

"But—"

"No buts. You won't do anyone any good if you're too exhausted to go on."

He had a point. I was also hungry, but I didn't tell him that. I hadn't seen any wraiths in the Abyss, and we couldn't waste the time it would take to return to Earth and feed. I wasn't so famished that it couldn't wait.

Leaning against the rock wall, I slid down until I settled on the pretty rocks that were as out of place in this land as the grassy field. Lifting his hand, Magnus rested his fingertips against the ceiling and stretched his back as he studied the entrance. His posture remained casual, but he couldn't hide his tension from me.

I couldn't help but admire him as he moved. I desired this man, but I was also beginning to realize, I liked him too. Maybe not in the beginning, but the more I got to know him, the more I admired his strength, determination, and loyalty to his friends. He'd stepped into the Abyss fully distrusting me and believing he was putting his life in the hands of an enemy, yet he still did it. There weren't many who could claim they would do the same.

He'd also sought to protect me by placing himself in between Olgon and me when he had to know Olgon would be more likely to go for him than me.

When he turned back to me, I glanced away and focused on the rocks again. "These rocks, that field..."

"What about them?" he asked when my voice trailed off.

"They don't fit here."

"No, they don't."

"But somehow, they *do* fit. Does that make sense?"

Magnus's gaze ran over the walls before settling on me. "No, but you feel things more deeply than me, and you are tied to this land."

"I am," I muttered not overly thrilled by the prospect. The grass, these rocks, and the waterfall were beautiful. The rest of this place made me itch to scrub the skin from my body.

Resting my cheek on my knee, I gazed at the rocks as I tried to puzzle out their presence here. Sleep tugged at my eyelids, I resisted giving in to it, but I wasn't sure I could stay awake for much longer.

"What is Absenthees?" Magnus inquired.

"Huh?" I asked and lifted my head to blink at him.

"The jinn with your parents, they said they would find you and bring you back to Absenthees. What is that?"

"I don't know," I said and stifled a yawn. "That's the first I've ever heard of it."

"Hmm."

"What's wrong?"

"I've been wondering about something since we escaped the jinn. The jinn are called forth by desire—"

"A *very* strong desire. It's not a simple one but one so deep it's all-consuming."

"And when the jinn finds this yearning creature, they get them to make a wish and ensnare them."

"Yes."

"So how were they able to draw *everyone* in camp into the Abyss if only *one* person or demon made a wish?"

"The wisher must have worded it in such a way that their wish included more than themselves in it. A group wish can draw more than one into the Abyss," I said.

"So, if someone said something like, I wish everyone in the camp was anywhere but here, it would affect everyone?"

"Yes."

He raised his other hand until they both rested against the ceiling. The short sleeves of his brown shirt fell back to expose the muscles in his biceps as well as his forearms. When he leaned toward me, a lock of platinum hair fell forward to curl at the corner of his eye. I suddenly wasn't so tired as my fingers itched to brush that lock aside.

"And this group wish would work to affect them all even if the wisher didn't specifically name the people or demons they wanted to be involved in it?" he asked. "Because I sincerely doubt the wisher named *every* single victim caught in here."

"I doubt that too."

"Are there enough jinn to pull off something like that, and are they strong enough to do so? They took a lot of palitons in what had to be a short amount of time as most of the victims were close to each other."

My fingers dug into my legs as my mind spun. "Well... no," I realized. "Everything has been so go, go, go, that I never stopped to think about it before, or since entering here, but they aren't strong enough to pull off a group wish of this magnitude. The jinn usually have to deal with their victims one-on-one, some can handle two at a time, but there are only forty non-Faulted jinn—the Faulted would have nothing to do with this!" I yelled as I sat up straighter and leveled him with a stare that dared him to disagree with me.

"I believe you, continue."

Taking a deep breath, I drummed my fingers on my shins. "There are forty jinn compared to how many from your camp?"

"There were a hundred twenty-five of us, one hundred twenty-one entered here."

"So many trapped souls," I murmured. "One jinni could bring one or two victims here, then wait until they were stronger before returning to Earth for another, but it would take time for them to gather so many."

"Someone would have noticed something before all of them were put under."

"Yes, they would. Even with a group wish, that's too many people and demons for the jinn to get *all* of them here without some help."

"What kind of help?"

"If those affected were somehow more susceptible to the jinn's form of mind control, then the jinn could get into their minds easier and wouldn't tire themselves out as fast. But, I have *no* idea what would make them all susceptible to that kind of mind manipulation, and there would still have to be a group wish."

I could practically see the wheels spinning in his mind as he tried to figure this out. "More susceptible how?"

"Well, like if they did *all* yearn for the same thing as the group wisher, and the wisher worded their desire in such a way as to include more than themselves in the wish. Then the jinn might be able to get into the minds of the others more easily too."

"What do you think the odds are of everyone involved in this *all* wanting the same thing?"

"Zero."

"I agree. What if the others involved didn't want the same thing as the wisher, yet they're still here?"

I rubbed my forehead as I tried to think of other ways the jinn could have manipulated so many with such ease. "The group wish could have taken out some of them, and the rest could have each made their own wish, but I'm sure someone would have noticed something before that could happen."

"So am I. Is there any other way?"

"If they were unconscious and more vulnerable to manipulation, then the jinn could get into their minds easier if there was a group wish. But they'd have to be deep under, and I'm assuming not everyone at the camp would be asleep at the same time."

"No, they definitely wouldn't be. It was the middle of the day, and we always have lookouts posted to keep watch for any threat."

"And it would have to be a *deep* sleep."

He stared at me for a minute before his eyes widened and a wave of fury washed off him. I braced myself as I knew I wasn't going to like whatever realization he'd just arrived at.

"Sloth," he hissed.

"What?" I asked in confusion.

"Sloth. The horseman. He could have left something or *things* near the camp that, when touched, put the toucher to sleep. Greed did something similar to us not too long ago. Or Sloth could have gotten close enough to the camp to put some to sleep while the jinn used their powers to trap the rest."

I'd never understood the saying "my blood ran cold" until it felt like my heart pumped chunks of ice through my veins. *A horseman? The jinn had worked with a* horseman *to do this!*

It was so much worse than I'd expected.

"The jinn might not be able to get into the minds of everyone the wish included, not normally, but if they were already in an unnatural slumber, they would have an easier time slipping into their minds," I said. "But if Sloth is involved, why didn't they kill everyone once they were asleep or in the Abyss? Their bodies were about as vulnerable as it gets."

"Because I'd bet that to get the jinn to join them, the horsemen and Astaroth promised the jinn lots of toys. You yourself said the jinn don't do well following orders or obeying anyone outside themselves. Do you think their hate for Kobal is strong enough for them to play second-fiddle to Astaroth if it got them the number of victims they have now? Especially if all those victims followed Kobal."

I bit my lip to withhold the tears welling in my eyes. Now was *not* the time to cry, but as the true depth of how entwined the jinn were with the craetons came to light, I felt hollow inside. I'd picked up on their anger over being imprisoned, but I hadn't expected for them to do *this*.

"Before today, no; but now, yes," I admitted. "What an awful mess."

"I have to go back and alert the others that there's probably a horseman involved in this."

Biting back a groan, I rose and walked over to him. "Let's go."

CHAPTER TWENTY-TWO

Magnus

WHEN WE RETURNED to the cave, I was relieved and dismayed to find three more humans awake and five dead bodies. Caim and Raphael were lifting two of the dead to take them deeper into the cave when we emerged from the Abyss. These five must have died right on top of each other if their bodies remained here.

One of the dead was Halstar, our newest telepathic demon and our communication link with Kobal. We'd have to send someone back for another telecommunication demon soon, most likely Raphael again, but it would have to wait until we resolved this mess.

Leaning against the wall, I was glad to find the skellein, Lix, awake. He held his skeletal head between his bony hands as if he had a headache. When he lifted his head, there were no eyes in his skull, but I felt his attention focused on me.

Lix wore a green tie with numerous Santa Clauses on it. All the Santa's were bent over to reveal their white asses as they looked behind them to grin out from the tie. Whereas before the tie would have been amusing, I didn't find any humor in it now.

Since coming to Earth, all the nearly identical skelleins had taken to wearing assorted accessories to differentiate themselves from each other. After the war with Lucifer, only twenty skelleins remained, thirteen of them lived at the wall with Kobal, and seven were with us.

Lix lifted the flask tied to his waist, uncapped it, and gulped the skellein's most recent brew. All the skelleins enjoyed their booze, but Lix consuming his entire flask before releasing it was out of character for him. The metal flask clattered against the rocky floor as Lix's attention returned to me before he focused on Amalia, and his jaw clenched.

I stepped in front of her, and my eyes narrowed on Lix. The skelleins loved their drink, games, and play as much as they enjoyed killing, but I'd never seen Lix so angry before. Bowing her head, Amalia edged back to lean against the wall of the cave. The angels lowered the bodies again.

"How is it going in there?" Corson asked me.

He sat with his back against the wall and Wren's limp body in his lap. Her pale blonde hair spilled over his arm; a couple of her fingers twitched before going still again. Corson's eyes glistened with a desperation I'd never expected to see from him.

"I think there's a horseman involved," I said and revealed to them what I discussed with Amalia.

"Sloth," Corson growled.

"But does he have the power to do this to so many for this long?" Erin demanded.

Caim waved his hand at the bodies. "Obviously, he does."

When I paused to take in everyone, I realized there were fewer bodies in here than I first thought. Only two skelleins remained, one of them was Lix.

An uneasy feeling grew in me as I looked to Corson. "Where are the others?"

"Dead," he said flatly.

I suddenly understood the look in his eyes and why Amalia had edged away from them and their emotions.

"Oh no," Amalia whispered.

Lix's head turned toward her and the hostility he emitted increased.

"Stop looking at her like that, Lix," I snarled at him. "She's trying to help us."

Lix's hand went to the sword strapped to his side before falling to the ground. Erin walked over to kneel beside him and rested her hand on his shoulder.

"How long were we in there?" I asked.

"In total?" Raphael asked.

"Yes."

"A day and a half," Raphael answered.

"How long did it feel?" Erin asked.

"About the same," I replied.

"Sloth shouldn't have that kind of power," Corson said, drawing the conversation back to the horseman. "Or at least he shouldn't have enough power to keep it up for this long. Sloth can make others lazy enough they eventually waste away and die, but this is a *big* undertaking even for a horseman."

"If he has enough power to put them under, even for thirty seconds, the jinn can get into their minds." Straightening her shoulders, Amalia stepped away from the wall. "You're assuming *all* the humans and demons went under at the same time. True, many of the bodies were centered in one area, but not all of them. You're also assuming this was all based off *one* wish, and because of the number affected, I did too, but I'm beginning to think there is more than one wish going on here.

"If some of the jinn moved through the humans on the outskirts of the camp, they could get people to make a wish without knowing what they were doing. Demons might have been more suspicious about what was going on, but not people, and maybe not even demons as they've had little to no interaction with the jinn before. Working this way, the jinn could take out solitary people until someone made the group wish. Then, with the help of Sloth, they could take them all down at once."

Everyone in the cave remained mute as they digested her words.

"What if we find whoever made the group wish, would there be some way to stop it if we brought them out of the Abyss?" Erin finally asked.

"Unfortunately, no, and that wisher may already be dead," Amalia said. "Mara said she wished for something, and if she was the group wisher, she's already gone. If she's not, then it still makes no difference."

"Then what do we do to stop it?" Corson snarled.

"Don't talk to her like that," I warned him.

Corson glowered at me while he cradled Wren closer. Then, some of his anger eased, and he took a deep breath. "I realize you didn't do this and you're trying to help," he said to Amalia, "but you have to understand—"

"I do," Amalia interrupted. "I can feel the sorrow and terror of *everyone* here, but yours is so raw and so..." Her voice broke off as she wiped away the tear streaking her cheek. "I understand."

Erin rose and started pacing while she spoke. "Okay, so there is no easy fix. Is there *anything* we can do? Can you bring more of us into the Abyss with you? Would that help?"

"I..." Amalia held her hands before her as she gazed helplessly at them. "I don't think that's a good idea. *We* barely got away from the jinn when they found us, and having more in there would make that more difficult."

"They know you're in there?" Lix inquired.

"Yes."

"I used the cloaking illusion to avoid them; I'm still a little drained from it," I said and told them about our encounter with the jinn.

"What if I go in there?" Raphael inquired when I finished speaking. "If I draw on the life in there, I may be able to bring the place down."

"You would intervene to save the lives of others?" Caim inquired, a sardonic smile curving his lips.

Raphael's violet eyes were chips of ice when they flicked toward Caim. Hostility simmered between the angels as Caim's grin widened.

"If they are still alive, I'm not intervening; I'm merely freeing them from a trap," Raphael replied.

"That's splitting hairs, brother, and you know it. Is Earth already having an impact on you? I cautioned you it would. Is it making you more humane, or perhaps feeding on the wraiths is already starting to turn you from your angelic nature?"

Raphael's shoulders became rigid. "Nothing is turning me from anything," he replied crisply. "I would not be healing anyone."

"But you could be interfering in their natural course."

"Enough," I interjected. "We have far too much going on without adding your childish bickering to it."

Both angels gave me an irritated look but remained quiet.

"Besides, I don't think bringing the whole place down is a good idea," I continued. "It may kill everyone in there."

"Let's not do that then," Erin said and glanced worriedly at where Vargas and Hawk remained immobile against the wall.

"Could we all go in and kill the jinn?" Caim inquired.

"No!" Amalia cried. "I won't allow that! I don't agree with what they've done, but I will *not* allow you to harm my family and friends!"

"Weren't they going to kill *you*?" Lix demanded.

"They're not happy with me, and my unshi Olgon is *furious* about what I've done, but they won't hurt me."

They all stared skeptically at her.

"It's true," I said. "I saw and heard the jinn when they were unaware we were there. The jinn may be ruthless when it comes to everyone outside of them, but they *do* love their own."

I didn't include her uncle in that assessment; he would kill her if she got in his way. I suspected Amalia knew this but was still holding out hope his love for her would win out and he would let go of the anger ruling him.

"Really?" Corson asked doubtfully.

"I didn't believe it either, but yes, they care for each other," I said.

"So where does that leave us?" Erin asked.

"I might have an idea," Amalia said. "I'm not sure it will work or if they'll help us, but I may be able to get the Faulted to intervene. There might be something they can do to help."

"And how do we do that?" Corson asked.

"I know where they live. I'll go to them."

Magnus

I stood at the edge of the grove of calamuts, stunned to discover the Faulted jinn had made their home amid the towering trees growing from the ruined remains of an area devastated by bombs. A couple of months ago, we'd come across another grove of calamuts on Earth, but we'd traveled too far since then for this to be the same one.

The calamuts originated in Hell, but they'd found their way to Earth and were spreading throughout the land. Twice the size of the tallest Earth trees when full grown, these babies were only a few hundred feet tall, but I didn't doubt they'd easily kill any threat walking beneath them.

The Faulted were less of a danger than I'd realized if the calamuts allowed them to live here. The calamuts didn't tolerate violence beneath their boughs, and if the Faulted resided in this forest, then the calamuts would protect them.

The black leaves shone in the sun filtering through them, turning them a more purple color as we strolled beneath the sweeping canopies of the calamuts' branches. Unlike the Earth trees in this area, which were barren in February, the calamuts retained their leaves, and small balls of growing prury fruit hung from the limbs of the more mature calamuts.

Broken bits of homes rose from in between the thick trunks, and a towering chimney nearly touched the bottom branch of a baby calamut. Scorched land crunched beneath my feet as did the shattered remains of some of the things humans once cherished.

Amalia bent and lifted something from the ground. Wiping away the soot coating it, she revealed the broken face of a child's doll. One blue eye stared out at us, but a chunk of the cheek beneath it was gone and the body was half rotted away.

"What is this?" she asked.

"A doll," I replied. "Human children play with them."

The look on her face said she didn't understand why. When a roach skittered out of the doll's rounded lips, she released the toy, wiped her hands on her dirty dress, and continued walking.

"When did the Faulted move here?" I inquired.

"A month ago," she replied. "They stayed in a few other places before this one, but I think they'll stay here."

"Corson and Wren encountered some jinn who lived in part of the ouroboro's den."

"Some of the jinn used that as a place to, ah... play, but they didn't reside there."

"Were you with them?"

"I was probably nearby, but I didn't join in the fun. No one ever mentioned running into two demons down there though."

"Wren was human at the time, and they slipped away before the jinn realized they were there."

"Wren was once a human?"

"Yes." I explained Wren's transformation to her while we snaked through the trees.

When I finished, she remained silent for a few minutes before replying, "I will save her."

"Amalia—"

"We're almost there," she interrupted, and the distant sound of laughter drifted to me.

CHAPTER TWENTY-THREE

Amalia

THE LAUGHTER DIED when the Faulted spotted Magnus and me standing amid the calamuts. Then, Rislen rose, and stepping away from the fire they were gathered around, she glided toward me. Her feet didn't seem to touch the ground as she moved, but a small crunch of debris accompanied her steps.

"Amalia," she greeted and clasped my hands.

A radiant smile lit her beautiful face, and her black eyes sparkled. Pulled back into numerous small braids, her black hair intertwined into a single braid that hung to her ankles. At eighteen thousand nine hundred fifty, Rislen was the eldest Faulted jinn and the one in charge of them. Her aura of love warmed me as she squeezed my hands.

Because the Faulted were also empaths, their ability deflected mine a little, but I was still able to pick up on some of their emotions. Rislen once told me this was because my empath ability was stronger than average, even though I wasn't immortal yet. The

Faulted were all confused about my arrival here with a demon, but they were also as happy to see me as I was them.

When Rislen released my hands and opened her arms, I stepped into them. "Rislen," I murmured.

"Easy," she soothed as she ran her hands over my hair and down my back. "Tell me what is going on."

Reluctantly, I released her and glanced at Magnus. Rislen followed my eyes, and I felt her uneasiness. "Why have your brought a demon here?" she inquired.

"I have much to tell you," I said.

She reclaimed one of my hands and drew me toward the fire, but her eyes remained on Magnus.

The other Faulted rose, and I made my way around the circle to embrace them all. Magnus's eyes held a steely gleam as he surveyed the Faulted while he followed me. He exuded displeasure when I hugged the male Faulted.

When I released the last Faulted, he clasped my elbow and gave each of the three men a look that caused them to shift uneasily. I frowned at Magnus, a bit surprised by his possessive hold. Yes, we'd skirted around sex, and he'd declared he would have me, but I'd never seen a non-Chosen demon act possessively of another before.

Then I realized that, if he hugged Rislen or any of the other women here, I wouldn't like that either. In fact, the idea made my blood boil a little. I didn't have time to think about my reaction as I sat beside the fire. The flickering flames warmed my face and warded off the growing chill in the air.

"Won't you sit?" Rislen asked Magnus when he stood beside me.

"I'd rather stand," he replied.

"The trees won't tolerate any fighting here," she said.

The leaves of the calamuts rustled as if in agreement and

turned over though no breeze stirred the air. Magnus glanced at the calamuts before looking at Rislen again.

"I understand; I've seen what they can do," he said.

Rislen focused on me. "Now, what has brought you and this demon here?"

The story poured out of me in a torrent of words and emotion. I struggled not to cry when I spoke about everything we'd witnessed, but I couldn't stop the tears from spilling as I recalled Corson's woe and Lix's desolation.

Rislen rested her hand on my knee. "You are still so young," she murmured as she patted my knee. "You are not as in control of your ability, or as capable of blocking what can be the overwhelming emotions of others. You will get there, and we will help you learn how."

"I don't doubt that," I told her. "But I'm not here to learn how to control my ability better."

Rislen's hand stilled on my knee, and a ripple of unease went through the Faulted surrounding me. "Then why have you come?" she asked and glanced at Magnus.

"I've come to ask for your help in the Abyss. Can you aid us in freeing the rest of the innocents trapped there?" I inquired.

"No."

Never before had I seen Rislen icy or distant, but she became both in an instant as she removed her hand from my knee and settled it in her lap.

"Rislen—"

"No, Amalia. We do not condone what our brethren do, and we will have *no* part of it, but we will not go against the other jinn, and we will not interfere in what they do. We do not stand with our kind in this, but we do not stand against them either."

"But it's not standing against them!" I cried, and Magnus rested his hand on my shoulder. The touch helped to calm my rising panic. "It's not, Rislen. It's helping those who *need* our help."

"It's helping those who kept us locked away," Aral stated.

"They didn't put you there," I said. "And there are humans involved in this. They had *nothing* to do with Hell."

Aral's blue eyes were intense when they met mine. The yellow freckles spattering his nose and cheeks matched his hair. "They didn't let us out either, and those humans willingly participate in this war."

"Can you blame them?" I demanded, and Magnus squeezed my shoulder again. "Look at what we have done since coming to Earth!"

"Not all of us," Rislen said.

"No, not all of us, but you condone the actions of the others."

Rislen's calm façade slipped a little. "We do *not* condone what they do."

"By doing nothing, you're allowing them to wreak havoc on this plane and its residents. They've joined with Astaroth, demons, and the horsemen who want nothing more than to rule Earth. Do you think any of them will be okay with you sitting on the sidelines throughout it all?" I demanded.

"The jinn will not allow anything to happen to us," Aral stated.

"So you believe Astaroth and the angels will allow the jinn or *any* demon to survive if they eliminate the palitons?" Magnus inquired.

Rislen glanced at him before focusing on a tree over his shoulder. "We will not go against our kind."

"Rislen, please," I breathed.

"I'd advise you to take the same course of action, Amalia. We all helped to raise you, and we all love you. If you do nothing to harm the jinn, you will be forgiven for trying to interfere, but if one of them dies because of this, you won't have a home amongst any of us."

My breath sucked in, and I would have recoiled if Magnus's hand hadn't kept me in place.

"I think it's time for you to go now, unless you intend to give up this traitorous quest and reside with us," Rislen finished.

"Many will die if we don't help."

"Many have already died, and many more will perish over the coming days and years of this battle. It is the natural way of things."

I gawked at her as I tried to think of something that might help sway her to our cause, but there wasn't anything I could say; she would not be moved.

"Can you at least tell me a little about the Abyss?" I asked. "I know nothing of it. How is it that the lightning is a life?"

Rislen didn't speak for so long that I didn't think she would reply; then, her eyes met mine. "It's not lightning but an actual life *force* is striking Absenthees, and when it strikes, that life spreads to all the jinn within the Abyss."

I rubbed my skin in a useless attempt to scrub away the remnants of life clinging to me.

"Absenthees is the monolith in the center?" Magnus asked.

Rislen's lips clamped together before she closed her eyes and nodded.

"What is it? What does it do?" Magnus inquired.

"It does what the jinn require it to do," Rislen replied.

"What does that mean?"

"That's all I'm going to tell you."

I buried my rising annoyance. It wouldn't get us anywhere with her.

"What is with the grass in there? Why is the Abyss so beautiful in some places and *so* hideous in others?" I asked.

"It was once *all* beautiful," Rislen whispered. "And then the lines crossed, and it was never the same."

"What do you mean the lines crossed?" I asked in confusion.

Rislen sighed before turning to face me. "Three hundred thousand years ago, the jinn and fae bloodline intermingled."

"Yes, I know." I hadn't known it was that long ago, but the jinn had told me about my ancestry. "It's why the Faulted are so different, but what does that have to do with anything?"

Rislen's black eyes held mine, but she didn't speak.

"Tell her, Rislen," Marhee urged. "She can't do anything with the information and neither can the demon. All the fae perished while we were behind the seal. There is nothing anyone can do anymore, and she deserves to know the truth. Besides, we planned to tell her when she reached adulthood and her time is nearing, we can all feel that."

I smiled gratefully at Marhee. At eighteen thousand twenty, she was the closest jinn in age to me. Her yellow eyes crinkled when she smiled back before ducking her head, so her yellow braid fell over her shoulder. With her coloring and matching freckles, she bore a strong resemblance to her brother, Aral.

"She's still young and not fully in control of her abilities, this might upset her," Aral said.

I gritted my teeth and tried not to glare at him. I understood why they treated me like a child, compared to them, almost everyone in existence was a babe, but I was tired of it. "I have made it through a day in the Abyss, seen things most of you probably haven't seen, and I'm still in control. If it upsets me, I *will* handle it."

Rislen remained pensive for a minute before speaking. "You are right, and I suppose it is time. We've kept our history vague with you because we felt it best you didn't know until you could cope better."

I had a bad feeling I was *not* going to like whatever they had to say.

CHAPTER TWENTY-FOUR

Amalia

MAGNUS BENT over me and clasped my hands in his. I frowned at him before glancing at my arms. I hadn't realized I'd rubbed my skin raw, but then I would do anything to rid myself of the life tainting my flesh. I had to stop; otherwise, Rislen might decide I wasn't ready to learn this.

"You've kept your history vague with everyone," Magnus said. "I spent a lot of time researching demon history and reading through the scrolls, but until recently, I'd never heard of the jinn and fae line crossing."

"Our history goes back to a time before demons started recording it," Rislen replied. "And once that started, there were some things the fae and jinn didn't want to be known."

I glanced at the circle of Faulted. All their faces were devoid of any emotion as they remained riveted on Rislen, but I sensed their uneasiness.

"Three hundred thousand years ago, the jinn and fae line crossed," Rislen said and placed her hand on my knee again. "And it wasn't just one fae and one jinni. Over the course of a few thousand years, more than a dozen fae and jinn found their Chosen with each other."

"Oh," I breathed.

"The fae initially controlled the Abyss, and it was once a *beautiful* place. The fae used Absenthees to harvest their emotions when the feelings of others became too much for them to bear. They would funnel those overwhelming emotions into the monolith, which spread them across the land and into the fae who were in the Abyss at the time. This bound the fae together and helped them to handle their empath powers by allowing them to share the burden. The good emotions such as love fed the land while the bleaker feelings were dispersed and borne by the fae.

"When the lines crossed, the resulting offspring were also able to enter the Abyss. Over the course of a hundred thousand years, the fae/jinn line spread until almost all jinn were offspring of the crossed line."

"How is that possible?" I asked.

"The original jinn were so heartless and ferocious they would often turn on, and kill, each other, but the introduction of fae blood to the jinn line bound the Fae-aulted jinn together and made them stronger. Their ability to enter the Abyss also strengthened them. Over time, the original jinn were killed off by each other, the Fae-aulted, and other demons until only the Fae-aulted jinn remained. And, as you know, some of that line is more fae than others."

"Like us," I murmured.

"So that is why when someone desires something deeply, the jinn know it and are attracted to them," Magnus said. "All jinn have at least some empath ability."

"Yes," Rislen agreed. "Before the fae and jinn intermingled, the jinn granted wishes and fed off their victims, but they more or less blundered their way into them."

"The crossing of the lines made them exceptional hunters."

Sorrow tugged at my heart, but I buried it. The emotion would only work against me here. "That's why all jinn, and not just the Faulted, can block my empath ability on some level?"

"Yes," Rislen murmured. "Your empath ability is the strongest I've ever seen, but you still don't feel an empath the way you do others because two empaths counteract each other. I think it's a survival mechanism. Could you imagine how horrible it would be to have two empaths feeding off the emotions of others, and then being in close enough proximity to feed them into each other? Such an influx would force them away from each other, thus weakening them and making them more vulnerable to attacks from others, and if they did stay near each other, it would probably drive them insane."

It would definitely drive me insane. "What exactly is the Abyss?"

"It's a separate plane that evolved with the fae."

"What do you mean it's a separate plane?" Magnus inquired.

"It's a plane, or if you would prefer, a separate universe, but unlike Earth, Hell, and Heaven it evolved much later and came from the abilities of the fae," Rislen said. "I'm sure there are many more planes or universes out there, perhaps connected to other planets and galaxies. The universe is far too big for there not to be more beyond our world."

"True," Magnus murmured.

"I believe the Abyss was more than a place for the fae to find release from the emotions of others, but also a place of protection for them," Rislen said. "The fae were so much weaker than *all* other demons, and they could hide in the Abyss. Or at least, they could hide there before the jinn took it from them."

I didn't have to ask who took it, that was obvious. "How was it taken?"

"Over the years the Fae-aulted line spread throughout the jinn, the jinn who entered the Abyss started to twist it into something more sinister. With the mix of their jinn and fae powers, they discovered a way to bring their victims into the Abyss and feed the life force of their victims into Absenthees, which in turn filtered it over the land.

"The suffering of those who were tortured and killed drove the pacifist, empath fae from the Abyss. With nothing good to feed on, the Abyss rotted away until it became the place you have seen. Most of the beauty is gone from it, but some remains, like the field."

"Why does it remain?" I inquired.

"Because there is still some fae in the jinn, they still feed at least a little good into the Abyss, and even the cruelest of us is not entirely destructive."

"Have *you* ever been to the Abyss?" I asked her.

"Once, many millennia ago, for a brief time. I would never return."

"Have any of you gone?" I asked the others.

"We've all gone. We did not spend much time there, and we will not return either," Marhee said.

"Why did the fae and jinn keep this history from being recorded?" Magnus inquired.

"Because it revealed a weakness in both the fae and jinn line," Rislen replied. "The jinn pushed the fae out of a land that protected them, and the jinn didn't want anyone to know they could possess what they saw as the weakness of the fae, so they hid the truth.

"The fae might have been the only ones who stood a chance of reclaiming the Abyss from the jinn, as they were the only others who could open a portal in and out of it. But it would've required them to fight the jinn for it, and they weren't capable of doing that."

"Why didn't they return there after the jinn were sealed away?" I asked.

"I assume, by then, the Abyss was so corrupted they couldn't tolerate being there for much time, if any," Rislen replied.

I pressed my hands over my aching heart. It was difficult for me to handle the Abyss, it must have been torture for the fae to be there. The fae had been so fragile, yet kind, and they'd lost the one place that could have saved them from the fallen angels.

"Hidden behind a waterfall, we found a cave with beautiful pink and yellow stones," I murmured.

"If it was hidden, then it most likely managed to avoid the corruption of the jinn," Marhee said. "I'm sure there are other such hidden treasures in there too."

"I hope so. How can two bloodlines be so different, yet both be a part of us?" I asked.

"That is often the way of things," Rislen replied and patted my knee again. "Night follows day, day follows night, both are complete opposites, yet this world needs them to survive. Throughout all the worlds, you will find opposing forces working in a symbiotic nature that supports life."

"True," I agreed. "We have to return to the Abyss; we have to try to help those trapped there. Are you sure you won't help us?"

"We cannot go against the others."

I placed my hands on the ground and stood.

"Stay with us, Amalia," Rislen said as she rose before me and took my hands. "You belong here more than anywhere else. *We* are not the fighters."

I squeezed her hands and released them. "Neither were the fae, and look at where that got them."

"But you are more fae than the rest of us," she said as she lifted my hair to let it slide through her fingers, "with your coloring and your telltale eyes. The Abyss is not for you."

"No, it's not, but I'm already involved, and I can't turn away from helping now."

Rislen's gaze shifted to Magnus. "You better keep her safe," she said.

~

Magnus

My eyebrows rose at the vehemence behind the jinni's words. For someone who claimed not to be a fighter, Rislen looked more than willing to tear out my heart.

"I will," I said and rested my hand on Amalia's shoulder. Beneath my hand, her collarbone felt fragile as it pressed against my palm. Mortal, and with her tender heart, she was more delicate than any I'd ever encountered; I'd do whatever it took to keep her safe.

The shadows beneath Amalia's eyes gave her a raccoon-like appearance when she glanced at me. I suspected she was more than just exhausted, but also hungry and beaten down by the emotions battering her for the past day. It might be time for her to give this up, but that was something we could discuss later.

"We believe Sloth is mixed up in this and that he helped the jinn trap everyone," I said to Rislen, and the jinn gathered around the fire gasped.

Rislen's chin rose. "Our brethren have chosen their alliances, but they are not ours."

"You will remain neutral?"

"We will."

I couldn't do anything to change her mind, it was their choice, and after what she revealed, I understood it more. Not only the Faulted, but *all* the surviving jinn were part fae.

If someone told me this last week, I would have laughed in their face and said they were crazier than a crantick demon. And the cranticks were known to run head first into walls and throw themselves over cliffs for the fun of it. When a group of them were together, they often howled at nothing. Many demons were afraid of them, and though they enjoyed a good fight, the cranticks were mostly innocuous and about having fun.

I now understood the bond and protective nature of the jinn toward each other. The most vicious demon species had bred with the kindest. They must have been the *strangest* couples in Hell.

"We have to go," Amalia said. "The longer we stay here, the more deaths occur."

The rest of the jinn rose and came forward to hug her. I resisted pulling her away from the men. It would only upset her if I did, and there was no rational reason for the impulse. But rational or not, I was tempted to tear their hands off while they embraced her.

When the last of them stepped away, Rislen clasped Amalia's hands once more. "I don't approve of this, but I bid you well, Amalia. I hope you return to us one day."

Gripping Amalia's elbow, I drew her closer. Her warmth and the way her body fit so perfectly against my side eased some of my tension. Savoring her scent, I led her through the shadows of the calamuts. As we walked away, the rustling leaves created a sad song.

CHAPTER TWENTY-FIVE

Magnus

"Fascinating history," I murmured when we stepped free of the trees.

We strode back through the burnt-out town on the border of the calamut forest. The glow of the full moon shone on the land, revealing the pitted road, broken homes, and dilapidated remnants of the humans who once thrived here. Even though it had been fourteen years since the gateway opened and the bombs were released in this area, the stench of burnt flesh and wood was still detectable on the air.

"Or sad." Amalia's skin turned red when she rubbed her arms again.

"It's both. You're hurting yourself," I said and grasped her hands.

She tugged her hands away from me and gave me a look of both anger and intense suffering. "Those lives touched me. They're *in* me!"

"Those lives are not in you," I said as I reclaimed her hands.

I held them against my chest as her ochre-colored eyes stared pleadingly up at me. Running my thumbs over the backs of her silken hands, I watched as her mouth parted, and my body quickened in response to her. Except, this time I longed to hug her against me and shelter her as much as I wanted to taste her again.

"But they are," she whispered. "I felt their strength flow through me."

"Amalia—"

She tugged at her hands again. When she grunted in frustration, I reluctantly released my hold on her, and she spun away from me. The edge of her dirt-streaked dress trailed on the ground, becoming browner in color as she stalked down the remains of the battered street. With subtle ease, she avoided the jagged pieces of asphalt jutting up from the broken road.

I hurried to catch up and fell into step beside her. "You don't have to go back into the Abyss."

She abruptly halted. "Yes, I do."

"We'll find another way to help the others, and we're not doing much good—"

"But we are doing *some* good. I don't care how much I despise that place, I'm going back in there, and you can't stop me."

A smile curved my mouth as I stepped closer to her. The impudent expression on her face was as amusing as it was alluring. Over the course of the past two days, some of her hair had straggled free from her braids and cleaved to her face. She didn't bother to push it away, but I brushed it back before I cupped her cheeks in my hands.

"I'm going back in," Amalia insisted.

"What if you open a portal and let me go in alone?" I asked as I stroked her silken cheek with my thumb.

"And how would you get back out if you needed to?"

"I'd find a way."

"There is no finding a way, if something were to happen, you wouldn't be able to get out."

"That's for me to worry about."

She blinked at me before she gave a derisive snort. "Silly, arrogant demon."

"We could arrange a designated time to meet up again."

"It seems as if they're the same, but time in the Abyss might pass differently than it does here. A few seconds or minutes could throw us off completely."

"I think it's the same," I replied. "Or at least I believe it is for anyone not caught up in the loops the jinn create."

She pondered that for a minute. "I think you're right."

"I usually am."

She rolled her spectacular eyes. "I *am* going back with you, and there will be no arguments about it." Patting my hands, she removed them from her face and stepped away. "We should return to the others and the Abyss."

"Not before you feed," I said.

"We can't take the time that will require."

"Shadows line your eyes and you look drained. We will *make* time for it. You're not going to do anyone any good if you're too hungry and exhausted to continue."

She opened her mouth to protest before closing it.

"Come on, Freckles," I said and claimed her hand. "With as devastated as this town is, there's bound to be wraiths somewhere close by."

~

Amalia

We found a mass of wraiths hovering over the red blocks of a wrecked building. Most of the blocks were singed black, and many of them had disintegrated to ash, but some were untouched and had a deep red hue.

The wraiths here were healthier than any of the wraiths who slipped inside the seals and been fed on by those lurking within. By the time most wraiths made it behind the seals, they were fed on to the point of barely being mobile anymore.

They'd kept me alive, but since coming to Earth, I'd been feeding on far healthier wraiths. Healthy or depleted, I loathed the spirits. They didn't deserve to be free of Hell. There were others who would say the same thing about me and the jinn, but there was little redeeming about the hideous human souls sent to Hell, and seeing so many wraiths in one place was usually a sign of a lot of death.

"Why are there so many wraiths here?" I asked as I studied the twisted, malevolent spirits darting through the air, plummeting into the ground, and rising again.

"It looks like this was a big place, a school perhaps. My guess is many of the humans gathered here after the gateway opened to seek comfort from each other and find strength in numbers, but something destroyed the place, most likely killing them all."

"How horrible," I murmured and lifted my hand to the sky to draw one of the depraved souls toward me.

The wraith's fathomless eyes stared out of a gray face, elongated into a grotesque mask. This wraith was new enough that I could still make out human characteristics such as its nose, cheeks, and flaking lips. The wraith squirmed in my grasp, but I held on as I drained more of its life from it.

Unlike many other demons, I took no joy in inflicting pain on it. I had to feed on wraiths to survive, but I couldn't stand the coldness of their spirit or the clammy way they made my skin feel and its vile emotions battering me as I drained it.

By the time I finished, it no longer had lips, and its face had extended and become grayer. When I released it, the wraith faltered until its flapping, black ends dragged across the ground before it swooped toward the sky.

No matter how much I despised feeding on them, when the wraith darted away from me, I felt rejuvenated and better prepared to return to the Abyss. I shuddered at the idea of the lost lives touching my flesh again, but I would deal with it when the time came.

Beside me, Magnus released his wraith, turned toward me, and claimed my hand.

"Let's get back to the others and the Abyss," I said.

CHAPTER TWENTY-SIX

Amalia

WHEN WE RETURNED to the others, we discovered Lix standing by the entrance of the cave with his head bowed and his shoulders hunched. At his side, Erin gazed morosely at the night.

"What happened?" Magnus asked.

"Two more humans and the other skellein have died," Erin replied.

My breath caught, and I resisted offering comfort to Lix. He wouldn't want it, and he may cut off my hand if I touched him. I shouldn't have any pity for a demon who would prefer to see me sealed away again or dead, but I hated not being able to ease his despair.

"Shit," Magnus muttered. "I'm sorry, Lix."

"To everything, there is a season," Lix muttered and uncapped his flask to take a drink. It was a different flask than the one he had earlier, and I suspected it had belonged to his friend.

"Will the Faulted help us?" Erin asked.

"No. They don't condone what the others have done, but they won't help us," I answered.

"They intend to stay out of the fight completely," Magnus said.

"*Fools*," Lix hissed.

"Maybe," Magnus replied, "but the calamuts are protecting them, so they aren't fighters, and after learning their history, I understand why."

Lix's head rose, and despite his sorrow, curiosity emanated from him. "What do you mean?"

"The jinn and fae have been keeping secrets from us," Magnus replied. "And I think you, with your penchant for puzzles and riddles, will appreciate this deception."

Lix's head turned toward me, and though he had no eyes that I could see, I felt his attention boring into me.

"She knew nothing of it, good chap," Magnus said in a cheerful tone that didn't quite fit the moment, but a trickle of amusement emanated from Lix. He may be grieving, but he enjoyed this banter. "The jinn were waiting until they believed she was ready to hear the tale and decided now was as good a time as any."

"I dare say," Lix said, "I'm intrigued."

"So am I," Erin murmured.

Lix and Erin fell in behind us as we strode back to rejoin the others. I told Magnus to take over the revelation as I wasn't up to it, and I needed time to absorb everything I learned earlier.

I mourned the lost fae, but I suspected it was a good thing the original jinn were gone. The jinn I loved could be downright savage; I couldn't imagine what they would be like if they *only* cared for themselves, like those long-ago jinn.

"I think the merging of the fae and jinn was an evolutionary survival tactic," Magnus said. "It wasn't a planned one, but one that came about as a way to preserve both species."

His words caught my attention. "What do you mean?" I asked and rose from where I'd sat against the wall.

Magnus turned toward me and spread his hands before him. The flames of the small fire danced within his silver eyes when they met mine, giving him an utterly demonic countenance.

"The fae weren't strong enough to survive Hell, not even with having the Abyss to retreat into. Whether the fallen angels entered Hell or not, they would have eventually been killed off. They didn't have active powers, and they had little, if any, inclination to fight. Their time would have inevitably come.

"The jinn were turning against themselves, and with their violent nature they would have wiped each other out, or more demons would have banded together to destroy them. The Fae-aulted were willing to fight for each other. They couldn't avoid being sealed away, but they evaded extinction, unlike the full-blooded jinn and fae."

My mouth parted and I started to reply, but I had no words for him. I'd been feeling sorry for the fae, but he was right. The fae lived longer than anyone believed they would, and the Fae-aulted continued their bloodline as well as that of the original jinn.

"So what do we do now?" Erin asked.

"Amalia and I will return to the Abyss and see what we can do there. Either Caim or Raphael must start searching for Sloth. You can't both go at the same time, as we need at least one of you should something happen to the other. We can't send out a ground search because we don't have the numbers for it, but the hunt for Sloth has to start. If we can find and destroy him, maybe his spell over them will break, and we can wake some of those here," Magnus said.

I was loath to pop the bubble of hope emanating from all of them at these words, but.... "They're ensnared already, destroying Sloth is a good thing, but it won't help anyone in the Abyss."

I noticed a slight droop in Magnus's shoulders I doubted the others detected. I was becoming more attuned to his body language, probably because I spent the spare time I had raptly watching him.

I resisted going to him and hugging him to ease some of his

distress. We'd nearly had sex, but that was sex, hugging was something else entirely. Hugging involved an emotional attachment of some sort whether it be friends or something more.

Then, I recalled the tender way he rested his hand on my shoulder to offer me comfort when speaking with the Faulted. Warmth had spread through me as he calmed me. *There are already feelings involved*, I realized, *but how deep do they run?*

I frowned as I pondered this. Demons weren't supposed to have feelings for anyone who wasn't their Chosen, except for their kin or close friends, and Magnus was none of those things to me.

Okay, maybe he'd become a friend throughout all this, but it was the start of a friendship and not a deep one. Besides, I had friends, and none of them made me feel as cherished or desired as Magnus did. They'd never acted as protective toward me as Magnus did either, and they'd never made me feel jealous as Magnus did when he hugged Erin earlier.

"We'll send Caim to hunt Sloth," Corson said. Shifting his hold on Wren, he settled her gently on the ground before standing.

Caim snapped his heels together and threw back his shoulders. "I will find the horseman and bring the lazy bastard down."

"Pride goeth before the fall, brother," Raphael murmured.

Caim laughed. "Then it's a good thing I have no pride; I'm just arrogant."

Raphael's eyes narrowed.

"It's time for us to get back," Magnus said.

"I still think more of us should go in with you," Corson told him.

"I think more of you are needed here in case Sloth, or someone else, discovers this cave."

Corson and Magnus gazed at each other before Corson's eyes fell to Wren. No matter how badly he wanted to plunge into the Abyss and pull her out, he wouldn't leave her body unprotected.

"We will see you soon," Magnus said to him before turning to me.

Amalia

We stepped back into the Abyss and the colorful cave we'd left before returning to Earth. Resting my fingers against a yellow rock, I couldn't stop the swell of sadness within me for the fae who once ruled this land. A land once full of color and beauty and now devoid of most of its original splendor.

"Can it be returned?" I mused.

I hadn't realized I spoke the question out loud until Magnus inquired, "Can what be returned?"

"The beauty, the life, and the love that once ruled here," I whispered.

"If places like this cave remain, then I think there's a chance it could be. We should go."

Reluctantly, I removed my fingers from the wall and followed him to the entrance of the cave. The waterfall misted my hair and clothes as we descended the rocks, but I welcomed the refreshing feel of it on my skin.

When my feet hit the ground, I stepped closer to cup my hands and slide them into the waterfall. The flow pounding against my palms pushed them down. I spilled my collection before I corrected my hands and gathered enough water to splash my face and hair with it. The cool water sluicing down my skin and soaking the dress washed away some of the lingering death adhering to my flesh.

Finished, I dropped my hands and turned to find Magnus's ravenous gaze fixed on my breasts. Glancing down, I realized the damp material of my dress clinging to my cleavage emphasized my areolas. The knowledge such a sight affected him caused my body to react to his as wetness spread between my thighs.

When he stalked toward me, I took an involuntary step back from the need he radiated until my heel connected with the rock wall. My palms flattened on the craggy surface, and my breath caught as my heart raced. Then, he was before me.

Tilting my head back, I gazed up at him as his silver eyes fastened on my mouth. When he leaned closer, the scent of him filled my nose, and everything in me screamed for *more* of him.

My chest rose toward him when he rested his hand on the wall beside my head. Dampened by the spray from the waterfall, his blond hair sticking to his head revealed more of the shiny, black horns I yearned to touch. His other hand claimed the end of my hair, and he wrapped it around his wrist until I was bound to him.

Using my hair, he drew me gently toward him until his face was only inches from mine. Unable to resist them anymore, I reached up to trail my hand over one of his horns. I brushed aside strands of his hair while I ran my fingers from the sharp tip, back along the side of his head, and toward the thicker end.

His head tilted into my touch, and my hand clenched around his horn as I rose on my toes to stroke it again. My movement brought me into contact with the rigid evidence of his arousal. Our eyes met as he thrust forward to grind his erection against my wet core. The movement and the pleasure it caused to spiral throughout me had my hand clenching around his horn as I cried out.

"Shh, Freckles," he murmured. "I don't think anyone can hear us over the water, but it's not a chance I'm willing to take."

Biting my lip to stifle my cries, my head fell back when he released my hair, and his knuckles skimmed down the front of my dress. I squirmed against him, eager for more as his thumb circled my nipple, but then, he stopped.

I was about to voice my displeasure over his hand moving away from my breast when the searing heat of his mouth settled over it.

When his tongue flicked the hardened bud through the thin material, I was lost to him as the world spun and my knees gave out.

Magnus caught me before I hit the ground, and in one swift move, he lifted me up and laid me down. I didn't feel the rock against my back or the spray of water coating us both; all I felt was *him*. Panting, wiggling, and desperate for more, I grasped his shoulders as he came down on top of me.

One of his hands slid down my belly and toward my thighs while the other propped him up above me. His hand entangled in my skirt, and he lifted it up. Entranced by the darkening color of his eyes, I couldn't tear my gaze away from his. Water dampened my legs when he pulled my dress up to my waist; I spread my thighs as he settled himself between them.

We shouldn't be doing this. We had to find the others and see if we could help, but I couldn't bring myself to part from him. Then his hand settled on my thigh and moved steadily toward my aching sex. Every slow, tantalizing stroke was a form of torture I wanted to end but craved more of it.

Lifting my hips and feeling nearly out of my mind, I couldn't bite back a scream when his hand slid over my sex. I squirmed beneath him when he spread my growing wetness over my clit before stroking it with his thumb. My hips rose and fell faster as my body came alive in ways it never had before.

There was something so incredibly wonderful about Magnus's body on mine as he dipped a finger inside me and held me close to him. Bending his head, his tongue slid over my lips before entering my mouth. He tasted me in slow thrusts that had my hips rising impatiently against his hand as my tongue entwined with his.

My fingers bit into the corded muscles of his back before I relaxed and lifted them to seize his horns. I dragged him closer until his mouth was bruising against mine, but I didn't care as I tried to get closer but couldn't get close enough.

His growl vibrated my lips as he parted me further and dipped another finger inside. When he moved his hand in such a way that his palm rubbed my clit, my back arched off the ground. So close, I was so very close...

His hand slid away from me, and I groaned a protest as I lifted my hips demandingly toward him, but he didn't give me what I craved. Breaking our kiss, his lips hovered against mine as he spoke. "Not yet."

I tried to grab him back when he lifted himself away from me, but he caught my hands and gave me a wicked smile as he pressed a kiss against the back of one. "Patience, Amalia," he said, and I saw the words forming on his lips more than I heard them over the water.

When I glared at him, he laughed. I was about to pull away when he bent to press a kiss against my belly. Torn between kicking him and curiosity, I remained unmoving as his mouth hovered over the place he'd kissed before his tongue flicked out to taste me. Moving steadily lower, he licked away the beads of water forming on my skin as he went.

His tongue dipped into my belly button before he nuzzled it with his nose and nipped at my flesh. I shivered and gave up any lingering irritation with him as his hands spread my thighs apart.

I bit my lip when he moved lower, and I recognized what he intended to do. Excitement tore through me; when I wiggled impatiently, his chuckle warmed my lower belly. Then his hands slid under my ass, and he lifted it off the ground. I bit harder on my lip when his eyes met mine as he dipped his mouth to my core. His warm breath against me created a tickling, entirely erotic sensation that caused my nails to dig into the rock. He continued to hold my stare as he tortured me with as much expertise as the jinn.

Then his tongue gave one, slow lick over my entrance and clit before making a teasing circle. *Horrible! Wicked demon!* I wanted to scream the words at him, but I couldn't speak through the lump clogging my throat.

He seemed to understand my torment as his eyes gleamed with amusement. He gave me another teasing flick with his tongue before plunging into me. My back arched off the ground; I cried out as he tasted me in deep, hungry thrusts that made me lose complete control. Releasing the rock, I gripped his horns and dragged him closer to me as I rode his tongue like it was his shaft.

When Magnus growled against me, it reverberated my clit and sent me over the edge. Releasing my ass with one hand, he used it to cover my mouth as I came apart with a wild cry. Joy suffused my trembling body as his pride over my pleasure beat against me.

Removing his hand from my mouth, he lowered me to the ground and gripped the button of his pants while my hands ran over his horns as if they were his shaft. A fresh jolt of excitement washed through me when he lowered himself over me again.

We were far from done.

I felt his button release against my belly, and his zipper slid down. Long and thick, his shaft heated my stomach after he freed it from his pants. When Magnus lifted his head to gaze down at me, his silver eyes were nearly black with desire, but there was also a strange curiosity in them I understood. Neither of us knew what to make of the other or what was happening between us.

Gripping his shaft, he shifted himself as he guided it toward me. My heart hammered when the silken head of it brushed my thigh. Then, he was rubbing it against my core and spreading my wetness before pressing it against my entrance. I opened my legs further when he started to enter me.

Gripping his horns, I drew him toward me for another kiss and froze when I saw the jinni stepping around the waterfall. I blinked away the water coating my lashes as I tried to figure out if what I was seeing was real or not. But Nalki remained standing there with his full lips pulled back to reveal his teeth and his blue eyes sparkling with amusement.

"Magnus, look out!" I cried, and with my hands still on his

horns, I clenched my thighs against his torso and jerked him to the side as Nalki rushed us.

Magnus tried to turn to see, but our rolling motion pulled him beneath me and his cock away as we spun under the waterfall. Water pummeled my back, battering my bones and bruising my flesh. Magnus embraced me firmly against him and yanked me under him, so he took the brunt of the water.

I caught a glimpse of Nalki through the thick curtain of water. And then we were falling.

It was a two-foot fall before we plunged into the pool and the force of the waterfall pushed us to the bottom. The water enveloping me calmed the rage Nalki emitted and doused my remaining lust. It also healed my battered body as it cleansed me of the remaining life force clinging to me.

Then, my foot touched a stone, and a wave of power flowed from the ground and into me. It tingled through my legs as it spread through my belly and up to my chest. My involuntary sigh drew a rush of water into my mouth. Choking, I tried to spit it out, but now that I'd opened my mouth, I couldn't cut off the flow of water filling it. My throat and nose burned as air bubbles erupted before me and the water stifled my scream.

Not immortal yet. I clawed at the water to pull myself up, but Magnus's legs kicked against mine as he dragged us out from beneath the crush of the waterfall and propelled us toward the surface.

When we burst free, I spit out water, choking and coughing as I greedily inhaled gulps of air.

"Are you okay?" Magnus demanded, his concern so strong it suppressed all other emotions. He pushed the hair from my face and wiped it from my eyes as I clung to his shoulders. "Amalia, *are you okay?*"

I opened my eyes in time to watch Nalki leap at us and catch Magnus by his shoulders.

CHAPTER TWENTY-SEVEN

Magnus

WHEN THE JINNI gripped my shoulders, I released Amalia and flipped myself back into the water. The jinni was beneath me when we sank below the surface; his fingers digging into my flesh drew blood as he retained his hold.

Trying to dislodge him, I twisted within his grasp until we were face-to-face. My chest constricted when the maneuver caused me to lose sight of Amalia. She was okay. I'd last seen her swimming toward the rocks, but were there more jinn somewhere nearby? If there were, they'd try to take her from me.

I'd only seen this one, but that didn't mean more of them weren't waiting to move in on us. My desperation to reach her gave me an unexpected rush of strength. Drawing my feet up, I planted them in the jinni's body and shoved off him. Scrambling to try and keep his hold on me, the jinni's fingers gouged my flesh before he clutched my shirt. When the material gave way, he lost his grip on me and spiraled toward the bottom.

Water surged around me; bubbles swirled past as I kicked

toward the surface. Bursting free, I twisted in the water in search of Amalia.

"Magnus!" I spun to find her kneeling on the rocks with her hand stretched toward me. "Hurry!"

"Are there more?" I demanded as I swam toward her.

"Not that I've seen."

"Are you injured?"

Water sluiced off and spilled around me when I grabbed the rocks and pulled myself out of the pool to sit beside her. Adjusting myself, I zipped and buttoned my pants.

"Nothing major." Her troubled eyes fell on the blood oozing from the gashes the jinni had torn into me. "Are *you* okay?"

"Fine." Taking her hand, I rose and pulled her away from the water as the jinni emerged and swam toward the other side of the pool.

"We should go," Amalia said and tugged at my arm.

I didn't budge as the jinni pulled himself onto the rocks and spun to face us. I recognized him as one of the jinn who spoke with her parents about keeping Amalia safe. He was the one who believed she was too soft and would be better off living with the other Faulted.

The jinni's eyes held a murderous gleam when they met mine as he stood. His sodden black hair trailed down his back in a thick braid. I would not leave here until this bastard was dead.

"Bring it, fucker," I growled at him as he sprinted toward us.

"No! Magnus, Nalki, this isn't necessary!" Amalia cried.

I pushed her behind me, using my body to shield her as the jinni leapt into the air. With his feet extended and his hands hooked into claws, Nalki pounced like a cat as he came toward me. I clutched one of his feet as the other one rammed into my chest and his hands clasped my horns.

He yanked my head to the side at the same time as I twisted his foot over. The jinni grunted, but when his ankle gave way with a sound like a breaking branch, he showed no sign of the bone piercing his skin hurting him.

And I gave no indication his twisting motion on my horns was pushing my neck to a snapping point. Releasing his foot, I swung up and smashed my fist into his chest. Flesh and bone broke and gave way as I dug into his body.

"Both of you, *stop!*" Amalia shouted, but I didn't ease up; to do so would be certain death.

The jinni released my horns and clutched my wrist. Using his good foot, still planted against my chest, he tried to shove himself off me, but I refused to release him.

"Stop!" Amalia cried.

The jinni released my wrist, clasped his hands together, and hammered them into my cheek. My cheekbone gave way with an audible crack; I spit out the teeth knocked free by the blow, and pulling my head back, I drove my forehead into his nose. Blood sprayed me and the jinni, Nalki, I recalled.

Twisting my arm to the side, I dug my hand deeper into the jinni's chest as his joined hands battered my face. I flung up my free hand, knocking aside his next blow. When my fingers scraped his heart, the organ gave an unsteady beat. Stretching further into his chest cavity, I clutched the beating heart in my hand. Yanking backward, I tore it from Nalki's chest and flung it aside.

Blood oozed from the hole I left in his chest; more spurted from his mouth as he choked it out. It wasn't enough to kill him, I'd have to decapitate him for that, but the removal of his heart would take most of the fight from him.

When I shoved him off me, he landed awkwardly on his uninjured foot and hobbled back. Gurgled sounds trailed behind him as he clutched at the jagged hole I'd left in his chest while I stalked after him. I'd rip this jinni to pieces for causing any hurt to Amalia.

I was so focused on Nalki that I didn't see Amalia until she gripped my arm and jerked me toward her. Anger radiated from her, but her eyes were an ochre hue when they landed on me.

"Oh," she breathed and stretched a tremulous hand toward my face. "What did he do to you?"

I turned my head away before she could touch my battered flesh and broken bones. "It will heal soon, and the teeth will grow back," I said, my voice slurred from my swollen cheek and missing teeth.

Her hand fell away, and her head turned to where Nalki had collapsed against the wall. Her eyes turned redder as she gazed at him while resting her hand on my arm.

"You can't kill him," she stated.

I blinked at her, sure I'd heard her wrong. "The fuck I can't."

"No," she said. "I won't allow it."

"Allow it? *He* tried to kill *me*."

When she bowed her head, her wet hair fell forward to shield her pretty features. "Yes, I know, but he didn't. I can't let you kill a jinni, not when I brought you here. If you killed him while you were fighting, that would be one thing, but you didn't. I won't let you destroy him if he can't fight."

I didn't know how to respond to this insanity.

"He's weakened," she said. "He won't follow us. To kill him now is cold-blooded murder."

"It's self-preservation and defense."

"No," she said again. "I will take you from the Abyss if you kill him."

"Amalia...." My words trailed off when she lifted her head, and I saw the despair in her ochre-gray eyes.

"It will be my fault if he dies, and I can't bear that."

"No, it won't." I turned my attention back to Nalki as he watched us with hooded eyes. He'd stopped bleeding, but his breath was so shallow his chest barely moved. "With as old as he is, he'll heal fast."

"We'll be far from here and maybe out of the Abyss by the time he does."

My fingernails dug into my palms as I resisted going over there and finishing him. Demons destroyed; we didn't show pity on those who wronged us. We took revenge, but how could I kill him after she'd asked me not to? How could I murder him in front of her?

She would never forgive me if I did, and no matter how badly I wanted Nalki's head in my hands, I desired Amalia's happiness more.

And she *would* take us from here. Lix would understand why I'd killed Nalki while knowing I'd be removed from the Abyss, and under normal circumstances, Corson would too, but this wasn't normal. Corson would never forgive me if we couldn't access the Abyss and Wren died. I also didn't trust anyone else to come back here with Amalia, if she even agreed to return with someone else.

"He deserves to die," I stated.

"He was wrong, but he does *not* deserve to die."

Glancing back at Nalki, I realized I couldn't kill him. "Fine, but we have to go."

I couldn't shake my need to kill Nalki, but when her eyes shimmered into a yellow hue, I knew I would make the same choice a thousand times over.

"Thank you," she breathed and squeezed my arm.

"Don't thank me," I grated, suddenly irritated by the strange thrall this woman had over me. The right thing to do was to kill the bastard, yet I'd caved to make her happy.

Is she my Chosen?

I'd been so close to learning the answer to that before Nalki interrupted us, and now the question would haunt me until I knew for sure. If she was my Chosen, I wouldn't know the answer until I was inside her, but the fiery, honeyed taste of her lingering on my lips and tongue still tantalized me even though my face throbbed with every beat of my heart.

"We have to go," I said brusquely.

Unlike the other time we'd encountered the jinn, I believed Nalki had just happened on us. Otherwise, the jinn would have all attacked at once; they would not give me another chance to escape them. However, I wasn't willing to take any chances more of the bastards weren't lying in wait somewhere.

Pulling my arm away from hers, I stalked over and lifted my shirt from where it floated on top of the pool. The tattered remains dripped water as I held it before me. The shirt was beyond salvation.

Tossing it aside, I was about to turn away when something at the bottom of the pool caught my attention. I frowned as, amid all the gray and black rocks, a single yellow stone resided.

I paid little attention to the bottom of the pool earlier, but I couldn't help feeling the yellow stone hadn't been there. Even with a cursory glance, I would have noticed the out of place rock, or at least I believed I would have.

Where would it have come from otherwise?

It must've been there before, but I'd been too caught up in Amalia and getting her somewhere safe to notice it. I couldn't allow myself to continue to be distracted in such a way anymore. From here on out, I would distance myself from her, or at least start thinking with my bigger head more often.

Turning away from the water, I stalked back to Amalia. "Let's go."

Nalki's shrewd eyes followed our every move until we were away from the waterfall.

CHAPTER TWENTY-EIGHT

Amalia

MAGNUS HADN'T SPOKEN since we'd left Nalki behind. His shoulders remained rigid, and anger radiated from him. My irritation grew with every step we took. Just because I'd denied him a kill, he'd turned into an asshole. It wasn't like I didn't tell him I wouldn't tolerate something happening to the jinn. I'd explained I would help him, but not at the expense of the jinn.

When I looked at his face though, I contemplated killing Nalki myself.

Shaking my head, I tried to rid myself of the absurd notion, but it wouldn't go away. The idea of anyone hurting him caused an irrational need to destroy whoever the offender was myself. Never before had the idea of killing someone entered my mind, but the black bruises on Magnus's face, which were already fading to a purple hue, and his still partially caved-in cheekbone made me feel murderous.

But fine, if he preferred to be a jerk, then he could screw himself because he wouldn't be touching me again.

I kept telling myself this, but my body remained oversensitive from our encounter earlier. Nalki's arrival had doused my passion, but staring at his bare chest and back helped renew it, as did the fact I kept replaying those moments in my mind. My toes curled when I recalled the intensity of the orgasm he'd given me.

What else he could do with that magnificent body, I wondered as my eyes locked onto his lean, flexing muscles more times than I would ever admit to myself or anyone else. Still damp, his skin glistened, and his hair was plastered to his face, revealing more of those horns I loved running my hands over.

He'd liked me touching his horns. I licked my lips at the memory.

What is wrong *with me?*

I resisted tearing my wet dress off as every step caused it to rub against me in ways that stimulated me further. If I believed it would help, I'd slip away for a minute and give myself some release, but I knew it wouldn't. No, the only one who could bring me any relief was Magnus, and he was an ass.

Tugging at the collar of my dress, I pulled it away from my stiff nipples and breathed a little easier when it helped to ease some of my discomforts. My immortality must be coming real soon, as I'd never felt this hypersexual in my life. I'd been told a demon's sex drive amped up right before and after they became immortal.

I hadn't believed it as I'd already started to experience a growing sex drive, but now, I considered jumping Magnus and having sex with him just to end this torment. My skin flushed at the image such a thought conjured, and I found it increasingly difficult to breathe.

Magnus sniffed the air before his head turned toward me. Ducking my face, I forced my expression into one of nonchalance though my reddened skin, the color of my eyes, and the scent gave away my growing arousal. I'd never felt awkward before, but I wanted to melt through the ground.

Then, laughter floated to me.

My head shot up as three more equally girlish ones followed the first laugh. I turned to search for wherever the laughter came from and spotted a small crevice between the rocks.

When I stepped forward, Magnus gripped my forearm to halt me. "I'll go first," he said.

Before I could protest, he slid past me and, turning sideways, slipped into the opening. I followed him into the fissure, but unlike Magnus, the rocks didn't scratch my chest and back as I sidestepped onward.

At the end of the opening, Magnus peered out before exiting. I emerged behind him and froze when I saw the group of naked women gathered on a plush, red bed. Pillows abounded on the bed, and a sheer, red veil hung around the edges of it.

One of the women was in the process of doing things to a pillow that would make a tree nymph blush. Some of the others moaned as they fondled one another. The remaining two women were laughing as they playfully hit each other with the pillows.

"Looks like they're having fun," I murmured.

"Yes, but someone isn't," Magnus said.

He nodded to a young man who was lying fifty feet away from the bed. I'd been so caught up in the orgie, I'd failed to notice the man sprawled out on the rocks with his hands propped behind his head, and his feet crossed at the ankles. A pair of sunglasses shadowed his eyes, but his head was turned toward the women.

"Hawk," Magnus murmured and started toward the man.

Sensing our approach, Hawk's head turned toward us. He lowered his hands and propped his forearms on the ground behind him as he gazed at Magnus. Well-muscled, Hawk was broad through his shoulders and chest and extremely good-looking. If my intense attraction to Magnus was because of my looming immortality, I expected to experience a wave of lust for Hawk, but I felt nothing as I took in the sculpted planes of his face.

Lifting the glasses, Hawk revealed indigo eyes as he looked Magnus up and down. "You must be real," he said.

"And why is that?" Magnus inquired.

Hawk's attention drifted to me, and his full lips quirked into a smile that I couldn't stop myself from returning. Not only was he good-looking, but he emanated a kindness few other demons did. Magnus's displeasure caressed my skin as he edged between us.

"Because," Hawk said and rose, "only you would be arrogant enough to parade around whatever this place is, looking like someone mistook your face for a punching bag, while half naked."

"Asshole," Magnus said, but he grinned.

"Very true," Hawk agreed. "What is going on here and where am I?"

"Someone made a wish allowing the jinn to take almost everyone in the camp into the Abyss."

"And what is the Abyss?"

"A place where wishes are granted and the jinn feast," Magnus replied. "Did you make any wishes?"

"I think I'd enjoy my time here more if I had." When Hawk's attention returned to the women, some of his amusement vanished and sweat beaded his upper lip. "A wish, huh? I knew something wasn't right, but I couldn't figure out how to make it *stop*."

"How did you know it was fake?" I asked.

"I didn't, not at first. I... uh... I lost myself for a bit."

"Only for a bit?" Magnus asked. "What kind of canagh demon are you?"

My breath sucked in at the revelation of the type of demon Hawk was.

"Not a very good one," Hawk admitted.

"You're a canagh demon?" I inquired and was surprised my voice didn't squeak a little.

I'd heard about, and been cautioned to stay away from, the canagh demons who feasted on sexual energy. They could snare a lover and turn them into withered husks of what they once were through sex. Like the jinn, not all canaghs fed off those they enslaved, but many demons feared them.

"Not by choice," Hawk replied.

"None of us have a choice about what kind of demon we are," I said, confused by his choice of words.

"Hawk was once human, but he was accidentally turned into a canagh when the blood of one mingled with his while he was dying," Magnus explained.

"Oh," I murmured.

"And you are?" Hawk inquired with an appreciative twinkle in his eyes as they ran over me.

"Off limits," Magnus warned.

Hawk's hands shot up, and he grinned at Magnus. "I didn't realize that, and I didn't mean any offense to the beautiful lady."

"None taken," I said, and Hawk gave me a grateful smile while Magnus made another, menacing sound. "My name's Amalia."

"Nice to meet you, Amalia. I'm Hawk."

I stepped around Magnus when Hawk extended his hand toward me. I recognized the gesture as something I'd seen humans do and, grasping his hand in both of mine, I gave it an enthusiastic shake that brought it up to our heads before down to our waists.

Hawk's eyes widened before he started to laugh. Though I could still feel Magnus's annoyance, he chuckled and stopped my next upward jerk.

"Easy, Freckles," he said. "Leave his arm attached."

I released Hawk's hand when Magnus's fingers gently pried mine away from his friend's. Magnus gave my hand a small shake up and down. "This is the traditional human way of greeting others," he explained.

"Oh," I replied and frowned at our shaking hands. "My way is more fun."

Hawk laughed as he shook out his arm. "It's more of a workout. So, where did you come from, Amalia?"

"From Hell; I was behind one of the seals. I'm a jinni."

Hawk's smile never left his face, but uneasiness washed out of him. The change in emotion was subtle and one I probably wouldn't have picked up on before. However, my empath ability was growing. I didn't know if it was this place causing it to expand, or if my immortality was closer than I realized.

"She's not like the jinn who placed you here," Magnus said.

"I see," Hawk murmured, and this time his eyes were more inquisitive than interested when they ran over me.

"So... did the women not please you?" I asked to distract him from his perusal.

"Oh, they pleased me quite well," Hawk murmured and licked his lips. "But something wasn't right."

"How did you know something was off?" Magnus asked.

Hawk gazed at the women before looking to Magnus again. "If this is a land of wishes, then I guess I didn't get mine."

"I don't understand."

"As a canagh demon, I feed on sexual energy. As a human, I had different partners because I was young and having fun. But I was also waiting for... I guess you could say the *right one* to come along. I wanted someone to love and to love me, someone to have my children and share a life with, when I was old enough and ready for that to happen, of course."

He wants that more than anything else, I realized when his longing coiled within my chest.

"Whoever put me here saw me only as a canagh demon and must have assumed sex was what I would want, but I already have this, and it's...."

Hawk's voice trailed off. Focusing on us again, he flashed a grin, but I'd already sensed the emotion he was about to name—lonely.

"Anyway, it appears the jinn misread me. Perhaps I was

thinking of sex when they took me, which is likely, or perhaps they took one look at my stunning physique and stereotyped me into the playboy role," Hawk continued.

He winked at me as he said this, and Magnus gave a throaty growl that had Hawk's eyebrows shooting up.

"Okay, no winking at you," he said to me while he gave Magnus a puzzled look.

"If you know this isn't real, then why are you still here?" Magnus asked.

"I tried walking away, but every time I leave, I find myself standing here again. So, I figured I'd settle in and wait for someone to come, and you did. How do I get out?"

"Unlike us, it's only your mind trapped here. Your body is in a cave with the others; you just have to return to it," Magnus explained.

"Are you telling me I'm like Dorothy and I've had the power to go home this entire time?" Hawk inquired.

"Who?" I asked, and Magnus looked confused.

"Dorothy, *The Wizard of Oz*, the scarecrow and some flying monkeys—"

"Where?" I asked, and my eyes shot to the sky. I once discovered a book of Earth animals in an abandoned home. I remembered liking the monkeys because they were cute, but I didn't think they flew.

"Demons," Hawk sighed. "It was a movie I saw when I was a kid. Dorothy went to Oz, and she had these ruby slippers and... You know what, never mind. It's not worth explaining."

"It, ah, sounds interesting," I said.

"It was." Hawk threw back his shoulders and clicked his heels together. "I'm done with this fucking place." Click. "I'm done with this fu—"

Before Hawk could finish, he disappeared and the women

vanished. I hadn't realized how loud the women were until silence filled my ears.

"I'm going to have to discover this *Wizard of Oz* thing," Magnus said.

"Oz sounds strange, but Hawk seems nice."

When Magnus shot me an irritated look, I smiled sweetly at him.

CHAPTER TWENTY-NINE

Amalia

Over what seemed like hours, but it was impossible to tell how much time passed in here, lightning struck the monolith a dozen more times. My skin increasingly felt like a slimy substance coated it as too many lives flowed through me. I would give anything to find another pool of water, jump in, and scrub the death from me.

The only good thing was we managed to find, and help free, more of those who weren't entirely trapped here. We'd found the demon Shax wandering the trails like Erin a while ago.

When he saw Magnus, he threw up his hands. "Did you create this place?" he'd demanded.

Magnus smiled. "Not even I am this demented."

"Then who?"

"The jinn."

"Of course."

And with those two words, Shax vanished. Magnus and I

stared at each other before continuing into what was increasingly beginning to feel like a labyrinth.

"The jinn will know Wren is Corson's Chosen, she's clearly marked," Magnus said after a while.

"They will," I agreed.

"I think she'll be at the center of all this if she's not already dead."

"Why do you say that?"

"Because she's the best leverage they have over us."

When I tilted my head back, I could only see the pointed tip of Absenthees from where we stood amid the rocky pathways. Another bolt hit the top, and a wash of life ran through me.

I bowed my head against it and rubbed at my arms to try and clean my flesh, but it cleaved to me. Capturing my hands, Magnus halted them on my arms. It was the first time he'd touched me since we left Nalki behind, and despite my annoyance with him, electricity jolted me where we connected. I didn't feel so gross or *dirty* when he touched me.

Unthinkingly, I stepped closer to feel more of him. When he hugged me, the urge to cry hit me, and not just small tears, but great, heaping sobs for everything happening here.

Instead, I wrapped my arms around his back and clung to him. My fingers dug into his flesh until the urge to weep subsided. Unlike all the other times we touched, desire didn't surge to the forefront. Instead, just standing in his arms and holding him contented me.

Resting my cheek against the smooth flesh of his chest, I inhaled his scent as his powerful arms cradled me closer and his head dropped to mine. His lips nuzzled my hair as his hands ran over my back.

I didn't know how much time passed, but when he reluctantly stepped away from me, I felt as cleansed by him as I had by the water.

"Are you okay to keep going?" he asked with his hands resting on my arms.

"Yes."

"Are you sure?"

Lifting my head, I met his gaze. Some fading yellow bruises remained, but his face had mostly healed. "I *will* get through this," I stated.

He released me and started to turn away before spinning back and claiming my hand. "*We'll* get through this."

I blinked at his use of the word *we,* but I smiled at him before following him through the Abyss once more. Carefully, I stepped over the broken remains of a small skeleton. There were numerous skeletons on top of the walls, but we hadn't encountered many on the path. I didn't know if whatever creatures they belonged to hadn't died down here, or if the years and many feet on the path had ground the other bones down here into dust.

"Wait," I said and tugged on Magnus's hand to halt him.

Releasing him, I knelt beside the skeleton and gently grasped the edge of it. I lifted one of the bones, but it was attached to the rest of skeleton and brought forth more bones until it was unfurling before me.

"It's a wing," Magnus said as he knelt beside me.

Keeping the wing in hand, I examined the body and the small skull with a hooked beak. "It was a bird, I think."

Lowering the wing, I was careful not to disturb the remains further.

"What was this place once like?" I pondered.

"We'll never know," Magnus said.

Unfortunately, he was right. Wiping my hands on the skirt of my now nearly brown dress, I stood and gazed at the walls surrounding us. Afraid to attract the attention of the jinn, neither of us climbed to the top, but I was itching to scale the walls and see what lay beyond.

"Come on," Magnus said.

He was turning away from me when a woman with hair the color of fire and red-hued skin rounded the corner fifty feet away from us. She froze as her vivid green eyes burned with hatred.

"Bale," Magnus breathed.

When she bared her teeth at us, she exposed a set of razor-sharp fangs before she charged at Magnus. "*You* did this!" she accused as she closed the distance between us far faster than I'd anticipated.

"Whoa!" Magnus cried and dodged the punch she launched at him. "What the fuck, Bale?"

He threw up an arm and knocked aside Bale's wrist, deflecting the next downward arc of her punch. She spun away, and her foot lashed out in a motion so fast it was nothing but a blur. Magnus leapt back in time to avoid the kick to his chest, but then she twirled to the side and bashed her elbow into his bruised cheek. His head snapped to the side as he grunted.

When she launched a punch at him again, Magnus jumped back and grasped her wrist. Pulling her arm back, Bale rammed her other fist straight into his face. His nose broke with an audible crack.

"Bitch!" I cried, and before I could stop myself, or consider my actions, I jumped forward and struck Bale in the gut.

Pain lanced from my wrist to my elbow as I'd never punched someone before and had no idea how to hit anything correctly, but the blow pushed her back a step, which was enough time for Magnus to grip her shoulders.

"What are you doing?" he yelled at her.

"*You* did this!" she screeched.

Hooking her fingers into claws, Bale launched herself at him, and they staggered into the wall. She kneed him in the gut before kicking him in the shin. Magnus's breath exploded out of him. He wasn't fighting her as he'd fought Nalki, but I suspected it was only a matter of time before he stopped seeing her as a friend and saw her as an enemy.

"This isn't his doing!" I cried.

Grabbing Bale's hair, I yanked it back. Twisting her head, Bale's fangs snapped at my wrist, and Magnus emitted a sound between a snarl and a roar. Releasing her wrists, he seized her throat and spun her so fast her hair was pulled from my hand.

"This is the world of the jinn!" Magnus shouted as he slammed her into the wall. "The *jinn* did this!"

Bale struggled in his grasp for a few seconds before his words sank in.

"The jinn!" she spat, and suddenly Magnus held only air.

Corson

Bale came awake with a vengeance as she leapt to her feet and unsheathed the sword strapped to her back. She surveyed everyone in the cave as if we were the enemies she would slaughter.

"Welcome back," I greeted dryly.

Content there was no enemy, Bale lowered her sword, but she maintained a two-hand grip on it as the blade settled on the rock. Shoulders heaving, she surveyed the cave again. Most of those still alive were awake and leaning against the wall. Vargas, Wren's friend Jolie, and a handful of other humans had come back to us over the past eight hours.

There were now eighteen humans awake and, including Magnus and Hawk, there were nineteen living demons free of the Abyss.

Only five demons remained asleep, including Wren, as well as six humans. The rest were dead. Almost three days ago, we numbered one hundred twenty-five. Now, with the angels, we were down to thirty-nine fighters.

"What is going on?" Bale demanded.

"It seems Sloth and the jinn teamed up," I said. "And they're wreaking havoc."

"Where is Sloth?"

"Caim has been searching for him without luck," Vargas said.

Sitting beside Erin, Vargas had his legs drawn up and his arms draped across his knees. Even with his olive complexion, he was abnormally pale, and his nearly black eyes with their flecks of golden brown were haunted.

No one came out of the Abyss eager to share what they experienced, but Vargas wouldn't speak about it at all.

Rising, Lix's skeletal feet clicked against the stone as he made his way around the much emptier cave.

Bale sheathed her sword. "Why don't I see Magnus's body?"

I explained what had happened as I stroked Wren's silken hair and let it slide between my fingers. The earring she wore for me lay against her cheek, and her hands twisted into my shirt.

A flutter of wings drew my attention before Caim sauntered in.

"I'm back!" he declared. "And so are you!" He ignored Bale's scowl when he clapped her on the shoulder. "How was the Abyss, Red? Did you see anything exciting?"

"I saw rock walls and misery. It was like being in Hell again," Bale replied. "Then I came across Magnus. I assumed he caused it, so I tried to kill him."

"Not the first time," I said.

Bale gave me a wan smile. "At least the other times, he deserved it."

"I'm sure he'll deserve it the next time."

She chuckled. "Most likely."

"Did you have any wish fulfillment in there?" I inquired.

"No. I roamed for hours or maybe days while trying to find a way out."

"Days," Raphael said.

"What?" she asked.

"You were gone for nearly three days," I said.

"I see," Bale murmured.

"Who cares about any of that?" Caim asked. "I found Sloth."

Ever so slowly, I lifted Wren, disentangled her hands, and set her carefully on the blankets I'd arranged for her. Then, I turned to face the angel. "Where?"

"Well, you see, the *where* is the tricky part," Caim said as he seemed to savor being the center of attention.

"Tricky how?" I demanded.

"Because Sloth is in the Abyss."

My mind spun as the implications of his words sank in. A horseman *in* the Abyss? *Sloth* in the Abyss with *Wren*. Taking a deep breath, I tried to clear my head of the anger and fear rattling it. I wouldn't do anyone any good if I couldn't think straight.

"It's the perfect place for him to hide, and the jinn will help him do so," I murmured.

"I believe there may be other horsemen in there with him," Caim said.

"Why?" I demanded.

"Because, as you said, it's a perfect place for them to hide. They may *all* be in there."

"Shit," Lix said.

"How do you know any of them are in there?" Hawk asked.

"Because Sloth would want to see the repercussions of his handiwork unfold, but I've searched everywhere, and he's not in the woods. Also, we wouldn't have the bodies here if he'd remained in the woods after the jinn sprang their trap. There was only four of us who remained free; they could have easily taken us down when we returned."

"They probably didn't know we weren't in camp when they set their trap," Raphael said.

"Maybe, but I think it's more likely they did know we weren't here. I think the craetons would be on the lookout for two angels; we're not hard to miss, especially not *moi*. But I'm just a simple fallen, and that's merely my guess," Caim replied and fluttered his lashes at Raphael.

The scowl Raphael gave him was anything but angelic as his hand fell to his sword.

"Enough," I warned, unable to deal with their sibling antagonism.

"I believe it is more likely, they didn't know when we would return to camp, and the jinn were unwilling to wait before starting to play with their new victims. Or they planned to return for us when they succeeded in slaughtering most of our friends," Caim continued. "Either way, what could be better than watching death and misery unfold from a secure location? The Abyss offers Sloth, the jinn, and the other horsemen all the security in the world while they unleash their havoc. Sloth is in the Abyss; I'd stake my life on it."

My gaze fell on Wren as the chill encompassing me spread into my veins and turned my blood to ice. "We have to warn Magnus."

"How?" Erin asked. "Maybe Halstar could have telecommunicated with him in the Abyss, but he's dead."

How do we contact him then? As hard as I tried, I could not think of an answer to that.

CHAPTER THIRTY

Magnus

"I... I SMELL WATER AGAIN," Amalia said, lifting her head and sniffing at the air.

Her hair hung lankly around her shoulders. After our last swim, her braids had come undone, and ever since we encountered Bale, she'd been distant.

"I have to... to... *wash*," she said and glanced at me from under the thick fringe of her multi-hued lashes.

"I understand."

We should continue our search, we were getting closer to the monolith, but she needed a break, and I couldn't push her when she looked so beat. Besides, the last time, the water revitalized her and hopefully it would again. The other jinn thrived on the life force they spread through here while every new one wilted Amalia like a plant denied sunshine for weeks.

Though, there hadn't been any lightning in a while.

I briefly contemplated going back to see if anyone from our

camp remained in here, but I didn't want to waste the time it would take to return.

Amalia headed for a crevice in the rocks that was barely large enough for us to walk side by side through.

"I hit Bale," she said after a few feet. "I pulled her hair too."

"I saw."

A crease ran across her delicate forehead as her pale eyebrows drew together over her nose. "I never believed I was capable of doing such a thing."

I now understood her brooding demeanor. "If it's any consolation, you didn't hit her very well."

A small smile quirked her mouth, but her eyes remained sad. "There was no need to fight behind the seal."

"There is on Earth and in here."

"I'm not a fighter."

"You're more of a fighter than you realize, and if you want to survive, you need to learn how to fight well. When we are free of this place, I will teach you."

"And I will learn," she murmured. "But I don't like it."

"Self-preservation is a *good* thing."

"I know that, but I didn't hit Bale for me, I did it... I did it because it made me so *mad* when she hurt *you*."

Her eyes reflected her confusion as they shifted to the color of honey. "It's not..." She shook her head and looked away. "I shouldn't have done it. I'm not violent."

"There is more than fae in you; there is also jinn," I reminded her, "and all demons are violent. The fae are dead now because they wouldn't fight."

"And the original jinn no longer exist because they were *too* violent. Just because something has always been one way, doesn't mean it should remain the same."

"You want demons to be less violent?" I asked incredulously.

Her hand trembled when she brushed her hair over her shoulder. "I understand fighting is necessary for survival, especially now, but I can dream maybe one day we will experience a better, more peaceful world."

I couldn't shatter her hope by telling her that would probably never happen. Besides, maybe I was wrong in my belief and she was right to dream of such things. No matter who was right or wrong, I determined that if I could, I would bring her this better world she envisioned.

The pathway opened to reveal a small pool of water at the end. Amalia kicked off her pink slipper shoes as she approached the pool, and I winced when she revealed the oozing blisters on her feet.

"Your feet," I said.

"They're fine," she replied. "The slippers have rubbed them raw since our swim, but they'll heal now that the shoes are off."

"You should have stopped wearing them."

"Hmm," she murmured, her attention already focused on the water.

I walked over to stand beside her and gazed down at mine and Amelia's reflections on the reflective surface. Either the water was the slate gray of the rocks lining the pool, or it was crystal clear.

"I'll be quick," she said and plunged into the water before I could reply.

I watched her sink toward the bottom before turning to survey the small space surrounding the pool. Stalking around the perimeter, I searched for another way into this place. After careful examination, I saw no one else or any other entrance into this place aside from the path we took to get here.

The walls rose thirty feet into the air, and at least fifty wilted trees dotted the top of the walls. Many of their barren branches leaned toward the pool.

∾

Amalia

Sinking deeper into the water, I relished the feel of it against my skin as it rinsed the death from me. Bubbles rose from between my lips as I scrubbed at my flesh. I smiled as I waved my arms before me and sank further into the water. The multi-colored hue of my hair fanning out around me reminded me of the sunrises on Earth.

I loved those sunrises, Earth, and anything beyond the seal, but there was something about this place, and especially the water, that called to me.

"But you are more fae than the rest of us, with your coloring and your telltale eyes. The Abyss is not for you."

Rislen's earlier words floated across my mind, and I wondered how right she'd been. The Abyss exuded loneliness, but a part of me belonged here, and it was not the jinn part.

By the time my toes touched the bottom, my lungs were starting to burn, but I wasn't ready to rise again. I could hold on for a minute more.

Gradually, I became aware of warmth spreading from my feet to my ankles and slithering around my calves. Closing my eyes, I savored the feel as the fire in my blistered feet eased and my skin repaired itself.

Rislen may have been wrong about the Abyss being more diffi-cult for me, but she was right about my strong fae connection. I felt the lingering power of the fae here all the way to the center of my being; I needed to experience *more* of it.

I became acutely aware of the growing discomfort of my thin dress against my skin and the fact it was keeping me from experi-encing the water *all* over me. Reaching down, I yanked the dress off and let it go.

The water moving freely over my bare flesh soothed me further. Running my hands over my breasts and down between my thighs, I cleansed myself of the last of the death as the heat from the stones climbed into my belly and spread upward.

Slowly, I waved my hands back and forth before me as the spreading heat encompassed my breasts and my nipples puckered. Tipping my head back, I discovered Magnus's face wavering in the water as he leaned over the pool to gaze down at me. Unexpected yearning ripped through me, and I nearly cried out from the intensity of it.

While I stared at his troubled countenance, the heat encompassed my entire body, and something clicked into place. At that moment, I realized two things... I'd come into my immortality within this pool of fae water, and I needed *him*.

CHAPTER THIRTY-ONE

Magnus

I WAS ABOUT to dive into the pool when I saw Amalia rising toward the surface with her arms at her sides, her head back, and her bare breasts exposed. My breath exploded from me, and my cock hardened so fast I groaned from the mingling pleasure and pain of it.

Then, she was breaking free of the water and gasping for breath. Her small hands fell on the sides of the pool ten feet away from me. When she lifted herself out, she revealed the curve of her round ass and lean thighs. The water spilling from her hair slid down her slickened body and emphasized every dip and hollow of her supple figure.

The scent of her arousal hit me, and when she crawled forward, she revealed a tantalizing glimpse of her sex.

Mine!

I'd felt possessive of her before, I'd *craved* her before, but something about her had changed in that water.

She needs me. Only me.

Without thinking, I unbuttoned my pants and pulled down my zipper. I kicked my boots off and barely registered their dull thump on the stone. My thoughts became a chaotic, jumbled mess as Amalia rose and turned to face me.

She smoothed her wet hair back from the delicate angles of her face. Her eyes were the vermillion color they became when she was impassioned, except now they were nearly burning coals when they landed on me, and she licked her lips.

Immortal! MY immortal.

I didn't realize I was walking toward her until my pants slipped further down my hips and my dick sprang free. When her gaze latched onto it, she swayed toward me as a bead of water slid to the end of one of her puckered nipples and hung enticingly there.

My entire being focused on her until nothing else existed. I somehow managed to remove my pants before I made it to her and was completely nude when my arms swept around her waist and I lifted her off the ground.

Her hands fell on my chest, her legs locked around my hips, and she rubbed her wet core against my cock. When her head fell back, she exposed her ripe, apple-sized breasts further as she lifted them toward my mouth. Bending, I ran my tongue around her nipple before pulling it into my mouth. The tug I gave it made her squirm more demandingly against me.

"I can't...," she panted. "I need you inside me. You have to, Magnus, you *have* to."

Before I could do anything, she reached between us and grasped my dick. Her hand enveloping my shaft caused it to jump; the sensation of her gripping me caused me to worry I'd come in her palm. Gritting my teeth, I somehow managed to keep myself restrained from thrusting into her fist and taking the release I sought.

When she rubbed the head of my shaft against her clit, I swelled further in her hand as she used me to tease herself. My hands tightened on her when her hand slid down the length of me and back up while she continued to stroke me over her clit.

"Amazing," she whimpered, "but need more."

I couldn't find the words to tell her to take whatever she needed; I was beyond words.

Her breasts pressed against my chest when she guided me down to the heat of her entrance. Ever so slowly, she slid the head of my cock between her folds and partially inside her. Her sheath enveloped me, and the further I pushed into her, the more something changed in me.

She felt right in a way nothing ever had before. The strange sensation of my upper and lower canines pricking caused me to prod at them, but I forgot about it when Amalia released my cock and her hands gripped my back. Her fingers dug into my flesh as she slid further down the length of me until I came up against an unexpected barrier.

Virgin.

I barely had time to register the knowledge before she thrust her hips forward and sank herself onto me. A shout of possession erupted from me as she cried out and froze. Her teeth bit her lower lip, and she trembled against me.

"Are you okay?" I asked in a guttural voice I didn't recognize.

"Fine! I'm fine!"

I gripped her nape as I drew her closer to inhale her sweet scent and savor in the sensation of her exquisite body flush against mine. Her thighs were steel bands around my waist; we were joined, yet I wanted something *more* from her. I didn't rush her, though mostly because I didn't want this moment to end.

Her passion-colored eyes held mine; neither of us moved while she adjusted to the size and feel of me. Bending her head, she kissed my neck before running her tongue over my skin. Then, her hands slid up to run over my horns. My dick jumped inside her as a shiver raced down my spine.

"I felt that deep inside me," she whispered. "I feel *every* part of you."

I knew what she meant by that. Even in the places where we weren't touching, she was branding herself onto me, and I could feel every movement of the muscles enveloping my shaft.

Using my horns, she lifted herself until only my head remained inside her before she slid back down the length of me. "Oh, yes," she moaned.

I gripped her ass with one hand while I tightened my hold on her nape with the other and dragged her down to claim her mouth. My tongue entangled with hers while her water-slickened body rose and fell against mine. My hand on her ass guided her movements.

My teeth...

Breaking the kiss, her head fell back, and her glorious hair spilled over my fingers as she ground against me and her breasts bobbed enticingly with her movements. I'd never experienced such exquisite gratification before; it was so extreme it bordered on pain as my cock swelled more than it ever had.

An unfamiliar pressure rose up my shaft, but I barely registered it as I focused on her and the fantastic way she felt. I lowered my head to run my tongue over her nipple. When I sucked it into my mouth, I nipped at her breast and my teeth—no, not teeth, four *fangs* pierced her flesh.

My shock over growing a set of upper and lower fangs I'd never possessed before was short-lived as Amalia went wild in my arms. Grinding, thrusting, clawing, she fucked me until I couldn't stand anymore and sank to my knees with her still impaled on me.

I bit harder as I laved her nipple and claimed what I now knew was *my* Chosen as those fangs were meant to mark her and only her. My movements became more frenzied, and I took her with an abandon bordering on savagery. I tried to reel myself in so as not to hurt her further, but her demanding body wouldn't allow me to hold anything back.

The pressure building in my dick was becoming unbearable, but now, I knew what it was. For the first time in my life, I was going to spill my seed inside a woman when I came. And that woman was *Amalia*.

The thought excited me further; I was on the brink of experiencing what so few demons did in their lives and with a woman who was better than I ever could have imagined.

∾

Amalia

The discomfort I experienced when Magnus first entered me was fleeting. Once my body started to heal and I got used to the size of him within me, pleasure swiftly buried any pain. From the tips of my toes to the tingling in my scalp, everything was alive with the new sensations coursing through my body. And some of it was more than the feel of Magnus's chiseled body against mine, some of it was the experience of being newly immortal.

Sights, sounds, and sensations were sharper than normal; my passion was running higher than ever before. But more than that, Magnus's emotions were fueling my empath ability until I couldn't tell his ecstasy apart from mine.

My curiosity about sex was finally answered, and it was better than anything I ever could have imagined, and I knew that was because I was experiencing this with Magnus. No other demon would have made my body come alive or possessed it as thoroughly as he did.

Before his fangs sank into my breast, I knew what he was to me, and I realized part of me had always suspected it, but as a mortal, I hadn't been ready to claim my Chosen. Now, I was more than ready.

Deep inside me, he grew thicker and stretched me further. *He's mine. All mine.*

Then, he released his bite on my breast and sank his fangs into my shoulder. His hand clamped around the back of my head as his growl reverberated against my flesh and his muscles bunched around me.

When my upper teeth lengthened into two fangs, I didn't hesitate before sinking them into his shoulder and marking him as mine. Two drops of his blood fell on my tongue, and the world spun away until it was only him and me.

The scent of our sex grew stronger on the air; the slick feel of our two bodies joined together became all I knew as we claimed each other.

Harder.

Faster.

Harder.

My body rocked against his as a tightening started in my lower belly and spread out. I recognized the feeling of impending release, but this was far more intense and demanding.

I grasped Magnus's horns and used them as leverage as I rotated my hips in just the right....

My eyes rolled back as my body splintered apart and ecstasy crashed through me. Deep inside me, I felt my muscles contracting around him and milking his shaft. His bite on my shoulder muffled his shout as he shuddered against me.

The pulsations radiating throughout his cock escalated my orgasm when he came inside me. I felt the heat of his seed spreading through me while he branded me as his from the inside out.

Contractions continued to run through me while he held me, and I replayed everything that happened. Nothing would ever be the same again; I was now immortal and bound to this demon for the rest of our lives. I found I was okay with that; in fact, it brought a smile to my face as I nuzzled closer to him.

Strong and protective, Magnus would make an outstanding Chosen and hopefully, one day, father to our child. I wasn't concerned about becoming pregnant yet, female demons who discovered their Chosen only produced an egg every ten to fifteen years. Newly immortal, it would be a while before my fertile time came.

Rousing myself from the haze still enshrouding me, I realized Magnus's horns had shifted forward in my grasp and now stood out from the sides of his head.

CHAPTER THIRTY-TWO

Amalia

"Your horns," I said.

"New development. They've never moved before, but you make more than one thing on me very erect." He rested his hand on my hip as his cock stirred within me. "The fangs are new too."

"The fangs," I groaned when I recalled the way they'd pierced my flesh.

"The fangs," he said and licked his lips as his gaze fell to my mouth. "And my Amalia."

"And my Magnus," I replied.

My body came alive and reacted to his when his fingers slid over my hip before dipping toward my belly.

"I should have gone easier on you for your first time," he murmured.

"I wouldn't have let you," I said with a smile. "I *didn't* let you. I wanted it as badly as you did, maybe more so."

His eyes shone with amusement when they came back to mine. "Oh, and why is that?"

"Because once I came into my immortality, your need for me amplified mine for you."

His amusement vanished as his finger stroked my cheek. "Immortal," he breathed.

"Finally."

"Do you feel any different?"

"My empath ability has amped up."

My nipples puckered as I recalled the way he'd reacted to everything and the emotions he emanated while we pleasured each other. We were still new to each other, but already I knew some of what thrilled him the most. He loved when I stroked his horns, but he also liked it when I bit his neck and licked his ear. I couldn't wait to learn more.

"I knew there was something different about you," he murmured.

"I can say the same, but it wasn't until I was in the water and I felt myself shift into immortality that I *knew*."

"It wasn't until you came out of the water that I did."

Bending his head, he nibbled on my lower lip before drawing it into his mouth and scratching it with an upper and lower fang.

I was starting to lose myself to him again when a life force washed through me. I froze as reality hit me like a boulder to the head.

"We have to go!" I gasped. He tried to snatch me back when I scrambled from his lap, but I moved away from him and jumped up. "The others!" Guilt tore at me as I realized what we'd been doing while someone was dying in here. "We have to...."

My voice trailed off as I gazed around with a dawning mix of awe and shock. *How did we not see? How did we not know?*

Because we were too caught up in each other to notice anything else.

But this? How could we have missed *this*?

Magnus rose beside me, and I knew the second he registered what had happened as his body became rigid beside mine.

All around us, the once deadened stone had returned to life. Oranges, pinks, yellows, blues, greens, and purples shone anew everywhere I looked in the small area surrounding the pool. The water was the same multi-hued combination as the rocks, and the stones inside the pool brimmed with color.

Tilting my head back, my mouth dropped when I saw the trees lining the edge of the wall. They were only half deadened as the branches closest to us had come alive and rose toward the sky. Orange-brown leaves and bright yellow and purple flowers decorated half the tree.

"What happened?" I breathed.

Magnus studied the surrounding area with a look that said it awed him as much as he distrusted it. Then, his furrowed brow smoothed, and he turned to me. "*You* happened."

"What? *Me?* How?"

"We have to get out of here. There's a good chance the jinn will notice those trees."

"Magnus, what did you mean *I* happened?"

He dove into the water and returned less than a minute later with my dress. His frantic energy beating against me overwhelmed me. My hand flew to my forehead as I stepped back and inhaled a shaky breath.

"You okay?" he inquired as he grasped my arms.

"Emotions," I murmured and took the sodden dress from him. "*Everything* is so much more now."

Clasping my chin, he turned my head back to him. Peace stole through me as I gazed into those beautiful silver eyes. "You will get used to it, and I will be here to help you through it all."

Those words stole my breath more than his chaotic emotions had earlier. "Thank you."

"No need to thank me." He pressed a brisk kiss against my lips.

"You're mine to protect, and I will do that every day of the eternity we'll have together. Now, get dressed quickly."

I tugged the dress over my head, and accustomed to being barefoot, I decided to forgo the slippers for the rest of the journey. I was ready before him as I watched him tug on his pants. Standing with my hands palm out at my sides, I savored the swell of power in this area. This is what the Abyss was supposed to be, what it *should* be, but I had no idea how to bring this beauty back to all of it.

Magnus clasped my elbow and led me toward the crevice we'd entered through. "Why did you say I did this?" I asked as I jogged to keep up with him.

"When we were at the waterfall, after we came out of the water, I noticed a single yellow stone at the bottom of the pool. At the time, I believed it was always there and I missed it in my rush to get you somewhere safe."

"And now?" I prodded.

"I know the stone was from you. You must have touched it. This place, or at least certain elements of it, are feeding on you."

"What? Why do you think that?"

"Because, for the first time in countless years, you are feeding this starved land something other than death. You funneled your emotions while you were claiming your Chosen into it, and fed it a whole *lot* of good emotions, especially ecstasy."

"Awfully certain of yourself," I muttered as I contemplated his words.

"I always am." His arrogant words couldn't hide his desperation to get me far from here.

"So that's why I've felt an affinity for this place since entering it. Beneath all the horror, the Abyss was straining to come alive, and it's been calling to the fae part of me."

"That makes sense," he said.

"Not much else does here."

"I agree."

When he grinned at me over his shoulder, he revealed that his teeth were back to normal, but I distinctly recalled his four fangs piercing my flesh. It seemed different demons developed different fangs to mark their Chosen, and I knew the Chosen bond also strengthened a demon.

My empath ability had increased before I emerged from the pool, but I felt it heighten further when Magnus and I claimed each other. Though there were numerous times when I saw my ability as more of a curse than a gift, it was powerful and *very* useful. When I learned to control it better, and I was confident I would over time, it would save lives.

I suspected Magnus's illusions would be stronger now too. His horns had flattened against his head again; as they were now, his horns weren't much of a weapon, but when they straightened, they could gut an enemy.

But will they straighten in battle as they did when I was gripping them?

There was only one way to learn the answer to that question, so I was content to remain curious for a while. Unfortunately, I didn't think we would have much time before the answer found us. We were too close to Absenthees not to encounter someone, and I didn't see how those half-alive trees could go unnoticed.

"Rislen also said the Abyss would be more difficult for me, and while it hasn't been easy, I've handled it better than the other Faulted did. I came *back,* and I will again, but the other Faulted said they would never return. Perhaps, they are more fae than me."

"They're not," Magnus said as we arrived at the end of the crevice. Poking his head out, he examined both ways before stepping out and pulling me with him. "Rislen said you're more fae than the others; your kindness and abilities are giving life to the Abyss again. This place resonates more with you than them, it makes you sadder, yet you refuse to retreat from it. You may be the youngest and the most fae of the jinn, but you are also the strongest of all the jinn."

"Oh, no, not me."

"Yes, *you*." Turning to face me, Magnus cupped my cheek in his hand and drew me closer. "You stand up for what you believe is right. In doing so, you went against the only family and existence you've ever known. That is far stronger than any of the jinn who are too angry to forgive or too scared to get involved, so they hide beneath the calamut trees. This place has been waiting for *you* to enter it."

"And do what?"

"Bring it some life."

"But what good will that do?"

"I don't know. Maybe none, but it needs you."

He kissed the tip of my nose before reluctantly turning away.

Needs me to do what?

I didn't voice the question as I worried I might not be able to survive whatever the Abyss and jinn had in store for us.

CHAPTER THIRTY-THREE

Magnus

I KEPT Amalia close to me as we wound our way more cautiously through the Abyss toward the monolith. Around every corner, I expected someone to leap out at us, but the pathway remained empty. I could put a cloaking illusion over us, but I preferred not to use it until we were closer to Absenthees.

After leaving the pool, I'd realized the jinn wouldn't hunt us in here anymore, not after I pulled my disappearing act and nearly killed Nalki. No, they would wait for us to come to them as all the paths led to one place. That didn't mean the newly resurrected trees wouldn't draw some of them into the Abyss.

Stopping, I leaned against the wall and drew Amalia into my arms.

She frowned at me, but I didn't let her go as I bent my head to kiss the top of hers. Her fingers curled into my back, and she bowed her head to rest it against my chest.

"Magnus?" she whispered.

"They'll be waiting for us at the monolith. You must be prepared for that."

Her fingers dug deeper into my flesh. "I am."

A mix of possessiveness and fear crept through me. I'd never known fear before her, but since meeting her, it had become an increasingly familiar emotion. Even in battle, I wasn't afraid; I did what I had to, and if I happened to die in the process, then so be it.

But with Amalia, I felt like someone had torn my heart out and placed it inside her; I could *not* allow anything to happen to her. Somewhere along the way, I'd fallen for this complicated woman who was so unlike anyone I'd ever encountered. I'd fallen for a preferred pacifist with the heart of a warrior. A woman who wore her every emotion in her eyes and knew so little of the world.

One day, I would show her everything she wanted to see and have her experience all she was denied while locked away. But first, we had to get through the many enemies out there who would prefer nothing more than to destroy us.

"I'm not going to lose you, Amalia."

"And I'm not going to lose you."

I gripped her closer as love swelled within my chest. I'd been determined to keep her at a distance, but it was impossible to do so with Amalia. With her unique spirit, loving nature, and spine of steel, she'd worked her way into my heart without me realizing it.

Amalia gave a small sob and nestled closer.

"Shh," I whispered. "I'll keep you safe."

"I know, it's not that." When she met my gaze, her eyes were the most vivid yellow I'd ever seen. She rested her hand over my heart. "Your emotions. They're so strong, and they're for *me*."

"Only for you," I said and kissed her tenderly.

When she leaned into me, I broke the kiss before it deepened into something more. We had a mission to complete, but this woman could distract the sun from its orbit, and I was nowhere near as strong as the sun.

"Only for you too," she murmured, and I claimed her hand.

"I'm going to put a cloaking illusion over us before we continue, so don't make any noise and don't let me go."

"I won't," she promised.

Digging into myself, I drew forth my ability to make us invisible to anyone beyond us. Typically, it was more difficult for me to weave the illusion as I found it easier to create layers of existence rather than hide them, but with Amalia's hand in mine and her claiming bite on my shoulder, I found it much easier to strip our presence away. When I finished, I didn't feel as drained, and I knew it was the Chosen bond strengthening me.

Kissing her again, I hugged her one last time and kept hold of her hand as we continued down the path.

Overhead, I barely saw the top of Absenthees poking above the high walls, but the monolith was only half a mile away at most. Turning a corner, we came to the end of the path and stopped five feet behind the jinni standing guard there.

A small jolt of surprise went through me, and Amalia's hand tightened on mine when Absenthees came into view. At the base of the monolith, boulders were piled at least twenty feet high against the structure. The silvery-black monolith shoved those rocks out of its way when it tore through the ground to rise high in the clearing.

And Absenthees rose far higher than I'd realized as I had to crane my head back to take in the top of the structure nearly three hundred feet above us. The smaller monoliths were silent as they rotated around Absenthees, and beneath them were mounds of earth around the four holes from which they'd risen.

The etchings I'd first suspected seeing on the monolith were some form of demonish, but I didn't recognize most of them. The ones I did recognize were the symbols of unity, strength, and bound. Instinctively, I knew the jinn didn't put those markings there. The fae or the Abyss itself had hewn them onto Absenthees' surface.

Most of the jinn, including Nalki, stood inside the pit. Two or three jinn stood guard in front of the seven other paths I could see leading into Absenthees. From what I'd witnessed at the top of the hill, two more paths led into the pit, but the monolith blocked them from my view. I'd bet more jinn guarded these pathways too.

At the bottom of the monolith, a few jinn stood on top of the boulders with their hands resting on Absenthees. The rest of the jinn in the pit were focused on it. Like one of the movies the humans were once so fond of, a scene played out on the monolith as if it were a screen.

The woman running through the woods was a Wilder. Her eyes were frantic as tears streaked her face and her arms pumped faster. I couldn't see what propelled her onward, but I suspected it was another of the jinn's torments.

Amalia crept closer until her shoulder brushed mine as the woman screamed, opened her arms, and threw herself off a cliff. The woods faded away while the woman plummeted, and I realized she'd thrown herself off the top of one of the labyrinth walls. The jinn all leaned forward as the woman's head smashed off an opposite wall and the impact threw her backward.

She was dead before she hit the ground, and lightning hit Absenthees less than a second later. The bolt lit the etchings as it traveled all the way to the bottom before flowing up again. Amalia shuddered when the markings at the base of the structure became the color of molten gold. Heat crackled across the open space separating us from the formation.

All the jinn stretched their hands out at their sides and turned their palms toward Absenthees. Their heads tilted back as they savored the life making Amalia shiver. I looked away from the spectacle of the jinn basking in death as the ones touching the monolith lowered their hands and stepped away. Four new jinn climbed the base of Absenthees while the ones standing there retreated. When the replacements rested their hands against the structure, a new scene unfolded before them.

On the structure, a demon having sex with three other males was revealed. The jinn watched for a minute before this scene faded away and a new one replaced it. And then, I understood how the jinn found us earlier.

The monolith was the equivalent of the humans' TVs. It showed one channel at a time, but the jinn could flicker through the different channels until they found something they wanted to watch. Through Absenthees, they watched different wishes unfolding, but they could only see one at a time, and the jinn would focus on the ones heading toward their tragic conclusion. They must have accidentally flipped to us with Dana while searching for something better to watch.

I examined the pit while I tried to decide what to do next. With the height of the walls and their rocky formations, climbing in or out of the crater without making some noise or knocking rocks free would be impossible.

The angles of some of the walls would make descending nearly impossible as in certain areas they curved in until some of them would have us hanging upside down. The place would be impenetrable if there were still two or three jinn at the end of this path, but we could slip by one.

I suspected the resurrection of the fae world Amalia created by the pool had caught someone's attention and drawn away the other jinn guarding this path. We'd somehow missed the jinn searching for us, or they'd tried to find us by stalking us from above.

No matter what they'd decided to do, or how they'd done it, they would be back, and we had to be out of here before they returned. Movement from the pit drew my attention back to Absenthees as, from around the corner of it, three of the ten remaining horsemen rode their mounts into view.

There are horsemen here!

It was a complication I hadn't seen coming but should have. I knew they were all in league with each other, and the horsemen would enjoy playing in the Abyss almost as much as the jinn.

At least the jinn hadn't invited any of the fallen angels to the party, or at least I didn't see any of them here.

Briefly, I searched the sky, but when I saw nothing there, I turned my attention back to the horsemen. If any of the fallen were here, they would have started hunting us from the sky long ago. Cloaking illusion or not, those pricks would scour the land ceaselessly until they found us.

My attention returned to the horsemen. In the center of the three, Lust sat proudly on her horse with her lush body on full display. Her white hair spilled over the ass end of her gray horse.

I recognized Pride by the way he carried himself. Like Lust, he sat bareback on his smoky, purple-gray horse. Out of all the horses, Pride's was the most beautiful with its thick, curved neck and its black forelock brushing against its nose. The horse's black mane and tail touched the ground, and its eyes were the neon color of lavender.

Pride's broad shoulders were thrust back as he sat taller on his mount than the horsemen with him. His black hair was brushed back from the planes of his angular face to reveal eyes the same color as his horse's. Not one speck of dirt or wrinkle marred him or his clothing from his black pants and shirt to the royal purple cloak he wore. An almond-shaped broach with a single, unblinking purple eye gazing out from its center clasped the cloak together.

Next to Pride, Sloth's pudgy frame slouched on the back of his horse. His legs barely wrapped around the horse's thick belly. The mane and tail of his brown horse were matted, and its forelock was a tangled knot between its ears. The horse had one lazy blue eye drifting toward the right and one lazy brown eye falling to the left.

Some of Sloth's tousled brown hair stood on end, and the rest of it draped across his round, florid face. Sloth personified laziness, yet the intelligence in his pale blue eyes didn't match his apathetic persona.

Amalia gave a subtle tug on my hand. When I turned to her, her red eyes burned with fury, but she'd paled visibly. *"They brought the horsemen here,"* she mouthed.

And if the growing pallor of her skin was any indication, the putrid emotions the horsemen emitted was battering her newly escalated empath ability. I had to get her out of here.

"Focus on me," I mouthed back.

Her jaw set before she pointed a finger at the horsemen. *"They should* not *be here. We can't allow them to remain."*

Then I realized the horsemen weren't just escalating her empath ability and fueling her anger; she was *enraged* at the jinn for bringing the horsemen into the Abyss.

Squeezing her hand, I turned my attention back to those gathered before us. We would have to return to the others and bring them here if we were going to fight the jinn and the horsemen. We couldn't face them with only the two of us.

A step drew my attention to the path behind us, and I froze. Coming toward us were three more jinn who would walk directly into us in less than ten feet.

Tugging on her hand, I turned sideways to slip past the jinni at the end of the path, and Amalia followed silently behind me. We hugged the steep walls until we neared the jinn guarding the end of the next pathway. Edging further into the middle of the pit, we stayed far away from the jinn to avoid causing a shift in air current and possibly alerting them to our presence.

I had to get her out of this pit and somewhere she could open a portal out of here. No one could see us, but I wouldn't be able to cloak the disturbance in the air she created with the opening.

Coming around the back of the monolith, I spotted a set of ruins sitting on top of the wall. Judging by the remains, the crumbling, sandstone structure once spanned hundreds of feet in length.

Most of what remained was only a few feet high, some of it was a single story, and in other sections, it was two. One area of the ruins stood three stories high.

The three-story section was mostly untouched and showed no sign it might collapse anytime soon, but the segment next to it was nothing more than a few feet of wall. A single tower stood beside that ruined section, and I suspected there were once more towers, but time ate all but the one.

If we could make it up there, we could find a place for Amalia to take us from here.

Her hand trembled in mine, and I felt a weakening in her. Turning, my breath caught when her eyes met mine; they were a sickly mustard hue I'd never seen before. Her skin was so pale her freckles stood out starkly.

Is this from the horsemen, or is something more at work here?

I went to scoop her into my arms, but she edged away from me. My teeth ground together when I stepped closer to her again; she avoided me.

"No," she mouthed. *"We both have to move freely. I'm okay. Go,"* her lips formed the words, but I found myself torn between carrying her out of here and listening to her. *"Go."*

I had no other choice; she would only fight me, and we could not stand here arguing about it. We made our way to the other side of the monolith, opposite the horsemen and most of the jinn. After a few more feet, a set of rocky steps rising from the pit and toward the ruins came into view.

We closed the distance between us and the steps in less than a minute. Chunks of crumbling sandstone fell out to roll down near my feet. Most of the railing had given way, and what remained of it lay on the ground beside the stairs. The steps didn't look as if they would support a flea, never mind the two of us.

I studied our surroundings again, but unless we intended to

hang out with these assholes for the rest of eternity, or until I couldn't hold the cloak anymore, we had no choice but to climb.

Amalia's fingers bit into my hand when I placed my foot on the first step and gingerly tested it. I worked to keep my concern for her safety buried so she wouldn't sense it as I placed another foot on the next step.

Amalia followed me as we carefully climbed the steps, but though the stairs looked like a breeze would topple them, they remained solid beneath my feet.

We were nearly three quarters of the way to the top when something shifted beneath my feet.

I froze, and behind me, Amalia's breath exploded out of her as for a minute nothing more happened. Then, the stairs turned into sand beneath my feet. I scrambled to find some purchase, but nothing substantial remained as we plummeted toward the ground.

CHAPTER THIRTY-FOUR

Amalia

As WE FELL, rocks and sand abraded my skin until Magnus somehow managed to turn over. Keeping hold of my hand, he lifted me and pulled me against him while the hundreds of pounds of debris battering us tried to tear us apart.

Then, he folded himself around me so that he took the brunt force of the rubble. He grunted once before riding the rest of the crumbling stairs to the bottom of the crater in silence. The dust and sand filling the air clogged my nose, but other than a rush of wind in my ears, the collapse was strangely hushed.

Our impact with the ground knocked me free of Magnus's hold, and I bounced away from him on my ass. Biting my lip until I drew blood, I remained quiet as every jarring impact threatened to break my bones.

I'd felt so strong after transitioning into my immortality; now, I felt drained from being in such proximity to the horsemen and their destructive, hate-filled nature. I could feel their depravity oozing from them like blood from a stab wound.

I loathed the way they made me feel and despised that they'd further perverted this once lush and thriving place into something vile.

When I came to a stop, I pushed myself onto my hands and knees and turned to search out Magnus. The cry I'd managed to keep suppressed tore free when I spotted him half hidden beneath a pile of rubble.

Scrambling on my hands and knees, I covered the distance between us with more speed than I'd ever possessed before. Not only did my new immortality fuel me, but so did the strength of our bond.

Magnus's silver eyes were dazed when his head turned toward me. Blood trickled from the corner of his mouth, but when he saw me, he jerked against the rocks, and his free hand stretched toward me.

"I'm going to get you out," I vowed.

I seized a hundred-pound rock and lifted it from him as hands fell on my shoulder. Screaming, I threw myself forward to tear free of the grasp. Lifting another stone, I spun and heaved it at whoever grabbed me.

My mother ducked to the side in time to avoid the rock, and when her eyes came back to me, they were wide with hurt. Then, her gaze latched onto my neck, her breath sucked in, and she stepped away from us.

"I'm sorry, I didn't... I didn't know it was you, Mohara," I stammered out an apology before digging into the pile again.

My fingernails splintered and broke away before starting to regrow; more of my blood continuously stained the stones I tossed aside. Able to move a little better, Magnus caught my hand when I reached for another rock.

"Run," he commanded in a gravelly voice as he stared at something beyond my shoulder.

They were coming for me, but it didn't matter. I would never leave him at their mercy. I yanked my hand away from him. "No."

"Amalia, run, *now*!"

Then more hands landed on me. The sound that came from me was animalistic and unlike anything I'd ever heard before. Kicking and squirming, I did everything I could to break free of the imprisoning hold. Turning, my eyes met Olgon's, and I went to kick him before someone else gripped my knees and raised them off the ground.

Olgon lifted my shoulders and hefted me above the ground while someone else claimed my feet. Twisting to see who held my knees, I met the sorrow-filled eyes of my father.

"Paupi, put me down, please!" I pleaded.

After a small hesitation, he shook his head.

I thrashed against their restraining hold as they carried me across the pit, away from Magnus. When they set me down, I saw the third jinni, the one who'd held my feet, was Nalki. The closing hole in his chest revealed the start of his reforming heart.

I lunged forward, but my father and Nalki grabbed my arms to restrain me as Olgon strolled a few steps ahead. Half a dozen jinn were forming a circle around Magnus.

"Don't hurt him!" I cried.

Magnus bellowed and started rocking himself back and forth until he tore himself free of the debris pinning him to the ground. Getting to his hands and knees, he crouched for a minute and leveled the jinn with a look promising destruction.

Then, Magnus sprang to his feet in a movement so fluid I barely saw it. His shoulders hunched as his horns curved out from the sides of his head. He didn't make another sound as he lowered his head and charged the jinni closest to him.

The jinni braced himself, but before Magnus reached him, three more versions of Magnus emerged from the original and circled the jinni. They were all identical to the original, right down to my bite on him. The jinni spun as he tried to figure out which one was real, and for a second, I was disoriented by the duplicates too, but when I focused on the one slightly to the left, I *knew* it was Magnus.

Then, Magnus buried his horns in the jinni's throat and jerked upward. The jinni's feet came off the ground before Magnus swung his head to the side and severed the jinni's neck in half. The jinni's head plopped onto the ground and rolled over.

My stomach twisted, and I tried to lift my hand to cover my mouth, but my father kept it pinned down. Death was the last thing I wanted for the jinn or Magnus, but more blood would spill before we escaped here. *If* we escaped here.

And that blood would forever stain my hands as I'd brought Magnus here, but the jinn started it when they aligned with the horsemen who they *never* should have brought here.

Fresh anger surged through me as I recalled the three monsters seated on their mounts close to Absenthees. I didn't dare take my attention off Magnus to look at them, but I could see their smug expressions from the corner of my eye.

What the jinn did to the Abyss was a travesty, and bringing those things here was a betrayal that cut far deeper than my bringing Magnus here. They were as eager to see jinn blood spilled as they were to see mine or Magnus's. How the jinn couldn't see that was beyond me, but the horsemen could *not* be allowed to remain here.

More images of Magnus sprang up around the pit. They weaved in and out as they circled the jinn until it was impossible to keep them all straight. I tried to remain focused on him, but a few times I lost him in the blur of movement.

Three more jinn fell at his hands while some of the others battled the illusions he created. Those jinn were left gaping at them when, if they hit them, the mirages dematerialized. The horsemen's twisted pleasure emanated from them as they watched Magnus destroy the jinn even though the jinn were their allies.

"Don't you see what the horsemen are? Don't you feel their malice?" I whispered to my father as the corners of Lust's mouth curved into a smile.

"Don't you see him killing jinn?" Olgon retorted without turning toward us.

My father's, troubled sun-colored eyes met mine before he glanced away.

"And you are trying to kill him," I said to Olgon before turning my attention to Nalki. "He has a right to defend himself, and he let you live when I asked it of him. Does that mean nothing to you?"

I sensed Nalki's uncertainty, but he wouldn't look at me as he whispered, "It does," so low that I barely heard him, but it didn't matter, there was nothing Nalki could do against so many.

Olgon's electric blue eyes were filled with hate when he looked at me over his shoulder. "He shouldn't be *here!*" he spat.

"And neither should the horsemen or the jinn!" I cried. "I spoke with Rislen; I know the truth! This was a fae land. We took it from them and twisted it into this atrocity!"

When Olgon turned dismissively away, fury blazed through me. I was *no* longer a child, and when it came to the Abyss, I understood it far better than the other jinn.

"Amalia, you are a sensitive being, but you must understand conquering is the way of all demons. Our ancestors took what they wanted and made it a land for the jinn, that is all," my father said as my mother walked over to stand next to him.

"Paupi," I whispered. "That's not all, and you know it. You must sense this place wasn't supposed to be like this. You are part fae too, you *have to* feel the Abyss aching to come alive again."

He refused to look at me, and I knew pleading with him would get me nowhere. "You feel it, don't you, Nalki?"

Nalki kept his gaze steadfastly on the battle. Even if they all felt it, they would never admit it. I blinked away the tears of frustration burning my eyes as Magnus destroyed another jinni. There were more than a dozen duplicates of him moving throughout the crater. The illusions couldn't kill but they provided a good distraction as Magnus made his way toward me.

Three of those mirages circled a jinni who spun as he tried to figure out if any of them were real. Two of the illusions dispersed when Magnus charged through them. The jinni turned toward Magnus as Magnus grasped his head, placed his foot on the jinni's chest and shoved him back.

The jinni's body flew across the pit while the head stayed in Magnus's grasp. Magnus released the head as if it were nothing more than a shoe he removed. Having regrouped enough to remain undistracted by the mirages and to focus on the real Magnus, four jinn jumped onto him.

"No!" I lunged against my restrainers hold on me.

Unprepared for the movement, or the ferocity of it, my father lost his hold, and I jerked Nalki forward three steps before my father snatched me back again.

"*NO!*" I shouted, nearly wrenching my shoulder from its socket as I struggled to tear free of them.

Two more jinn pounced on Magnus, and the sickening thud of fists hitting flesh filled the clearing. My stomach lurched when Magnus's legs gave out and he nearly went down. Catching himself before his knees hit the ground, Magnus lurched forward and sank his horns into the belly of a jinni. The woman screamed as Magnus propelled her into a wall, but the other jinn were already tearing him away from her and dragging him down.

"If he dies, I die, Paupi!" I screamed, and my father's eyes swung back to me. "He's my Chosen. Don't let them take him from me!"

Magnus managed to tear the heart from the chest of another jinni before they succeeded in pinning him down. He thrashed against their hold, but they yanked his hands behind his back, and two of them sat on his torso while two more kept his legs restrained.

Magnus's silver eyes were black with wrath when they met mine. Restricted like that, there was nothing he could do. None of the jinn would fall for his illusions, and cloaking himself would be useless while they held him.

I could not stand here and watch him die. I jerked forward again, but my father and Nalki didn't budge this time.

"Olgon, do not kill him!" my father shouted as Olgon approached Magnus.

A sneer curved Olgon's mouth when his gaze swung back to us. "*Don't* kill him?"

"He's Amalia's Chosen."

"Please," I pleaded. "I'll take him from here, and we'll *never* come back."

"And will you return their lives to them?" Olgon inquired and waved his hand at the six dead jinn littering the ground. I hadn't realized how much destruction Magnus waged until they succeeded in taking him down.

"You would defend yourself and your Chosen if you had one," I said. "That's all he was doing. You shouldn't have taken me from him."

"Until you brought him here, he had no reason to defend himself against us. We would not have attacked the Chosen of one of our own."

"But you did attack his camp, and you are attacking the Chosen of one of his *friends*! She may be dead already! You have also killed numerous friends of his! What you did to them and what you are continuing to do is wrong, and you know it! You *never* should have brought the horsemen here, and now you're allowing those *things* to cloud your judgment!"

"Things?" Lust purred.

Magnus jerked against the jinn holding him as a cold chill ran down my back. Lust's emerald eyes glittered with amusement when they swung toward me, but malevolence oozed from her.

"Now, now, I'm sure the child meant no insult," Pride said. "She's frightened for her Chosen."

"You could have helped us to bring the demon down," Olgon said to Sloth. "Before he killed so many of us."

Sloth covered his mouth with his hand as he faked a yawn. "Why would I?" he inquired. "I do so much enjoy a good show; the demon provided one for us. I was duly entertained and impressed."

"I must agree," Lust murmured. Full-blown rage tore through me when she licked her lips and eyed Magnus like a treat she intended to devour. "And what an attractive, enticing demon he is. I wonder...." Her voice trailed off as she ran a hand over her breasts and turned her attention back to me. "Perhaps we could keep him alive, but you must be made to pay as you did betray your kind and you did call us *things*. I've killed for less, and I could never allow such offenses to go unpunished."

My heart lodged in my throat when she nudged her horse, and the beautiful beast made its way toward Magnus.

"You *both* must be punished as this one follows the king." Lust swung from the back of her horse and landed on the ground. Her step was so light she seemed to float across the rocks as she made her way toward Magnus with her white hair trailing across the ground. "And the show this demon put on and the destruction he wrought is just so... *arousing*."

CHAPTER THIRTY-FIVE

Amalia

THE HUNGER EMANATING from Lust beat against me and left me with a hollow sensation. The jinn sitting on Magnus looked ready to bolt from her approach, but they stayed where they were, and Magnus remained helpless to escape them.

"I'm sorry! I didn't mean it!" I cried as Magnus shrank away from Lust.

"What must it be like for one Chosen to watch their lover fuck another," Lust pondered.

"No," I moaned. When she knelt at Magnus's side, my legs gave out. My father and Nalki kept me up, and my father cradled me closer to him.

"Olgon, stop this," my father said. "For Amalia to witness such a thing is a punishment worse than death."

The look on my mother's face mirrored my father's words as she spoke. "Olgon, do not allow this."

Olgon didn't acknowledge my parents as he remained focused

on Lust and Magnus. The indifferent air surrounding my uncle shredded my heart further. Until then, I'd held out some hope he would let his anger go and become the loving man he once was, but that Olgon was lost forever. This vengeful man had taken his place and would destroy anyone who he felt stood in his way.

"Let me take Amalia from here!" my father pleaded.

"She stays," Olgon stated.

"No!" my mother cried. "You don't understand! You don't know the bond! This will *destroy* her!"

"So be it."

"I'm taking you from here," my father said to me.

"Stop them if they try to leave," Olgon said to the jinn closest to him.

"*Kill* them if they try to leave," Pride commanded.

"Olgon—"

"Kill them if necessary," Olgon said to the jinn.

Nalki's hand tightened on my arm, not to keep me held back but because shock gripped him at this command. The same emotion radiated from some of the other jinn. My father stepped toward Olgon and the horsemen, but before he could speak, I did.

"It's not worth it, Paupi," I whispered. "Even if I don't see what happens, I'll *know* it did."

The lost look on his face blurred when tears spilled down my cheeks. My mother fell to her knees beside me. Wrapping her arms around me, she held me close.

"Don't watch, baby," she whispered.

I couldn't look away as Magnus attempted to lunge at Lust. His fangs snapped, and inhuman sounds issued from him while he struggled against the jinn. None of them looked thrilled about what they were doing, but their terror emanated from them and left a metallic taste on my tongue. They would not go against Olgon or the horsemen.

"Stay away from me!" Magnus spat at Lust.

Avoiding his fangs, Lust rested her hand on his forehead. The swell of her power rocked me backward. The jinn closest to her leaned away, and one of them fondled his crotch before shaking his head to clear it of the effects of Lust's powers; effects targeted at Magnus.

Any hope I held Magnus might be able to resist Lust's power vanished when he went completely still.

Panting for breath, I tried to keep myself under control as it felt like my heart fractured in my chest and the shards of it slipped into my bloodstream. Those shards shredded everything they came into contact with.

Nalki looked from me to Magnus and back again; his face reflected his dismay, but he didn't release me.

"Olgon—" Nalki started.

"Let him go," Lust commanded the jinn restraining Magnus. They didn't hesitate before they released him and scrambled away. "Rise, demon." Lust placed the tip of her finger under Magnus's chin and lifted his face toward her.

Magnus blinked, looking confused, but he rose. Lust stepped back, surveying his body while she circled him. I couldn't tear my gaze away from Magnus as he stared straight ahead with a glazed look in his eyes. Blood coated his chiseled face, hands, and clothes.

I wasn't much of fighter, but I'd kill everyone here for this, especially Lust. Red blurred my vision when she stopped before Magnus and grabbed his crotch.

"Oh," she breathed. "Perfect."

Magnus's brow furrowed when she touched him; a muscle in his cheek jumped before he started to recoil from her. Hope surged within me, but it was doused when Lust ran her finger over his lips, and he stilled again.

"Shh," Lust soothed.

"I'm going to kill her," I whispered.

My mother released me to lean back on her knees. She cupped my face and turned it toward her. I don't know what she saw there, but it caused her hands to tremble.

"Amalia?" she inquired.

But my attention returned to Magnus as his mounting confusion and distress beat against me. No matter what kind of thrall she had him under, he did *not* want this, but he couldn't break free of the hideous bitch.

My eyes ran over the jinn and horsemen blocking the way between him and me. I was outnumbered and probably the worst fighter here, but I would not allow this to happen without attempting to stop it. I didn't care if they killed me in the process. Watching this happen, having *Magnus* used in such a way while I did nothing, wasn't an option.

Not only would it destroy a part of me, but it would also destroy him. It didn't matter if this was his fault or not, what Lust planned to do to him would eat at him for the rest of his days. We hadn't known each other long, but even if Magnus wasn't in love with me, he cared for me deeply. I felt those emotions from him less than an hour ago.

We'd both be better off dead than have this happen, but I had to wait for the right moment, or I'd succeed in nothing more than the horsemen seeking to punish us further.

When Lust ran her hand across Magnus's chest, she smeared the blood over him before wiping it over her breasts. She left bloody streaks across her flesh as she caressed herself. "I am so going to enjoy this," Lust murmured.

My mother rose to stand beside my father. "Can we stop this?" she whispered to him.

"How?" he asked. "Olgon won't listen, and the horsemen and jinn are with him...."

Lust brought one blood-coated finger to her red lips before sucking it into her mouth. Everyone in the pit focused on her as the scent of her arousal grew stronger on the air. It was now or never.

Lurching forward, I broke free of Nalki and my father, though they'd both barely held me anymore. With natural grace, I leapt to my feet, sprinted around my mother, and raced forward. I may not be the fighter the rest of the jinn were, but I was faster than them, especially now that I was immortal and had a Chosen in danger. I dashed in and out of the jinn who sought to cut me off while others didn't bother to intervene.

Magnus! Get to Magnus!

Only twenty-five feet away.

Twenty.

Fifteen.

Magnus's eyes flicked to me, but I saw no acknowledgment in them. *I can't have lost him already, I just found him. Please don't take him from me!*

Ten feet.

From the corner of my eye, I spotted Lust's horse cantering toward me. *Fuck you! And the bitch who rode you in here!*

Bits of rock and sparks flew up as the horse skidded to a halt in front of me, cutting me off from Magnus with only five feet left to go.

Teeth snapped inches from my face, fetid breath washed over me, but I darted back to avoid the horse's jaws. The horse pivoted on its two hind hooves, planted its front, and lashed out with its back legs.

The hooves came at me in a blur that, even with all my speed, I wasn't fast enough to avoid. When they slammed into my chest, my breath exploded out of me. Some of my ribs gave way with an audible crack as I was lifted off the ground and flung backward. Air whipped around me; the world was nothing but a blur before I hit the ground on my back. I skidded across the rocks and came to a halt only feet from where I initially knelt.

Nalki and my parents had rushed after me when I first charged at Lust and were now twenty feet away from me. Their heads turned toward me; their wide eyes revealed their shock and worry. They ran back to me as I strained to draw air into lungs I was sure were deflated.

"Easy," Nalki said as he knelt next to me. "The more you fight, the worse it will feel. Relax."

Turning me on my side, he patted my back while I coughed up the blood threatening to suffocate me. Finally able to draw air into my brutalized chest, my vision cleared enough to see Magnus.

"Oh, that looks like it hurt," Lust taunted as her laughter echoed around the pit.

My mother knelt at my other side and brushed the hair away from my face while my father stood protectively in front of me.

Then, a thunderous wrath hit me so forcefully that my vision blurred again. Unable to understand the depth of the rage, it took me a few seconds to realize it was coming from Magnus and not me. Struggling to clear my mind, I blinked until I could focus again.

Magnus's eyes were nearly black when they met mine, and blood trickled from where his fangs pierced his bottom lip. He leapt at Lust, who had her back to him while she continued to laugh at me.

"You *whore!*" he bellowed as he dragged her down beneath him. His fists moved so fast his arms blurred while he pummeled her.

"Magnus!" I croaked in warning when Lust's horse spun toward him.

Magnus didn't show any sign of hearing me as Lust's beautiful face became a bloody, broken mass beneath him. For the first time, Sloth sat upright in his seat and kicked his horse's sides.

"Magnus!" This time my voice came out stronger, but he still didn't react to it as he remained focused on destroying Lust.

When Sloth rode up beside him, a wave of his power emanated across the pit. Magnus was drawing his arm back to hit Lust again when he froze and his arm fell limply to his side. Then, Sloth leaned over and rested his hand on Magnus's head.

My mouth went dry when Magnus collapsed on top of Lust. Ignoring the discomfort in my brutalized body, I staggered to my feet, but my father held me back.

"No," he murmured. "Now is not the time. They're not going to kill him."

"You don't know that," I whispered.

"Yes, I do. He's one of the king's men, and they want him alive. They would have already killed him otherwise."

Any further protest I might have made died when Pride rode up beside Magnus and Sloth. He gazed at Magnus's back before he lifted his head and those neon purple eyes met mine. "It seems," he said, "the Chosen bond is stronger than we realized. Interesting."

No one spoke, no one even breathed as he kept those eerie eyes focused on me.

"Take the demon and lock him away with the other one until we decide what to do with him," Pride commanded.

"And her?" Olgon asked with a backward wave at me.

"She remains here," Pride said. "The two of them will be kept apart, indefinitely."

Anguish filled me over not being able to see him, but I kept my mouth shut. At least Magnus would live, for now, and neither of us would have to endure Lust abusing him anytime soon. As long as we remained alive, there was a chance we could get out of this. I had no idea how, but I refused to give up hope.

"Take him away," Pride said and stared pointedly at some of the jinn. They rushed forward to lift Magnus off Lust's unmoving body. When one of the jinn reached for her, Pride held out a hand to stop him. "Leave her. Let her lie there and live with her failure."

My skin crawled at his callous words, but my gaze remained focused on the jinn carrying Magnus's body toward the pathway closest to what remained of the stairs. The jinn disappeared down the path before reemerging a few minutes later near the ruins.

CHAPTER THIRTY-SIX

Magnus

"Magnus. Magnus, wake up."

The persistent voice gradually penetrated the thick fog of sleep clinging to me. My head felt like a leporcháin demon battered it for hours with their caultin and a dull ringing resonated in my ears.

"Magnus! *Wake up!*"

The incessant voice was female I realized, and desperate.

"Amalia?" I murmured.

"Come on, Magnus, open your eyes."

I did as the woman commanded, only because I had to see Amalia again. Light burned my retinas, and I closed them against the searing pain it created. A groan issued from me before I silenced it.

"Stay with me, Magnus," the woman pleaded.

Not Amalia. The voice was familiar, but it wasn't Amalia's. Who then? What happened? *Where is Amalia?*

Memories surged back into my mind. The stairs, the jinn, *Lust!*

My newfound fangs lengthened at the memory of being frozen

before that hideous thing and the sickening feeling of her hands on me; all while Amalia was forced to look on helplessly. I bolted upright as I worried the woman speaking to me might be that *bitch!*

I'd kill her this time. I wouldn't let my temper get the best of me and only beat her. No, this time, I'd tear Lust's head from her shoulders and force her blood down the throats of Pride and Sloth. I would make them choke while they feasted on her.

My teeth clenched when I recalled watching Amalia fly through the air after the horse kicked her. The sight of it finally pierced through Lust's hold over me, and I would never allow that bitch to get her hooks into me again.

Slowly, I took in my surroundings as I tried to get my bearings. I sat with my back propped against a wall, and when I glanced at it, I saw it was made of solid sandstone, as was the ground beneath me. They'd taken me to the runes after Sloth knocked me out. There were bars in front of me, bars to the right, to my left were more bars, and... *Wren!*

She stood, staring down at me from her cell. A sad, crooked smile curved her lips when her blue eyes, flecked with green, met mine. Her pale blonde hair, pulled into a disheveled knot, hung against her nape. Always slender and athletic in build, she'd lost weight while here as her cheekbones were sharper.

"Hello, sleeping beauty, or bruised beauty might be the better description," she greeted.

"Wren?" I asked.

"That's my name."

"What are you doing *here*?"

"I'm guessing the same thing as you. Where's Corson?"

Her imprisonment had worn her down, but it hadn't dimmed her willful nature. I couldn't stop myself from scowling at her. "You're probably not doing the same thing here as me, as I'm physically here while you're only mentally present. And Corson isn't in this place; he was never trapped."

"He's free," she breathed, and tears shimmered in her eyes. "Oh, thank you." Then she lunged at the bars and encircled her hands around them. "Is he okay?"

"He's holding up," I assured her.

"Good. Good." She inhaled a jerky breath as she took a minute to compose herself. "Mentally here," she murmured. "That makes sense."

"Why does that make sense?"

"I've tried everything to get out of this place without success. However, I'm assuming it would be more difficult to break out of a mental prison than a physical one. You can physically flee your surroundings, but you can never escape your mind."

"True," I agreed.

I sat and waited for her to vanish now that she'd learned the truth, but she remained where she was.

"What?" she asked and rubbed her face. "Do I have a booger or something on me?"

"When the others fully realized they didn't belong here, or it was all in their minds, they disappeared."

"Where did they go?"

"The jinn's spell on them broke, and they returned to their bodies. Those who returned are fine."

"The jinn," she spat the word like she'd tasted something sour. "I should have realized those *assholes* had a hand in this."

"And so do some of the horsemen."

"Of course they do."

"Did they bring a woman in here with me? Have you seen someone named Amalia?"

"No, some guys brought you in, dumped you in the cell, and left. There are some more cells down the hall, but there's no one in them. Who is Amalia?" Her gaze fell to the marks on my neck. "Is she your *Chosen*?"

"Yes, and I have to find her."

"Good luck getting out of here. I've tried everything."

"Then we'll try everything again, plus some."

She stared at me for a minute before grinning. "Yes, we will." Then her smile slid away. "Wait... you said those who *returned* are fine. What about those who didn't return, and how many were affected by this, and *where are we*?"

I explained to her everything that happened while she was in here. By the time I finished, she'd settled on the floor with her shoulder against the bars and her head leaning on them.

"So many lives," she murmured. "But why am I still here? I knew this place wasn't right before the bars appeared."

"I don't know," I said. "And what do you mean before the bars appeared?"

"When I first got here, there were no bars, and I was a part of the show. However, though I was a part of it, it didn't feel right, and I don't think I ever left the vicinity of this cell."

"What show?"

Placing her hands on the floor, she pushed herself up. "Come here."

She walked to the front bars and turned expectantly back to me. Every muscle in my body felt like they'd been run over by a truck, but I gritted my teeth and rose. Shuffling forward, I drew on the strength of the Chosen bond as I willed myself to heal faster with every pain-filled step.

Amalia was still alive, I would know if she were dead, but where was she and what were they doing to her? While I remained a walking bruise, I would never be able to get out of here and to her.

Stopping at the bars, I slid my arms through them and craned my head to look for the other cells Wren mentioned. The movement made me wince, but I spotted the cells diagonally across from Wren's. Their doors were open, and no one was inside as Wren had said.

A solid wall was ten feet across the hallway from me, and

judging by the near perfect condition of everything, I suspected we were in the third-story section of the ruins.

"It's starting again," Wren murmured.

I turned my attention forward as the sandstone walls of the hallway faded to white ones. The sudden beep of a machine sounded in the distance and chairs materialized against the wall as blue swinging doors replaced the bars of the other cells.

It took me a minute to realize the hallway had been replaced with one of the humans' hospitals. People in white lab coats, carrying charts or pushing wheelchairs, rushed back and forth. They scurried around as they barked orders at each other while shouting for medical supplies.

Other people walked around as if in a daze, their hands to their heads or with bandages swathed around their arms. The details were vivid enough that the fluorescent lights above gleamed off the white floor and sneakers squeaked on the tile.

The set of blue swinging doors burst open, and a gurney wheeled into the hall. A man pushed the gurney while a woman straddled the patient lying on it. She used her hands to pump his chest up and down; when they got closer, I realized the woman was Wren. Sweat dripped from her forehead, and her pretty face was scrunched with determination as she worked on the man.

"Originally, I felt the man's chest beneath my hands and was a part of it, but once I realized it wasn't real, I was relegated to the cell," Wren explained.

"Yet you continue to be in the scene," I murmured.

"I think part of the fun for them is making me watch over and over again."

"Watch what?"

"You'll see."

The scene shifted to reveal Wren standing outside a door marked operating room. Another young woman and two men about her age stood with her. Wren's blue scrubs were replaced with a pair of jeans and a blue sweater.

When the door swung open, a doctor emerged to let Wren know the patient would live. She smiled and politely thanked him, but when the doctor went back through the doors, she let out a cry of joy. One of the men enveloped her in a hug, lifted her off her feet, and swung her around. Then, they kissed.

In the cell beside me, Wren cringed and bowed her head.

"Who is he?" I inquired.

"I don't know," she said, "but apparently in that world, he's my boyfriend or something."

The man set her down and kissed her again. "We have to go out and celebrate!" he declared.

"I can't," Wren replied. "I have to meet my parents for dinner."

"After dinner?"

"After dinner," she promised.

Then, the scene shifted again to reveal Wren sitting in a restaurant with her napkin on her lap. She had a forkful of food lifted halfway to her mouth, but she ignored it as she eagerly regaled the couple sitting across from her with the details of her day.

Gray tinged the couple's hair and wrinkles lined their eyes and mouths. Judging by their similar features to Wren and the love in their eyes, these were the parents she'd told her boyfriend about. Parents who, in this world, had been killed when the gateway opened.

"And then the doctor came out and said he's going to live!" Wren gushed before shoving her spaghetti into her mouth.

"That's fantastic," her mother said.

Her father rested his hand on Wren's. "We're so proud of you."

Beside me, I scented Wren's tears, but I didn't look at her. She would hate it if I saw her cry.

They exchanged more stories about their lives, and I came to realize this was a weekly dinner date for them. It was a time for them to catch up with their daughter, who was a resident in a hospital an hour away from their home.

When the meal came to an end, they exchanged hugs, and her parents promised to let her know they'd arrived home safely before saying their goodbyes.

"I miss them so much," Wren whispered beside me. "This... this is what they would look like now if they'd lived. I *know* it is. They would have come to visit me weekly, and I would have looked forward to *every* one of their visits."

I glanced at her as she wiped the tears from her eyes and straightened her shoulders. Then, the scene shifted again to reveal Wren sitting in her car. She dialed her phone, and I realized she was speaking with her boyfriend when she told him she'd meet him in twenty minutes.

Wren hung up before pulling out of the parking lot and driving through a green light. She was halfway through the intersection when a truck barreled through a red light and toward her car. Brakes squealed but not in time to stop the truck from crashing into the driver's side door of her car and spinning it around into another vehicle. The screeching of metal reverberated outside the cell before Wren's car skidded to stop a hundred feet away from where it was initially hit.

Within the car, Wren's head lulled at an awkward angle on her broken neck.

Then, the scene vanished.

CHAPTER THIRTY-SEVEN

Magnus

"Every few minutes it loops through the same thing," Wren said and turned away from the bars. She walked to the back of the cell and slid down the wall to sit on the floor again. "Thankfully, you can't see or hear it from back here. There's only so many times I can watch myself die, although the first time, I actually heard and felt my neck snap. It was horrible."

"You experienced your death?" I asked.

"Yes. Well, sort of. The mortal version of me died in that world, but I was still alive when the scene started over."

"Your torment is different from the others we witnessed, probably because the jinn and horsemen want you alive."

"Why?"

"Because you are Corson's Chosen and few are closer to the king than he is."

Fire blazed from her eyes when they met mine. "They're in for a rude fucking awakening then because I won't allow them to use me for anything."

I smiled at her before glancing at the hall. "What made you realize something was wrong in here?"

"His kiss," she said. "Real or not, it felt so *wrong*. I went through the entire play once, but when he kissed me the second time, I almost threw up and my hand went to Corson's marks." Lifting her hand, she rested it against the fading marks on her neck. "Touching them woke me up to what was happening."

"Then what happened?" I asked.

Gripping the bars, I braced my feet against the cell door as I attempted to pull the bars apart. They didn't so much as groan, never mind bend or move in any way. My shoulder popped, my injuries protesting every movement, but I strained harder on them. Nothing.

"Then, I woke to find myself in here, and that... *that* playing over and over again. Do you want to know the weird thing?"

"Always."

"I think it's real. I mean, I know it's some kind of movie or something, but I think that's the way my life would have gone if the gateway never opened. I think I would have gone to school to become a doctor and dated the cute resident. My parents and I would have remained close, but it all would have come to a screeching halt the night I died in that car accident."

I stopped yanking on the bars to look at her. "The jinn cannot reveal the future in such a way, and none of our paths are set for us. Free will tends to get in the way of that."

"Maybe, but something about what happened out there feels *right*. For so long, I wished many things were different in my life. I wished my parents had lived and the gateway never opened, but I think if it remained closed, I would have died young. I think the death I was supposed to have in *that* world transferred over to this world when Greed's horse pummeled me beneath its hooves and becoming a demon is the only thing that stopped it."

"That's not the way things work."

"Then why does it feel so real?"

"Because the jinn are very good at imprisoning people in their thoughts. Before coming here, did you make a wish to someone?" I asked.

"No."

"You didn't wish life could be different? Or that the gateway never opened and demons never came to Earth?"

"I said *no!*" she retorted. "I realized years ago longing for things I could never have was pointless. Besides, I *never* would wish for it now that I have Corson. *Never!*"

"I believe you."

I turned my attention back to the bars. I was still weakened from my fight and probably feeling some lingering effects from Sloth's ability, but I should be able to do something with these bars.

"I told you, they don't budge," Wren said.

"Hmm." I made my way around the cell, jerking on every bar I could, but none of them moved.

Glancing around the cell again, I stared at the sandstone floor before turning my attention to the ceiling where I spotted the large, circular symbol carved five feet over my head.

The circle encompassed a rotated square forming a diamond and another square imposed behind it. The squares held numerous lines etched into different angles that became a maze throughout them. At the center of the maze, a monolith shape rose tall.

"I don't know what those markings are," Wren said, and I realized there was an identical etching in the ceiling of her cell.

"Ancient symbols. When I saw them on the monolith, I assumed they might be some form of demonish, but it's something different."

"What?"

"I think it's a binding mark."

"But if they're not demonic, then what are they?"

I rubbed my chin as I pondered this. "If they're on the monolith, then they must be fae. But why would the fae need a prison? Unless...."

My voice trailed off while I inspected our surroundings again. My mind spun as I tried to puzzle it out.

"Unless what?" Wren prodded after a few minutes.

"Unless the fae had more abilities than anyone realized. They didn't have abilities that manifested themselves physically, like your talons or my illusions, but inner ones that revealed themselves in this world and in their symbols."

"Like they're witches or something?"

"The fae could be where the legend of witches came from, though they were known for their fair beauty and didn't wear pointed hats. They also didn't cast spells."

"Or maybe they did," Wren said as she rose to her feet. "Not like a cauldron kind of spell, but maybe some other type, and maybe those markings are their spells."

"It could be possible. There is power in symbols as evidenced by the ones that once held up the seals. I'd bet the fae learned the power of these symbols from Absenthees. The mark above us is something they took from the monolith to help them fight their enemies. We'd assumed the fae were pushed out of the Abyss without a fight, and maybe it didn't become a physical altercation, but they did try to resist the jinn. The fae must have placed some of the jinn into these cells before they were overrun, and that symbol made it so they couldn't escape."

"So how do we get out of here?" Wren asked.

"Have you tried destroying the symbol?"

"No, but I didn't think it was a mystical binding thing either."

No, she probably wouldn't have put the two together. She'd never seen the seals.

"Besides, I'm not entirely sure destroying some ancient,

mystical binding thing is a good idea," she said. "When the seals fell, they pretty much destroyed Hell."

"Maybe it's not a good idea, but it's the only one we have."

Grasping the bars, I locked my legs around them and started to climb.

CHAPTER THIRTY-EIGHT

Amalia

I KEPT my attention diverted between the horsemen and the ruins where they'd taken Magnus. Having slightly recovered, Lust dragged herself into a seated position a few minutes ago and propped herself against the wall.

I couldn't help but feel pleased she looked as bewildered as she did beaten. She'd never imagined someone might be able to resist her once she unleashed her power on them, but she'd never encountered someone like Magnus before.

He resisted her because of me.

Tears pricked my eyes, and my heart swelled. Not only was I terrified for him and worried about where they'd taken him, but I'd also fallen in love with my Chosen. I think I'd been in love with him since he handed me those flowers.

There had to be a way to get out of this and get to him, but I had no idea how—not while they were surrounding me. I was already healing. My ribs were only fractured instead of broken, and my internal bleeding had stopped. Soon, I would heal enough to make a move, but I needed a plan for when that time came.

Think, Amalia.

My head spun as the jinn who'd taken Magnus away returned to the pit. *I will get us out of this. I will figure this out.*

I didn't know where he was in those ruins, but if the jinn had returned, then he was secured somehow. He was still alive, I would feel it if they'd killed him, but what had they done to him?

My parents stood beside me; my mother's hand rested on my shoulder while my father surveyed everything with his arms crossed over his chest. Their disapproval thrummed against my skin as did their love for me. They'd followed Olgon, they'd picked this path, but they did not sign up for this.

But then, they probably hadn't expected me to do the things I'd done either. No matter our different paths, they would try to protect Magnus as they understood the Chosen bond, and they wouldn't risk losing me should the horsemen decide Magnus should die.

Olgon and Pride stood near Absenthees, occasionally glancing at me while they spoke. This close to the monolith, its power electrified my skin, but I could also feel its wrongness, just as so many things were wrong in the Abyss.

Behind Pride, his horse shifted, and its tail twitched in annoyance while it surveyed the crowd. Nalki moved to stand a few feet in front of us and to my left. Some of the jinn still blocked the pathways leading into the pit, others clustered into a small group, and the rest stood near the monolith. All of them were unusually subdued; their uneasiness drifted from them in waves reminding me of ripples spreading across a pond.

Thinking about water made my heart ache as I recalled my too brief time with Magnus beside the pool and the life we'd returned to that area of the Abyss. I glared at my uncle before studying the ruins again. There was still no sign of Magnus or anyone who may be up there watching over him.

They wouldn't leave him alone, would they?

No, there is no way they would feel confident in doing that. Unless it was impossible to escape wherever he was located, or maybe Sloth could keep him unconscious for hours or days.

"We won't let them hurt you," my mother said for what felt like the hundredth time.

I believed she would try to keep them from doing so, but what were the three of us versus the jinn and three horsemen? Not much at all considering Sloth knocked Magnus out with a touch of his hand.

And I didn't want anything to happen to my parents.

Olgon and Pride broke apart. The smirk on Pride's face as he sauntered toward us caused my hand to fist with the urge to hit him. Walking beside Pride, my uncle's face was expressionless, but I sensed his fury.

Taking a deep breath, I lifted my chin. There may not be much we could do against them, but I refused to cower before these *pricks*.

"Have you come to a decision?" I asked as I held Olgon's gaze.

"We have," Pride replied.

Knowing it would infuriate the most arrogant of the horsemen, I refused to acknowledge Pride. "And?" I asked Olgon.

Pride kept his face impassive, but a wave of annoyance washed off him. I bit back a smug smile. *I'm an empath, asshole; you can't hide your feelings from me.*

"And," Olgon said, "if Rislen revealed our heritage to you, that means you have spoken to her recently *and* returned to the Earth plane."

A shiver of foreboding raced down my spine. I didn't know where he was going with this, but I suspected it wouldn't be good.

"So?" I inquired with more bravado than I felt.

"You are Magnus's Chosen, we hold you both prisoner, and we also hold Corson's Chosen. Magnus and Corson are friends of Kobal's, but Astaroth tells us Corson is closer, and we want him too."

"And you are going to return to Earth and bring us to Corson," Pride said. "You must have met him if you encountered Magnus."

"I haven't," I lied.

"Your eyes give you away, Amalia," Olgon murmured. "Do not lie to us; it will be *your* Chosen who suffers the consequences of it."

I almost spat at him that he was family, but I bit the words back. I was family too, and I brought an enemy into the Abyss. It didn't matter to Olgon I did it to save lives. He was determined to destroy those lives.

"Even if Corson is close to the king, you have to know Kobal won't risk everything to come here and try to save him," I said.

"Of course he won't," Pride purred.

"Then why do you want Corson?" I asked Olgon.

"Because Corson knows things about the king no one else knows," Olgon replied.

"He'd never tell you anything that could be used against his king."

"Maybe not normally," Pride said. It took all I had to keep my focus on Olgon. "But he'll do anything for his Chosen, and he most certainly won't be able to stand seeing her tormented in any way."

Don't react. Don't react. Even if my eyes gave me away to Olgon, Pride wouldn't know how to read my emotions yet.

"I'm not bringing you to Corson," I stated.

"But you are," Pride purred.

Behind his back, Lust rose to her feet. Swollen and bruised, her face resembled a half-smooshed tomato, but she was healing fast. Grasping her horse's mane, she pulled herself onto its back and settled there. I hoped one day I'd get to watch her and her asshole beast meet with a horrific fate.

Lust's head lulled forward before snapping up. She nudged the horse toward us and stopped beside Pride's steed. Sloth remained near the monolith with his eyes closed; he appeared to have fallen asleep, but I suspected he was listening.

"She and that filthy demon will be cut apart piece by *tiny* piece, and they will watch it happen to each other!" Lust vowed. "Then, I will feed them to each other before starting the process all over again."

I inwardly recoiled at the prospect of such a thing happening while Lust's green eyes burned into mine. I didn't know what possessed me, but I smiled at her. *Drop dead, bitch.*

I'd never known someone so beautiful could become so ugly, but her face twisted into a rage that blurred her features into something hideous and unrecognizable. For a second, Lust's face mirrored her insides.

"I'm going to kill her," Lust snarled.

Pride held up a hand, forestalling her when she went to dismount. "Not yet," he said.

"Look at what that demon did to me!" she spat at him.

"You should have suspected the Chosen bond would make him capable of withstanding your power. Your hubris did that to you. Do not forget, you are Lust, not *me.*"

If Pride could feel the hatred Lust emitted when she pinned him with her stare, I suspected he would have killed her, or at least tried. However, after her brief lapse with me, she'd composed her face into a blank expression again. Outwardly, she showed no signs of loathing toward her fellow rider, but inwardly she seethed with it.

The horsemen are not as close as they seem.

"We need her alive to do as we bid, and if we kill the demon, she'll be useless to us," Pride continued.

Some of Lust's hatred waned until it smoldered beneath the surface like a burning ember.

"Now, child," Pride said to me.

This time when I refused to look at him, his hand shot out and he gripped my chin. His finger dug into my flesh, bruising it but not drawing any blood as he forced my head toward him. I tried to break free of his touch before he could poison me with his overly arrogant ways, but he was keeping his power confined, for now.

My mother shifted beside me, and her hand tightened on my shoulder. "This is my daughter," she hissed from between her teeth. "Do *not* hurt her."

Pride's eyes flicked toward her; I tensed to defend her as I waited for him to attack. *No* one told *Pride* what to do. But he glanced dismissively away from her.

"I'm not playing games with you, child." Pride's fingers dug into my chin until my skin broke, blood trickled free, and his nail scraped my bone. A muscle twitched in my clenched jaw, but I didn't make a sound. "I'll tear those beautiful eyes from your head and personally hand them to your Chosen unless you do what I command."

"She's not to be hurt," my father said and stepped toward him.

"Paupi, no!" I cried and threw out my hand to snatch his back before he could touch Pride.

The horseman may not be infecting me yet, he needed me for something, but he would have no qualms about taking down my father.

"You are going to take us to where Kobal's followers are hiding," Pride said.

"No, I'm not," I replied.

"Yes, you are, because if you don't, I'm going to take you to Corson's Chosen and I'm going to make you watch as I cut off her hair. Then I'm going use her hair to tie a pretty blonde bow around the ears, lips, and nose I'll also cut from her. I'm going to make sure you *personally* hand the package to Corson when you do agree to take us to him."

My belly clenched at the possibility, and when Pride smirked, I knew my eyes had shifted colors to give away at least something of my emotions.

"You don't like that," he purred as he rubbed my chin. "And you don't know his Chosen, do you?"

"We've... ah... we've never spoken," I admitted.

"Yet the idea of her suffering in such a way upsets you, how sweet. You truly do have the loveliest eyes, child; I knew some fae before we were locked away. Exquisite creatures, spineless, but exquisite." Lifting his head, he focused on something over my head. His expression became distant as if he were remembering something, and a smile curved his mouth. "One time, I tore the spine from a fae for fun; her screams were as enchanting as she was."

Where his finger dug into my skin, a spreading sickness seeped into my system. I could feel his rot seeping into me, and it took all I had not to knock his hand away, but he'd make me pay if I did.

"Now," Pride said, and his attention returned to me, "I'll tell you what I'm going to do to *your* Chosen. First, I'll cut off his cock, and while he's still screaming from that"—he seized my hand before I saw him move and lifted it before me, gripping my index finger—"I'm going to cut off his fingers, but not all at once. Oh no, I'm going take them apart knuckle by knuckle before starting on his toes and doing the same. Then, I'm going to slice him from groin to gullet and dissect him one piece at a time until—"

"Stop," I moaned.

He leaned so close to me that our noses nearly touched, and the neon lavender of his eyes deepened to a purple, the same color as the calamut leaves. The sexual arousal emanating from him caused my sick, tainted feeling to grow. I didn't want to give him the satisfaction of looking away, but I couldn't hold his gaze anymore.

His breath tickled my nose and lips when he spoke again. "Everyone thinks Death is the worst horseman, but they're wrong. It's *me*. And do you know *why* it's me?"

I shook my head no, and his finger scratched against my chin bone. I barely registered pain, but I cringed at the sound it made.

"Speak up, child. I can't hear you," Pride purred

"No," I whispered.

"No, *what?*"

"No, I don't know why you are the worst of the horsemen," I said.

Releasing my chin, he rose to his full height again. "Then, let me educate you!" he cried with a zeal bordering on insanity. "The humans dubbed me the deadliest of the sins, but as you know, the dimwitted humans separated the sins from the horsemen when we are all one in the same. I suspect this is because, as mortals, humans believe nothing can be worse than death. We both know that's wrong though, don't we?"

"Yes," I said when he paused long enough that I realized he expected an answer from me.

"Ah, yes, so the humans fear death the most," he sighed. "But my fellow rider, Death, simply kills you, but there is no fun in that. The fun is in the *play*. I am the horseman who takes great *pride* in making suffering an exquisite, eternal thing. *I* am the horseman many humans called the boogeyman and hid under their beds from; I am the one demons *cower* from.

"I am the horseman *no* one can avoid. Not everyone falls victim to gluttony or sloth. Not everyone gives in to their lusts and greed. Not everyone goes to war or experiences famine; there are even those rare beings who never know envy. Many know rage, but there are some who *never* experience true wrath. And, if immortals play their cards right, they may never experience death. I mean, look at how old some of the angels are. Look at how old *we* are."

I had no idea how old the horsemen were; I wasn't sure anyone knew. They'd been sealed away after the jinn, but that was only because the horsemen had probably been harder to trap.

"But everyone, and I do mean everyone, experiences at least

one second of pride in their lives. *Children* take pride in things before they can name the emotion they're experiencing. All the other horsemen can be avoided, but no one avoids *me*."

He was so smug he didn't realize his arrogance would be his ultimate demise. If that time ever came.

"And I am far more twisted than my fellow riders," he said.

I couldn't help but glance at Lust when I felt the smallest trickle of apprehension from her. *She's afraid of him.*

I gulped before meeting Pride's beautiful eyes again.

"You're going to take us to the others now," he said to me.

I opened my mouth to say no, but the word froze in my throat. I'd rather die than give into these creatures, and I could say no if this were as simple as my death. I would sacrifice myself to help stop the spread of the horsemen's evil, but what Pride intended to do to the three of us was a fate far worse than death.

And what will he do once you give into him? He's not going to let you walk away; he's not going to free Magnus or Wren. And with Corson in his hands, what could he learn about the king?

"No," I croaked.

The simple word was the toughest one I'd ever spoken, but once it left my mouth, I knew it was right.

There was a moment in which it didn't seem as if he heard my response, and then fury emanated from him.

"I was hoping you would say that; more fun for me," he lied.

I didn't get a chance to reply as he turned, grabbed my mother's head, and tore it from her shoulders before anyone could react. I recoiled when her hot blood sprayed over my face and clothes. A scream rose and lodged in my throat when her body toppled in front of me. Pride released her head, which thumped on the rocks before rolling to settle near my mother's shoulders.

The scream burst free of me as I collapsed to my knees. "*No!*"

Pride's hand landed on my shoulder. Bearing down on me, he dug my knees painfully into the rocks as he pinned me in place.

Through tear-filled eyes, I turned my bleary gaze to my father as strange, choked sounds tore from him. Collapsing beside me, he gathered my mother's body into his arms and sobbed while he rocked back and forth.

"Vya," he whimpered in a voice I didn't recognize.

I did this to him; to her. I did this!

No, he did this!

Lifting my head, I glowered at Pride as my heart shredded into a thousand pieces.

CHAPTER THIRTY-NINE

Magnus

W HEN I MADE it to the top of the bars, I kept my legs and one hand locked on them. From here, the mark was only a foot away from me. I stretched out with my free hand and felt over the symbol. I'd expected it to be etched into the ceiling, or maybe branded onto it, but it was smooth against the sandstone, almost as if it were a part of it.

Frowning, I pulled my hand away and examined the marking more closely. "There has to be a way to break it."

Rereleasing the bar, I used the side of my hand to rub at the mark. I scrubbed until my skin scraped off and my blood stained the ceiling, but the symbol remained untouched.

"You know," Wren said, "I think if it were as simple as rubbing a piece of the symbol away, they wouldn't have put it within easy reach of the bars."

I didn't reply as I rubbed harder, but the mark remained fully intact. Drawing my fist back, I ignored the discomfort in my body as I battered the ceiling. My knuckles broke open, more blood spilled free, but I ignored it as I was determined to tear through the symbol and rip it to shreds.

Minutes later, sweat slid down my cheeks, my battered body ached, my hand was broken, and I hadn't made so much as a scratch on the surface. The only difference in the marking was my blood drying on it.

"*No!*" The scream tore my attention away from the symbol as the word rebounded down the hallways and echoed throughout the ruins.

Amalia! I recognized the voice instantly and the anguish in it.

What had they done to her? What were they *doing* to her?

I'll kill them ALL!

Releasing the bars, I landed on the ground as her scream reverberated in my head. My shoulders heaved, and my horns curved away from my head. The still new sensation of them sliding forward was strange, but it came with a rush of power that I felt all through my body.

"Who was *that?*" Wren stared at the back wall of her cell as if she could somehow see through it. When her head turned toward me, her eyes were haunted, but then her jaw dropped. "Magnus, your horns!"

I have to get out of here! I have to get to her!

Clutching the bars again, I forgot any pain as I ascended and, without thinking, battered my horns into where my blood stained the ceiling. Whereas my fists had failed to penetrate the symbol, my horns caused bits of sandstone to break free and rain down on me. I pulled my head back and slammed my horns into the ceiling again.

As more dust broke free, the bars wobbled and a faint grinding noise sounded from somewhere above me.

"Magnus," Wren said slowly. "I... ah... I'm not sure that's a great idea. It sounds a little—"

The rest of her words were drowned out when I rammed my

horns into the symbol again. My horns took the brunt of it, but this blow jarred my spine all the way to my tailbone. Head throbbing, I pounded the ceiling with my horns again.

I don't care if I break every bone in my body, I'll destroy this thing.

Pulling my head back, I was about to ram the symbol again when the low grinding noise became an ominous groan.

It's booby-trapped.

I had only a second to register this, release the bars, and lunge toward the front of my cell before debris broke free from above to pelt my shoulders and back. A chunk of building the size of a boulder hit me between my shoulder blades and knocked me to one knee.

When another one crashed onto my other shoulder, I fell to my knees. Debris piled up on my back so fast I was certain it would bury me alive. Dust clogged my nostrils and filled my mouth when I drew in a breath.

Choking, I tried to spit out the cascading rubble, but there was no escaping it. My next breath brought the debris all the way into my lungs.

"Magnus!" Wren's scream barely penetrated through the thunderous clatter of my grave falling around me.

Amalia! I have to get to her.

The thought of her gave me a fresh wave of strength. When I stretched my arm out, my fingers curled around a large rock, and I used it as leverage to pull myself out from under the crushing weight of debris. Rocks slid away from my back as I strained to pull myself forward inch by excruciatingly slow inch.

And then, some of the weight gave way enough for me to scramble to my feet. The rubble causing the floor to rise beneath my feet forced me to run in a hunched-over position toward the front of the cell. I would have only one chance at freedom before everything collapsed on top of me.

Lowering my shoulders, I ran full speed at the bars.

Amalia

Pride lifted my mother's head from the ground and held it before me. I recoiled from her unseeing eyes and gaping mouth.

"Are you going to tell me no again?" Pride asked as he waved her head at me.

He wanted to see me break and watch me crumble, and I was so close to doing that, but I couldn't. If I did, he'd destroy me, and I would *never* give him that satisfaction.

"You bastard," I whispered.

My father lunged for the head, an inhuman sound issuing from him. His hand snatched at the air and came up with nothing as Pride swung it beyond his grasp.

"Give her to me!" my father bellowed.

I winced at the raw agony pouring from him, but gradually his sorrow became replaced with a building rage that would make the erinyes proud. And the erinyes demons more than lived up to the name the humans had given them—furies.

When my father leapt at Pride again, I dove forward and wrapped my arms around his waist. I managed to stop him from grabbing the horseman. "Paupi, please no," I pleaded.

The death of my mother also doomed my father, but I craved a few more minutes with him, and I did not want Pride to destroy him. The lump in my throat threatened to choke me as my father's emotions poured from him. My parents had spent over eighteen thousand years as each other's Chosen.

I could only hope Magnus and I might have the time they'd shared, but to lose someone after so many years, and after enduring so much with them, was a loss I couldn't fathom, but I felt it from my father. He may still be breathing and speaking, but he was essentially a living corpse.

When my father struggled to break out of my arms, Nalki intervened and helped me restrain him.

"No, Eron," Nalki murmured. "Your death will solve nothing."

My father collapsed like someone pulled the bones from his body. Sobbing, he gathered my mother's body to him again.

"Now," Pride said, his eyes focused on me. "Will you take us to them, or shall I get *your* Chosen?"

Around me, the shock of some of the jinn was fading to become replaced with disbelief and anger over the murder of my mother. Their postures were rigid as they glanced from my mother to Pride and back again. In his arrogance, Pride miscalculated the depth of the jinn's loyalty to each other compared to him. And so had Olgon as some of them turned angry eyes toward my uncle.

But not all of the jinn were angry; some were fine with what happened, and they would allow Pride to do as he pleased. Olgon was one of them. The knowledge his brother would die hadn't fazed him.

"Child—"

A sudden vibration rocking the ground caused Pride's words to break off. I stared at the rocks beneath my knees, half expecting the ouroboros to have returned to life and burst from the rocks.

Embracing my father, I pulled him closer, and Nalki released him. My heart thundered in my chest. I waited for a fissure to race across the ground as the earth split apart to swallow us whole. Maybe the Abyss finally had enough of being abused and decided to destroy us all. I wouldn't blame it if it had.

My father shook in my arms, but his tears had dried and his eyes burned with rage. Except this time, he wasn't glaring at Pride. No, he focused his hatred on Olgon.

The rumbling became a crescendo reverberating throughout the valley and quaked the walls behind me. Debris broke free and bounced down the wall before pelting my back. My father grunted when a large stone caught him in the head, but he didn't attempt to protect himself from further injury.

I tried to pull my father away from the rubble jarring loose behind us, but Pride remained in our way, and I didn't want my paupi anywhere near that monster. Beside us, Nalki hunched over and threw his arms protectively over his head.

What is going on?

I folded myself over my broken father to protect him from the more massive falling rocks and gritted my teeth when they pelted my back. And then, the rain of them eased, though the ground still quaked. I chanced a glance up to discover Nalki leaving himself less protected as he knocked some of the larger rocks away from us.

Then, the ground heaved and thrust us all forward as a rending noise filled the air.

"Amalia!" my father cried. He wrenched free of my arms, threw himself over me, and pinned me to the ground. This brief return to reality for him wouldn't last, but this glimpse of the man he'd been before these bastards destroyed him was wonderful to see.

Then, the ground stopped shaking, and I found the ensuing quiet nearly as terrifying as the disturbance.

Lifting my head, I looked up in time to see rocks and sand blow outward from the ruins. The thick cloud of debris exploding over the top of the crater sent some of the jinn scurrying away as boulders whistled through the air before crashing to the ground. Rocks hit the monolith and bounced away, but none of them left so much as a scratch on the metallic surface.

"*Magnus!*" I screamed, somehow knowing he'd done this. "*Magnus!*"

Clawing at the ground, I started to drag myself out from under my father when he released me. Probably because he wouldn't have let anyone stand in his way of getting to my mother.

I leapt to my feet as more boulders crashed into the pit, shaking the earth and leaving craters in the ground. A few of them nearly took out a couple of jinn, and Sloth finally stirred on his mount. When he kicked his horse, it grudgingly plodded forward.

Without thinking, I ran toward the path where they'd taken Magnus. I went to dodge around Pride, but his hands fell on my shoulders, and he released a bone-chilling snarl. His fingers digging into my collarbone pierced my flesh and drew blood. Before I could formulate a thought, my feet left the ground.

Lifting me, he flung me away as if I weighed no more than a pebble. A scream lodged in my throat as the world whipped around me and the wind tore at me. The ground became a dizzying blur until I had no idea where I was.

And then I hit the earth.

Breath burst out of my lungs when I crashed onto my side, and my back screamed in protest as I skidded across the ground. The rubble still raining down from the ruins pelted me; I threw my arms over my head to shield it before I crashed into the rocky base of the monolith.

Lying there, I panted through the pain in my ribs as I tried to get my bearings. Overhead, the cloud of smoke cleared to reveal more of the red sky, but from my angle, I couldn't see what happened to the ruins.

Turning myself over, I clawed my way up the pile of rocks until I arrived at the top and settled only a foot away from the monolith. My heart sank when I finally saw the ruins again.

Or at least I saw what remained of them.

A perfect single square piece of the three-story section had collapsed. If anything was in that section, it was dead.

CHAPTER FORTY

Magnus

WHEN I CRASHED into the bars of my cell, they held firm before bending outward with a low screech.

Come on! Come on! Come on!

Gritting my teeth, I pushed harder as rocks battered my body. One of them crashed onto my heel, turning it to the side until something popped and I nearly went down.

Amalia.

Her name became a mantra in my head compelling me to continue as the world narrowed to a pinprick of light and thought around me.

The bars broke in half as they finally gave way beneath my weight and my determination to be free. Momentum carried me across the rubble spilling out of the cell and into the hallway. I had to keep my head bowed and my shoulders hunched to avoid smashing them off the ceiling. When my cell collapsed, the shockwave of the force lifted me off my feet. I curled into a ball to avoid breaking my neck on the ceiling as I flew across the hall.

I saw the wall coming but was helpless to do anything to stop myself from being slammed into it. My entire body jerked and twitched when I collapsed onto the rising debris. Lying there, I inhaled large gulps of dust and sand while the thunderous noise dimmed and a few rocks clattered into place.

Opening my eyes, I blinked away the thick coat of dust caking them. The layer of rubble coating me fell apart as I rolled to the side and rose to my hands and knees to survey the destruction. In this position, the ceiling scraped the tips of my horns. The debris packed the hallway, and closer to where my cell had been, it rose until it was impossible to tell the ceiling from the floor.

Wren!

I should have expected this kind of booby trap, but I was so focused on getting to Amalia that I hadn't stopped to think the fae might have worked into place something designed to kill their enemy should they discover a way to break free.

Tricky little extinct race, and more vicious than I'd believed.

But then, I suspected they were pushed to more brutal means in an attempt to keep their home. And those means had failed.

Crawling forward, I made my way toward Wren's cell. My heart battered my ribs with every passing second as I made my way across the unsteady ground. When the area narrowed further, I slid to my stomach and dragged myself through the destruction. The stones abrading my flesh, smeared more of my blood across the Abyss as I battled to reach Wren.

She has to be alive. I would never forgive myself if I'd killed her. I liked the feisty ex-mortal, and I couldn't be the one who entombed her under a mound of ruins. I didn't let myself consider that I might also be buried in here; it wasn't an option.

I listened for any sound from Wren. A footstep, a breath, or a call, but all I heard was my labored breathing as dust billowed off the rocks before me with each breath. I didn't dare yell out for her; the jinn and horsemen already knew something happened up here, letting them know I'd survived it by calling for her would only bring them here faster.

The bars of Wren's cell came into view, and I slithered toward them at a faster rate. The ceiling pressed against my back and rocks dug into my chest as I pulled myself forward to peer through the bars. My heart sank when I saw the wall of debris ending only inches from the ceiling all the way around her cell.

It would take days to dig her out, but if her head had been crushed, there would be nothing I could do.

A flicker of something on the other side of the cell caught my attention. From the way my face was positioned against the bars, the debris looked as if it stretched all the way across the cell. When Wren moved again, she broke the optical illusion, and I spotted her on top of a two-foot mound of rubble. She stood with her back pressed against the bars opposite my cell.

Despite the destruction wrought on my cell and the ring of rubble around hers, the rest of Wren's space remained remarkably untouched by dirt and rocks. Not one pebble made it beyond the symbol on her ceiling.

I suddenly understood why the three-story section of runes had remained intact. The symbols had protected this area of the structure from collapsing until I broke one of them.

"I'm coming," I said to her.

She gave me the finger.

Smiling, I pushed myself away from the bars and wiggled through the wreckage toward the corner of her cell. It widened out again when I neared the bend, and on my hands and knees, I scuttled around the side of Wren's cell.

When the rubble dropped off dramatically, I slid down the rocks to stand on the smaller pile outside her cell. Her eyes swung toward me, and though she grinned, she looked as gray as a ghost.

"Were you trying to kill me?" she asked.

"No, and thankfully I didn't."

"Yeah, thankfully, dumbass."

I smiled at her before inspecting the bars; I hoped they would give way from this side without her having to destroy the marking. Neither of us would survive more ruins filling this place. However, I suspected the symbol was only meant to make it impossible for those inside the cell to breakout.

The booby trap was more malicious than I'd expected from the fae, but they wouldn't make it so their prisoner could never exit once they were inside.

But what if they'd made it so the only way someone could walk freely out of the cell was through the door? I glanced at the scant foot of space available between ceiling and floor where Wren's cell door was located.

If that were the case, I'd find out soon enough as I didn't have enough time to dig through all of that and get her free before the jinn returned.

Gritting my teeth, I ignored the pop in my shoulder as my muscles strained while I worked to separate the bars. For a second, they didn't give, and then, with a low squeak, they began separating.

"Oh," Wren breathed.

I pulled the bars more than a foot apart and stepped aside. "Hurry," I urged. "They'll be coming for us soon."

"I can't believe that actually worked," she muttered as she gripped the bars and started to wiggle out. "I should have destroyed the thing days ago." Her chest came free, then her torso. "I'm so mad at myself. Thank—"

The second her feet slid free of the symbol, she vanished. One minute she was before me, and the next, she was nothing but air. I gave silent thanks she was free and back with Corson before turning to search for a way out.

Too bad it wouldn't be that easy for Amalia and me.

Amalia

Tears streamed down my face when I buried my head in my hands and wept loudly. Magnus was still alive, I could feel him through our bond, but I would never let Pride or any who stood with him know. When I thought of my mother, the tears came easy.

They all had to think Magnus was dead. It might be the only chance we had of getting out of this place.

While I cried, I tried to think of some way for us to escape. How could I get to the ruins without someone stopping me? And what if Magnus was trapped beneath that mess?

One problem at a time.

Cracking my fingers apart, I assessed the others with blurry eyes. Lust ordered some of the jinn to check the ruins and report back to her immediately. A few of them hesitated, but they all obeyed her command.

What if *I* went back to get the others? What if I returned and brought some of them here to help us fight? Would they believe me about what had happened, or would they think I was trying to set them up?

They would know I was Magnus's Chosen; they'd have to see that all I'd want was for him to be safe, but would they think I was plotting something against all of them?

No, that was *not* an option. I would *make* them believe me because I had to do something, and staying here wouldn't do Magnus or me any good, not against these numbers and the horsemen. I hated leaving Magnus alone here for even a second, but it was all I could think of to do, and I wouldn't leave for long.

"Someone get that *pathetic* bitch down from there," Lust sneered.

Now or never.

Lowering my hands, I pushed myself to my feet. The rocks surrounding Absenthees were solid, but some of the debris from the collapsing ruins shifted beneath my feet. I stifled a cry and flung out a hand to steady myself before I fell over.

When my hand connected with the monolith, I froze as a bolt of power raced from it and into me. This wasn't like the hideous jolt of energy that came with the life going through me after someone died here.

No, this was more like when the pool of water enveloped me, only this was so much *more!* I felt electrified with the power suffusing me. Everyone had believed the fae to be weak with an inactive ability, but in this place, they had created a thriving world of life and power.

"Oh," I breathed when beneath my palm, one of the symbols warmed and a faint hint of orange light illuminated its edges.

"What secrets do you hold?" I murmured.

A rock clattering nearby drew my attention away from the monolith. While I was focused on Absenthees, a handful of jinn had started climbing the rocks toward me.

I didn't want to let go of the monolith, but I couldn't stay here. I had to get to the others, and the jinn were closing in on me. When I jerked my hand away from the tempting structure, the light vanished. I glanced longingly at Absenthees before waving my hand in front of my face, and opening a portal, I stepped into it.

"*No!* Stop her!" Lust screamed.

But she was too late as I was already entering the cave while the portal closed behind me, officially sealing me off from Magnus. Panic rose within me, but I shut it down. I had to be calm and reasonable when talking with the others. It was the only way I'd be able to make them understand Magnus needed help.

I opened my mouth and started to gush out an explanation of what happened. "You have to help...."

My voice trailed off when I realized I was speaking to an empty cave. I stood, gawking at the shadows hugging the spacious area as somewhere in the distance water dripped onto rock.

What? Where? I couldn't form an answer as the only hope I had of saving Magnus exploded into pieces around me.

They wouldn't leave Magnus behind, I was confident of that, but why had they gone? Then, I realized they'd either been forced to move or were dead. Had Astaroth or someone else somehow uncovered their location? Had Magnus's illusion covering the front of the cave crumpled when the ruins collapsed? Magnus wasn't dead, but was he so severely injured that he couldn't hold an illusion anymore?

No matter what had happened here, it all equaled the same thing; Magnus and I were on our own.

CHAPTER FORTY-ONE

Wren

I CAME AWAKE WITH A START, jerking against whoever held me and flinging myself forward.

"Wren!" Corson's arms constricted around me.

The fight went out of me when he pressed me against his chest. "Oh," I breathed and draped my arms around his neck. I inhaled his scent as my lips rested against my fading bite on his neck. "It's you. I'm... I'm... back."

I had a vague memory of having gone somewhere without him, but where had I gone and what happened?

"You're back." Distress and relief resonated in his voice as he stroked my hair. "You're back."

"I missed you."

"And I, you."

I let myself drift into his comforting embrace, but I turned my attention away from his neck when my fangs pricked with the impulse to sink into his flesh and mark him. However, I sensed others around us, and I wouldn't share our private bond with them.

"Others went with me, didn't they?" I asked.

"Yes."

"How many remain wherever I was?"

"Just Magnus and Amalia."

Leaning back in his arms, I smiled when his beautiful citrine eyes met mine. I cradled his cheek as love swelled within me and his eyes danced with joy. I was so focused on him that it took me a minute to notice the dark purple leaves and arching branches over his head.

We certainly hadn't been anywhere like this before... before...

Total recall danced at the edges of my mind, but the memory of where I'd been continued to elude me. Then, I forgot about trying to recall my whereabouts when I realized we were in a grove of calamuts.

"Where are we?" I asked.

"Trying to get help," he said, "and failing."

"Where is Amalia?" an unfamiliar voice demanded.

I turned my head to find a striking woman with black hair and black eyes staring intently at me; I guessed she was the speaker. I didn't respond to her as my gaze traveled over all those gathered around us. I'd never seen the six men and women standing with the woman who'd spoken, but I recognized the ones gathered close to Corson. However, there were far fewer demons and humans here than there should be.

"Where is everyone else?" I demanded.

Lix grunted before chugging from his flask; Erin rested a hand on his shoulder. From over Corson's shoulder, Jolie gave me a wan smile.

"This is all that's left," Corson murmured. "There are twenty-three demons, including Magnus, two angels, and twenty human survivors."

There's only forty-five of us left!

My stomach turned over at the realization. Yesterday, or

however long ago it was before all this occurred, there were one hundred twenty-five of us. *Eighty* had died while I'd been wherever I was. If I were still human, the knowledge would have made me puke.

"Oh," I breathed as I took note of all the *missing* faces. For years, I'd fought relentlessly against those who sought to kill us, and I'd aligned with the demons in the hopes of keeping the Wilders alive, but I'd lost so many of them in one fell swoop.

"This is not your fault," Corson said as he guessed at my thoughts. "You could *not* have stopped this. None of us could."

It was true, but it didn't matter; I still blamed myself. *If Randy is still alive, he's going to be so disappointed in me.* He'd left me in charge while he went to find a safer place for us to live, and I'd failed.

No, you didn't, and he won't be disappointed. The reasonable voice in my head replied. And the reasonable voice was, of course, right, but I couldn't shake the feeling I'd let Randy down and that I'd failed all the Wilders who were lost.

"Well, that's not entirely true," Lix said in a tone so icy I half expected to see frost billowing from his jaw as he spoke. "Some of those gathered here might have been able to stop it, or at least *attempted* to stop it. They definitely could have stepped in to save a couple of lives. Just *one* life would have been better than none, right, Rislen?"

"We cannot go against our kind," the beautiful woman who'd spoken to me stonily replied to him.

"Your kind?" I inquired.

"Rislen is a jinni," Corson said.

"Jinni," I snarled.

Before I could control them, my five-inch long talons sprouted from the backs of my hands. They'd grown over the past couple of months, but they still weren't as long as Corson's, and they may never be. They were lethal though, and I'd seen enough of the jinn to know I'd happily slice and dice them.

"Easy," Corson murmured and rubbed his fingers over the back of one of my hands. "Rislen is Faulted, as are the jinn standing with her. We came here in the hopes of getting their help."

"And we're not leaving until we do," Hawk stated.

Overhead, some of the calamut leaves stirred when a shadow soared above them. Tipping my head back, I watched as Raphael swooped over the trees before disappearing. Caim must be up there somewhere keeping watch with him too.

"Faulted?" Lowering my head, I focused on the others again. The word niggled at the back of my mind, begging me to recall something.

"There are some jinn who are more Fae-aulted than the rest. It's a complicated story, but—"

"I know it!" I cried, cutting off Corson as some of the pieces locked into place. "Magnus told me about the Faulted!"

"You saw Magnus?" Corson demanded.

Did I? I must have seen him if I'd said that, but where and how... Then the fog dispersed and memories flowed forth.

"Yes, the jinn brought him up and imprisoned him in the cell next to mine. He told me everything that's been going on and about Amalia, his Chosen."

"His what now?" Vargas blurted.

"His Chosen," I said. "Put me down." I flattened my palm against Corson's chest. I didn't want out of his arms, but I had to stand. When he set me on my feet, he kept his arm around my waist. "You didn't know he'd claimed her?"

"No," Erin answered. "The last time we saw them, there was no indication of anything like that."

"He was pretty protective of her when I saw them in the Abyss, but I saw no marks on either of them," Hawk said.

"Where is Amalia?" Rislen interjected, her composure slipping as she pinned me with a harsh stare.

"I don't know." I quickly informed them about everything I went through, what Magnus had told me, and how he'd freed us. "I never saw Amalia. The horsemen and other jinn kept her with them. They'll know something is wrong now that Magnus destroyed the symbol, and they're going to hunt for him."

"They'll use Amalia against him, Rislen," Corson said in the tone I recognized as his "don't fuck with me" voice.

"Our brethren allowed *more* than one horseman into the Abyss," Rislen murmured. "Why would they do such a thing?"

"They shouldn't have allowed *any* of the horsemen in there," another jinni whispered to her, and Rislen bowed her head.

"They let them in because they're angry about being locked away," another jinni said, "and they have a right to that anger. We all do."

"You do," Corson agreed, "but does the whole world have to be demolished for them to sate that anger? And what if the horsemen and fallen angels aren't satisfied with getting vengeance on Kobal and the rest of us; what if they seek more afterward? Maybe your fellow jinn will want to call it quits if Kobal is destroyed, but do you think Astaroth and the horsemen will let them? And what will they do when a new varcolac rises to replace Kobal? Will they blame that varcolac too? This is a *never*-ending cycle, Rislen."

Rislen kept her head down, but a muscle in her cheek twitched.

"You know how twisted the angels and horsemen are. They won't be satisfied with anything less than complete annihilation," Corson pressed. "Maybe they'll maintain enough control to leave some humans alive, and not destroy themselves in the process of getting their revenge, but maybe they won't. That will be *so* many more lives lost, Rislen, and many of them will be *innocent* lives.

"Think of all the suffering that will be created in this world. With your Faulted status, you will *all* feel it because not even the calamuts can shelter you from that much anguish. Not to mention, Amalia. Can you imagine what the horsemen will do to her? Are you going to let that happen?"

I thought he might be getting through to her when Rislen's eyes flicked toward him, but then she became expressionless again.

Amalia

"Help with what, dear?"

When the voice spoke from the shadows at the back of the cave, I nearly jumped out of my skin. Straining my eyes, I tried to see who'd spoken, but I didn't spot Caim until he stepped away from the wall almost a hundred feet in front of me. The shadows hugging his body like a second skin caused me to gulp.

Until recently, I'd had nothing to do with the fallen, but I'd heard enough about them to know I preferred to keep my distance from them. I didn't get any bad impressions from Caim. Mostly he projected amusement, yet he still unnerved me.

Was he somehow capable of hiding his emotions from me? I knew so little of the angels that it could be a possibility. Raphael came across as indifferent to almost everything, with a bit of boredom mixed in, but Caim, for all his smiles, was trickier to figure out. And why was he here when the others were gone? Had Caim turned against them like he'd turned on Lucifer to fight for Kobal's side?

"I didn't mean to scare you," he murmured.

"You didn't," I lied and badly.

He smiled at me, but it didn't reach his onyx, rainbow-hued eyes. The tips of the spikes on top of his wings caught what little glow remained from the dying fire and reflected it. Those spikes could skewer me in less than a heartbeat. I itched to open a portal and plunge back into the Abyss, but if the others *were* still alive, he might know where they'd gone.

"What do you require help with?" he asked.

"Where are the others?" I was proud my voice came out stronger than I'd expected.

"They've gone to speak with your Faulted. They left me behind in case you and Magnus returned while they were gone."

"No," I moaned. "That's too far; it will take too much time for me to reach them."

Caim's eyes flashed to the bites on my neck, and his smile vanished. "Where is Magnus?"

"The horsemen ordered him taken away, and the jinn took him to the ruins. Then the ruins collapsed, and now, I'm not sure where he is!" I blurted. "I *know* he's still alive; I feel it through our bond, but I don't know if he's buried underneath it all, if he somehow managed to get free, or if he's somewhere else entirely!"

By the time I finished speaking, I could barely contain my mounting terror. I took a deep breath to help calm me, but the longer Magnus stayed in the Abyss alone, the more something might happen to him.

"The horse*men*?" Caim inquired.

"Yes, the jinn brought Pride, Lust, and Sloth into the Abyss. Pride killed..." I had to stop to swallow the lump in my throat before I continued. "He killed my mother."

Caim blinked at me before tilting his head to the side and running his gaze over me. "I will return to the Abyss with you and help you get Magnus away from them."

I had no idea how to respond. Did I dare trust a fallen angel when I'd felt the distrust of the others toward him?

Then, I realized one thing—I didn't have a choice. Even if Caim flew me to the Faulted, it would take more time than I was willing to spend on Earth to get there, and I couldn't send him to retrieve the palitons while I returned to the Abyss.

I might never get this chance to bring help back to the Abyss again.

Caim continued to study me in that unnerving, bird-like way of his. "Do you not trust me?" he asked.

No. But I bit the word back as I sought to figure out a solution to my problem.

Then, I felt a slip in the humor he projected. A twinge of sadness slipped through his emotions before he smiled at me, but I still felt the sadness behind his smile. He couldn't keep his feelings from me, but somehow, he was better than the others at suppressing them most of the time.

His sadness tugged at my heart, and I found myself softening toward the perplexing angel. He couldn't fake that feeling, no matter how hard he tried. It was impossible to fake emotions. He wanted... no, he *needed* to be trusted. He was once as golden as Raphael, once one of the elite, and now he was the one left behind to wait in caves.

He was trying to atone for his past; maybe the others didn't see that yet, but I did.

"I understand your distrust of me," Caim said. "But remember almost *everyone* on Hell, Earth, Heaven, and your Abyss want me dead far more than you."

I almost protested his words, but there was no reason to lie to him when we both knew the truth.

"Right then," I said firmly. "Here's what you have to know." I filled him in on the scene I'd left behind and what he could probably expect if he returned with me. "Would you still like to help me?"

His grin revealed all his teeth as he skipped away from the shadows and toward me. Watching a fallen angel skipping across the open space may have been one of the strangest things I'd ever seen, but somehow it fit this peculiar being. As he skipped, both his index fingers swung back and forth in front of him like he was composing a song only he could hear.

Gulping, I realized two things. Yes, Caim did indeed seek to help, but he might also be a little bit... no, he was *full*-blown crazy.

And I believed this crazy was precisely what the horsemen would *loathe*. Things were about to get interesting in the land of the fae.

"You know—" He offered his elbow to me and a new emotion wafted from him—comradery. I accepted his arm without hesitation. "—back in my golden days, when I was *much* more of a bore, I was a bit of an empath myself. I lost the ability when I fell, but I've felt twinges of it again since returning to Earth. It's how I knew you were different from the other jinn."

"Of course," I murmured as it all made a little more sense. He wasn't keeping his emotions suppressed from me; his ability was deflecting mine as the jinn's did.

"My ability wasn't as strong as yours, I can sense that from you, but I would get impressions from the other angels. However, I think my empath readings are more to do with the raven in me than an actual empath ability."

"Why do you think that?"

"All animals sense things beyond what mortals and immortals do. Their instincts are better than ours in so many ways. But my empath ability was strong enough that I felt for other creatures when the rest of the fallen stopped caring at all," he murmured.

My breath caught when I realized Caim was something akin to the lone Faulted amid the fallen angels. For me, it was lonely enough being Faulted, but at least I had six others like me, even if I'd been torn between them and my parents.

Life must have been incredibly lonely for Caim in Hell. It must still be lonely living with a group who didn't fully trust him and might never do so.

I vowed that, if we survived this, he would have a friend in me who would trust him and understand him a little better. But first, we had to return to the Abyss. I'd only been back here for a few minutes, but that was hundreds of seconds in which Magnus was left alone.

Panic shredded my chest, and when I spoke again, my voice trembled. "When we return, if you grab me and fly as fast as you can, we should be able to avoid any jinn who might be waiting to pounce on us."

"And the horsemen?"

"I'm hoping Pride and Lust are too arrogant to climb to where I was, and Sloth is too lazy."

"That would make sense," he said with a chuckle. "I'll take you to Magnus if I can."

"Yes," I breathed.

"And then I'm going to ruin the lives of some horsemen and one woman, of course."

I opened my mouth to protest, but he continued speaking before I could.

"Nothing too crazy, my dear, I promise. When you're ready to vamoose from the Abyss with your Chosen, I'll be prepared to go with you, but you must let an angel have *some* fun."

His grin leaned toward the side of madness, but who was I to deny an angel their fun?

CHAPTER FORTY-TWO

Magnus

After climbing through the rubble and slipping out a hole I found in the side of the ruins, I moved toward the front of the building in time to watch Amalia vanish from beside Absenthees. I hoped she never returned, but I had no doubt she would. She'd gone to bring back help, and she would come back with the others.

And when she did return, I *had* to be near her, because the jinn were already settling in to wait for her near the monolith.

I stopped to erase the few footprints I left behind as I moved. Earlier, I'd seen some of the jinn break away from the others and head toward a pathway I was sure would lead them to me. When they arrived, they couldn't know I was heading toward them instead of away. I could have cloaked the prints with a small illusion, but it was more important to focus my energy on healing and keeping myself cloaked.

Besides, I hadn't left a print since I'd moved past the area closest to the collapse, where the sand and dirt of the ruined building was fresh and thick. Further away from the collapse, the ground was the color of sand, but as solid as a rock.

From around a corner of a boulder, four jinn emerged and started toward me. Ducking back, I gripped the top of a three-foot section of wall and boosted myself over it without a sound. Though I'd cloaked myself and moved out of their way, I still crouched down when they neared.

My horns had finally returned to normal, but now they slid forward again as my body pulsed with the need to kill. Amalia's kind or not, I'd had enough of these fucking assholes. However, I remained where I was; to kill them now would let those below know I'd survived the collapse and was coming for them.

My fingers clawed into my palms as the jinn strode passed me with an arrogance that infuriated me. It was the kind of arrogance I'd always exhibited—a *"you can't touch me"* approach to life I no longer felt because I could so easily be destroyed now.

Before Amalia, I'd never cared if I died and would have done so with a smile and a big fuck you to whoever killed me as I took them down with me. I'd been willing to give my life for my king, the cause of destroying Lucifer, and to keep Earth as intact as possible. Nothing had scared me before because there'd been nothing I cared about losing.

I had so much now. I would still die for this cause—we'd all die if we didn't fight the craetons—but I wouldn't go into anything with the same arrogant indifference I'd possessed before. If I died, then so would Amalia. And if I lost her....

For the first time, I understood terror as it settled in my gut and chilled my skin. I would level anyone in my way if it meant keeping her safe, and if necessary, I would do precisely that to get free of this place.

When the jinn were out of sight, I moved away from the wall and toward the path.

The fifth jinni stood at the head of the pathway with his arms crossed over his chest. He stared straight ahead, unaware I stood behind him though I was practically breathing down his neck.

Gritting my teeth, I turned sideways and edged passed him. I ached to bury my horns in his throat and rend his head from him, but I slipped by and raced toward the monolith.

I came to a halt at the end of the pathway and behind a sixth jinn. The path here was too narrow for me to pass him without touching. Standing behind him, I stared at his neck. He had to die, but I'd have to wait until Amalia returned before making my move. The second his body hit the ground, the others would know I was here, and I needed to maintain my element of surprise until Amalia returned.

Lifting my gaze from his nape, I stared at the spot where Amalia had vanished as I waited for any sign of her return. I spotted a subtle ripple in the air before she emerged in Caim's arms. Red filled my vision; my lips curled back as jealousy seared like a hot poker straight into me.

Caim's wings unfurled with a crack of air, but before he could take flight, two of the jinn crashed into the side of him. Swinging a wing out, he battered the jinn with it and knocked one of them back.

Where are the others?

As the question crossed my mind, I seized the head of the jinni before me. I tore it from his shoulders and lobbed it aside. Before it hit the ground, I created a duplicate image of myself and sent it forth. As the image ran forward, more than a dozen identical illusions broke off from it and ran toward Absenthees.

I ran straight up the middle of the splintering figures as I headed for the monolith and Amalia. Caim gave up trying to fly and punched the other jinni in the face, but more jinn were converging on the two of them. Lifting his right wing, Caim turned it over and plunged the silver spike at the bottom of it into the eye of another jinni.

"Go!" Amalia shouted at him when half a dozen jinn closed in on them. "Find Magnus!"

Caim could have gotten free without her, but he remained by her side and, for the first time, I felt a twinge of respect for the fallen angel, even if I would still like to kill him for touching her.

Some of the jinn rushed forward to attack the duplicates of me, which vanished when touched. As they were disappearing, I sent more forth until over a dozen mirages of me filled the cavernous space. I resisted my instinct to slaughter the jinn I ran past; I didn't dare give away my location, or the fact I was cloaked again before I reached Amalia.

One of the jinn ran past Caim's wing and barreled into Amalia. With his shoulder in her ribs, the jinni lifted her off her feet and propelled her into the monolith. A cry escaped her when her back slammed into the structure; I barely suppressed a bellow as her voice echoed in my head. I'd tear the jinni apart for harming her.

Arriving at the rocks mounded around the bottom of Absenthees, I climbed them faster than I'd believed possible as Amalia fought against the jinni trying to get a firm hold on her. A thunderous look crossed the jinni's face when she wiggled free of him again.

Have to get to her. Have to get to her.

The jinni succeeded in getting one arm around her waist and was trying to lift Amalia when she pulled back her hand and punched him in the nose.

Her face twisted in pain and she shook her hand while the jinni adjusted his hold on her. When we were free of this place, I would teach her how to fight.

Halfway up the rock base, the coating of debris from the ruins shifted beneath my feet, and I almost went down. I managed to catch myself, but I couldn't cover the rocks and dirt skittering away from me and tumbling down the base of Absenthees. They would know I was not one of the illusions.

The noise drew the attention of the few jinn still climbing toward Amalia and Caim. They turned toward me, but I'd already risen away from where the sound was centered. One of them started toward where I'd almost fallen, but two others looked in the direction of where I was heading. They couldn't see me, but they'd surmised it was me and were trying to figure out where I was.

They guessed too accurately for my liking.

Like locusts, a handful of jinn swarmed Caim while the others moved beyond him to Amalia. The jinn had all gotten too close for Caim to continue using his wings as weapons, and he was starting to lose the battle. Clutching his arms and legs, the jinn were about to lift him off his feet when he shifted into raven form.

Some of the jinn yelped and stumbled away as Caim rose into the air. The three-foot-tall raven was easily a hundred pounds and had six-inch long talons curving into lethal hooks. Turning, Caim tucked his wings back and dive-bombed the jinn with a ferocious shriek.

One jinni threw himself backward and toppled down the rocks. I darted out of the way when he bounced passed me. Another jinni wasn't fast enough to avoid the raven; he staggered away with both his eyes and a good portion of his face missing. Caim rose higher before diving again at the jinn still swarming the rocks.

Unaware I was there, Caim came straight at me to get at the jinn who had started in my direction after I dislodged the debris. I threw myself to the ground before he took me out with the three jinn he knocked onto their backs.

Rising, I raced back up the rocks, uncaring about any noise I might make as four jinn surrounded Amalia. The jinni she was fighting with the whole time finally succeeded in lifting her. Amalia hit his shoulders before rearing back and smashing her forehead off the bridge of his nose. The jinni squealed and released Amalia as if she were on fire.

Blood pooled from between the jinni's fingers as he clutched his nose and stalked toward her. When Amalia's back connected with the monolith, it stopped her from retreating any further. The jinni pulled back his arm to punch her.

No!

I covered the distance separating us in three large bounds. Coming up behind the jinni, I gripped his head and yanked it to the side. One of his hands flew up to mine but not in time to stop me from ripping his head from his body.

Amalia pressed against the monolith with her eyes closed as she waited for the blow to land. When it didn't, she cracked open an eye as the jinni's body hit the ground and I released his head. She blinked, her mouth parted on an O before excitement lit her face.

"Magnus!" she breathed.

Amalia

"Amalia."

I still couldn't see him, but his whisper caused his breath to caress my face, and then his hand cupped my cheek. I turned my head into his palm as a wave of his love swept over me.

And then, he was gone.

Opening my eyes, I discovered three jinn tackling an invisible mass onto the rocks. As they rolled, Magnus's feet came into view, then his extended horns and head. The disconcerting, patchwork way he shed the cloaking illusion made my breath catch. His legs and torso remained invisible until a punch to his gut knocked the breath from him, and his upper body reappeared, followed by his legs.

Resting my hand against the monolith, I rose to my feet and turned to face the two jinn coming at me. A thrill of power raced into my palm and up my arm as the warm glow lit the symbol beneath my hand again.

I wanted to turn to look at Absenthees, but I didn't dare tear my eyes away from the approaching jinn whose loyalty only went as far as anyone who didn't stand against the horsemen, I realized with a heavy heart. Behind the seal, we were all so close; there hadn't been this hatred toward each other and the world. There was resentment, of course, but not to this degree.

The falling of the seals did more than set us free; it also released all the hatred and bitterness the jinn suppressed over eighteen thousand years of captivity.

They'd kill me to get what they sought, and I'd fight them to the death, theirs or mine before I let them return me to the horsemen. My life, and Magnus's, might as well be over if those abominations had control over one of us again.

Kill or be killed.

Bracing myself for a battle, I removed my hand from Absenthees and fisted them before me. When this was over, I was going to learn how to punch as I'd broken my thumb when I hit the jinni earlier. It was healing, but not fast enough.

I was about to launch my first blow when Magnus plowed into the side of one of the jinn and shoved her into the other. The strike took them both out. With no jinn before me, I could see what was happening below. Though at least twenty jinn swarmed the monolith and were climbing toward us, almost a dozen remained below, uncertain about jumping into the fray.

Nalki and another jinni restrained my father while he struggled against their hold. Olgon stood between Pride and Lust; their attention was focused on us, and their fury was a hot ray I felt from nearly two hundred feet away. Sitting beside Lust, Sloth yawned as he surveyed the fight with a bored air.

I didn't know why they hadn't set their powers free to put an end to this, but then I realized that if the horsemen unleashed their abilities, they would trap all the jinn too. Doing such a thing might render the jinn useless to them and might make it so the horsemen couldn't escape the Abyss.

And Pride had told Lust she should have suspected the Chosen bond would make Magnus capable of withstanding her power. They loved to create death and destruction, but they preferred to do it without getting their hands dirty. Magnus had almost killed Lust once already; they wouldn't take the chance such a thing could happen to one of them again.

Still, I didn't want to see what would happen if the horsemen decided they had no choice but to free their abilities.

We have to get out of here, now!

Stepping back, I pressed against the monolith and flattened my palms on it as Magnus brawled with the two jinn he'd tackled. When another jinni came toward me, I remained where I was and hoped my face reflected my fear. I kept my eyes lowered so they wouldn't see the rage simmering in them while I waited for her to get closer. Then, I'd surprise her by shoving her backward.

I had crossed a line when I brought Magnus into the Abyss, but what they planned to do to us went *far* beyond that line. I was looking to save lives, they were looking to *end* ours, and any loyalty I might have felt toward anyone standing with the horsemen died with my mother.

Now, I would play the role they expected of me, helpless and frightened. I may not be the best fighter, but I would *not* go easy, and I would not let them destroy my love for Magnus.

Love?

I would always believe peace was better than war; it would always be my preferred course of action, but whereas before I would have walked away from this and let the jinn do what they wanted, I would *not* back down.

Magnus, the Abyss, the humans, the world, and *I* were all worth fighting and dying for.

The jinni was only a foot away from me when, keeping my head down, I leaned against the monolith, lifted a foot, and smashed it into her chest. Her mouth formed a startled O, and her astonishment hit me like a hammer as she clawed at the air. However, there was nothing she could grasp to stop herself from falling over, and I watched as she toppled head over heels down the rocks.

I took no pleasure in having beaten her, but I did take satisfaction in it.

Magnus succeeded in throwing one of the jinn away from him before bashing the head of the other off the stones and tossing their limp body aside. Overhead, Caim swooped down to pluck another jinni from the rocks.

The man screamed as Caim flew across the cavern and released him over Pride's head. The sound the raven released sounded like laughter as the falling jinni flailed his arms. Pride jerked his horse out of the way in time to avoid being hit by the jinni. The man hit the ground with a resonating crunch.

Pride fixed hate-filled eyes on Caim as, against my back, Absenthees heated further.

CHAPTER FORTY-THREE

Magnus

Turning back to Amalia, I took one step toward her and froze when my eyes fell on the monolith. The jinni stalking her hesitated before stumbling away. With her head bowed, Amalia's hair shielded her face from me when I desperately wanted to see her.

"Amalia," I breathed, but she didn't respond as she kept her gaze turned away.

The jinni fled down the rocks as a molten gold hue started to burn from the symbols etching the structure; the color illuminated each of them as it spread higher. Light radiated out from Amalia's palms, and the orange-yellow hue burned hotter with each passing second.

I took a step toward her to pull her away from the monolith before stopping. I had no idea what was going on here, but she wasn't in pain, and something about this felt right. The memory of what she'd done by the pool drifted back to me. She'd awoken so much beauty there, and she could do it here too.

She is a part of the Abyss and it's a part of her.

A stirring of air from behind the monolith drew my attention to the portal forming there. My eyebrows rose when Rislen and the other Faulted stepped into the Abyss. Rislen's gaze locked with mine, but from her position, she couldn't see Amalia or the glow spreading toward the sides of Absenthees.

Then, Rislen turned to take in the death and destruction scattered around the monolith. Her eyes shone with displeasure when they met mine again, but her attention was drawn swiftly back to the symbols now illuminating all sides of the monolith. Rislen stepped forward before halting abruptly.

When her eyes shot questioningly back to me, I mouthed, "*Amalia.*"

Longing speared across her face before she composed it into a blank mask.

Amalia lifted her head, and when she looked at me, a radiant smile lit her face. I'd never seen her look so beautiful before. *This* was what she was meant to do.

"Magnus," she whispered.

The second she released the monolith, the light vanished from it. And that could not be allowed to happen. There was a chance this place coming back to life would *not* be good for the horsemen. It might not be good for Caim and me either, but we'd hurdle across that bridge if we came to it.

When Amalia stepped toward me, I clasped her hand. Her smile grew as I lifted her hand to my mouth and kissed the back of it before turning it over and flattening her palm against the monolith again.

"Whatever you do, Freckles, don't let go of this."

"What?" she asked as Absenthees glowed beneath her touch once more.

I released her hand to rest mine against the structure. The sizzle and pop of my flesh crackled in my ears before I yanked my hand away. The monolith had seared away the first layer of my tissue and left blisters behind in seconds.

Lesson learned. I suspected only someone with fae blood could touch this without paying the price. Too bad we couldn't get the horsemen up here so we could fry their asses with this thing.

"Magnus!" Amalia cried and released the monolith to reach for me.

"I'm fine," I assured her, and using my good hand, I caught hers and set it against the structure again. "No matter what, don't let go."

"Wait!" she cried when I released her. With her other hand, she grasped my arm. "Oh," she breathed as a starburst of illumination erupted behind her palm on Absenthees. The light became a fissure racing across the metallic surface. "Oh."

"Kill her!" Pride barked. "*Now!*"

My head snapped toward him, and I bared my fangs as he thrust a finger at Amalia. I'd tear him to shreds for issuing such a command. Many of the jinn had retreated from Amalia and Absenthees to stand by him and the other horsemen. When Pride issued this order, a few of the jinn exchanged a look and stayed where they were, but the others started toward the base of the monolith again.

"Caim!" I shouted, and the raven descended to land beside me.

With a ruffle of feathers, he returned to angel form, and his ebony eyes reflected the spreading light of Absenthees. "That's an interesting development," he said to Amalia.

"She's breathed life into this place before," I informed him.

"That makes sense," Caim murmured. "This dying land is craving the return of the fae. She's like drops of water on a sun-scorched land to it."

"Stay with her," I said to him.

"Where are you going?" Amalia demanded.

"After the horsemen."

Her fingers dug into my arm. "I'm coming with you; Pride killed my mother."

A twinge of sorrow for her tugged at my heart. Wrapping my hand around her head, I drew her close and kissed her forehead. "I'm sorry. I will make him pay for it, but you must stay here. What you're doing could be what we need to drive them out of here."

For the first time, she turned her head to look at the awakening structure. In the growing radiance it emitted, her hair and eyes became more yellow as her face lit with awe and joy.

When she looked at me again, sadness filled her gaze. "The Abyss is awakening."

"Because of you. You must stay here."

She looked about to argue with me, but then she closed her eyes, gave a brief nod, and focused on me again. "Be careful," she whispered and released my arm to rest her hand on my cheek.

"I will," I vowed.

"I love you, Magnus."

My heart swelled to the point of bursting. To have her love me as I loved her was more than I ever could have asked for from my life. I ran my lips over her forehead before turning my head to rest it on hers. I relished the feel of her silken hair against my cheek while I inhaled her sweet scent.

"I love you too, Freckles, forever."

I clasped her hand with my healing one and pressed it against my face before placing it on the monolith too.

"I'm coming back for you," I vowed.

"You'd better," she said, but her smile couldn't hide the sadness and fear in her eyes.

Reluctantly, I released her and turned away. I didn't look back as I raced down the rocks toward the jinn and horsemen; I was afraid if I did, I would change my mind and flee from the Abyss with her. And there were far too many lives that counted on us destroying the craetons to run away from here.

I wasn't up to full strength after my last cloaking illusion, but I weaved one over myself again as I ran. Once done, I still had enough power to send out a few duplicates of me. As I ran, I zigzagged back and forth to throw my enemies off my location further.

Behind me, the light of Absenthees grew stronger, and for the first time since arriving in the Abyss, my shadow appeared before me.

"This place is lies and shadows." I recalled Erin saying when we encountered her in here. There were no shadows then, but if Amalia succeeded in bringing the Abyss back to life, there would be again.

∼

Amalia

I BOWED my head against the encompassing light to keep it from burning my retinas. However, I didn't miss that the colors spreading higher through the monolith were the same as my hair and eyes. Nor did I miss the new fractures racing across the surface of Absenthees.

The heat beneath my palms intensified until I was sure it would melt the flesh from my bones before dissolving them, but my skin remained unmarred, and the sensation wasn't unpleasant.

I watched Magnus fade away, but this time, fewer duplicates of him were sent forth to confuse the others. *He's weakening.*

"Caim, he needs help," I said.

Caim held his wings open and over his head to block some of the brightness from Absenthees. "And you need protection," he replied as some of the jinn started up the rocks toward us again.

"I'll be okay."

"I know you will because I'll be here to make sure of it."

"Caim," I moaned.

I almost tore my hands away to grab him and shake some sense into him, but I stopped myself before I did. The Abyss was yearning to be free of the cruelty reigning here for far too long, and I wouldn't deny it.

Movement to my right drew my attention, and Caim tensed to pounce. "It's okay," I said to him when Rislen and the other Faulted emerged from behind the monolith.

Their awe beat against me and shone on their faces as they tipped their heads back to take in the spectacle of Absenthees. Slowly, Rislen touched the structure with her fingertips. She hesitated for a second before flattening her palm on it.

"Amazing," she whispered.

"Yes," I agreed as, with her touch, the fissures raced faster over the structure. "It is, but there are jinn who don't want this." When she looked at me in confusion, a burst of anger raced through me. "That means *you* will have to take a stand against *your* kind."

Her eyes flickered toward the approaching jinn, and I sensed a weakening in her steadfast stance to remain neutral. I didn't know what finally convinced them to come here, and I didn't care.

"You told me if I did nothing to harm the jinn, I would be forgiven for trying to interfere, but if one of them died because of this, I wouldn't have a home amongst any of you. There are dead jinn here, Rislen. Magnus and Caim have killed some of them, and *Pride* killed my mother," I said.

Horror wafted from her when she looked at me again.

"I want peace as much as you, but unfortunately, we must *fight* to earn it. The craetons will destroy us all if given a chance, and you know it. If you stay here, then you are choosing a side, and there are jinn who will *not* be on it. Take a stand, Rislen, or leave the Abyss and take any who would prefer to hide with you."

I didn't look at her again as I focused my attention on Absenthees once more. She had to understand what was on the line here and that things between the jinn could never be the same as before they were sealed away. We could use their help, but if she didn't understand what was on the line here and what would have to be done to save us all, then she had to leave before she got the Faulted killed in here.

Beside me, I saw Rislen rest her hands on Absenthees again. When I looked at her, she held my gaze. "We will take a stand against those who would destroy us," she murmured, and relief washed over me.

As the rest of the Faulted spread around the monolith, they hesitatingly placed their hands against it. A ripple of astonishment went through them and into me as they connected to Absenthees and the life that once thrived within the Abyss.

CHAPTER FORTY-FOUR

Magnus

I WAS NEARLY at the bottom of the rocks when Amalia's father broke free of the jinn restraining him. With a ferocious shout, he raced across the clearing and pounced onto the back of his brother. I'd been expecting him to go for Pride, but he drove Olgon onto the ground. Grabbing the back of Olgon's head, he smashed it off the rocky earth.

Blood sprayed outward before he lifted Olgon's head and battered it into the ground again. I closed in on them, my legs moving faster as I ran toward the horsemen.

"I think it might be time for us to go," Lust's words drifted to me. "Things are getting a little too... bright here for my liking."

"I must agree," Sloth murmured.

Pride rose taller on his mount, and his chin lifted arrogantly. "We are horsemen; we do not *run*."

"No one is running; I plan to saunter on out of here, but we have no idea where Magnus is or what those Faulted are going to bring forth. Do not be so prideful it condemns you," Lust murmured.

I circled to the backs of their horses, searching for a way to take the three of them down at once. I wanted them all dead, but I had to be careful. If I only got my hands on one, the other two would bolt or attack me.

"Death would never allow himself to be caught in such a place," Lust continued.

There must be a rivalry between Death and Pride as Pride's head snapped toward her. "Coward," he sneered at her.

"Call me what you will, but I'll be alive." Lust turned dismissively away from him. "You," she looked at Olgon and rolled her eyes as Eron twisted his head around. "You should probably help your lover," Lust said to Pride.

Pride glanced at the brothers before shrugging. "I'll find a new one. I was growing tired of him anyway."

"He's a powerful aid to our cause."

It didn't matter what Olgon was as Eron succeeded in decapitating him. He roared as he lifted Olgon's head into the air and shook it.

Lust turned and pointed toward a male jinni. "Open a way out of here for us, *now*."

The jinni started to wave his hand in front of his face. If he succeeded in opening a portal, then it wouldn't matter if I could find a way to take the three horsemen down at once, as they would all flee. Racing toward him, I seized the jinni's head and twisted it around before he could open a doorway out. Tearing his head from his shoulders, I spun and heaved it at Lust.

It spun rapidly through the air, and with a startled cry, she yanked her mount back to avoid its trajectory toward her chest. The horse pranced away until his ass bumped into Pride's horse, who snorted and shifted to shove Lust's mount away.

The urge to go to sleep hit me at the same time blood rushed into my groin, and I became semi-erect. And all the while, I resisted shouting the boast of my kill to all the Abyss. Momentarily overwhelmed by the conflicting emotions, it took me a minute to realize the horsemen were unleashing their abilities.

Drawing on my bond to Amalia, I resisted the horsemen's effects as Lust spun toward the other jinn.

"All of you!" she commanded. "Open a portal for us to get out of here, now!"

I couldn't kill all the jinn, and she knew it. Some of them edged further away from the horsemen, but more of them came forward.

"No!" Eron shouted. Lifting the headless body of his brother, he spun it and smashed it into three of the jinn closest to him. "*No more helping them!*"

I didn't need Amalia's empath ability to feel the madness oozing from her father. The severing of his bond to his Chosen had broken him.

The emotions Lust, Pride, and Sloth released amplified until I found my head bowing and my eyelids drooping. The jinn closest to the horsemen started to react to the horsemen. A couple of them sat, three of them started tearing the clothes from each other, and another stood haughtily by while fluffing her hair. Those farthest from the horsemen hadn't been affected yet, but it was only a matter of time.

Caught up in their spell, the illusions I'd sent forth started to fade.

I have to fight this for... for... I struggled to recall what was happening, where I was, and then a flash of freckles and multi-hued eyes burst through my mind. *Amalia! I have to fight for her!*

Lifting my head, I focused on Amalia standing in front of the monolith. The jinn who had started toward her again were frozen halfway up the base of the monolith. Caim stood ready to take them on, but they didn't look willing to go any closer to Absenthees.

More of the metallic color cracked and chipped away from the monolith. The vivid glow of the waking Absenthees suffused Amalia in a radiance nearly as dazzling as the sun. The symbols on the structure all burned a brilliant white, and as it grew brighter, I felt the effects of the horsemen weakening further.

When the last of the metallic color fell away, four bolts of light burst out the top of Absenthees and struck the smaller, rotating pieces of stone. Fissures zigzagged across the surfaces of those smaller structures as Absenthees started to emit life once more, instead of absorbing it as the jinn forced it to do for thousands upon thousands of years.

"We have to go," Lust said, unable to keep the hint of panic from her voice.

While I'd been focused on Amalia, and fighting against the horsemen's powers, a jinni succeeded in opening a portal next to Lust. She turned, and without looking back, disappeared into it.

Shaking off the last of their effects on me, I ran toward Pride when he started to follow her, but Amalia's father got to him first. Grasping Pride's leg, Eron yanked the horseman from his steed.

Pride hit the ground with a small grunt, but it was the only sound he made before he turned and lunged at Eron. Enclosing his hands around Eron's throat, he rose again as he drove Eron to his knees. Pride squeezed until Eron's face turned a florid red.

Arriving at their side, I drew back my fist and hammered it into Pride's face. His cheek caved beneath the blow and knocked his hold on Eron free. When my punch connected with the horseman's cheek, the last of my illusions faded away, including the one cloaking me.

"Pride goeth before the fall, *bitch*," I snarled at him.

Pride fell to the ground as his mount charged me. I tried to leap out of the way, but I wasn't in time to avoid the horse's head from bashing into my side and flinging me back a few feet. Mouth wide open, the horse grabbed Eron's arm when he threw it up to protect himself. The beast lifted Eron off the ground and flung him into the air.

Eron's breath exploded from him when he hit the rocks a few feet away, but he was already regaining his feet when Pride whistled, and his mount spun toward him. The beast's hooves clattered off the stone as it galloped at full speed toward its master.

Pride seized his mount's mane when it raced by him and swung himself onto its back in one fluid motion. Sloth's mount followed at a much faster speed than I would have believed possible for the rider and his rotund beast.

They raced for the portal as Eron launched at Pride again. Eron caught Pride as I ran at Sloth and, leaping into the air, hooked my arms around his thick neck and yanked him to the side.

My momentum carried us over the side of the horse and toward the ground. When we hit the earth, my grip on Sloth was knocked free. I bounced across the terrain before crashing into the base of Absenthees. As I rolled, I realized the rocks forming the ground of the crater were losing their dark coloring and becoming the same multi-hued stones that surrounded the pool and been hidden behind the waterfall.

Sloth landed a few feet away from me, and I watched as he stumbled to his feet before staggering forward.

I expected the jinn to rush forward to help him, but some of them were either fleeing through the open portal or creating their own to escape through. The ones not fleeing the Abyss were staring at the monolith or Eron and Pride as if they were trying to decide what to do.

Shoving myself to my feet, I ran for Sloth as his horse galloped toward him. I poured on the speed, determined to beat his mount to him. Lowering my head, I ran my horns straight through Sloth's neck.

Sloth jerked, choked, and then gasped when the tip of my horn burst out the other side of his throat. His hands clawed at the horn as I lifted Sloth off his feet before tossing him to the ground. Slamming my foot onto his back, I pinned him down and yanked my horn free.

His mount snorted, and smoke billowed from its nostrils as it closed in on me. It was only three feet away from me when I lifted Sloth and spun him toward his steed. The horse's hooves tore up chunks of pale pink and orange rock as it tried to stop itself from crashing into its master, but it was too late.

Waiting until the horse was nearly on top of us, I released Sloth and dove to the side. Rolling across the ground, I bounded to my feet in time to see the steed trampling its master. Sloth's thigh bone burst free of his skin, his other leg twisted awkwardly, and one of his arms flopped to the side as blood spilled from his mouth.

I ran toward the broken horseman as his mount turned back to charge me again. Falling at Sloth's side, I sank my fingers into the wound I'd left in his throat as his horse's nearing hoofbeats thundered in my ears. Its breath heated my cheek as I tore Sloth's head free.

Three inches away from me, Sloth's horse burst into a cloud of brown dust that coated my clothing and filled my mouth as it showered me. Blinking away the dust coating my lashes, I lifted my head in time to watch Pride toss aside Eron's decapitated body. The horseman dropped Eron's head on the ground before his horse strolled through the portal.

Amalia, I thought sadly, a second before a swelling light filled the Abyss.

CHAPTER FORTY-FIVE

Amalia

WHEN THE LAST of the black color faded from the four smaller monoliths, the light from Absenthees became blinding. It stretched over the land until I was sure the spreading tendrils of it illuminated every crevice of the Abyss. Bowing my head, I turned it away from the structure.

The heat of Absenthees still didn't burn me, but instinctively I pulled my hands away from it, as did the other Faulted. The power swelling within Absenthees crackled against my skin, and I knew it would not be contained.

Run!

No sooner had the impulse hit me than Caim turned toward me with his arms outstretched.

But it was too late.

Light flashed outward in a concussive blow that lifted me off my feet and flung me away as if I weighed no more than a speck of dirt. Caim's spread wings filled my vision before I closed my eyes.

Though it threw me backward, the light was also comforting

and empowering as it enveloped me like a mother with her child. The sense of rightness stealing through me was nearly as deep as when Magnus was inside me, claiming me.

This is what the Abyss is supposed to be.

A smile tugged at my lips before I hit the ground and skidded across it.

The rocky ground abraded my ass, but the smile didn't leave my lips as warmth spread throughout the land. That warmth scrubbed away the lingering life force coating me until I felt *clean.*

I didn't stop skidding until I crashed against one of the walls, the breath burst from my lungs, and my smile faded away.

I lay for a minute, taking stock of my body. My ass throbbed so bad, I didn't think I'd sit for a week. My back and legs were swollen and probably covered in bruises. My chest was still sore from the kick Lust's horse had given it, and the rocks against my back poked my shoulder blades through a hole in my dress. Blood trickled from a wound in my shoulder, but I was intact.

Magnus! My father! Where are they?

Cautiously, I cracked open one eye. When I discovered the light had died down enough not to sear my eyes from my head, I opened them both.

Magnus was rushing toward me; his face strained with tension, and his bloody horns turned outward. The happiness suffusing me at the sight of him gave me a rush of strength. Pushing myself up, I winced when my body protested the movement, but I rose onto wobbly legs.

Behind Magnus, I spotted Caim rising unsteadily to his feet as well as the Faulted and the jinn who hadn't followed the horsemen. I searched for my father as I stretched my arms out to Magnus. Pulling me into his embrace, he lifted me off my feet and clutched me against his chest.

"Are you okay?" he demanded.

"I'm fine, are you?"

"Yes," he said as he buried his face in my hair.

"My father?" I croaked, afraid of the answer.

When his arms tightened around me, I knew my father was gone before Magnus spoke. "I'm sorry."

Tears burned my eyes, and my fingers dug into his shoulders as I clung to him. My father wouldn't have survived the loss of my mother, but I'd wanted the chance to tell him how much I would always love him and how much they both meant to me.

"How?"

"Pride killed him, but your father killed Olgon before then."

"Good." It was a word I never thought I'd say about the death of my uncle, but after he stood by and watched Pride kill my mother without so much as a hint of remorse, he stopped being family to me. He would have killed Magnus and me; his inaction killed my mother.

I buried my face in Magnus's shoulder while I battled my fury and sorrow. My fingers threaded through his hair as I sought comfort in his steady presence and his love for me. It took a few minutes, but eventually, I felt stable enough to part from him.

No matter how badly I yearned to hold onto him and give in to my emotions, I couldn't. There was far too much to deal with before I could take the time to grieve.

"I'm okay," I whispered and pulled my head from his shoulder. "You can put me down."

I sensed his reluctance, but he set me on my feet and kept his arm locked around my waist as he stepped away. Once I could see behind him to the world beyond, shock shivered up my spine. A sense of unreality descended as I took in my new... no, not new... *reawakened* surroundings.

In the center of the crater, Absenthees had shed its black coating to become a solid white, crystalized stone. Four pieces of white rock branched out from it and formed bridges to the smaller monoliths. Those bridges had pierced the smaller structures and made it so they no longer rotated around Absenthees.

Unlike Absenthees, those smaller monoliths had each taken on a different hue. One was a pale orange, another a rose pink, the third the color of lavender, and the fourth was the color of the sky on a cloudless day. Power crackled as it flowed between all the monoliths, and I realized this was the way Absenthees should have always been. The jinn's abuse of its abilities broke this connection between the structures, and when it broke, the land died.

Now the reawakened land was thriving with life once more. The rocks around us were multi-hued pastels. The leaves on the trees lining the tops of the walls were mostly orange, but a few had sprouted green leaves, and one large tree had leaves that matched the colors of the smaller monoliths.

The tree's multi-hued flowers were the size of my hand as they stretched toward a sky that reflected the color of the rocks. Those numerous colors swirled throughout the sky, and like Earth, a few puffy white clouds floated across it. The ruins remained mostly piles of rubble, but the rest of the land was coming alive again.

In Magnus's arms, I'd finally found the place where I belonged, but in this land, I'd found the place where I fit.

"It's magnificent," I breathed as the other jinn and Caim wandered around with their mouths open.

A melodious call broke the hush of the land. Another answered the first call and then another. From between one of the cracks in the walls, a small yellow head emerged. The creature's round, black eyes took in its surroundings before it crept out from its hiding spot with more than a dozen of its species following it.

Waddling like ducks, the creatures were the size of a squirrel as they craned their heads back and forth on their short necks to inspect us and the land. Exceptionally cute with their fluffy yellow feathers, orange beaks, and plump bodies, they emitted curiosity and excitement as they squawked, stomped their webbed feet, and bobbed their heads up and down.

When their yellow wings unfurled to reveal the multi-colored feathers underneath, I realized they were the same creatures as some of the skeletons we'd come across. They must have been in hiding, or perhaps hibernating since the Abyss became a wasteland.

With another sweet song, the first one spread its wings and took to the sky with the others following it. From all around the Abyss, more filled the sky until their lovely song echoed throughout the land.

I gasped when, from behind the multi-hued flowers on the large tree, small creatures crept forth and rose into the air. Tinier than the birdlike animals, these creatures were of such various colors that it was impossible to name them all.

"They're butterflies!" I gasped as more of them rose from other areas of the Abyss. Or at least they were similar to Earth's butterflies, but these were larger and possessed more color variations.

"They are," Magnus murmured.

"What else is going to come alive again in here?" I wondered.

"I suspect many things."

"And all of them will be wondrous."

Magnus drew me closer against his side and nodded to where the others were starting to cluster near the base of Absenthees. "We should join them."

"Yes."

"You did this," he said as we walked over to the monolith. "You brought life to this place again."

"We all did this," I replied. "And we are *all* going to protect it." I focused on Rislen when we stopped before her. "The fae didn't fight for this land before, and they lost it. For thousands of years, our loyalties kept the jinn bound to each other, but those who left here with the horsemen have chosen them over *us*. The horsemen slaughtered my parents; they will destroy Earth, the humans, and anything else in their path. They would destroy this place again, and so would the jinn who left here with them."

I waved my hand at the marvel the Abyss had become as I pinned the non-Faulted jinn with a remorseless stare. "The Abyss will *never* again be used to hurt others. If you have a problem with that, then leave now and don't come back, or there will be a battle. I will *not* allow anyone to destroy this place again."

"And neither will we," Nalki said. "We would have left with the others if that was the side we chose, but we stayed because—" His voice trailed off as he looked at Absenthees. "—because this feels *right*."

"Yes," the rest of them murmured.

I pondered if these jinn had a little more fae in them too. Not enough to be Faulted, but enough to feel that this was the true way of this land more than the others did.

"We will also fight for this place," Nalki stated, and I realized he'd risen to take over Olgon's role as leader of the remaining non-Faulted jinn.

"You might have to fight the other jinn," I pressed, knowing neither the Faulted or non-Faulted would be eager to do such a thing. "Especially if they come back here with the horsemen. I will destroy anyone who tries to ruin the Abyss again."

"We will protect this place." Rislen's gaze drifted to Absenthees before rising to the creatures soaring through the sky. "It *must* be protected."

All the others followed her gaze, and their faces shone with awe, but more than that, I sensed their growing protective feelings toward the Abyss.

"We will protect it," Nalki vowed.

"All of you?" I asked.

"All of us," some of them murmured while others nodded.

I didn't question if they were lying or not, the truth of their conviction and loyalty to the Abyss radiated from them.

CHAPTER FORTY-SIX

Amalia

Magnus, Caim, and some of the jinn carried the dead through the field of grass where Magnus and I first entered. Sloth's body was at Absenthees with four jinn watching over it. He absolutely would *not* be buried in the Abyss. We would remove him from this place as soon as the burials were over, and then we would burn his remains.

Before making this journey, I'd gone with Caim and Magnus to the cave on Earth. We gathered the shovels they had in camp and returned to the Abyss. We'd considered removing Sloth from here then, but none of us were willing to let his body out of our sight until he was nothing but ash.

The grass soughed as it blew in a breeze I could now feel against my skin. This time, instead of sounding melancholy, there was an exultant tone to the swaying field that hadn't been there before. Despite its joy over the Abyss coming back to life, it seemed to sense my melancholy as it caressed my hands in a gesture meant to comfort me. Some of the fronds coiled around my fingers before releasing me.

Butterflies flitted down to land on the feathery ends of the grass, or they perched on my shoulders. Their supple wings caressed my cheeks, and their antennae twitched in the air before they flitted away and another replaced it. I understood my obsession with earth's butterflies better now. Some part of me instinctively recognized that Earth's butterflies were a distant relation to these beautiful creatures.

The birds landed in the grass around us, and some of them rose to brush against my hands or brush a wing against the top of my head before soaring away.

Oh yes, I would fight and die for this place. Anyone who tried to take it from me would regret the action and learn what Hell hath no fury *truly* meant.

Arriving at the side of the water, the others placed the bodies near the shoreline. The water no longer held a red hue but reflected the beauty of the multi-colored sky. I struggled against my tears but couldn't keep them withheld when the shovels broke the ground. Nine jinn had perished, eighteen left with Pride and Lust, and eighteen remained with us.

My hands fisted when my mind briefly turned to Lust and Pride; I would see them both dead by the time all this was over.

I kept my gaze focused on the water as the graves were dug and the bodies placed inside. In Hell, demons didn't entomb their dead, but to leave their bodies out to rot in this place or on Earth seemed wrong. Magnus had said the practice of burying and marking a demon's final resting place was becoming more common amongst demons on Earth.

When the jinn were laid to rest, Rislen stepped forward and said a few words before the jinn and Caim retreated to Absenthees. I remained standing by my parents' graves long after the others left. My uncle was buried today too, but I'd made sure he was far away from where they lay. I didn't know if they marked his grave or not, and I didn't care.

Magnus stood by my side, his arm around my waist as he sought to comfort me. I didn't know how much time we spent there, but eventually, the sky darkened and an amber moon rose on the horizon. The colors shifting through the sky all day became dancing lights flickering across the horizon.

The butterflies and birds settled into the grass for the night while some nestled on the shoreline close to us, and a few gathered around my feet. Their tiny bodies warmed me as they snuggled close.

From the grass, a few dozen rodent-like creatures the size of a rabbit emerged. Their small snouts and purple eyes were almost lost in the thickness of their fluffy brown coats. They sniffed the air before coming closer to join the birds and butterflies. Their coat was the softest thing I'd ever felt as they nuzzled my ankles and curled up around my toes. With every passing second and new discovery, I was falling more in love with the Abyss.

"I will fight for this place," I murmured.

Magnus kissed my temple. "You humble me, Amalia."

"You? Humbled?"

"Yes," he murmured and lowered his head to mine. "Because of you, I know love and became a man who is terrified of losing it. Because of you, I know I cannot defeat or laugh off everything anymore."

"You won't lose me," I promised.

"No, I won't," he growled.

And I knew there wasn't anything this magnificent demon of illusions wouldn't do to protect me, but there wasn't anything I wouldn't do to protect him either.

≈

Magnus

We stepped out of the Abyss and into the grove of calamut trees with Rislen and some of the other jinn. Rislen had informed us that Corson and the others had gone to see her and were waiting for us. What they revealed to her finally made her decide to enter the Abyss, but she hadn't wanted to bring them with her until she knew what was happening.

Caim swaggered through the portal with Sloth's body draped over his shoulder, and Nalki carried his head. As Rislen had said, the palitons were waiting for us when we exited the Abyss through her portal. When we stepped out, any who were sitting leapt to their feet.

"You're okay!" Wren blurted.

I didn't get a chance to respond before the calamut leaves rippled overhead and an ominous creak filled the air. Silence descended over those in the clearing. Grabbing Amalia, I tugged her against my side and sheltered her there seconds before the trees burst into motion.

The branches of the calamuts rose high before slamming into the ground all around us to create a cage. When the earth heaved, it staggered most of us back, though everyone managed to keep from touching the trees. Jarred by the sudden movement, prury fruit broke loose, fell to the ground, and shattered.

Then, more branches shot through the cage as the trees struck out at us.

Caim yelped and ducked out from under Sloth when multiple limbs plunged into the horsemen's body. The trees pierced Sloth from shoulders to feet, covering every inch of his back and holding him suspended five feet off the ground.

Then, the branches groaned again, and rising higher, they ripped the body to pieces. When more branches slithered through the cage, Nalki threw the head in the air. Before it could plummet to the ground, limbs punctured it through the eyes and mouth and yanked it apart.

No one dared to move as the trees continued to creak and sway. Then, numerous roots tore free of the ground; they dripped dirt and worms from them as they pulled themselves free of the Earth. Anyone unfortunate enough to be standing on one of the roots danced back as if their feet were on fire.

The fine black hairs lining the thick roots enveloped Sloth's shredded pieces and dragged them beneath the ground. Amalia released an explosive breath when the branches settled back into place. The freshly upturned soil was the only indication they'd broken free as the leaves danced overhead.

"Holy shit," Wren murmured; her skin was paler than normal, but so were the faces of everyone in the grove.

No one else spoke for a few minutes, no one dared to move, and then Lix unscrewed his flask and gulped down some of its contents. "You know," he said to Erin, "that makes me think of a riddle."

Erin's eyes widened before she gave a small smile of sadness and joy. The skelleins had tried and failed for months to stump her with a riddle, but now Lix was the only skellein who remained in the Wilds. I doubted he'd been much for puzzles and games since losing so many of his friends and family.

This small reversion to his more jovial self was a relief to see considering he'd removed all his accessories and wore nothing but the flask strapped to his side. He looked as he had in Hell when the skelleins were almost interchangeable.

"And what is that?" Erin asked.

"An apple tree has apples on it. A storm comes through, and there are no longer apples on the tree, but there aren't any apples on the ground either. How can this be so?" Lix asked.

Erin rubbed her chin. "Let me think about it."

"Take your time," Lix said and took another swallow of his

brew. "So how did you off Sloth?" he asked me, and I gave everyone a brief account of what happened in the Abyss.

"We have to report to Kobal and let him know everything that happened," Corson said.

"Since Halstar's dead, we'll have to send someone back," I said and looked at Raphael.

Raphael's jaw clenched, and his hand fell onto the hilt of the sword at his side. "I am *not* your carrier pigeon whenever you need to communicate with your king."

"He's your king here on Earth too, and it's either you or Caim," Corson said. "We have to get word back to him soon, and traveling by foot will take too long. Not to mention, Kobal and River have probably moved on from where they were the last time you saw them at the wall. Wings will make finding them far easier."

"Send Caim then," Raphael stated.

"Oh no, brother, I'm *not* to be trusted!" Caim said and threw up his hands. "There are way too many temptations for a wicked angel such as myself. I might never come back. I might not even arrive there!"

I didn't believe that, not after what I'd seen Caim do for Amalia in the Abyss. We'd all distrusted him from the beginning, and with good reason, but I believed he was an ally.

He *had* to be an ally if Amalia brought him into the Abyss; she wouldn't have done so if she felt anything secretive or distrustful from him. However, Caim looked highly amused right now, and I suspected he was enjoying pissing off Raphael.

Raphael's nostrils flared, and his hand tightened on his sword. "What shall I tell Kobal?"

Corson smiled at him before giving a rundown of details for him to tell Kobal. "With the number of fighters we've lost, I don't think it's wise for him to send more troops back. We can't risk losing more of them, but we do need another telepathic demon so we can communicate with him," Corson finished.

"And we're keeping this one alive," Raphael growled from between his teeth. Before anyone could reply, he shoved off his feet and streaked straight into the air so fast the calamuts barely had time to move their leaves out of his way. The leaves shuffled with annoyance when they settled back into place.

I couldn't help but smile after the angel, and when I looked around, I found almost all the demons smiling too. Ruffling the feathers of the arrogant, golden angel was fun.

"I know the answer to the riddle," Erin said to Lix.

"And?" Lix inquired.

"The tree only had two apples, so when one fell in the storm, the tree and the ground both had only *one* apple. So neither had *apples*, but they each had one apple."

Lix grinned at her. "Right you are, as always."

"You'll get me one of these days," Erin said.

Lix's smile slid away. "Perhaps."

"He's so sad," Amalia whispered to me.

Pulling her close, I kissed the top of her head. "He will learn to cope with the loss."

"As will I," she murmured with a hitch in her voice. Then she pulled away from me and smiled. "I think it's time to show you all the Abyss."

"I don't think that's wise," Rislen said.

"It is," Amalia stated in a tone that didn't tolerate any argument. "Because if we need help to defend the Abyss again, then they have to know what we're asking them to protect. We will help them against the craetons trying to destroy us all, and they will help us."

My eyebrows lifted at Amalia's stern command. She may be the youngest jinn, but she'd been the first to breathe life into the Abyss, and she was like a mother protecting her young. Despite her age, I suspected none of the jinn would be able to push her around or give her orders again.

When it came to the Abyss, it was hers, and I could see that understanding dawning in the eyes of the jinn. But then, she also belonged to the Abyss. I'd seen the way the grass and the creatures in there reacted to her, none of them behaved the same way with the other jinn.

"And the palitons may occasionally require somewhere to hide; we will allow them to do so in the Abyss," Amalia continued and gave the jinn a look that dared them to argue with her.

Pride swelled in my chest when they all remained silent.

"Come," Amalia said, and stepping from my hold, she waved her hand before her to open a portal. She edged away from the portal and gestured for the others to enter. "For some of you, it is *far* different than the way you left it."

The others started forward as Amalia stepped back and into my arms again. Closing her eyes, she rested her head on my chest. "I will protect the Abyss and you," I promised her.

"I know," she said.

The last to come forward, Corson and Wren stopped beside her. Corson rested his hand on her shoulder as he spoke. "I'm sorry for the way I behaved toward you in the beginning."

"I understand why you did; you didn't know about the Faulted or really anything about the jinn other than the destruction they can wreak," Amalia said.

"True," he said. "But I still shouldn't have treated you that way. Thank you for helping to bring her back to me."

Amalia ducked her head. "No Chosen should be separated from their partner."

"No, they shouldn't," Corson agreed and released her shoulder. "Magnus is a lucky man."

"He is," Amalia agreed, and I chuckled.

"I'd like to thank you too," Wren said and held her hand out. Amalia stared at it for a second before clasping it in hers and giving it a small shake. "I'm Wren."

"I know," Amalia said with a small smile, and Wren grinned at her before releasing her hand.

Corson and Wren entered the portal as some branches of the calamuts dipped low and their leaves stirred. Their movement created a breeze that tugged at Amalia's hair and ruffled mine. Caught up in the wind, seeds from the broken prury fruit danced on the air before sweeping into the portal.

"Oh," Amalia breathed.

"And it seems the calamuts will help protect the Abyss too," I told her.

"Yes."

Taking her hand, we crossed back through the portal to discover the others gazing in amazement at the Abyss and Absenthees. The prury seeds floated through the air before some of them settled onto the stones surrounding Absenthees. Others drifted higher and further away as they spread out to protect a land I'd initially believed to be a horror, but the Abyss had proven to be as magical and proud as the woman standing beside me.

Wrapping my arms around her, I lifted Amalia off the ground and spun her around. I couldn't believe I'd once considered her weak in her immortality and reluctance to fight. She was one of the strongest creatures I'd ever encountered, and she was *my* Chosen.

"I love you," she whispered, and the shifting lights in the night sky danced as if they heard her words.

"And I love you, Freckles."

Love was something I'd believed myself incapable of feeling; I'd been arrogant enough to think myself above it, but I'd only been waiting for a young Faulted to fly free of her cage and turn my world upside down. Placing her palm against my cheek, Amalia kissed me tenderly, and I lost myself in the wonder of her.

The End.

Look for Hawk's story in *Kiss of Death*, Hell on Earth, Book 3, to release October 2019:
brendakdavies.com/KDwb

Stay in touch on updates and other new releases from the author by joining the mailing list.
Mailing list for Brenda K. Davies and Erica Stevens Updates:
brendakdavies.com/ESBKDNews

Join the Erica Stevens/Brenda K. Davies book club on Facebook for exclusive giveaways, to discuss books, and join in the fun with the author and fellow readers!
Book Club: brendakdavies.com/ESBKDBookClub

FIND THE AUTHOR

Erica Stevens/Brenda K. Davies Mailing List:
brendakdavies.com/ESBKDNews

Facebook page: brendakdavies.com/BKDfb
Facebook friend: ericastevensauthor.com/EASfb

Erica Stevens/Brenda K. Davies Book Club:
brendakdavies.com/ESBKDBookClub

Instagram: brendakdavies.com/BKDInsta
Twitter: brendakdavies.com/BKDTweet
Website: www.brendakdavies.com
Blog: ericastevensauthor.com/ESblog

ABOUT THE AUTHOR

Brenda K. Davies is the USA Today Bestselling author of the Vampire Awakening Series, Alliance Series, Road to Hell Series, Hell on Earth Series, and historical romantic fiction. She also writes under the pen name, Erica Stevens. When not out with friends and family, she can be found at home with her husband, son, dog, and horse.

Made in the USA
Middletown, DE
18 December 2022

19315278R00195